IRON CITY
CONSPIRACY

A Novel

Stewart Lytle

Copyright © 2015 by Stewart Lytle
All rights reserved.
ISBN-13: 978-1511675031
ISBN-10: 1511675039

Library of Congress Control Number: 2015906055
CreateSpace Independent Publishing Platform
North Charleston, South Carolina

For the Very Reverend Doctor Guy Fitch Lytle III
who inspired, challenged and loved me.

ACKNOWLEDGEMENTS

Several people have contributed to this novel. Some worked with me at various newspapers. A few served as models for characters, including my first editor, the late Duard Le Grande, and Bill Cornwell, a longtime friend, newspaper colleague and the best writer I know.

Other friends, particularly Cornwell and veteran television news anchor Troy Dungan, were kind enough to read drafts and provide valuable critiques. Louisette Morin, a Montessori kindergarten teacher, read the novel and taught me a lot about spelling, punctuation and sentence structure.

I deeply appreciate the assistance of Jeff Becker with Haynes and Boone, a steadfast friend and one of the best intellectual property attorneys, and Steve Bloom, a genius at social media and web site design.

This novel would never have been finished had it not been for the encouragement and love I get every day from Mary, my wife, who persevered to read draft after draft with a pen in her hand.

And I dedicate Iron City to my brother, the Very Reverend Doctor Guy Fitch Lytle III, who was the Dean of Theology at the University of the South. I don't know where I would be without his inspiration, guidance and love.

PROLOGUE

Samuel Grey started speaking at five minutes after seven on Wednesday night. He had written the speech days before in long-hand on a yellow legal pad and rehearsed it in front of a mirror, which was unusual for him. He normally spoke without notes or even gave his speeches much thought in advance. But this speech was different. He had rewritten the opening and closing paragraphs twice. He had read again speeches he admired, including Dr. Martin Luther King's *I Have a Dream* at the Lincoln Memorial. He felt he had been preparing to give this speech his whole life.

He never dreamed it would be his last.

A tall, broad-shouldered man, Grey was forty one, but seemed older, his hair more salt than pepper. He wore a black suit with pin-stripes, and in a gesture to the flag that stood behind the pulpit he had selected a bright red and white striped tie on a blue shirt. He was distinguished looking, often complimented for his attire, but his face was that of a man who had lived hard, which attracted a lot of attention from women who liked men they thought were bad boys.

As a county commissioner in Iron City, he walked on the proverbial water with black voters. He scared most white people, who worked in the tall buildings downtown and lived in the suburbs, the richest of which were south of the mountain.

Grey was a natural public speaker with a voice that seemed to roll up from deep in his chest. His cadence at times was lyrical, at others staccato, ending at times in crescendos that brought crowds to their feet. In little more than a whisper he began speaking to the packed house in the small, historic Sixteenth Street Baptist Church. People leaned forward in the polished wooden pews to catch every word. He recited the progress African Americans had made in Iron City in the half century since dogs and firehouses were turned on civil rights marchers in the downtown park across the street from the church.

Schools were integrated legally, he told the crowd. But few black and white students actually went to school together. Black men and women can sit in any seat on a bus and travel anywhere in the city, but each person sitting in a pew that night knew that only poor whites and even poorer blacks rode the buses in Iron City.

A black man had been elected mayor several years before, but Grey did not mention it because the mayor had been accused of taking bribes from construction companies and forced to resign to keep from going to prison.

In Washington, D.C., the first black President has been elected, Grey said, his voice rising to the church ceiling.

A few amens rose from the audience.

"Yes, black folks have made lots of progress in America and even here in Iron City." He paused for effect, building the suspense. The hundreds of voices in the congregation were silent. No babies cried. Even the teenagers stopped whispering. Like their parents, they were mesmerized by Grey.

"But the gains that we have made in the past mock us today. We are not all the way free or, God forgive me, equal with the white man. The road we travel is long. It is no longer all uphill, but it is not so easy as the road traveled by white folks."

The congregation erupted in a chorus of "Amen."

"We are no longer slaves, the property of white masters. But remember the whites only and colored signs on the toilets and the drinking fountains? A few of you older folks recall how it felt to be thirsty on a hot afternoon and be told you could not drink from a water fountain a few feet away. Or heaven help you, if you had to use the toilet. Those days are gone now. Thank the Almighty Lord. But once, not so many years ago, they defined us. Now we can be served in any restaurant, cafe or bar as long as we got the green or the plastic. But are you satisfied?"

"No!" came the chant from the congregation.

"Do you have a job that is as good as you can do?"

"No!" shouted the entire church audience.

"Are your children learning in school what they need to compete for jobs in this age of computers, cell phones, iPods, iPads and whatever new technologies are coming next?"

"No!" came the answer.

"Are your children safe when they walk home from school?"

"No!" the congregation shouted. Their shouts rocked the small church.

"Can you rest easy when your children, like my two little girls, leave the house? Do you believe they will be safe and protected by the police? Or do you worry that they will be harassed, arrested or, God forbid, shot by a police officer?"

An angry murmur of ascent went through the church. It was common knowledge that the police arrested blacks more often than whites. Recent shootings of black men were still fresh on everyone's mind. It happened too often in the streets of Iron City.

To the mothers in the audience, he asked, "If they are arrested, are you afraid your children or your husband will be beaten and abused by the white jailers?"

"Yes," shouted the audience. A few shook fists in the air.

Reverend James Smallwood stood up from one of the three high-backed, wooden chairs with gold-colored velvet that lined the pulpit's red-carpeted platform. He came to stand beside Grey. Dressed in a black robe with a gold and white, embroidered collar, the reverend lifted his arms high above his head. The two men standing together at the front of the church worked well together, one a church leader, the other a government official. They had stood together on several protests, facing down the white establishment. Most recently to secure better treatment for black men in the Iron City jail, they had marched arm and arm beneath the tall downtown buildings, leading hundreds of demonstrators to stand with placards in front of city hall, the courthouse and the jail. The speeches and signs had demanded that more black guards be hired at the jail. Sheriff Ned Peebles had ignored them.

Reverend Smallwood had planned this special Wednesday night service for more than a year. The service was being held in mid-September, in honor of the anniversary of that fateful day a half century ago. It was a turning point then in the Civil Rights Movement, when Ku Klux Klansmen set off sticks of dynamite in the church, killing four teenage girls.

The church was rebuilt, but in recent years had become as much a tourist attraction for black families as the religious sanctuary and seat of power it once was. The congregation was smaller. The passion that once made this church a focal point for the national civil rights movement had dissipated like smoke from a chimney on a dark night. Now it stood in the shadow of Iron City's skyscrapers, a dwarf among giants. Its blue neon cross, orange brick and stained-glass windows had long been a comfort to black people. Across the street, a museum dedicated to the Civil Rights Movement had been built. Constructed with bricks and mortar, paid for largely with money from national corporations, the museum made sure no one ever forgot that Iron City was the cradle of black liberty in America.

In a time when some pundits claimed racial prejudice was a thing of the past, Smallwood had come to Iron City to reverse the downward slide of passion and power, not just within his church, but the city's entire African-American community. He wanted this service to rekindle the spirit and galvanize black people to action once more. He asked Grey to speak because the county commissioner could move a crowd, and he wanted to give this young man the chance to stand out on this historic evening as a rising star on the national stage.

The well-publicized service attracted African American dignitaries from as far away as Los Angeles. Congressmen, mayors and NAACP executives flew to Iron City to attend and especially to be seen at the service. The Black Educational Television network was recording the service for a special nationwide broadcast.

Smallwood, a stooped, stick-thin man, his thick hair gone to white, no longer aspired personally to national power. But he could deliver a lot of black votes in Iron City. Like a father feels for a talented son, the minister believed that Grey was destined to be a better, more enduring spokesman for the African-American community than several of the national leaders who sat pompously in the congregation.

Standing on the orange tiled steps at the front of the church before the service began, Smallwood had told the BET television crew, a few reporters from magazines and newspapers that served black readers and one lone white freelance reporter, "Those four girls, who died in the bombing of this beautiful church, would be middle-aged women now, maybe members of this church with children and grandchildren of their own. It was a tragedy we must never forget." He paused for effect. "And tonight we won't."

Smallwood predicted that Iron City would never again be the same after this service. The minister smiled as he walked back into the church. The ushers were in place, wearing purple and gold sashes to signify their importance in the church hierarchy. The choir was singing the third song, a medley of old civil rights protest songs that ended with *The Lord is On Our Side*. They stood behind the elegant wooden divider that separated the choir loft from the stage in front of tall, gold-painted organ pipes. Everyone agreed it was a beautiful church.

On Wednesday nights the service usually drew only a few devoted souls. Tonight people stood three rows deep in the back and along the side of the church, below the stained glass windows. The deacons sat in the front two rows in the center. One of the oldest deacons, seventy-eight-year-old Jimmy Marshall, wearing a dark blue suit with a green tie on a white shirt, sat praying as he relived in his mind the glory of his youth when he first met Dr. King. The great man had come to Iron City to work with Dr. Fred Shuttlesworth and other local black ministers to organize protest marches. King and Shuttlesworth mobilized an army of non-violent protestors to stand against Iron City Police Commissioner Harrison "Bull" Wainwright and his ruthless band of segregationists. Marshall was one of the young men who faced down the dogs and fire hoses and spent weeks in jail for joining the forces marching against segregation. Now a great grandfather, Marshall could see in Grey a man who had King's charisma, vision and fearlessness. He felt young again.

Grey hit the top of his vocal range. He was in rhythm. He paused and leaned against the solid wooden pulpit, the weight of the world on his shoulders. He began again, slower, more forceful.

"We all remember the stirring words of Dr. King in Washington, D.C. standing at the majestic memorial built to honor the Great Emancipator. He told the world there at the feet of Abraham Lincoln that he had a dream where justice would prevail, not just for the white man, but for the Negro, too. One hundred years after Lincoln freed many of our forefathers and mothers, Dr. King declared 'the Negro still is not free'."

Grey sighed deeply as he went on to quote King, words that everyone in the audience had learned as children. "'One hundred years later, the life of the Negro is still sadly crippled by the manacles of segregation and the chains of discrimination. One hundred years later, the Negro lives on a lonely island of poverty in the midst of a vast ocean of material prosperity. One hundred years later, the Negro is still languished in the corners of American society and finds himself an exile in his own land.'"

The silence was broken in the church with several "Amen, brother." Grey held his hands high above his head. "Tonight, it is time we demand our full rights, not just our political rights. It is time we demand that black companies and businesses get more contracts from city hall and from the county courthouse. Our people can build schools and roads, run the stores at the airport, own finance companies and sell insurance policies the city and county buy from white men who live in the big houses over the mountain. It is time that our businesses reap the rewards without fear of retribution."

Many in the congregation nodded. They understood what he was talking about. Grey paused to wipe sweat that beaded up on his forehead. The congregation slowly broke into a chant of support. They knew what was coming. They wanted to hear it. They clapped and chanted, urging him on. Grey stood quietly for a dozen heartbeats. He cast his eyes down. He sighed deeply and his shoulders heaved.

"It is time, my brothers and sisters, to break down one last barrier. It is only one job. Just one job. I am not talking about the man who lives with his beautiful family in the White House, as great as his election as President was. But here in the cradle of the Confederacy, there is a job that is the ultimate symbol. If a black man had that job, there would be no stopping the march of progress for blacks in our time."

Grey paused again to let the suspense build. "It is time ... it is time ... I say, it is time for us to demand that a black man coach the University of Alabama Crimson Tide football team, to lead the young men, those gifted young men who play football for the glory of the university."

There was hushed silence in the congregation. To suggest that one of their own walk in the footsteps of the legend, Bear Bryant himself, was revolutionary. There were other black men coaching college football teams, even one in Texas. But Alabama was different. It was sacred ground for the mostly white alumni who graduated from the university in Tuscaloosa.

"The Crimson Tide football team is more black than white." Grey's voice boomed through the church. "It is the skill, hard work and sacrifice of our young black men who win the games and championships for the university. But it is a white man who gets the credit. On national television who is it that the cameras always show standing on the sidelines barking orders on a fancy headset?"

"A white man," chanted the congregation in unison.

"Yes," he shouted. "It is a white man who gets the huge payday for calling the plays that our young men run. The men on the field may be strong and fast, and many of them have skin the same color as yours and mine. But the world believes that the brains of the team, the man with the clipboard, belong only to a white man."

One of the deacons sang out, "You right, brother; do right, brother; be right, brother." That was followed by cries of "Amen" and "Mercy" from every pew. Grey waited until the church was quiet again.

"We are not just good at toting the bale and pulling the barge. We can work with computers and the latest phones and tablets. We are doctors and lawyers and teachers. Black men and women can run companies. And believe me," his voice rose to its highest note, "a black man can coach the great University of Alabama football team and win a national championship.....

A blast rocked the church to its foundation. The bomb blew the stained glass out of the windows. Choir members flew through the air. The pulpit where Grey had been speaking was gone.

The county commissioner with his fist held high and his eyes looking to Heaven died at that instant, his body blown apart, his last words on Earth drowned out. He delivered his call on the Lord for his Almighty help directly to Saint Peter.

Smallwood was killed at the same instant when the blast drove a shard of flooring through his eye into his brain. His body rose almost to the roof, as if on its way to Heaven, before it fell lifeless back onto the splintered wood of the stage, a few feet from where Grey had been speaking.

The choir members landed in heaps with broken ribs, legs, ankles and arms. Two choir members, a man and a woman, would each lose a leg. Blood flowed from cuts that created brown stains on their gold robes. Covered in plaster and debris, they looked like they were wearing white makeup as some screamed and cried. Others lay unconscious in the debris.

The blast was heard blocks away as the music died down at the Iron City Symphony Hall. The mostly white audience, many of whom had driven north over the mountain to attend the concert downtown, sat silently wondering what could have made that sound. Some began to whisper, and a few men stood up and walked out through the lobby to stand on the sidewalk to see if terrorists had struck Iron City. It was difficult to see anything in the dusk of the evening. But then they heard sirens. Women in furs and men in tuxedos walked quickly toward the exits.

Of the deacons in the front rows of the church, four died instantly. Three others died hours later from head and chest injuries. Only three survived. Two had sat on the ends of the pew. The bodies of their fellow deacons sitting next to them blocked the shock waves and the flying wood and metal shards that killed the others. They sustained only broken legs and arms when heavy-bodied men landed on them.

Jimmy Marshall was unhurt. He claimed later, because he was called on often in the coming weeks to tell the story of how he survived, that he was praying hard to Jesus and Dr. King at the moment the bomb exploded. He said he felt King's strength from the grave had blocked the explosion and kept him safe.

"I don't know why I was not killed with the others," he told television and newspaper reporters. "I suppose God has something else for me to do."

Marshall found himself lying under the pew with the body of Harry Welds, another deacon, on top of him. He pushed Welds' wide body off him and stood up. What he saw was horrific. The church was filled with smoke. He assumed the building was burning, but saw no flames. Children and adults wailed. A few ran up the aisles to the exits. Some tried to crawl under the pews. Injured parishioners lay moaning in the dark. Marshall recalled later that he had not panicked. If he had not been killed by the blast, he thought, why should he worry about being killed in the aftermath? He decided to check on the other deacons and choir members near him while he waited for someone to rescue him.

The uninjured spilled out of the church into the night. They staggered in a daze down the front steps. Standing on the sidewalk, they searched for family members and friends. Parents rounded up children and hugged them in relief. Friends clung to one another and wept. Others talked with one another about what had happened, what had caused the explosion.

Some said they had seen the minister and several choir members flying in the air. No one had seen what happened to Commissioner Grey. He was speaking one minute; gone the next, his body parts, found later, were scattered across the front of the church.

Fire engines rolled to a stop beside the church. Fireman bolted out of the giant trucks, looking to see what they faced. As they began moving people away, ambulances blocked the streets. Several firemen ran up the steps to begin rescuing those inside, while the driver of one truck talked on a radio, describing the scene to the bosses. Nerves across the city were already fraying. As the firemen carried out the injured, they were laid on blankets on the sidewalk and in the street.

Several men gathered stood on the steps of the church, surveying the carnage and watching bleeding bodies being brought out of the beloved church. They looked across the street at the Civil Rights Institute. Through the smoke, lit up by the flashing red lights of the fire engines and ambulances, the statue of Dr. Shuttlesworth in front of the institute appeared to levitate, his hand out-stretched in friendship.

"Never again," shouted a short man in a black suit, standing on the top step of the church, his fist punching the air. "Never again. They're not going to do this to us, no more. Get your guns, my brothers, we're taking this war where it belongs - to whitey."

1

Mark Hodges died weeks later and miles from the church, but he was just as much a casualty of the church bombing as any of those who died that night.

I sat under a tall old elm thinking about my friend as a digging crew cranked up the small backhoe that had dug his grave. There weren't many flowers. There had been few mourners. I was the only person who threw some of the red Iron City clay on his casket. It was sad that a person as special as Mark had so few people standing by the grave to see him off to the next life. I was his best friend, probably his oldest, certainly the longest suffering. Mark made being his friend difficult at times, his drinking bouts and occasional disappearances were almost legendary. For me, although not for others, his talent and delightful personality made all the challenges he presented worth any effort.

Pain squeezed my chest, loneliness engulfed me as I watched his coffin lowered into the ground. I thought of Sheila as they had closed her inside a box for eternity. My wife had looked so tiny and fragile, lying there on pink silk cushions. I knew she was not really there and much happier where she was. She had welcomed death, after years of pain. But I was as miserable then as I was today.

I watched the crew working around the grave. Theirs were the only sounds that broke the afternoon silence in the cemetery between airplanes landing and taking off at the nearby Iron City International Airport. Mark and I had joked that in another life we must have been two halves of the same person, opposites in many ways, one white, one black, two personalities that were poles apart in many ways, but connected in others. He could finish sentences I started, and on occasion I had to finish his.

Now I had to complete something much more difficult that he had started. If I had known, those famous last words. If I had known then how much of a challenge he had left me, I might not have accepted it so readily. Oh, right. Who am I kidding? I live for such challenges. That is why I became a newspaper reporter right out of college. Of course, I wanted to finish this story, no matter what the cost.

In the back of my Blazer I had a six pack of Coors Light in a cooler. Mark and I had often kicked back with a few long necks, while we talked about stories. Mark had great insight about stories that few newspaper reporters are blessed with. He had a way of seeing a story, the twists and turns it would bring, long before it was written. He had more chutzpah than any reporter I knew. There was no one he wouldn't interview, or at least try to. There was no story he wouldn't take on. He did not write as well as some, but his epitaph should read: Here lies a great reporter.

Mark's weakness was his unpredictability. Some, including a couple of the editors who work for me, called it "piss poor" behavior. It made his writing for a daily newspaper with a small staff like the *Iron City Post* impossible. He might disappear just when we needed him most. If he didn't think that a story was important, he would let it drift for weeks. At times, he simply couldn't be found. Reality was hard for Mark. He preferred living in other people's worlds, writing about things beyond himself. When reality got too close, when he worried about his marriage or his mounting debts or why he hadn't made more of his talents, he drank.

I loosened my tie and laid my suit jacket on the grass beside me as I leaned back against the base of the tree that would shade

Mark's grave. I looked at the jacket and smiled. It was normal for me to be dressed in a suit and tie, gold-plated cufflinks at my wrists. But not Mark. He probably should have been buried in a pair of his jeans, a blue blazer over a knock-off polo shirt that he loved to wear, especially when chasing a story. But his wife wouldn't have it. Seeing him in that casket with a suit, white shirt and one of my better ties seemed out of place, but she might be right. He should be well dressed to meet Jesus.

The diggers were pushing dirt over the coffin. A small flatbed truck rolled up with the headstone on the back. Two men struggled to pull it off and set it in place. The temperature was still in the eighties, although the Alabama summer mugginess showed signs of breaking. The light breeze brought the smell of a coming rain, and the prospect of a cooler fall rippled through the Mimosa trees.

When I popped the top of the first beer, one of the crew, an older man dressed in mud-stained overalls, his black skin glistening under a bright orange t-shirt, turned and watched me. In a few minutes he walked over to pick up a piece of litter that lay near me. "You a friend of this man?" he asked, pointing to the grave. I nodded. "I'm mighty sorry he be dead then." I reached in the cooler and pulled out one of the beers and tossed it to him. He caught the can of beer in one large hand, his fingers spread wide. He looked at it, nodded his thanks and moved off, opening the beer. When the white man driving the truck looked up and saw him swig the beer, he shook his head in disgust.

Mark and I had started as young reporters at the *Iron City Post*. We broke a few big stories, ran a couple of disreputable politicians out of office and had a glorious time doing it. There is probably no headier feeling than being young and having the power of a daily newspaper at your fingertips. Now I am the editor of that newspaper, the youngest and the first black man ever to occupy the corner office. I had risen fast through the ranks, covered city hall for a few years before Howard Blake, the editor then, my mentor and friend, sent me to Washington to write about the Alabama congressmen and senators and anything else the federal government did of interest to Iron City readers. I am the son of a banker. My father was one of the first black men to rise to be a vice president of a downtown Iron City bank. And I am the grandson of a steelworker who was Irish to the core. I am the third Joe Riordan in our lineage.

My heritage gives new meaning to the term black Irish.

As editor of a morning newspaper and our around-the-clock Internet Web site, I have a managing editor, seven section editors and almost fifty reporters, photographers and copy editors on my staff. Mark wanted only to be a reporter. He liked to chase the stories himself, not tell others how to do it. He chided me for giving into the lure of management, of being an editor, but there were times when he seemed to envy my ascent in the ranks.

Not long after he turned thirty, life soured a bit for Mark. His wife tired of his late nights of drinking and chasing stories, too often in the morning passed out in the bed or on the couch until after she left for work. Newspaper reporters are rarely well paid, and she expected a lot more. When he drank or bought lottery tickets with his meager earnings, they had to live on her salary, and she made him pay. I got to know the signs. The more she ragged on him, the more sullen he became and the more he would drink. It was a downward spiral. And now the spiral had hit bottom.

I started on my second beer and saw my new friend from the grave crew amble back in my direction. "Could my associate here have one of your beers? He can pay." I smiled at the insincerity of the offer and reached into the cooler. I tossed him a can for the other gravedigger. "We gonna drink to your friend," he said.

Mark would like that.

He died when his car landed at the bottom of a deep ravine. Iron City, the tail end of the Appalachian Mountain chain, has a topography that has proven treacherous to many drivers. Its deep gorges and steep mountainsides make Iron City beautiful, but they create steep, sharp curves more like Switzerland than most

American cities. Mark was just one of the lives that had ended in what folks around here call a holler.

My friend was never a good driver. I hated to ride with him, and in recent years I had insisted on driving. He believed it was because I thought he was buzzed, and he would protest that he was sober. The irony of it was that he was probably less a danger to himself and others when he was driving a bit loaded. He paid more attention. When sober, he was tense or bored, a caged, hungry lion. The radio never played the right song. He either talked to me or spoke or texted incessantly on the phone. He was always taking his eyes off the road. When he looked away, his right foot lifted off the gas, then he would turn back to watch the road and speed up. It made for a jerky ride. I often teased him that his curiosity would someday get him killed.

Bad joke now.

When they reached his car at the bottom of the ravine, the rescue workers found several empty Pabst Blue Ribbon beers on the car floor. The police report blamed drunk driving for the accident. But the autopsy, which I had to insist on, showed he was slightly buzzed, but not drunk. And though PBRs have developed a new following among younger drinkers today, I never knew him to drink that brand. Maybe he was becoming more hip, or was it the only brand the store had? Or was he broke and it was on sale? A Brad Paisley disc was cued up to one of his favorite songs. I hoped he had been singing what I teasingly called his hillbilly tunes when he met his end.

Before he died, Mark, like hundreds of other newspaper and television reporters, magazine writers, FBI agents and Iron City police officers, was knee-deep in the investigation of who bombed the Sixteenth Street Baptist Church and killed the minister and a local county commissioner. Mark was working it freelance. He was competing against some of the best reporters from national newspapers, who had numerous sources in the FBI, White House and Congress. He was up against New York-based television news reporters whose networks broke into daytime entertainment shows for days to allow their well-known anchors to regurgitate old and re-hashed news about the bombing. That included CNN, which broadcast for two days after the bombing from the Civil Rights Museum across the street. Iron City was deluged with reporters and camera crews, running from the bombed out church site to city hall, where daily updates gave them little new information.

If Mark could break a new angle on the story, he would have had his choice of newspapers and magazines, all with checkbooks in hand to buy breaking stories on the bombing. It would also be his redemption. A year ago, the pressures of writing freelance had gotten to him. He had sold a story to a local magazine about an attorney that had dipped into the trust fund for one of the local playboy heirs. Mark had written the story, quoting the attorney and the young heir, giving a very colorful account of the rich kid's lifestyle and his derogatory comments about his attorney. When the story was printed, there was only one thing that the attorney and his client agreed on. They had never uttered the words Mark's article quoted them as saying.

Mark stood by his story, but he had not recorded the interviews. So he had egg splattered over his face, a tough lesson reporters often learn too late. I believed Mark, but some of my senior editors thought there was too much smoke not be some fire in the accusations by the attorney and his client.

I hadn't seen my friend much lately. He and I had talked only once about the bombing story. He hadn't told me he had a tip on who the bomber was. I wouldn't expect him to call us if he got something. The *Post* may have given him his start as a reporter, but he had left our ranks to become a freelancer. My bosses didn't pay freelance writers much, and he knew too well what some of my editors thought of him.

I smiled when I got his voice message:

"Hey, buddy, just dropped something pretty damn special in the mail. You run this, and the shit will really hit the fan. You get first crack at it. If you want it, and you are going to want this, we'll work something out. I know it's hard to squeeze blood out of a turnip, but maybe this is good enough that even the jerks you work for will cough up some real cash. Joe, thanks for hanging in there. You're the best friend. Thanks for everything. See ya."

I hated that I had erased the message. I never dreamed it would be the last time I would hear his voice.

The day after he drove his car off the cliff, a brown envelope arrived with his distinct scrawl. It was mailed, I knew, because he was old school. He never trusted anything important to email. He believed, with good reason, that someone was reading whatever bounced off satellites.

Inside the envelope was his article on who bombed the church. There was also a disc with a recorded interview with a man who claimed he was the bomber. After I read the article and listened to the interview, I was as excited as a young reporter with my first page one story. More than anything, I wanted that story. That's what we live for, those articles that stir things up and sell newspapers. They are what keep life interesting.

If Mark had lived, there would have been problems publishing his article, but far fewer than the ones his death left behind. "Damn it," I said out loud. I needed him here to talk to. He would chuckle at the problems his death had caused. I could see him now. He would throw back his head, laugh and lift the long neck bottle with his thumb and index finger like he always did. The twinkle in his eyes would give away his thoughts, the amusement he found in life.

"Yeah, life throws you a curve, but you learned to swerve," he would say, quoting one of his favorite Rascal Flats songs.

I wished I could hear that one more time. He knew he had a world-class scoop, for both of us. He also knew there was more to this story than he had found. He needed help finishing it.

As I sat under that elm and watched the crew covering his grave, I opened another beer. For that moment the cemetery was quiet. The whole town seemed to be quiet. Maybe everyone was taking a breather. It was too much to hope that the violence was over. There was still too much anger, too many people who wanted payback for all the years of pain from real or perceived injustices. One explosion in a small church had set the city ablaze.

The night the church was bombed, the newsroom had been in slow motion, a routine Wednesday night. I had just complained out loud that we hadn't had a good story in weeks: something good to investigate, a page one hummer that would help circulation and break the monotony of the summer news cycle. God must have been listening.

Maybe the best thing about the newspaper business is that it rarely stays boring. The phone rings, the police scanner squawks, a junior reporter wanders back to the office scratching his head over a story he doesn't understand, and off we go chasing something new.

That night it was the police scanner, then the phones. Pat Galloway, our police reporter, called to say he was headed to the church. The newsroom was suddenly organized chaos. More reporters plus photographers were dispatched to the church. Other reporters worked the phones, calling local officials, Sheriff Ned Peebles for comments. Editors worked on deadline, pulling together a story about the explosion, speculation at first, then confirmation that it was a bomb, more speculation on who might be responsible, estimates on the number of dead and injured, the ties back to the first time this church was bombed, the reaction around the country and the world. We got a newspaper out that night, barely. Given the time constraints working against us, the last editions were damned good. We had information that no other newspapers, television networks or Internet sites had. Many quoted us or picked up our story from our web site.

I finished the third beer, stood up and headed back to the car. It was so hard, facing life, knowing I would not see Mark, hear his voice or laugh at his jokes again. The last beer in the cooler looked like an orphan. I laid it on the grass and waved to the old gravedigger to come get it. The beers I drank had helped dull the pain. I turned on the car, but did not put it in drive. I reached into the glove box and pulled out an Ipad that I had been listening to on the day he died. He had given me an old Kris Kristofferson download and asked me if I thought the Rhodes Scholar, singer, songwriter and sometimes movie star could be the best writer ever.

The Pilgrim, his favorite song, was cued up. I listened again. It fit my mood after the burial of my best friend who might have been a model for Kristofferson' song. I sang along as the melancholy song played. It was now my favorite song too. Every time I heard it, I would feel like I could touch Mark once more.

On the passenger seat was Mark's story. I pulled it out and read it again. I brushed aside my suspicion that his death had not been an accident. It had to be. I told myself I was just getting paranoid. With all the violence in the streets, buildings gutted, people dead in the streets, it was easy to let your fears rise from dark places.

Mark had found the bomber. Not the FBI nor the Iron City police. Not CNN or the *New York Times*. Mark, a talented reporter, but with hardly the resources of some of the major media outlets chasing this story, had tracked down the man who had bombed the church. My friend, lying in his grave, had solved the case. At least a big part of it.

His article said the bomber was a county constable named Lonnie Crenshaw. He was a violent redneck, a man who didn't just hate blacks, but a man who had little problem killing a dozen people just because of their skin color. The article quoted Crenshaw word for word from an interview. Mark was a master at opening the door for people to do that to themselves. Crenshaw might as well have held out his arm for the needle.

But Mark had not been content just to name Crenshaw as the bomber. His article speculated that Crenshaw had been hired to plant the bomb and kill Grey. The article did not name anyone else. Mark's article left the conspirators in the shadows.

9

He knew we would not run the story as he wrote it. We would have to find and re-interview Crenshaw. There had been too many kooks wandering into newsrooms, FBI offices and police stations claiming to be the bomber. It was not just our reputation on the line. It might spike more tensions in the streets. More people might die.

Did Mark expect me to identify the men behind Crenshaw? Or was the article he sent me just the best he could do in the time he had?

I wished he were here to ask.

At more than six feet tall with prematurely white hair, Mark could not have hidden in the crowd at the church. He was there to write an article on Grey for the *American Progressive*, a magazine written for liberals. The readership of the magazine had peaked when the President, capitalizing on the political fiasco the opposing vice presidential candidate had created when she could not name any magazines she read, listed the *American Progressive* as one of his favorites. Lobbyists and staffers of every stripe inside the Washington Beltway put a run on the copies that were trucked to the District of Columbia in hopes of knowing what the President was reading.

Mark's article would have traced the rise of the young county commissioner and his determination to improve the living conditions for blacks in Iron City. He stood in the back of the church to observe Grey and the crowd's reaction to him. Grey had not trusted Mark and kept him at a distance, but had finally relented.

"He just got tired of this white boy dogging him everywhere he went," Mark told me, excited like he always got when stories were coming together. Grey had scheduled the interview after the Wednesday night service.

Mark came away with a far better story. Suddenly he was in the middle of a breaking news story that would run on every front page the next morning. He had tripped in the church, fell and hit his head against a pew. Blood rolled down the side of his face as he interviewed survivors. Mark got some of his best comments from two of the out-of-town dignitaries while they were in near shock at the bombing and seeing a white man bleeding with them. Later the dignitaries would put on their public faces and regret their comments to Mark, but not before those words had run on numerous Web sites, morning television shows and in newspapers across the country. Mark had fed the story and quotations to the wire services. Out of old loyalties, he had phoned Clay Johnson, my city editor, but Clay, influenced by the stories he had heard about Mark, did not trust him entirely and had used only a couple of the quotations.

Other newspapers were smarter. Mark's article on the bombing, complete with a byline, ran the next morning on page one in several of the nation's largest dailies. He gave me a copy of the *Washington Post*, where his article ran with his by-line.

The article read:

> *Iron City, AL. - In a gruesome repeat of the church bombing here a half century ago, the Sixteenth Street Baptist Church in downtown Iron City was bombed Wednesday night, killing County Commissioner Sam Grey, the church minister and 10 members of the congregation.*
>
> *None of the nationally prominent civil rights leaders, who attended the service in honor of those who had died in the first bombing, was killed or injured.*
>
> *Following the bombing, rioting and looting erupted in Iron City. Fueled by anger and frustration at the second bombing of the beloved church, black men, women and teenagers rampaged through downtown Iron City and attacked stores and buildings north of the downtown area. Police mobilized to quell the rioting.*
>
> *Police and FBI spokesmen said they had no clues yet as to who placed the bomb.*
>
> *Grey was considered a rising political star in Alabama. He was elected to the County Commission three years ago.*

The same church in downtown Iron City was bombed in 1963. Four teenage girls were killed in the first explosion, one of the bloodiest single incidents in the civil rights era. Four men, believed to be members of the Ku Klux Klan, were identified as suspects. One died before standing trial. Three others were sentenced to life in prison and have since passed away.

The out-of-state leaders who came to Iron City to attend the service included U.S. Rep. Emory Johnson (D-GA) who called the bombing "a despicable act of cowardice." He blamed the "racist policies" of Alabama Governor Sam Kitterage.

"That bigot in Montgomery might as well have put the bomb in the church himself," said the congressman, who was clearly shaken by the bombing.

Rev. James Rathburn, a Chicago minister, was hit by flying debris. Bandaged by an emergency medical technician, Rathburn called on the FBI to send 100 agents to Iron City to solve this crime. "We don't want any whitewash like there was in '63. We want the bastards who did this," he said.

He said the President had assured him there would be a thorough investigation. "That's why we worked so hard to get one of our own elected President – to make sure these white (men) don't get away with atrocities like this."

An unidentified member of the congregation echoed the anger that many of the congregation felt. "Those white (expletive) klansmen down here tried to do it to us again. We are not going to put up with this (expletive) no more."

By noon the next day, the wire services, CNN, FOX and the other networks had stopped using Mark's story. There was new material, including footage of sympathy protests in other cities across the country, but little new information about the Iron City bombing. Billy Bates, the Iron City Chief of Police, was becoming a familiar face on television screens in households across the country. He speculated in one press conference that the bombing may have been a vendetta against Grey on a personal matter. He would not say what the personal issue was, commenting only that Grey was an attractive and popular man. He dismissed any links to terrorists.

Other media focused on the arrival of Deputy U.S. Attorney General Allison Keene, who flew to Iron City to open the federal civil rights investigation. The White House issued a statement condemning the bombing and urging calm in the streets. The President with his attorney general beside him told the White House press corps that the full power of the federal government was being deployed to find the bomber and bring him to justice.

Bates, who had been police chief for only six months, welcomed the federal agents, but promised his department would have the bomber in his jail before "all those FBI guys find the Holiday Inn." The Justice Department and the FBI, paying Bates little attention, flew in a team Thursday afternoon that consisted of two dozen investigators and two public affairs spokesmen. Keene, the flamboyant and beautiful deputy attorney general, toured the site of the bombed church. She also reassured the public that the bombing was not the act of foreign terrorists. But having more political smarts and experience than Bates, the deputy attorney general stopped short of promising a quick arrest.

The federal agents confiscated the security camera footage from across the street at the Civil Rights Institute, looking for any photo of someone who could be a bomber. A few delivery drivers to the Institute were interviewed. There were no security cameras at the church itself. Any fingerprints or DNA on the bomb itself or where it had been placed had been obliterated in the blast. The FBI said there was no Internet or phone intercepts that were helpful. No group claimed credit for the bombing. We were told, but the FBI would not confirm that it had asked the National Security Agency in Maryland if there were any satellite surveillance of Iron City during the bombing. Apparently nothing proved fruitful.

In the days and now weeks after the bombing, the Justice Department and FBI spokesmen had added little in their daily news briefings for reporters. They seemed to be focused on the white supremacist/neo-Nazi movement in Alabama. Almost everyone with white supremacist leanings had been hauled in for an interrogation. But no one was detained for long.

"What'd you expect?" Bates told our police reporter privately. "You send in a bunch of Yankees who need a seeing eye dog. They ain't gonna find nothing."

Much has been written about Iron City and how it has different roots from most other southern cities. Founded years after the Civil War, Iron City was a boom town by the early twentieth century. It was one of the South's first industrial centers, more like Pittsburgh than Charleston or Mobile. Workers, like my grandfather and namesake, came from the tough mill towns of the north to work beside men who had moved away from southern farms looking for better pay and more excitement in Iron City. The jobs created by the mills also lured black men by the thousands, many of them sharecroppers and the sons of former slaves. In recent years Mexicans and Central Americans had come to work in construction and take jobs that once belonged to the mill workers' sons and daughters.

It made for a spicy dish.

Iron City sits on deposits all in one place of iron ore, coal and limestone, the ingredients for making iron and steel. Civic boosters, the bankers, real estate developers and utility executives downtown, tried once to change the name to Steel City. They thought it sounded classier. Other than for one large car dealer who advertises on television and in the two newspapers, the name change didn't take. To my grandfather and other men who forged the city out of the steep, rocky slopes, Iron City was the right name, a tough, brittle place like the pig iron they forged in the mills. There was little that was ever soft about Iron City.

The city's symbol is Vulcan, the Roman God of the forge, an ugly creature, cast off Mount Olympus in Greek mythology. A statute of Vulcan stands on top of the mountain, looking out over his city. Several national newspaper columnists and television talking heads thought it clever to note that Vulcan is the root word for volcano, an apt metaphor for a city with daily eruptions in the streets.

Fifty tons of cast iron, the statue has a hammer in his left hand, an anvil by his side. Unveiled at a World's Fair, Vulcan was brought to Iron City and placed on a high perch. For years the god of the forge carried a spear in his right hand, until the good ladies of Iron City, wanting a gentler, kinder symbol for the city, replaced the spear with a light that glowed green if no one died that day in a car accident. A few years ago, when leading citizens raised money to refurbish the deteriorating statute, they gave up on the light and returned Vulcan's spear to his right hand. The spear seemed more fitting for the guardian of a city with so much bottled up anger.

Sitting in my car at the cemetery, I read again Mark's latest article on the bombing, the one that no one else had seen. Compared to this one, his first article on the church bombing was tame. I laid the piece of paper inside the innocuous looking file folder in the glove box, then started the Blazer.

The short drive from the cemetery to the newspaper building downtown frightened and depressed me. Thickening dark clouds overhead felt like the final pillow mercifully snuffing the life out of a terminally ill patient. Driving out through the gates of the cemetery with its long green lawns dotted with white headstones was like stepping out of Eden. The neighborhood northeast of downtown had long ago transitioned from poor white to poorer black. Since the riots started, houses and businesses had been burned out. Others were boarded up, waiting for the riots to lose steam. But there seemed to be no end in sight.

I wondered what the President thought every morning when he got his briefing that included the latest toll of death and destruction, not in Kabul, Kandahar or Paris, but in Iron City. I remembered the words from his first Inauguration speech, so full of promise and redemption.

> "...*why men and women and children of every race and every faith can join in celebration across this magnificent Mall, and why a man whose father less than sixty years ago might not have been served at a local restaurant can now stand before you to take a most sacred oath.*"

That speech had filled me with hope, a moment in time when everything seemed possible.

Not now. My city had changed in the blink of an eye. Before the bomb exploded in the small Baptist church for a second time in a half century, Iron City had looked, at least on the surface, like most other New South cities. New restaurants were opening. Younger people were moving back into the city, particularly on the south side near the medical center where a growing number of trendy shops had sprung up. The city's economy had diversified away from the huge, out-of-town-owned steel and pipe industries that built it. Now it was home to some of the world's best health care facilities. My mother used to say, "No place better to get sick than Iron City." She would know. She was in and out of the hospital fighting colon cancer for years. The chamber of commerce had a lot to brag about, like the new minor league baseball stadium, several national trucking firms, a handful of health-care companies and there were a even resurgence of innovative steel pipe companies.

On the surface race relations in Iron City had seemed to be improving. College educated, young black men and women were being hired in a growing number of professional jobs. A lively urban social scene had emerged where blacks and whites mingled. Personally I rarely felt the humiliation of discrimination. But below the surface, there was always tension. Blacks felt they were targeted and threatened more by police. And in numerous stories we had written the statistics seemed to confirm that police harassed, ticketed and arrested blacks far more often than whites. There were certainly a higher percentage of young black males in the Iron City jail and state prisons. Older, wealthier whites avoided blacks beyond telling them where to plant the azaleas or polish the silver. Many whites had retreated into the suburbs and came downtown only to work in the tall skyscrapers where they interacted only with blacks who were accepted by the establishment. Having grown up listening to my father's anger and frustrations, I knew a lot about that type of segregation.

Then the bomb exploded in the church. Shock waves rolled out across the city, a chain reaction of angry men and women burning, killing and looting as they quenched life-long frustrations on anything that stood in their way, concrete, metal, glass, wood and flesh. Police tried to quell the riots with a show of force, tear gas and dummy bullets, but that only heightened the anger and swelled the ranks of those taking to the streets. And there were too many rioters, locals and a growing number of outsiders, who joined in the street battles with police who could not be at three or four riot sites at the same time.

Corinthian Boulevard, north of downtown, was hit hard. Once the main thoroughfare north before the interstate highway was built, the street was lined with businesses that served downtown residents, office workers and the surrounding neighborhoods. Sammy's Barbecue Palace had dished out some of the best chopped pork. Ethan's Hardware had sold paint, screws and lawn mowers for generations. My Dad used to take me there on Saturdays, where he would spend hours talking with old friends, while I roamed the store looking at the interesting tools and trinkets. The row of businesses included a laundromat and dry cleaners, a framing shop, a small pharmacy, a storefront whole-life ministry, and of course, Harry's, which claimed to be the largest beer and wine store in the South.

Harry's had gone the first day. The old brick warehouse-style building did not have a window or door left. The rioters, hardly shopping for a rare Bordeaux, had pulled off the doors to use in hauling away the cases and bottles of alcohol inside. Ethan's, I was sad to see, had been ransacked for any tool that could be turned into a weapon. The framing shop and cleaners were burned out. Only Sammy's stood largely untouched, maybe out of respect for good barbecue. But now it was closed, and we had quoted Sammy's son saying that he would not reopen.

The fires and destruction had stopped for only a few hours as people packed the convention center downtown for the funeral of Commissioner Grey, Reverend Smallwood and the other victims of the bombing. It was a long, emotional day of prayers and weeping and of promises by officials from Montgomery and Washington that the bomber would be brought to justice. The Vice President came and standing with Commissioner Grey's widow and two daughters prayed for calm in the city, and he too promised justice. Reverend Al Sharpton flew from New York City for the funeral, held a press conference in the park across from the church and broadcast his cable network talk show from the Civil Rights Center. Surrounded by black ministers, officials and businessmen from Iron City, Sharpton praised Grey and Smallwood and lamented the loss of their leadership. He too called on Heaven and Washington to bring the bombers to justice.

The riots started again that night. Few had much faith in the politicians' promises.

I turned south toward downtown and passed two police cars. A third had pulled over a relic of a car, and the police officers were frisking two black men as they lay face down on the sidewalk. It had become such a common scene I hardly noticed it.

Gangs of black teenagers, led by angry men in their twenties and thirties, had torched several of the major buildings. The saddest was the burning of the Church of the Advent. The beautiful church in the center of downtown, where I had attended a Good Friday service last spring, had gone up in flames. In our story on the burning of the Church of the Advent, we quoted a note delivered to the newspaper that said only: "A whitey church for one of ours." The fires burned right through the sanctuary. The stained glass windows, depicting the Last Supper and Sermon on the Mount, melted in the blaze. What was left after the flames burned the beautiful building and gardens had been destroyed by the fire crews dispatched to save them. This church would be rebuilt, but it would never again for me or anyone else who watched it burn be the quiet refuge in the center of the city.

Across Main Street a group of about a dozen men had attacked the new Commercial Bank Tower, an elegant glass and steel skyscraper, a symbol to many of the new Iron City. The rioters had peppered the building with shotguns, poured gasoline throughout the lobby and lit it. The *Post* carried photos on page one of the burning tower. The police evacuated everyone in a Herculean effort while the firemen fought the flames leaping toward the upper floors.

Leaving the bank tower a charred relic as Iron City's new image broadcast on television and the Internet around the world, the gangs turned to other downtown buildings. Black smoke blocked out the sun for days. Police and fire crews battled the rioters and the flames with little success.

Police in riot gear now patrolled the streets. But there weren't enough officers, not enough jail cells. The rioters struck unexpectedly, seemingly at random, with lightning-fast raids, burning and destroying. As quickly as they came, they were gone. The police were baffled and frustrated.

"These riots are really strange," said Walt Simpson, a longtime friend and savvy political adviser to the Iron City political bosses. He called me from his Cadillac as he watched a building being torched. "It seems organized. Who the hell ever heard of a planned riot?"

The better question was who was planning them and why.

I made a left turn onto Seventh Avenue. A teenage boy, wearing a white t-shirt with some logo I didn't recognize, ran out of the old housing project next to the new charter school that was heralded as the solution for all that ails Iron City public education. He had ear buds in, listening to some music that made him almost dance along the sidewalk. I paid him no attention. He was just another teenager among dozens hanging out, until he bent down and picked up a brick. He turned and threw it at my car, cracking the windshield of the Blazer into a spider web.

What the hell had I done to deserve that? Was he blind? My skin was as dark as his. Maybe it was the suit and tie.

Policemen in two cars, cruising slowly one after another, stopped, jumped out of their patrol cars and chased the boy into the housing project. One officer talked on the radio, while the other three ran after him. When the officer finished reporting in, he slammed the door and raced after the others. They carried only their handguns and batons. Barely able to see through the windshield, I pulled the car to the curb. I told myself I shouldn't drive it. But really I was so annoyed at the shattered windshield, I couldn't resist watching the chase.

The old housing project had been there as long as I could remember. A hundred units were spread over several blocks. The federal Department of Housing and Urban Development gave it a facelift several years ago to make it look less like the bunker-style projects the government once used to warehouse poor people. But the surgery was only skin deep. Housing officials touted these apartments in press releases and speeches as a stepping stone for the poor. Mostly the one-story apartments served as a permanent downtown ghetto. Few flowers or grass grew out of the mud. The play areas were littered with broken glass. Only one child with an older sister watching played on the plastic slide and swing set. Otherwise the area was desolate.

The policemen, weighed down by their tactical gear, helmets and Kevlar-lined vests, waddled in the wake of the boy. They made it halfway down the narrow corridor between two of the buildings when a group of black men stepped out at the far end. Some carried baseball bats. A few held garbage can lids for shields. Others brandished knives and tire irons.

Behind the policemen at the near end of the buildings, several more armed men stepped out of apartments. One, talking on a phone, directed the attack. He yelled at the teenage girl and her brother to get inside. She hustled her brother off the slide and dragged him into an apartment as he cried at having to stop playing, or maybe because he felt his sister's fear at being caught on a battlefield. The trap was well laid. The four cops, outnumbered and outmaneuvered, even with their guns and riot equipment, were going to be badly hurt, probably killed.

No one cared that I was still there. My car had served its purpose, the bait to lure in the cops. I locked the doors and almost drove away. No one would expect me to get involved. As a newspaper editor, I am supposed to remain neutral, and my skin color might raise the question of where my loyalties lay. But journalists, despite the prevailing view of us, do have a conscience.

It was all surreal, watching the prelude to battle. Things moved almost in slow motion. The attackers did not advance immediately. They seemed to be enjoying the panic they had created in the policemen they hated. I shook my head, bringing me back to reality. I dialed 911 and told the operator what was about to happen. She bounced the call to the police station a few blocks away.

"Commander Howell, this is Joe Riordan. I'm editor of the *Post.* I'm in my car watching a battle about to start. Four of your men are trapped in the housing project off Seventh Avenue. They are in big trouble."

"Yeah, I know who you are. You say you're in the project? Four of my men are in trouble? Big trouble?"

I described the scene and gave him the exact address.

"Okay, we're on our way. Get out of there. Now. We don't need any more civilians killed, especially you. But, ... thanks." As he disconnected, I thought he sounded surprised that I had called.

A yell went up from the attackers. The ones with garbage lids banged them like drums. I knew the promised rescue would be too late, even if Howell got troops here in minutes. And then what? If four white cops were killed by a gang of black men, any hope of ending the riots peacefully would evaporate in a hot wind. The fighting would escalate: black against white, civilian versus cop. Iron City might as well change its name to the I Don't Want to Live Here city.

The Blazer needed a new windshield anyway. I gunned the engine, the car jumped the curb, crossed the sidewalk and hit the dirt between the two buildings. Six men with their backs to me stood in my path. When they heard the engine, they jerked their heads just in time to see my car headed toward them. They stepped aside as I sped passed them. One hit my car with a bat. A few feet behind the policemen, I hit the brakes and the horn. The policemen, their guns and sticks drawn ready for what was probably their last fight, did not have to be asked twice. One opened the front door and slumped in the seat, mumbling a thank you. Two scrambled onto the car roof, holding on to the luggage rack and aiming their guns at the crowd. One was perched precariously on the hood with little to hold onto. I shifted into reverse and started to back the Blazer out, slowly this time.

The attackers threw the bats and tire irons. A few picked up rocks and hurled them at the retreating car. The windshield shattered more, but the plastic held. The pounding got worse. I could hear cries and grunts from the cops outside. I reversed in as straight a line as I could. The attackers caught up with the car and in the hand to hand battle with our survival on the line, they tried to pull and knock the men off the car. The Blazer rocked on its axles. The fury aimed at us felt like we were caught in a tornado.

No shots were fired. A bat hit the policeman on the hood in the head. He fell back against the windshield. A cop on the roof grabbed his arm to keep him from falling or being dragged off. The man with the phone shouted and gestured wildly at the other men. He wore wrap-around dark glasses, and I doubted I could recognize him if I looked at mug shots or ran into him again.

A few more feet, and we bounced off the curb and sat in the middle of the street. The two cops on the roof jumped down and joined the cop who had been sitting beside me. They were ready to fight. One of the policemen held his right arm that looked broken at a grotesque angle between the elbow and wrist. I hid in the Blazer, praying the attackers wouldn't see me.

The black men chased the policemen into the street. Then I heard it. A police helicopter swooped in and hovered over us. Its giant rotors churned up a whirlwind, blowing the attackers off stride. An officer in the helicopter turned on a speaker and shouted "Police. Stand back. Drop your weapons." The calm, firm voice rained down. Few sounds had ever been so sweet. In an instant, the helicopter shifted the advantage to the police. It took only a few minutes for the reinforcements the commander had promised to arrive, screaming down the block in several vans and cars. They bolted out of the vehicles, wearing full tactical gear and ran toward us in rows with their batons outstretched in front of them. The attackers, now outnumbered, scattered quickly. They disappeared into the housing project as quickly as they had come.

The man with the phone watched at his army melt away. His whole body shook in anger. He bent over and started to slam his phone to the ground, but stopped his arm in mid-swing. He shrugged, then jogged off in the same direction as his men. I so wanted to know who was on the other end of the phone.

With police surrounding the officers and my Blazer, I stepped out to look at the damage. The beloved car looked like it had rolled down a cliff. I dreaded telling my son. He and I enjoyed it on our Saturday outings. I hoped the insurance company would pay to put it back together.

"Christ, I thought we were dead," said the cop with his broken arm. Another cop hugged me. Tears rolled down his face. "Man, I don't believe it." He was young, and it was probably the first time he had faced death.

Cops and reporters are often at odds. It was nice for a moment to be on the same side. We joked that we knew how Custer must have felt and thanked the commander for bringing the cavalry. It didn't occur to me until later that I was the lone Indian standing among the cavalry.

An ambulance arrived, and the medics began treating the unconscious policeman, now lying on the asphalt of the street. He was out, but breathing. They immobilized the other cop's broken arm. The others had escaped with bruises and scratches where their gear didn't cover. I was less sure about their psyches, or mine.

2

The newsroom at the *Post* is home. Littered with stacks of old newspapers and half-empty Coke cans on desks, the large, mostly open room is a constant buzz from noon to midnight when the last editions roll out. While newsrooms at other newspapers have evolved to look more like insurance company offices, the *Post* newsroom remains open. There are few cubicles, just desks. Telephones ring constantly, people swear, laugh or yell across the room, police radio scanners squawk in an on-going cacophony.

I love it.

Standing there now, my Blazer towed away to the body shop, I felt both relief and a sense that everything familiar was unreal. My head spun. Half of my brain expected that the battle I had just witnessed would have transformed at least something. The other half of my brain was having trouble believing it had happened.

"The circulation figures are on your desk," said Joiner, one of the *Examiner*'s underlings. Joiner, I don't think I ever knew his first name, was the liaison between us at the *Post* and his bosses at the *Iron City Examiner*, our partner and at the same time our rival in the two-newspaper town. Joiner's was a thankless job.

"How much space are we getting today?" I asked automatically.

"Uh, well, that hasn't come through yet," Joiner answered.

Snap. I was back in the real world. "You know it's due by three. Where is it?" I was annoyed.

"We're just running behind today. A little snafu."

"Playing the game again, maybe, huh?" I said.

Joiner shrugged his shoulders with his hands held out, palms up. A non-response. There never was. The two newspapers loath one another, but were forced to work in tandem and in the same building. The *Post* and the *Examiner* co-exist in a joint operating structure that the Babcock Newspaper Syndicate in Alexandria, Virginia had negotiated fifteen years ago with Robert Daniels, Sr., who was then publisher and owner of the *Examiner*. Old man Daniels was dead now, and his heir, the pompous, arrogant, powerful Robert Jr., is the publisher and majority stockholder. The agreement continues, apparently making money for both, while keeping us on a taut leash.

We publish a morning newspaper, which in most cities was the dominant newspaper with the larger number of readers and advertisers. But in Iron City the *Examiner*, which published the afternoon paper, had the larger circulation. This phenomenon, I was told, came from the 1930s and 1940s when the mill workers went to work early and came home early. They wanted their newspaper when they got home, not before dawn when they were headed to work. My grandfather always read the *Examiner*.

The *Examiner* also publishes the Sunday edition, the only day we aren't allowed to print a paper. That Sunday edition generates more than forty percent of the *Examiner's* weekly revenues. It also gives the *Examiner* clout we can't match with just six-day-a-week newspaper. Our Saturday edition is puny. A reader once wrote to complain that he could read our Saturday paper and still have a quarter cup of coffee left. I started to write back and suggest he drink faster.

"I have to know the size of our news hole for tomorrow if we are to get out a paper by six," I said.

"Okay, Joe, chill out. You'll have it."

It was just a daily reminder from the Fifth Floor of how dependent we are on the *Examiner*. Daniels and the other *Examiner* brass seem to enjoy these little games. They can hassle us without killing us, a kind of slow death.

The afternoon news meeting had already started. I could hear the excited discussions going on, as the section editors argued stories and placement. Normally I loved being in the middle of it. But today I was in another world. The real story was Mark's. It gave me a sense that a small piece of my friend was still alive. And it was the story of a lifetime.

The television in my office was on. I pushed the button on the DVD machine and played again the BET recording of the church's last service. On the television, Reverend Smallwood opened the service. The choir sang old hymns I remembered from childhood while sitting between my parents at church. The minister prayed and welcomed the dignitaries, introducing several of them by name as life-long friends and "soldiers who had fought long and hard for our people." The camera panned to show the celebrities in the audience. There was a sea of heads in the packed church.

Smallwood introduced Grey. I watched as the commissioner worked the crowd into a frenzy. It was great theater. I thought about the first time Grey had walked in my office. He was more than just a natural politician. He was a chameleon, capable of adapting to any environment. In my office asking for the *Post*'s endorsement in front of my managing editor, editorial page editor, city editor and me, he was as buttoned down as any silk-tied lawyer. Riding with one of the county's road paving crews, he could be one of the men who put on thick gloves and hard hats everyday. And once I had watched him sing in a nightclub. Barry White couldn't have done it better. After the meeting, he had asked for a word in private. Our chat lasted for an hour.

He filled up my small office. His height and charisma dwarfed the collection of knickknacks scattered around the office and the series of portraits of Indian princes that I had inherited from my first editor. Howard, my old mentor and friend who occupied this office when I was a rookie reporter, must have loved hovering over us in that meeting. His ghost still seemed to haunt the room. The commissioner and I talked of personal things: my son, his twin daughters who were about to graduate from high school. I waited for the real Samuel Grey in that pinstriped suit to let down the mask.

"How is it here?" he said waving his left arm toward the newsroom.

"Good," I told him. "They are like family."

"I thought it might be hard, you being the first of us to be editor," he said.

I shook my head. "It's what I always wanted."

He paused and looked around the office. "I know your father."

"Everybody knows Dad."

"Seems like a nice guy," the commissioner said, not meaning it. I nodded.

"He must be really proud of you, being editor and all."

It was time to cut through the bullshit. "Not really. Dad always wanted me to be a banker. As you probably guessed, he was a bastard at home. Not like when he was at the bank or out at the cocktail parties. There was, probably still is, a lot of rage in him."

My father, tall, strikingly handsome with a stride like a general on parade, was half white and half black in a world where that was the thing people noticed first, ahead of your competence at your job or your character. He did his job well, but without love or passion. The First State Bank, in its quest to be a progressive southern bank, needed a black officer to help African American customers feel more comfortable. He also was tasked to tell them that their accounts were in arrears or they were not getting the mortgage they needed to buy a house or the loan to expand their business. Being black, the owners thought, would make a bitter pill easier for the black customers to swallow. With a black man is telling them the bad news, they believed the customers would not think it was because they were black that the bank wouldn't help them. Hiring him also showed the world that Iron City and the bank had changed, that it was no longer the bastion of racism. My father, the first in our family to graduate from college, walked out of the all-black Mission College and straight into the bank's junior executive training program. At the time, he was one of a few black professionals in Iron City. Now there were many more doctors, lawyers, insurance brokers and bankers.

After five years as a teller and junior loan officer he was given an office on the first floor to make sure everyone saw him. He rarely missed a charity luncheon or dinner. He was never chairman of the chamber of commerce, but was always appointed to visible committees. The Irish side of him gave him a quick smile, an endless banter of jokes and a lighter shade of skin color. His black side kept him frustrated with the world where he was neither fish nor fowl. Both sides of his genetics made him drink.

I wondered what Grey knew about my father.

"Drove him home a couple of times when he had a snoot full. We talked some. A lot going on there." The large man looked down at his folded hands on pressed trousers. "Tough old world out there. Tough to be caught in the middle wanting to be in the white world, but not able to give up being black. Things seem better for you. You know who you are, what you want. You're father do that for you?"

I shook my head. "I had my mother. She was my world. And my grandfather. When he breezed into my life, all my little fears floated away."

He nodded. "I think things will be better for my girls. The world's changed, at least on the surface. You know we've got two girls just like the First Family in the White House. Ain't that something?"

He paused and looked at me without really seeing.

"I wanted to be a surgeon, but couldn't make heads or tails out of chemistry. They told me to be a lawyer. I certainly had the bullshit down pat. Went up to Fisk, but hated it. Came home and got married. Worked for a while, made some friends, got involved in a few elections. Then I let myself be talked into running for county commissioner. Pretty simple resume."

Sitting in the chair opposite my desk, Grey told me I was a source of pride in the community. I thanked him, but knew he thought I had been named editor for the same reason my father got his carpeted office at the bank. He thought I was the token black man in the Babcock chain, an African American with a big title who could be waltzed out by the owners and managers on special occasions to quell criticism from the Congressional Black Caucus or the NAACP that the newspaper chain was not progressive enough in hiring minorities in management. "Look," they would say and probably had said, "we have an African American editor, not in New York or Cleveland, but in the heart of Dixie, in Iron City."

I had wanted to tell Grey that it was not like that. But I didn't know how to say it without sounding more than a little naive. We sat there in the corner office, two men who could hardly have set foot in here only a couple of generations before, much less belong there. I think we understood one another.

Grey then turned to what I assumed was the real reason for his visit. He talked about his vision for Iron City's future. He dreamed of a city where there was collaboration between the traditionally powerful white business executives and government officials with the growing African American communities. He wanted to create enterprise centers that promoted black entrepreneurs in the health care fields, spin offs of the large University of Alabama medical center. And he wanted to make sure every black child had the opportunity to succeed. He talked of creating after school and Saturday school programs that would teach black children new skills for the modern world.

It was an impressive agenda. I told him so.

"So join me. You and me. We are more alike than not. We can change this city. People respect this newspaper. It may not be the largest, but I would bet it is the best read. Folks respect you. Together we can make a real difference. We need to finish what

Shuttlesworth and King started. They had a dream for achieving equality for black folks. We've made a lot of progress. But we are not there yet. There is more to do, a lot more. With you and me working together, we can finish what they started in the churches and the parks and the streets. Remember they didn't have a newspaper that reported the news fairly."

We shook hands and agreed to work together. I explained that there were limits to what stories we could write. He said he understood our ethics code. I promised we would support him where we could in our editorials. We would look for opportunities to write news articles that educated the community on issues he cared about and about the successes and failures he had in achieving that agenda. I promised him that he would not be ignored.

"That is all I can ask," he said.

When he left, I thought we had forged an understanding and hoped we would have a long, productive friendship that would do good for Iron City. The best plans often go awry. It only took one redneck and a bomb in the basement of a church.

I looked at the television screen. Grey held the congregation enthralled. I watched as he took the crowd through the accomplishments African Americans had made in Iron City. From Bull Wainwright, who had run the Iron City Police force like his personal gestapo, to Barack Obama, we have made it down a long and bumpy road at a very fast pace.

On the television, Grey shouted: "But the gains that black folks before us have made in the past mock us here today. We are not all the way free or, God forgive me, equal with the white man. The road we travel is long. It is smoother and straighter than it was, but it is not so easy as the road traveled by white folks."

The congregation yelled "Amen."

"We are no longer slaves. There are no more white and colored restrooms. We can eat in any restaurant as long as we got the green or the plastic. But are you satisfied?"

"No!" came the chant from the congregation.

I muted the sound, but left the disc playing. Funny how I did not feel a part of the rich history that made my people who they are. I was not even born in the 1960s, when students were jailed for sitting at a North Carolina department store lunch counter or when Rosa Parks, a black woman in Montgomery, refused to give up her seat on a bus. I had learned about the protests, the riots, the jailings from books, at church and on television. My parents rarely discussed it.

I opened the door to the conference room. The daily news meeting had already begun. I looked around the table at close friends, men and women I had worked with for years. Those who bothered to wear ties had pulled them down. Several slouched in their chairs, leaning back, eyes closed. Coffee cups, Coke cans, candy wrappers littered the long conference room table competing for space with newspapers, laptops and iPads.

They had all been there with me when Sheila died and stood by me when I had gone off the deep end, when I was my own worst enemy. No one had judged me harshly. They could have. I could have hurt not just my own reputation and set the tongues wagging about a black man who was promoted above his station, but also the newspaper's image and everyone who worked for it. Through the years I had been to their homes in times of crisis, driven them home when they were drunk, exhausted or depressed and fought for them when the owners of the Babcock chain of newspapers issued edicts from their office building overlooking the Potomac River that squeezed salaries and trimmed staff. We worked together to produce a newspaper we took pride in. We forged a bond that transcended friendship. Our lives were mixed up together like clothes of several different people twisted together in a washing machine. Newspapers built those kinds of relationships.

"Look, you morons, this is a good story." Amanda Franklin, the Lifestyle section editor, was again fighting for one of a story. An anorexic woman who favored long, sweeping skirts, Amanda had edited the Lifestyle section for five years. She fought hard for her

THE NEW YORKER

☐ 23 ISSUES FOR JUST $1.74 AN ISSUE

SAVE UP TO 81% OFF THE COVER PRICE

Plus get the New Yorker Canvas Tote — FREE!

Name _____
(Please Print)

Street _____ Apt. No. _____

City _____ State _____ Zip _____

E-mail _____

Bonus: to get the 90th Anniversary **Book of Cartoons FREE**, order at newyorker.com/go/cartoonbook1

Best Deal! → ☐ I prefer 47 issues for only $1.49 an issue

☐ Payment enclosed   ☐ Bill me later

J5H5J2

NO POSTAGE
NECESSARY
IF MAILED
IN THE
UNITED STATES

Get the 90th Anniversary Book of Cartoons:

newyorker.com/go/cartoonbook1

Offer valid in the U.S. only. First issue mails within 3 weeks.
Please add applicable sales tax.

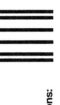

BUSINESS REPLY MAIL
FIRST-CLASS MAIL   PERMIT NO. 107   BOONE IA

POSTAGE WILL BE PAID BY ADDRESSEE

THE

NEW YORKER

PO BOX 37684
BOONE, IA 50037-2684

stories, but often lost out to wire services stories about some entertainment scandal or the latest from the *New England Journal of Medicine*.

"Boring. Bor-ring," hissed the copy desk editor. A tall, thin man, who always wore a white short-sleeved shirt and his seven year Alcoholics Anonymous pin, took great pleasure in taunting Amanda. I thought her free spirit threatened him in small box he had to live in to keep at bay the temptation to drink. "We've got a war out there in the streets. We don't have room for fru-fru stories," he said.

She took the bait. "The problem with this newspaper is that it has Dracula working the damn copy desk."

At the far end of the table, Ed Simmons smiled in relief when he saw me standing in the doorway. He was the managing editor, my right hand and long-time friend. "You want to sit here, Joe?"

I smiled and shook my head. This was his problem.

The daily news meeting was scheduled for three fifteen every afternoon. Some days it even started on time. The editors for the separate sections gathered to discuss the stories they had their reporters working. They competed for placement of stories with the best going above the fold on page one. National and international news generally took up more than half of the front page. But we took pride in knocking off some of the wire service stories with local stories. It was the way we beat the *Examiner* and got to hear the radio and television guys reading our stuff the next morning, a good reason to get up after a long night.

Amanda's story was about new diabetes research at the university. She knew I had a soft spot for diabetes stories because the damned disease had eaten up my grandfather and was slowly killing my father. Ed resolved it by telling her to make sure she got an interview with the doctor and a good photo. "I don't want to read a rewrite of a press release and one of those glamour shots of the doctor."

"What else we got?" Ed asked looking around the room. "The *Examiner* had a good piece on some interdenominational ministers group meeting to develop a plan to stop the riots. Any reaction from the cops or City Hall on that? The mayor and governor hold press conferences, saying they are working to bring the riots to an end, but don't really say a damn thing. What are they doing? Anything? We need a follow up."

Clay Johnson, the city editor, nodded, his head down making notes.

The wire editor cleared his throat. "The Justice Department has a report out on hate crimes. We made it high on their list again, mostly because of the church bombing. The stats are broken down by state, but not by city. They recorded fifty-seven in Alabama last year."

Ed looked at me with his eyebrows raised, his way of asking what I thought. I waggled my hand to say it was just an okay story, not great. "Can we get the list of the hate crimes in the state?" Ed asked. "The list would make it more interesting."

The news editor said he would call the Justice Department in Washington and ask. "Maybe Ms. Deputy Attorney General Keene would like to comment," Ed added, his voice thick with sarcasm. "She hasn't had much to say in the last couple of weeks about Iron City. We're probably due."

I had never asked him, but wondered, not for the first time, if there were any public officials that Ed liked. He was typical of many in the newsroom. Most newspaper reporters and editors are cynics by nature, forged by the amount of tragedy, stupidity and evil that seemed to confront them each day. I prefer to think of us as more as optimists without illusions, thrilled when someone actually showed some leadership, but realistic that it rarely amounted to much.

Bob Karem, the business editor, announced that the city had lost another major convention. He seemed about to cry. The riots had crippled the city. More businesses were threatening to move out of town. No new business or industry would now even consider expanding into Iron City. Major conventions had canceled. And the Alabama-Tennessee college football game, which was scheduled to be played at the Veterans Memorial Field in Iron City, had been moved to Knoxville this year. The loss of the one game would cost hotels, bars and restaurants millions. The mayor was screaming about the loss in sales taxes.

"That's not really new news. Put it on your page, okay?" Ed said. In our space crunch, we allocated only one page to business. It was usually a section front page, followed by what was left of the classified ads after the Internet had finished stealing most of them.

The state editor reported that our capital reporter had talked with the governor, who was getting antsy to take some action about the riots. He was threatening to send in the National Guard. "Our guys think he's getting nervous that his annual trip to Europe might have to be canceled," the state editor said, causing the room to break up in laughter.

Ed continued around the room. Bud Shaw, the sports editor, opened his eyes and sat forward in his chair. He said more college football recruiting scandals were being investigated. "The NCAA is looking into some hot shots at Alabama buying cars and jewelry for the boys." He pantomimed a player showing off his new ring. A burly man with a wide florid face, who always wore his tie loose from his collar, Shaw was almost a legend among our readers. His column probably sold more papers than even the comics.

That story would have to be on page one. College football reigned supreme in the state, evenly divided between those who loved or loathed Auburn University and the University of Alabama. The entire population of the state seemed to hold its breath at Thanksgiving, waiting to see which team would win the Iron Bowl, the annual football rivalry. If Auburn won, Alabama fans seethed. Auburn fans took no pride in Alabama's recent championships. The battle was fought as much with bumper stickers as on the field.

Ed asked if there was news on what college, Eugene Crabtree, a promising young tailback from Woodlawn High School, was considering. We had run several stories on the young man, comparing him to legendary running backs. Shaw said he called Ms. Crabtree daily for updates on her son. "She's warming up to me. I think in another month we are going to start dating."

My thoughts were still on the street outside. College football seemed almost irrelevant after seeing the anger in the eyes of the men attacking the cops. It disturbed me more that it was not spontaneous. I couldn't shake it off. Maybe I had been at a desk too long. My reporting days had ended six years ago and for five years before that I worked in the Babcock Newspaper chain's Washington bureau, covering Congress. That was more of a nine-to-five job than most reporting positions. For me breaking news was no longer a contact sport. Today I got a closer view of the action than I cared to.

And then there was Mark's article. Depending on what we did with it, his article would propel not just me, but all these friends into one of our biggest battles. They would be called 'nigger lovers'. Some would be shunned socially. We would get hate mail and threats. Maybe even one of us, or a member of our families, could be hurt.

We had printed tough stories before. We had been threatened before. When I was a rookie, a city councilman had held Mark Hodges and me at gunpoint in his office. But in those days death didn't seem real. We felt invincible. I didn't believe a councilman would shoot us in city hall. He didn't. He was just being dramatic.

If we ran Mark's last article, would the city be better off for it? Or was it just news, something to sell more papers?

"Joe, what do you think? Is Mike's story page one?" Ed asked.

I shrugged. I hadn't been listening. Ed and I worked together long enough that he knew it and told me what I had missed in the last few minutes.

"Mike's chasing a story that the council is ready to ask the mayor to make the police chief go public with what he's got on the bombing. Bates has been pretty tight-lipped lately on any leads he's got."

"Probably because he hasn't got any," came the inevitable cynical comment.

I nodded. "That's fine." Mike Rose, the city hall reporter, was young with good instincts on a story, and despite my best efforts to recruit more, he was one of our few black reporters. I had a fond place in my soul for city hall reporters. I had been one for several years. Because he was also black, I saw Mike as a younger version of me.

"Let's couple it with a riot story I witnessed on my way in today. Get Pat to talk to the cops. It was pretty hairy. I'll give you the details."

"Where was it?" asked Clay Johnson.

"Around on Seventh."

Clay, who supervised the city reporters, pulled out his phone and sent Pat Galloway, our police reporter, a text.

It was nearly four. The news meeting broke up and everyone headed back to finish editing and laying out for the first edition. Ed stood up slowly and started for the door.

"One more thing, Ed." I stopped him in his tracks. A few times before I had dropped a bomb on him with the same words. It usually meant something new from our owners or a battle with the *Examiner*. He frowned at me and sat back down.

"We've got a ball buster that Mark Hodges wrote before he died. You and Clay read it in here and let me know what you think. It needs a lot of work. But if it checks out, and I believe it will, this information will blow the lid off of things," I said.

Ed raised one eyebrow. Clay put down his phone and looked at me.

"The bottom line, I think we know who bombed the church." Just saying those words I felt a flutter in my chest.

"No shit!" Clay said. "You trust it? You trust him?"

I tossed a hard copy of Mark's article at them. "I'll let you decide. But only the two of you read this. And give it back to me. No leaks."

Clay's young assistant, whose firm, heart-shaped ass and tight pants made almost every guy in the news room lust after her, stepped into the room. Pat was on the phone, she announced, then turned and swished back toward the city desk. We all stared as she walked. Clay looked at his watch, swore, threw down his copy of Mark's article he had only started to read and went to take the call. Ed continued reading.

Three minutes later, Clay was back. "Pat's on the riot story on Seventh. He said he had already gotten a tip on it. Something about you saving several cops. True?"

I shrugged.

"What happened?"

I gave him the short version. Clay shook his head. "You gonna write the story or you want someone to interview you?" I smiled at the deference. Nobody but the editor would have that option.

"I can still write a story."

The *Examiner* was squeezing us again. When I stepped back in my office, the overdue space report was on my desk. I'd have to live with it today, but it was time to visit Daniels and his henchmen upstairs in their Fifth Floor inner sanctum. Taking on Daniels was not something I enjoyed, but seemed to be something that I had to do about every six months. Henry Jenkins, who was the editor of the *Post* after Howard died, refused to take him on, and our news hole shrunk steadily for the first two years he ran the paper.

A few months after I came back from Washington to be the *Post*'s managing editor, I volunteered to meet with Daniels and his senior staff. I expected Jenkins to say no, but he jumped at it. Daniels' big personality scared him. Tall, handsome and always better dressed than anyone around him, Daniels seemed to like intimidating people, so I decided I would never give him that satisfaction. After the meeting, Jenkins heard from one of Daniels' flunkies that I had been "argumentative" and "uppity." He was told that Daniels did not want me, the second in command, representing the *Post* in the future. Jenkins lectured me that I shouldn't have bothered "Mr. Daniels," but the *Examiner* increased our pages for the next several weeks. I told Jenkins I thought I should continue going to the meetings. He could feign having the flu or be out of town. He agreed, a wave of relief cascading across his face, but he warned me not to annoy Daniels. In effect, I became the editor of the *Post* that day,

The elder Daniels died of lung cancer during my second year at the *Post*. He had built the company that owned the *Examiner* into a financial giant with four television stations and several daily and weekly newspapers around the country. For all the money his television stations made him, his love was the newspapers and particularly the *Examiner*. I like to think he had ink in his veins.

Old man Daniels used his media company to wield power that stretched to Washington and New York. Alabama governors returned the elder Daniels' phone calls faster than their most generous contributors. Bankers called him back quicker than they did their largest depositors. Nothing big moved in the city or the state without the old man's okay. He lived in a world of privilege, as his son did now. In what seemed like a throw-back to the plantation era, the Daniels father and son were served lunch daily by a tuxedo-clad, black man in a private dining room off the publisher's office. It was in that room that many decisions were made, what candidates to endorse for office, whose businesses should be promoted, whose reputations were destroyed. To be invited for lunch meant you had made it to the inner circle of Alabama power. Of course, I had never seen the inside of the room.

Before the cigars he chewed and the smoke he breathed eroded the linings of his lungs and stomach, he could be found most mornings standing near the giant printing machines, waiting for the first paper to roll off. That's where I met him the one and only time. Dressed in a rumpled black suit, he grabbed the paper from the copy boy and opened it. He studied the front page behind a pair of bifocal glasses, running a long, thin finger over the headlines and picture captions. He chuckled to himself. When he turned and saw me watching him, he smiled and said, "Having your own newspaper is better'n bourbon."

I knew what he meant.

The younger Daniels, now in his late forties, reveled in the wealth and ego-massage the *Examiner* gave him, but he lacked his father's passion for it. The newspaper's quality had declined. With his father at the helm, the *Examiner* had won some good prizes, including one Pulitzer Prize for photography. Today it lacked a sense of urgency. Politicians and socialites still kissed up to the younger Daniels, but he did not possess the skill or ambition to deliver the punch his father had. He seemed disinterested in the daily coverage. When he did get involved, he was heavy handed. Where a rapier was required, he used a club.

Clay stuck his head in the door a little before five o'clock. I was just finishing my weekly call to my boss in Alexandria. "Wow, you left a little out of the description of your role in the fracas today."

"Don't get carried away and blow it all out of proportion," I said.

"Yeah, well there's a lot of difference between saving a couple of cops' asses and taking on an angry mob in your car. Pat says the cops are down there singing your praises. According to their version, you came on like an avenging angel."

I chuckled to myself. Whoever said there was no good irony left in the world. A black editor of a daily newspaper risks his life and car to save four white cops from being killed by an angry mob of black men. That was rich.

"Run it with the jump off Mike's council story," I said. Most jumps, the continuations of stories off page one, usually ran about page six. That would be far enough inside not to cause too much of a problem.

"Right," Clay said dripping sarcasm. "I don't care if it is you. This is a helluva story. Lots of drama and action, cops' lives on the line. I ought to make you write a first-person story like in the old days."

"Howard didn't make Percy write up his story," I said.

Clay left laughing. It was a story from the *Post*'s folklore. This one had reached the status of a legend. When I was a rookie reporter, Percy Sims, our religion page editor, was arrested at the Paris Bookstall, an X-rated bookstore, on Sixth Avenue. He was a strange man, whose body looked like one of those Russian dolls, an overly large round head on top of an even rounder body. Percy, who lived with his mother, wore the same thin black tie with food stains on it every day. He had two loves in life, Jesus and pornography.

When Percy was arrested, Howard asked Pat Galloway, the veteran police reporter, to talk the officer into filing his arrest as a disorderly conduct, not indecent exposure or lewd public display. Percy would have been publicly humiliated, and more important to Howard, could not spin a story to his church friends. It was the newspaper's policy then that if you did something that violated the law, you wrote your own story and it went on page one where no reader could miss it. It was never a good policy and was now gathering dust in the human resources manual. Pat wrote Percy's story that night, and Percy kept on writing the religious news.

Howard was one of the newspaper's best editors and prompted two local professors to write his biography that lauded his impact on the city. He spent his whole career at the *Post*, and I doubt he could have imagined working anywhere else. Raised as an only child by his modestly wealthy, widowed mother in a small south Alabama town on the banks of the Tombigbee River, Howard didn't care much about dogs or football or fishing. He didn't play golf or hang out at the country club. He like producing the *Post* and studying people. Even late in life when cancer had eaten a hole in his colon, Howard could sit in his hospital room and tell me what was going on at the newspaper. He told me being editor was easy, all you had to do was read minds. Only then, he told me, would I be a good editor. A newspaper, I learned from him, is not the printing presses, the ink, the paper, the Web site and Facebook accounts or even the advertising that brought in the dollars to pay for it all. It was the people who wrote stories about other people.

The day after he was arrested, Percy was back at his desk, twirling around in his chair, an extra-long telephone wire wrapped around his plump torso. In a grating voice so high it sounded like a seagull's call, he told ministers and choir directors an elaborate tale about how he had been assigned to write a story on the protests in front of the Paris Bookstall. When he went inside the shop to get a comment from the clerk, he said he had become outraged at the sight of "those filthy magazines" and started throwing them at the man behind the counter. Percy neglected to mention that he spent a chunk of his check each week buying the same magazines. Under his desk as he was concocting his lie, there were several magazines stuffed in an old satchel-style briefcase that went home with him every night. He told his church contacts that he had been arrested for yelling at the clerk, not that he had been unlucky enough to be caught with his pants around his ankles in the back plugging quarters in the video machine.

I was shocked that we had knowingly published a false story. I charged into Howard's office full of indignation to ask why we hadn't told the readers the truth. After all, truth was something we stood for, I said self-righteously. Howard laughed at my naivete.

"Sometimes, not often, but sometimes, the truth can hurt more than it helps," he told me. "Besides, who else could I get to write that damn religion page?"

Twenty years later, sitting in Howard's chair, I knew why he had published a less than truthful story about Percy's arrest. If we had, Howard would have had to suspend or fire Percy, who had since retired and still took care of his aging mother. Without the *Post* and his status among the church crowd, his life would have spiraled downward. Instead, Howard allowed him to keep his job on the condition that he visited a therapist once a week. He put the person ahead of the principle.

After I hit the send button, forwarding my story to Clay, I stepped out out of my office, where I often felt claustrophobic, and found the newsroom abuzz. Clay had told the staff about my afternoon adventure. Several of the veterans came over to shake my hand and clap me on the back. Most seemed to appreciate the irony of the situation.

As I walked by the city desk, Clay looked up from editing my story, smiled and gave me a thumbs up. I had promoted Clay to be the city editor shortly after I was named editor. He had good instincts for what made a story interesting and managed his limited number of reporters well. Ed Simmons, who had been city editor, was elevated to my old job as managing editor. Although Ed's shoes were a bit large for Clay to fill, they made a good team.

Small and wiry, Clay was a physically strong man in his mid-thirties. He had been an Army sniper for six years before opting out for civilian life and college. Over his favorite dinner, a cheeseburger, fries and Dr Pepper at the Elite Grill two blocks from the newspaper, he often regaled us with stories of how he could sneak up on targets behind enemy lines. He talked about learning patience to crawl inch-by-inch for miles to set up for the right shot. We teased him that few of his reporters, and certainly not his ex-wife, would ever associate patience with the name of Clay Johnson.

He had mellowed with the years, but they had not improved his fashion sense, always wearing one of three hideously ugly ties. Like many journalists, Clay's personal life was a bit off kilter. After being married and divorced young, he had found a woman who made him happy, a topless dancer with the stage name of Nightingale. She was good at taking money off gullible guys who paid to see her take off her bra and hoped for something more. But she went home after 2 a.m. to Clay, who also worked late putting out the last edition. They often ate dinner, he told me, at 3 in the morning. When he first took me to meet her, he hadn't told me much about her. I thought we were stopping for a beer at a bar over the mountain. When Nightingale came on stage, Clay went up and put a ten-dollar bill between her ample breasts. He told me she was the love of his life and showed me a photo on his phone of them together. My mouth fell open, then I almost pissed my pants laughing.

The senior copy desk editor, who was responsible for writing a headline, hovered over Clay as he edited the story. They would all want banner headlines, *Post Editor Saves Police From Attack*, but knew I would nix that. I wanted a one-column head next to an ad for a credit card debt relief service where few of our readers would notice it.

Some editors and publishers like Daniels love being famous. Hardly a week went by that the *Examiner* failed to carry a photo of its owner accepting an award and speaking at some dinner. He sat on the board of almost every major civic and charitable organization. He had been the chairman of the chamber of commerce, the symphony board, the United Way and a half dozen other organizations. I had no such ambitions. Being the first black editor of a major newspaper in Iron City brought me enough recognition. I had dreamed of being the editor of the *Post* since the day I walked in the door and met Howard. Sitting for the first time in his office looking at those Indian chief portraits on the wall, I knew this was what I wanted. My father was adamant that I use the college education he had partially paid for to follow in his footsteps at the bank. But counting other people's money never got my juices flowing.

Howard and I would sit in his office many mornings talking about the newspaper business. He never had a son and, at that point, I needed a different father. He taught me about power and how it moved best when quiet. He admired Teddy Roosevelt and had a bust of the old Rough Rider in his office. Howard was a gentle spirit and usually walked softly, but liked having the newspaper as his club.

"If you use it right," he smiled as he said, "you can knock the crap out of people."

Damn his cancer. Howard had planned to live to a ripe old age, writing columns for this and other Babcock newspapers. That never happened. If he were alive today, he would find my dilemma over coverage of the rescue amusing. I could sure use his advice on the Crenshaw story.

3

Ed Simmons came into my office and shut the door. His skin was so pale and thin, one could almost count the blood vessels in his cheeks. He had busted his knee in the Marines before he was twenty. Scar tissue had built up in the knee and made him limp, particularly when he was tired, worried or if it was raining. Now approaching sixty and carrying forty pounds too much from the nightly raid between editions on the candy and chips machine, he limped as he threw the copy of Mark's article on my desk. He sat down and rubbed his knee.

"So what do you think?" I asked.

"Christ Almighty, you know what I think." Ed's tone sounded like a mother talking to a wayward five-year-old. "It's great that maybe he found out who the bomber is, incredible really. But who can trust Mark Hodges?"

"Don't speak ill of the dead," I said.

Ed worried about everything and everybody, especially me. If anything was happening in the newsroom, I only needed to ask Ed. I relied heavily on him. He had a long memory and was totally unflappable in a crisis. When I was hired at the paper, he had been the assistant city editor and sometimes I thought he still saw me that way. Mark had also worked for Ed, who had put up with Mark's drinking, a common malady in the newspaper business, but he could not stomach Mark's disappearances. Ed's German ancestry and the demands for producing a daily newspaper made him a stickler for delivering articles on time. Mark, more Irish and French than Hun, rarely did. I tried saying his stories were worth the wait. It fell on deaf ears.

"I'm sorry he's dead. Especially for you. He never did drive well. His car, whatever he was driving, was always a patchwork of dents. But, damn it," he waved his arms at my desk where the article had landed, "his dying just makes this piece impossible to run. We've got no way to verify any of this."

I knew all the arguments. I turned my chair to the small floor safe that stood beside the credenza. I opened it and pulled out a recorder and set it on the desk.

"You mean you've got ...."

"Just listen." I pushed the play button.

Mark's voice came through the speaker like he was sitting in the room with us. It was hard to believe I had just watched him lowered into his grave. Mark was talking with a man who spoke in one of those drawls that set even other Southerners' teeth on edge. He stumbled over his words and used a lot of "uhs," "ahs," and "you knows." It sounded like they were in a bar and the man Mark was talking with had been there awhile.

"..them darkies getting way too big for their britches. They thinking they as good as white folks. Pretty soon they be wanting to be better'n us, ya know, trying to screw all our women, not just the whores. You hear on TV, how they got bigger dicks than us. Well, I seen a few in the showers when I was doing basic training in the Army. They didn't look so big to me."

"So what're you gonna do about it?" Mark's voice asked.

"(giggle) Well, I don't know 'bout you, uh, but I done my part, you know," the man said.

There was a pause and you could hear chatter and music in the background. "Oh yeah, what you done?" Mark said.

"You want to know what I done? Well, I don't know if I want to tell you," the man said.

"Hey, bartender, my friend here needs another one of those drafts. Bring a shot with it," Mark said. The recording picked up all the sounds around them, making it hard to hear all of their words. Music played on a jukebox. Glasses hit the bar. Mark thanked someone.

"Nectar of the gods, right?" Mark's voice said. "What'd old Ben Franklin say, 'Beer is living proof that God loves us and wants us to be happy.' Ain't that right on?"

"Really, he said that. Ben Franklin. The old guy with the kite? That's funny."

"So tell me, what'd you do to fix black folks?"

There was a long pause while we heard only the sounds of the bar. Ed looked at me and raised his eyebrows to question where the tape was going. I motioned to him to wait.

You could hear the glasses hit the bar again. "Good beer, huh?" Mark said. "Not that cheap watered down stuff. This stuff really stands up."

The other man grunted. Only music and muffled noises came through the recorder for several minutes.

"So, my friend, what is it you done to fix black folks?" Mark asked again.

He ordered two more beers. The bartender, apparently talking to the man with Mark, asked how he was doing. "Might have to cut you off," he said.

"No, no. We're doing fine," Mark said. "I'm taking care of my friend here. We're good. Thanks for worrying about us."

More noise from the bar. Ed was getting impatient. He looked at his watch.

Then the man, slurring his words more than before, said, "Well, I done took care of the biggest nigger of 'em all, around here any-how. Took a few of his pals too. Know what I mean. They know they been got. That's why they been burning and all. I fixed 'em good. You bet I did."

"Wow, that's great. How'd you do it?" Mark was working him, playing the role of the groupie.

"Well, I ain't talking about that." There was silence. A Toby Keith song played in the background. Closer, a glass came down hard on the bar. "Hey, gimme 'nother one," the voice said.

"Here, here, let me get that for you. I wanna hear this story," Mark said.

I chuckled at my friend's tactics. Ed didn't.

"Well, seein's how you's one of us, and all, you gonna love this, man." There was another pause, then he said, "I got the commish himself."

"You did? No shit, you did that? The church? For real, man? That was you? Wow, I'm proud to meet you," Mark said. There was a long pause, then Mark continued, "But how, I mean, how did you come to do it? That's amazing."

An even longer pause on the tape with just sounds from the bar and the jukebox.

"Well, I guess it'll be all right. I mean you ain't with the FBI or nothin'?"

"Me, nawh. Do I look like an FBI man?" Mark said.

"Nawh, I guess you don't. You don't look like some g-man, no fucking Elliott Ness, now do ya?" Both men laughed, and we heard their bottles clang as in a toast.

"This guy, you see, he comes and finds me on the job," the voice said finally. "He knows a lot 'bout me, and all. He knows I got no love for Neegg-roes and shit, so he comes to me and says, 'Why don't I hep 'im get rid of this one big Negro.' I asked who he means, and he tells me the commissioner, the head fuckin' nigger in the county. I laughed and told him, he ain't grey, he's black, real black, like he just came off the boat from Africa or somethin'. That's how it got started. This guy, well, he liked that. We talked 'bout how to kill him, shoot 'im, stab 'im or put 'im down some hole."

"Yeah," Mark said.

"He says Grey been messin' with things that he need'n be messin' with. He says he and some other guys in town wanted him out of the way, you see," the man said.

"He say who those guys were?" Mark asked.

There was no answer for forty seconds. I actually timed it.

"So how did you decide to blow him up?"

"Well, there was this other guy. He calls me on the phone. Says he is a friend of the man I been talking to. He knows all 'bout me and what I been talking with this other guy about. He says it is important that it be real big, send all them darkies a message about who's the boss. Blow 'em all up. Bunch of them all at one time."

"Wow, ain't that something?" Mark said. "D'you know much about blowing things up?"

"Hell, I guess it weren't no secret. I learned to blow up shit like IEDs out at Fort Leonard Wood and then in the badlands, Affuckinganistan. I know about blowin' stuff up. It ain't hard once you know what you doin'. And I do."

"You were in Afghanistan? Damn. Let me shake your hand."

Mark ordered another round and waited until the beers came. "Here's to you man. So, you decided to blow him up. How'd you know about the church meeting?"

"Uh, well, I didn't. You know I never even knew that some good ol' boys years ago had blowed up that same church. Pretty cool, huh? But this guy, the one who called me on the phone, well, he said I should do it at the church, lots of folks there, you know. It'd set the niggers in Iron City back a long way. Back like they were before Martin Luther the Almighty King." The man laughed at his attempt at a joke. "Yeah, he says to me that all white men in the world would 'preciate what I'd done."

"He was right, wasn't he?" Mark said. "Did he pay you?"

"Oh, yeah, well, the first guy did. When we met, he gave me a wad of hundreds and said more would be coming. No problem."

"So what happened?"

"Well, I done it. I got this shirt from a friend of mine with some air conditioning company's name on it. I bought the C-4 from an ol' boy I used to run with down home. Then I went over to the church on that Wednesday afternoon before the big, fuckin' deal was happening. I told the women sittin' in that office next door that I needed to service the air conditioners in the basement. Those women fannin' themselves. They so fat. One of 'em asked me to try to make the air conditioner work better. That was funny, wadn't it? I had the bomb, the detonator and fuse all right there in my bag. They never knew what it was." He giggled. The beer was really going to his head.

"Wow," Mark said encouraging.

"I asked them women if I could see where the preaching was done. They told me to go on in the church, I wouldn't bother nobody. They said the TV boys would be comin' in later to set up. I stepped off how far it was from the front wall to the pulpit. That's where they told me that the head Neegg-rows would be. Then I went down in the basement where they had a big room, lots of photos on the walls and in glass cases of old Negroes. I stepped it off. I got a stepladder out of a workroom and crawled up in the drop-down ceiling. There was a beam runnin' right under the stage, just like it was waitin' on me. I had soften the brick up, twisting it while I sat in the car. I put it on top of the beam. It was perfect. Right there I stuck the fuse in and set it go off twenty minutes after seven, just like the guy on the phone told me too. When I went upstairs, two of those fat women were standing there gigglin'. One of 'em asked me how I liked their church. I told 'em it was better'n any church I'd ever seen. They liked that. I didn't tell 'em it was gonna all be blowed up real soon."

There was a pause. Reba McIntyre was singing a sad love song. The bar noise was getting louder.

"So what'd you think when you heard your bomb blew up the church and killed those folks?" It seemed a risky question to ask. Crenshaw might feel some latent guilt and shut down.

"Aw, shit, why would I care? I was sittin' there in my car. I saw the whole thing. They shouldn't be here. They should've gone back to Africa. Most of 'em were trouble makers. Good riddance," he said. He paused to drink and set his glass down hard again on the bar. "And I got 'em real good too, didn't I?"

Mark was reading the guy well. "Boy, I'd say. People gonna be talking about what you did for years. That guy who called you was right, wasn't he? You sure set 'em back a long way."

"Yeah, I sure did." There was a smile in his voice. "Yeah, I sure did."

On the jukebox, Travis Tritt's song *I'm Gonna Be Somebody* played in the background. The man started humming, then singing the words, "on the harder side of town, where it's hard for a poor boy to find the money." He hummed a few lines, then broke into the chorus:

"I'm gonna be somebody
One of these days I'm gonna break these chains
I'm gonna be somebody someday
You can bet your hard-earned dollar I will."

"That's right. You know, I think that old boy was singing about me," the man said.

"How 'bout another one? Hey, bartender. We're dry over here." There was a pause. "There, how about that? Yeah, here's a ten. Thanks. Keep an eye on us. We don't want to run dry."

The conversation drifted to other topics. They talked about women in the bar, what kind he liked, did he fish or hunt? A George Strait song started on the jukebox. Some guy nearby sang along. Ed shifted in his seat and looked again at his watch. I waved at him to keep listening.

"You're right. Folks everywhere will remember what you did," Mark said. "You say you got paid for what you did?"

"Yeah, paid pretty good. And I can have more if'n I need it to get outta town or for some jackshit lawyer. But nobody knows. And s'long they got that dick chief of police, he couldn't figure this out if I laid it out for 'im. The only thing I worry about is the feds. That's who I gotta watch out for. But hell, I heard some guy on TV say the FBI took twenty years to figure out who done blowed up this same church the first time. Those guys who done it were ol' men. Damn, why should I worry? Besides, I got a few friends like the sheriff who would help me if 'n I need it."

"So who's the guy who's paying you? How much you say he's paying you?" Mark asked.

There was a long pause. Then the man said, "Nope, I ain't talkin' about him or any of those motherfuckers. He's a mean son of a bitch, you know, and he's got the money and whatever it takes to buy what he damn well wants. You know what I mean. He and his friend, who is even meaner, could get me wasted, quick as shit through a goose. I plan to spend this money, get me a little honey and get her to suck the rust off my pipe here."

Mark refused to give up. I knew what he was thinking. He was so close, and this was the biggest story of his life.

There was a sound of a table being knocked over and someone getting hit. Some guy yelled "Yee-hi."

"Wow, d'you see that?" the voice said. "That woman knocked the shit outta that ol' boy. He musta tried to feel her up or somethin', you think?" The glass thudded on the bar. "What the shit's this world comin' to? Can't even grab some ass in a joint without gettin' a fist in the ol' kisser. Guess I'll hav'ta watch myself. "

"Damn shame, the way the world's going," Mark said. There was a pause in the conversation, while they probably watched the guy get up. There was a lot of laughter in the background and chairs scraping around. Someone was yelling, but was too far away to make out the words over the music.

After things quieted down, Mark said, "Well, he must be an awful tough guy to scare a big guy like you thata way."

"Who?"

"You know, the man who paid you."

"Yeah, believe it. Nobody fucks with this guy. He's got everybody scared or bought off. I mean judges, congressmen, the mayor. The sheriff even told me I was playing with fire talking with this guy, but I think it may have been the sheriff who told him about me. So fuck 'em all. Maybe I'll get outta town and enjoy my money. Get me a little honey, like that one over there. What'd you think?"

"Yeah, she's something. I think you need another beer. She'll look even better then. How about it bartender? Couple more over here," Mark said.

"You're a good guy. What you do?" the man asked.

"Aw, this and that. Ain't got no regular job. Like that song, I ain't made for working, I'm made for drinking," Mark said.

"Yeah, me too," the man said. The beers arrived. "But you got money to pay for your fun."

"Yeah, my ol' lady's got a good job. I take some from her. She don't mind s'long as I come home regular," Mark said. I marveled at how easily the lie rolled off Mark's tongue. His wife, Peggy, didn't make much money at the insurance company, and what she brought home she would not have liked giving to Mark for beer.

"That's good," the man said. And they drifted off into other conversations. Ed looked antsy again.

The jukebox played Lynyrd Skynyrd's *Sweet Home Alabama*. There was a lot of noise in the bar, chairs scrapping, people yelling. Then what seemed like the whole bar, full of people, joined in singing. "We gotta stand up," the voice said. "That's the national anthem."

I could envision Mark standing up with his hand over his heart, while *Sweet Home* played. When it was over, the voice said, "Love that song."

Then there was a long pause and some more yelling before a Kenny Chesney song blared out.

"Well, if I ever get in trouble, you got somebody who can help me?" Mark asked. He sounded surprisingly sober and was still probing. I wondered where the beer was going, if not into his bloodstream.

I could feel Mark's tension as he hoped the guy would loosen up a little more. "You ever hear of a bunch of guys call themselves the Jacksons or something like that?" the voice said finally.

"Nawh, you mean like Michael Jackson?" Mark said.

"Hell, no. Not that faggy Negro. D'you see how fast he went from freak to saint when he died? Shit. No, I mean a bunch of white guys who get together and, you know, talk and do stuff."

"Like what stuff?"

"Oh, like who's gonna be mayor and who's gonna get the contracts to build the streets and run the schools, shit like that. They decide all that stuff," he said.

"No. I never heard of anybody like that. Who are they?" Mark asked.

"Oh, I don't know. Sheriff Peebles told me about them. To watch out for them. Hell, I better go home. I'm pretty drunk. I talked too much a'ready."

"No, don't go home. We're just getting started. What you got at home that looks better than that?" Mark said, probably pointing at one of the women in the bar.

There was a lot of mumbling and scraping noises. A door opened. It sounded like they were outside. The music was muffled. There were street sounds. Then the man said, "Look, you seem like a good guy. Just leave it be. Don't mess with it. It could get you killed and, for shore, me too. These are mean fuckers with a hell of a lot of money. They went to college and wear thousand dollar suits. If they can get me to blow up that church, what'd you think they could do to you and me?"

A vehicle door opened and closed. It sounded like a window was rolled down. "Thanks ol' buddy for the beer and all. See ya."

"Sure. Any time. You're a hero," Mark called. An engine started and we could hear the crunching of the tires on gravel. There was a long pause on the recording. Then I heard Mark blow out and yell, "Hoeee!" He knew the story would rock the country.

I reached over and turned off the player. Ed just sat staring at it. "You're the only other person who's heard this."

Ed sat thinking. I could watch his mind wrapping itself around the issues. He was an old pro, whose only real agenda was printing the best newspaper we could every day.

"This guy didn't know he was being recorded. They can't really use that in court to indict. And we've only got Mark's word for who he was talking to. He never called his name or identified him. We've got nothing to compare the voice to."

I nodded in agreement. "If I had known Mark was not going to be around, I would have gotten him to notarize a statement or something to make the lawyers a bit happier."

"Christ, so what have we got? A story by a dead reporter and some unidentified guy talking into a recorder in a bar. The dead reporter tells us his name is Lonnie Crenshaw. And this guy says he placed some C-4 on a beam below the pulpit at some church, killing the commish, who we assume is Commissioner Grey. Anybody could claim that. Dozens of good old boys drinking beers and shots probably talk shit like that. Maybe he just wanted some sucker to buy him his beer," Ed said.

I hated it, Ed was right. These were the problems with Mark's article I had been wrestling with. We knew from the police forensics that it was C-4 that exploded in the church and it had been placed on a beam under the pulpit. But anybody with police connections as this guy probably had or could buy a newspaper and read what the police were saying publicly could know that information. We were a long way from an ironclad story. There were holes a truck could drive through. But I knew we were on the right track. I trusted Mark.

Nailing Crenshaw would be hard, but not impossible. Even harder would be nailing who paid Crenshaw. Mark's conversation with Crenshaw had narrowed the field. We could be pretty certain that the guys behind Crenshaw were white, male, powerful, close to politicians, rich or have access to money. They belong to the Jackson Group, which I only knew a little about. And according to this Crenshaw, they were willing to kill. And what was the sheriff's role in this?

"We still have our work cut out for us, don't we? At least, we have a direction now," I said. Ed nodded, waiting for the other shoe to drop. "Let me ease your mind on one thing. We're not running any story we can't back up. If I didn't have concerns about Mark's story, we would be running it tomorrow. Damn, I wish we could. I wish I had a chance to discuss it with him. But he just dropped it in the mail, left me a message it was on its way and then went and drove off the mountain."

I shook my head at the tragedy of it all. Just as my friend was about to become world famous and recognized for being the great reporter he was, he died.

"So here's what we're going to do." For the next few minutes Ed and I discussed a plan that should fill the holes in Mark's story and uncover who ordered this bombing. My greatest fear, reinforced by my claustrophobia in the office with the door shut, was that we were going to get beat on the story by some national newspaper, a television network, a blog or the FBI. I wanted it all done yesterday.

We brought Clay in, played him the recording and told him the plan. He could hardly sit still. I knew the feeling.

The *Post* had a small staff of reporters. I could stand in the doorway of my office and see most of them. So when we assigned two reporters to one story, it cut deep. We could get by on more news wire copy for a week or two. But when we needed a third reporter, then the newsroom really was depleted.

Pat Galloway covering the police and Mike Rose at City Hall would continue to work their beats. They would devote time to specific issues: background on Lonnie Crenshaw, the shadowy Jackson Group, others who might be involved, including some elected officials, the mayor and sheriff. They would continue to stay on top of the FBI and police investigations.

We needed to interview again the women who were in the office at the church. If they could identify Crenshaw's photo, we might have enough to run with a story. We also needed to backtrack in Mark's footsteps. How had he identified Crenshaw? Most important, we had to find Crenshaw and confirm what he told Mark. Maybe we would have better luck getting him to tell us who had paid him. Mark was good, one of the best investigative reporters, but he was one guy against dozens of well-motivated FBI agents and dozens of other reporters with vast resources at their disposal. How had Mark found the needle in the haystack, and they hadn't? Did he get a tip? As any reporter will tell you, most stories are broken because of tips from the public or government officials. Who might have pointed Mark at Crenshaw? If we knew that, we'd be a lot closer to the men who had paid Crenshaw.

I walked over to the city desk, always the eye of a storm on a busy night. Two desks back up to one another with a third jammed up against the other two on the side. It makes for a large working area, but every inch is needed for computers, scanners, phones, reference manuals, address directories, the ever-present style manuals and the ever-present caffeine-loaded beverages.

From this position Clay and his assistant could survey the newsroom at a glance and see who was working on stories and who could take a breaking one. The city staff spreads out at desks toward the front windows of the building. Tonight about half of the fifteen city staff reporters were out on stories. The rest had a phone to their ear, while they typed notes into a computer.

The sports reporters lounged at desks behind Clay. There was something different about men and women who write about sports. They seemed always to be leaning back, feet on their desks talking on the telephone. They never appeared to work, but every day they turned out one of our best sections of the paper. The photographers camped in a small space behind the sports reporters. The copy desk, where the headlines were written and the pages laid out, was in a u-shaped configuration with five copy editors, all within shouting distance of the city desk. There always seemed to be tension brewing between the copy editors and the city staff. The closer we got to a deadline, the more they shouted.

The newsroom was designed for quick conversations and snap decision-making. Privacy and personal space were low priorities. To outsiders the arrangement looked unstructured, noisy. Some recruits balked at the lack of privacy. But the system was built over years and worked.

"Clay, you talk with Pat and Mike?"

"Yeah, they're right on it."

Both were solid reporters with good contacts and knew how to work on a short deadline.

"I think we will need Rachel full time on this too. What'd you think?"

"Yep. Okay," Clay said. "I may be a little light on feature stuff for a while, but if we can break this one open, well .. no problem. It'll be worth a hundred feature stories."

Rachel Stanton was one of our youngest reporters, but one with tremendous potential. Thin with very long legs, Rachel could outrun most men and write circles around them. On any given day she might write a feature on a new cosmetic product, help out on the understaffed business desk with a CEO profile and interview the parents of a kid who had died in a drive-by shooting. The diversity of stories was good training, but most reporters want a more stable beat where they can build contacts and know the background on stories. They usually get that beat after a few years. Rachel had been on general assignments for three years. She was ready to take on something serious.

Clay sent Rachel into my office. The overwhelming impression I had, as she sat down, was how young she was. Her skirt stopped about her knees. She sat down on the couch, her knees were on the same level with her shoulders. She was gangly, like a teenager, but I had seen men stopped in the middle of Fourth Street to watch her walk across the street. Out of college for five years and with us for four, she had started on the copy desk, working the late shift. For her, the copy desk was a cage. She asked Clay to consider her for a reporting job. Always on the lookout for talent, Clay found her a spot. It was a move he had never regretted. I hoped I would not regret putting her on the bombing story.

I handed her a copy of Mark's article. "Read this in here and don't discuss it with anyone. And I mean no one, except Clay, Ed or me."

Her eyes got wider. She stretched her legs out on the coffee table, settled back into the couch and started reading. She read the first paragraph and put it down with two hands in her lap. She stared at me. "Wow," she said almost in a whisper. I smiled, and she went back to reading, the excitement building in her face, not just about the story, but that she was being brought in on it. She knew what that meant. I left and shut the door behind her. I didn't want anyone coming in while she was reading, but I couldn't stand to be in the office with the door closed for more than a few minutes. I sat at a desk and started going through the mail, but my mind was on what she was reading.

When she finished, she opened the door. I went back in and sat on the edge of my desk as we went over the details of the story. I outlined the steps needed to get the story ready to publish. She had to round out what Pat was working on with the police and what Mike was working on at city hall.

"Are you up to this?" I asked.

She stood up, and I slid off the desk to stand facing her. Eye to eye with her, I felt like a military officer giving a young recruit a battle assignment. I saw no hesitation or doubt in her eyes. She looked at the copy of the story in her hand. "This is really important. This is why I wanted to be a reporter, to work on stories like this. But it's more than that. I didn't know Mark Hodges. He must have been awfully good. Now I hear he is dead. I'd like to help finish the work he started. That would be something worth doing."

Mark would have liked that.

As I left the building for the night, a copy girl came running after me to hand me a copy of the first edition. She usually met me as I was leaving to give me a paper, but I was ahead of schedule tonight, ready for home, time to stop thinking about riots and bombings.

"All the guys upstairs said to give you a high sign. They liked what you did," she said and gave me a thumbs up as she turned and ran off.

Ed, Clay and the copy desk had played the story below the fold on page one, but the headline was across three columns. Half the page screamed *Post Editor in Heroic Rescue*. They carried a photo of my bashed Blazer. They knew better than to run one of me.

Inside next to the jump there were head shots of the four policemen, scattered in a graphic that depicted a city under siege. It was too much. I called Clay from the car and told him to kill the graphic for the later editions. But I knew I was just spitting in the ocean. The story would move up the page for the city editions. By then, I'd be at home and unable to stop them. The old adage of better to ask forgiveness than permission prevailed.

As I drove, I thought that the city probably couldn't take a lot more. Governor Kitterage would have already sent in the National Guard and imposed martial law if there wasn't a budget crunch at the state Capitol. Allison Keene, the deputy attorney general in Washington, was annoyed with the governor's inactivity and had threatened to send in federal marshals. The Republican governor postured for votes from the Capitol in Montgomery. Keene, who worked for a Democratic administration, made points in press conferences from the Justice Department offices on Pennsylvania Avenue. Iron City was caught in the political crossfire.

The house was quiet when I opened the front door. I had grown accustomed to being greeted, in order, by a dog, an older woman pushing food and a shout of hello from the den where my father-in-law was usually watching television. My son would be asleep by that hour.

Tonight I didn't get any greeting. The dog was outside. My family was doing some early Christmas shopping. The empty house felt lonely, and I wanted someone there. I thought about calling Nicki, the woman I was dating, but she was working and probably unreachable.

A note in the kitchen said I could find dinner in the oven. My mother-in-law had prepared a meat loaf with corn and mashed potatoes with gravy, one of my favorites. A major joy of having my in-laws live with us is the way Sheila's mother cooked. She had never heard of low-fat cooking, and I had added about ten pounds to my waist.

The census bureau classifies the Riordan household as a family of four, plus a dog, sometimes a goldfish. The difference from the Ozzie and Harriet 1950s image of the American family was that the four residents include my five-year-old son, my wife's mother and father, who are in their seventies, and me. Sheila and I were married for ten years before breast cancer attacked her lymph nodes and ate up her frail body. There were still moments when I turned into our bedroom, I thought she was in the bath with the door closed while she dried her hair. But the bath was empty and dark. She would never dry her hair again.

Fortunately our marriage left me the greatest of gifts, Christopher James, a bright eyed, happy little boy, seemingly content that he was the center of attention for three adults. He would know what his mother looked like and what her voice sounded like from videos I had of her stored on the computer.

But he would probably not remember what she felt like to touch, what she smelled like or how it was to have her arms wrapped around him. That broke my heart. But every day his bright smile and cute comments filled up much of the hole Sheila's death had left in me.

Sheila's father had retired from managing a steel-fabricating plant. He had not relished the idea of his daughter marrying a black man, but he came to like me. When he and his wife had grown tired of living in their small house on a pension, they sold it, banked the money and moved in to help me raise Chris.

We lived together in a rambling old house, built in the 1930s as Iron City began to spread south up the mountain slope. This house, now just one of many along the mountainside, had once been a local marvel because it was built into the rock. An architect designed it to establish his reputation in the city. And it worked. He was called on to build other similar houses on the mountain's rocky slope.

What I liked about it most was the balcony on the back of the house and the views of Iron City it offered. Actually a large deck suspended thirty feet off the ground, it was called a balcony because it had no stairs. There I surrounded myself with overflowing flower pots. Mums were blooming now, my least favorite flower, but having flowers around me made me feel close to my mother, a dedicated gardener. Every spring she and I would pack up the car, leave my father behind, and drive south to the Bellingrath Gardens in what is called LA for Lower Alabama, the Gulf Coast. There we walked, often hand-in-hand, among giant azaleas, camellias and dogwood trees. It was some of the happiest moments of my childhood.

My house was on the north side of a winding street appropriately named Cliff Road. At night I love to sit on the balcony and watch the lights flickering across the city, making it one of the great places in the world to sip a beer, prop up your feet and think. I took my dinner out on the balcony. It was there that I felt I could really breathe. There is something about small rooms, and most rooms like my newspaper office are small, that seemed to take my breath away. I have always been that way. I knew why. The shrinks I talked to until they weren't helping me anymore told me it stemmed from my childhood fears. They were right, and I knew what fears they were talking about. It didn't help knowing why. I still didn't like small spaces. I liked wide open spaces, especially at night before I fell asleep. I always prayed the openness of the balcony would keep my worst nightmares at bay, the ones where I was locked in a small, dark room listening to cries and grunting that seemed to go on for hours. Sometimes it was a prison cell. Screaming and grunting came from the next cell. I always woke in a sweat.

I found a beer in the refrigerator and turned on my favorite Usher download. My in-laws came in, chattering away about the shopping. My father-in-law handed me a sleeping Chris. I undressed him and put on his Atlanta Falcons pajamas, tucked him into his bed and watched him sleep from a chair. He was different from his mother, more outgoing than she was. His constant chatter was so unlike her long silences. But asleep his facial features looked more like her than me. His skin color was closer to mine, but lying on the pillow his face looked almost identical to hers in a photo I cherished. We had gone skiing in North Carolina. The artificial snow was too treacherous for beginners, so mostly we had stayed in the rented house and enjoyed being alone. I shot a lot of pictures, one of Sheila taking a nap, face relaxed, her blond hair flowing over the pillow. She didn't like the picture and made me promise I would throw it away.

It was one promise I did not keep.

4

J. Harrison Pitts was waiting outside my office the next morning. The special agent in charge of the FBI's Iron City division sat in one of the chairs that lined the wall under a row of windows which looked out onto Fourth Avenue. Pitts, the first African-American FBI chief in Iron City, looked unhappy at being kept waiting for his ten o'clock appointment.

Pitts played his role to the max. He insisted on being called Harrison. When one of the rich Alabama good old boys would clap a hand on his broad shoulder and call him Harry, he would scowl. His press release factory ran overtime. Our databases were full of photos of him accepting awards, making speeches and handcuffing criminals from kidnappers to counterfeiters.

Our relationship perplexed him. He expected us to be close, two educated black men near the same age who had risen fast to senior positions in white-run organizations. What he did not understand was that I was a newspaper editor first. Being black was only my skin color.

Seated next to Pitts was a man I knew only from news broadcasts and wire photos. He was a frequent guest on the network and cable public affairs television shows, one of the Justice Department senior lawyers called on to discuss new policies. Wayman Wright had flown into town two days after the bombing to head up the

Justice Department's strike force investigating the church bombing. He had brought with him an army of federal investigators and prosecutors.

Wright was on the fast track in Washington. According to the Washington news corps, he was in line to succeed Allison Keene as the number two person at the Justice Department if she were named to be the next attorney general or to the Supreme Court. Born in Georgia, Wright had risen fast in the ranks of the Justice Department. He had been sent to Alabama, a southern lawyer, to prosecute the church bomber and to do it quickly to stem the riots. So far there was not much to show for weeks of the high-profile investigation.

When I had promised Pitts a few minutes, he hadn't mentioned Wright. If I had known a celebrity was coming, I might have been on time. It had been a busy morning. Chris had been full of the "I wants." He wanted a rabbit. I promised to consider it for Christmas. He wanted to play on a YMCA basketball team. I told him he was too little, but he said his friends were going to play. He wanted to go fishing in a big boat like the one he and his grandfather had seen on television. I told him to talk to his grandfather about it. And I escaped.

"Gentlemen," I called as soon as I was within earshot across the newsroom. "I apologize for being late. Please come in."

I hoped I sounded like Howard, my old editor, who seemed to be able to put people at ease with just a word or a gesture. My voice echoed through the empty newsroom. Mornings are quiet at the *Post*. Only a few people who cover regular daytime beats work at that hour, and they are rarely in the newsroom then. Not until noon would the newsroom become a beehive.

The two men stood and we shook hands. They looked like they were cut from the same bolt of grey cloth, one black, one white. Both wore tailored suits on athletic frames. I spent a moment studying Wright at close quarters. You could see why he was a star in the Byzantine world of Beltway politics. His quick charm and firm handshake was complemented by long graying hair he swept back over the top half of his ears. He looked the part of a successful lawyer, turned politician and media darling, tall with chiseled facial features, a quick smile in front of white teeth.

As we walked into the office, I could feel him sizing me up. I was as tall as he and Pitts and could wear a suit as well, but maybe not as handsome as Wright. I had thicker lips and a bigger nose, and I was not as tough looking as Pitts, whose large head, hands and prominent scar over his right eye made him look like a man you didn't want to meet in a dark alley.

Since his Georgetown law school days, Wright had been studying opponents. I wondered what his thoughts were behind that plastic smile. Pitts opened the meeting. Camille James, my assistant, brought in coffee and tiptoed out. She could barely contain how impressed she was.

"We believe we are closing in on the individual who perpetrated this heinous crime. We have more than a hundred FBI agents and technicians assigned to the investigation of the church bombing. Standing by are dozens more if they are needed. This investigation is the top priority of the department and the bureau. Deputy Attorney General Keene is briefed on our progress daily. She briefs the attorney general and sometimes the President almost daily."

"Yes, so we have reported," I said.

"Well, yes, and we appreciate the *Post*'s coverage. It has kept the investigation in front of the public and encouraged the public to cooperate with us."

I waited for the bullshit to stop flowing. But as Pitts took longer and longer to get to the point, I felt a tightening in my stomach. Was it because I now viewed the FBI as competition? We were so close to solving the bombing ourselves. I did not want the Washington boys mucking up our story. They had been all over town, kicked up dust, made a lot of noise and come up with few leads. I did not want to wait for them to find Crenshaw and announce it to the national media, the wire services, the television news and, of course, the Internet, leaving us just another media outlet.

Wright took over the conversation. He probably had taken over every meeting he and Pitts had gone to since Wright had landed on Pitts' turf. The FBI bureau chief looked away, but not before I saw his lips and brows turn down. The two senior officers of the federal government's investigation into who bombed the church were having a personal power struggle.

"What we would like to ask, if we are not too far out of line, is some special cooperation from the *Post*," Wright said. "We need your help. We are after a terrorist. Just like Timothy McVeigh in Oklahoma City and other home-grown terrorists." His sincerity dripped on the carpet. He stared straight at me. There was tension in his body, but it was well hidden under his well-fitting suit, expensive tie and Gucci loafers.

I should have expected something like this. Mark's article may have been seen by one too many people.

With my best smile on, I said, "Sure, we are always glad to assist the law enforcement authorities." Editors spin bullshit too.

"We have reason to believe that one of your reporters has information that would be of value to our investigation," Wright said, pausing to assess my reaction. When I gave him only a blank stare, he continued, "Your government, from the President to every agent working the case, would appreciate it if you would share this information with us. We believe it could bring our investigation to a speedy conclusion and allow everyone in this beautiful city to return to their normal lives."

I said nothing. I was pissed, but did not want to show it. He pressed on. "We know your reputation and that of the *Post*. We know that the news media has rules, but we are facing an extraordinary situation here. The sooner we wrap up this investigation, the sooner we can all get on with our lives."

"Joe, please," Pitts said, leaning forward in his chair to make his pitch. "If you've got something, give it to us. We'll protect your source."

I sat forward in my chair, mimicking Pitts. "If we had something solid, we'd print it. And you would be the first to know. If you understand anything about this newspaper, it is that we are very aggressive. None of our reporters, I hate to admit it, has come up with anything useful. We're just like every newspaper, TV station, web site and blog covering this story. We are working hard to develop some leads, but our staff reporters have come up with nothing solid yet."

"You're absolutely certain?" Pitts implored. "Our information on this is pretty good. It would really help stop all these riots in our community."

His reference to "our community" was not about Iron City. It was his less than subtle appeal to me, brothers with the same skin tones.

"Well, there may be something I'm not aware of. I'll bring it up with my editors. It would help me if you could share with me, confidentially, of course, how this information came to you. I'll protect your source," I said.

I loved irony.

Wright sighed and stood up. Pitts looked annoyed. If he was, Wright kept it to himself. It was a standoff. The FBI had heard something. Where was our leak? We needed to find it and close it fast. That leak might be flowing not just to the FBI, but to others. That could hurt the story and maybe get someone killed. Wright shook my hand. Pitts stood up, looking disappointed. He didn't offer his hand.

"Well, I hope that if you do come up with something, we'll hear from you," Wright said.

"Yes, yes, of course. My first call."

As they left, Wright and Pitts passed Clay, coming to work. "What'd they want?" he asked.

"They want us to solve their case for them," I said and pulled Mark's article out of the safe.

"Oh? And did you?"

I gave him a get-real look. "Right. I told them we were dumb fuckers, sitting around with our thumbs up our butts."

Clay nodded. He knew I was angry. So he waited to see where my anger was directed. I stood up and walked out in the newsroom. I yelled for Ed and waved for him to join us. I told them about the conversation with the FBI guys.

Ed got red in the face. When his blood pressure went up, the veins in his face and neck looked like a Google map. He hated disloyalty of any kind. "We got a leak?"

I nodded.

"I guess it was inevitable. Too much to keep quiet about. Shit, I hate stupidity," he said.

We sat thinking about the problems a leak created.

"Maybe we just asked the right question in the wrong place," I said, not believing what I was saying.

Clay brightened at my suggestion. "Yeah, maybe when we started asking questions about our boy, it got back to them. Do you want me to slow the guys down?"

I shook my head. "No, speed it up. Tell them to be careful."

Now we had two investigations, one on the outside hunting for Crenshaw, the other inside hunting for our leak. Did we have a traitor? Or was someone just stupid enough to confuse the difference between patriotism and being a lackey for the authorities?

Iron City has its share of Christian bigots. One of the loudest and probably best known, or at least his assistant, was holding on the telephone line as I reviewed the return call messages that had backed up. The mayor wanted to give me an award. The police auxiliary was sending a dozen roses in my honor to some retired policemen's home. I couldn't imagine why a bunch of elderly policemen would want a bunch of roses.

On the phone was the Reverend Jonathan Webster, the senior minister of the Church of the Redeemer in an eastern suburb. Webster had his own local television show, *Onward Christian Soldiers*. He claimed to be a great admirer of the Medieval Crusades, not one of mankind's and particularly Christians' finer moments. He argued forcefully on most Sunday mornings that white Americans are on a modern crusade to maintain their values and heritage from an assault by other races, and of course, the liberal press. He liked to preach the doctrine of an eye for an eye.

"That was a fine thing you did for those policemen yesterday. I hear they would have been dead were it not for your courage. You're a genuine hero," Webster said in his melodious tones.

I deflected the compliment, saying I only did what others would.

"Well, that's what we would all like to believe. But listen, Joe, I'd really like to have you come on my show this week. My audience would be thrilled to see a real live hero, a black hero, on the screen, telling how you fought back and helped those white policemen keep from being killed," he said.

I shuddered at the thought. "Thank you, Reverend Webster, but I have to decline the invitation. It was an experience I would rather forget than promote."

"Big mistake, son. Promotion is everything. Image matters. Get on those airwaves, and you'll be selling more papers than you can print." He paused, and it sounded as if he was mouthing words to someone on his end of the telephone line. "I understand how you feel. The conflicts you must feel, siding with the white men against your black brethren. Well, it gives you goose bumps, don't it?"

I tried not to let him to get to me.

"You know I went down there to that show they all put on at the convention center for those folks that died in the church. What a show that was, a real good send off for Reverend Smallwood. He was the real troublemaker. I hate to say that about another man of the cloth. But its God's truth. That Commissioner Grey, he was just following what Smallwood told him."

I was getting a headache gritting my teeth.

"Well, folks asked me, why'd you go down there with all those Negroes? You know what I tell him?" He chuckled. "What I tell them is that I went down there to make sure the good reverend was really dead. I wanted to send him on his way." His chuckles turned to laughter.

I tried to stop myself, but I couldn't. "Whatever happened, Reverend, to love for thy fellow man?"

"Well, you have to understand, son, when you read the Bible carefully and completely as I have, you will know that the good scriptures do not include all people. Yes, sir, the Lord has shown me the light."

I was in no mood to argue.

"Did you catch my show last night at seventy thirty on channel thirty nine? That's prime time, you know," he said. I told him I had missed it. "Well, I never got so many calls, emails and texts off one show. You know what my message was? I told them to prepare for the worst, lock their doors and get their guns, shoot if you have to. We may just have to take the fight to them."

Webster, built like a block of wood, stocky on a short frame, was pouring gasoline on a smoldering blaze. Simmering twigs could suddenly erupt into a forest fire. Webster was inciting frightened white people to come out armed into the streets.

"Now don't get me wrong. The Bible commands us to take care of all his children. And you black people and the browns are all God's children, but nowhere does the good book say we're equal or have to live close to one another. Now does it?"

"No. U.S. law is pretty clear on that point," I said.

"Well, I answer to a higher calling. And so do you, don't you forget that. Oh, goodness, I've got to go, got to tell my producer you won't go on the show. Too bad, would have been one of my best. He and I and the viewers, well, we will all be disappointed, you know, but if that's your answer, so be it."

I tried returning the calls that came in about the rescue. Most were painful. Some black people accused me, among other things, of selling out. To them, when I helped rescue the policemen, I had declared myself on the side of the white establishment and against my own people. I tried to explain that I was trying to save our city from destruction and a handful of men from being killed, that I was not on either side. There was little neutral, rational ground left in the city.

My next call made me smile.

"Hey, homeboy, how they hanging?" said the voice of a man I had known for a dozen years. Henry Thomas Jones, affectionately known as H.T., was a small-time black political activist. H.T. worked hard to develop his mind and body. He was well read. His interests included politics and philosophy. He could talk eloquently about Chinese and ancient Indian mystic philosophers. H.T. had also transformed his slight frame through extensive weight lifting and probably steroids. He now had a huge chest, arms and back, which looked even bigger because he was short, maybe five foot six. Two years ago, H.T. shaved his head probably to make him look more menacing, like the ancient warriors he idolized.

When I first knew him, he would sit in the audience of city council and county commission meetings and banter with the elected officials, white and black, making scurrilous comments. It was a time when H.T. was working hard to develop a reputation for being bad. He wore black t-shirts with black jeans and boots.

When I covered city hall and local politics for the *Post*, I found him amusing. We used to drink coffee in the cafeteria while he told me how the council was wrong, corrupt or evil. I occasionally quoted him in stories. Nothing made him happier.

"Some of the brothers don't care much for what you did to save the pigs," he said.

"Well, you know how it is," I said.

"So all this fussing in the streets has puckered your asshole too? Typical. When we get scared, we revert to type. You're no different," he said.

"Yeah, well, we've been scared for two hundred years that you field hands will overrun the manor house and throw us house slaves out in the cold," I joked.

"Yeah, that's right. You still in the big house, ain't ya? But we're coming."

H.T. was a barometer for what was happening on the north-side, predominantly black neighborhoods. He had graduated from heckling council members to running a small political organization of young men. He claimed he could deliver five thousand votes, depending on how large his check was. The real number was probably no more than a thousand votes, but in a close election that could make the difference. He claimed he could elect whomever he wanted to the council seat for north Iron City.

He and his guys also provided muscle where needed, intimidating people who supported rival candidates, pulling out yard signs, trashing the opponent's campaign headquarters. He would never admit it, but he was probably better at stopping people from voting for a candidate who didn't pay him.

H.T. preached self-discipline, self-determination and self-respect. No drugs. No booze. No sex without condoms. In a strip center he had built a dojo where he taught martial arts and enforced discipline on the lives of the young men who followed him. Dozens were drawn to it. He introduced them to Asian philosophies, insisted that they do their school homework after they cleaned the dojo. What money they earned from jobs they brought to H.T. for the common good.

I once told him he would have made a great Jesuit. "The Jesuits were pussies," he said.

H.T.'s story was almost a cliche. His mother had died when he was eleven. He never knew his father, nor did I ever hear him say he wanted to. He cared a lot about his mother. She was only seventeen when he was born, a child raising a child. When I asked him how she died, he didn't answer for a long time. He sat in the cafeteria staring down at the checkered linoleum. "My mother got thrown out of school on account of having me. She started cleaning white folks' houses. My Nana raised me. My mother came home tired and went in and took a bath, got herself dressed up. Then she went to work at the bars."

"A waitress?" I asked.

"Yeah, that and whoring. She worked hard. And she really wanted a man. I could hear her lying in her bed crying. Every man she brought home was worse than the last. Most hit her. Some hit me. She wouldn't stand for that."

He paused and looked long at me. "Life's shit, ain't it?"

I nodded.

"One night she didn't come home. Nana sat in the kitchen for days and cried. It wasn't until the day of the funeral that anyone would tell me she was dead. I learned later that some guy tried to stiff her on her money after she did him out back of the club. When she bitched him out, he cut her and left her to bleed out."

H.T. paused to get control of his emotions. "He even took her tip money. I heard him say years later that she didn't need it."

The *Post* had interviewed him a couple of times about his youth program and the challenges young black men faced. He talked about how at risk they were. Black girls, we quoted him, were also at risk, especially when they got pregnant. But girls are tougher and more focused than the boys, he said. He was a realist.

"White folks who read your paper don't want to hear about black folks and their problems," he said, when he called to thank me. "They just want to go quietly to their nice houses and not worry too much about what's happening over here on the northside."

From the angry letters and emails we got, I was afraid he was right about too many of our readers.

"Tell me what's going on out there," I asked. "The out-of-town folks working the collection plates and some of your friends trying to step up into Commissioner Grey's shoes?"

"Yep. It's a convention of well-dressed brothers in town, that's for sure. They've been working the churches here on Sundays and the big corporations during the week. Their bank accounts are getting fat. But then, you know, it's been a long dry spell. Nobody much cared what happened to us down here in old Iron City until somebody blew up the commish," he said, breaking into a Hip Hop accent.

"Who's stepping up?" I asked.

"Bunch of folks, including me. We'd all like to take on the mantle of the great man. Good bucks and lots of strut in that."

"You? After calling all of the commissioners sell outs all these years, you going to join them?"

"Yeah, well, you know. We all grow up. How about you helping me out some, being a friend and all?" he said.

"Uh oh, here it comes. Hold my checkbook," I teased him.

"That'd be something, a rich, Ivy League-educated Negro like you writing me a check. But nawh, you got something better'n money. How about you printing an article saying I'm one of the leading candidates to win the election? Would you do that?"

"If you are, you know I will. You think you can win?"

We had written a couple of stories about the special election to fill the vacancy Grey's death had created on the county commission. I knew several candidates were running. The job of county commissioner paid well, much better than a city council or state legislative seat, and there were only five commissioners for the whole county. Grey's district covered much of the northern part of the county. A black candidate would probably be elected. I made a mental note to ask Clay if Mike Rose was writing profiles on the candidates.

"Hell, yeah, I can win," H.T. said. "But I gotta get ahead of a few of the brothers first. I need them to think I got some stroke."

"Okay," I said a little doubtfully. I was having trouble seeing H.T. getting elected.

"Be sure and mention that I was in the church that night. I could've been killed just like the commissioner and the reverend. You write that, so people will remember," he said.

I wanted to change the subject to something more important than his political aspirations, but when dealing with H.T.'s ego, it was always best to move with some care. "Tell me, H.T. what's the word around about who set the bomb? I know you know."

"Oh, that's easy. The pigs did it."

"What?" I asked.

"The cops. Them oinks you saved. Same crowd. Why you think the brothers set that trap? Retribution for the church, for Grey, for all the crap they put us through every day, that's why. We know no cops will ever be brought down for what they did. That's for sure."

I wondered if Crenshaw being a constable had fueled this belief on the street.

"Oh, yeah. It was them, kluxers all dressed up in dark blue. Now we're going to get our own justice. One by one. Two by two. That way we know we'll get them who done it," he said.

H.T. was beginning to sound too much like the Reverend Webster, one black, one white, both caught up in the hate. "But, H.T., you know a lot of the cops are innocent. Some are actually pretty good guys, really. Some are brothers."

"There you go, sounding like your old man. No good brother is a cop. He just another pig, no matter what color his hide is. If they didn't do it to Grey, they did other things. Don't go feeling sorry for no dead pigs. Make great barbecue," he said.

"H.T., the riots come down on the police, the Guard will be in here with heavy guns and tanks patrolling the streets."

"Let them come on. We'll fight them, too. Same crowd, different shirts," he said.

"Please, H.T., we're close to knowing who really did plant the bomb. We'll print his name and demand that he be brought to trial. Give it a rest. Be a leader, H.T. Quiet things down for a while," I said.

"No percentage in that. River's running the other way." He paused. "You really know who it is?"

"We're getting close. We are trying to confirm what we have been told," I said.

"What you been told? Who did this? The cops, right?"

"No. You know I can't tell you," I said.

"That's right. Tell your white masters up in Washington, but not your brother down here in Iron City, working hard to make things better for our people."

I let that go. There was no response to such racist bullshit.

"If you find him, you going to write that he planted the bomb?" he asked. I told him we would. "If you don't find him, you got no story, right?" H.T. said.

"Maybe. I don't know. It depends on several things," I said.

"What if he's dead?"

"Why would he be dead? You think he is dead?"

"Hell if I know. You're just like all the brothers who want to be white. You're either going to print his name and let everybody know it was some cop who blew up the church. Or you're an Oreo, just like your old man. Make up your damn mind. Shit or git off the pot."

With just the dial tone to listen to, I sat staring at the copy of Mark's article on my desk. It looked so innocuous there among all the other papers and files that littered the top of my desk. But now I knew it could shape the city's future or destroy it. I didn't know which.

My last call before I escaped for lunch was from my boss in Alexandria. Maury Weitzman, a veteran of the New Jersey newspaper wars, called to tell me the story about my heroics made the national wires and NBC's *Today Show*. The national newspaper, *USA Today,* wanted to interview me. I told him I would prefer not to have the publicity. Weitzman, a sarcastic man who rarely let personal feelings get in the way of running a dozen newspapers around the country, told me he would have preferred that I not engage in such "antics." But since I had, I should play it for all its worth. It sold newspapers. Hell, he sounded like Webster too.

He was right about increasing sales. The rack sales on the city edition had jumped twelve percent today with the headlines about the rescue attempt. Heroism, I told myself, was still appealing. I just wished I felt like I had slain the dragon and rescued the damsel. Instead I felt anxious. Even with the door open, my office walls seemed to be closing in on me. The knot in my stomach seemed to know what my brain was trying to tell me better than I did. With Mark's article and the recorded interview locked away in my safe, I walked out into the newsroom. It was always comforting to stand in the midst of the buzz all newsrooms generate. As I watched my people typing on computers, talking on phones, yelling at one another across the room, I realized I had made myself a lightning rod in the middle of the city's worst electrical storm.

5

Very little rattles Camille James. A woman in her early sixties, tall and thin, and even on her small salary, she was
always impeccably dressed. A proud woman, Mrs. James
regularly told me she didn't know how the *Post* or I would survive
when she retired. Her only quirk was her selection of glasses. I
had counted four pairs, each a different color, pink, green, white
and purple. She alternated them, matching her glasses each day
with her outfit. She never wore the same glasses two days in a
row.

Her title was assistant to the editor, but she was really far more
valuable as my historical reference point. If the *Post* was a museum, she would be its curator. Although tough as any old Scotch-
Irish madam with a deep faith in her Presbyterian roots, nothing
in the life of this Southern lady had prepared her for the riots on
the streets outside or the delegation of three black men who sat in
the chairs along the wall outside my office.

Relief swept across her face when she heard my voice. She had
never worked for a black man before and told me I took more than
a little getting used to. She seemed genuinely afraid of black men.
Despite my efforts to dispel her concerns, she whispered once that
she was afraid her fate was to be raped by a black man, an event that
was hard for me to imagine.

I was actually back ahead of schedule. Interviews with two local television stations had gone faster than I expected. I was the hot story for one day at least. As I turned the corner from the elevators and walked up the three steps into the newsroom, the three men stood and took turns shaking my hand. We often had walk-in visitors. I liked it that people thought they could come to the newspaper any time, sort of like a church or at least how churches used to be before they had to start locking their doors. I had told the guards downstairs to take a good look at visitors and weed out those who appeared to be potential terrorists, but let anyone else upstairs.

We had to be concerned, but I considered it unlikely that self-respecting terrorists would pick the *Post* as a target. What were they going to do, hold the writers, editors and layout guys at gunpoint and demand that we print a story to their liking? The only real risk, I thought a bit naively, was that someone would bring a gun and start shooting. But I thought that risk worth taking. So we kept to our open-door policy long after the *Examiner* firmly shut out anyone who did not have a confirmed appointment.

I offered the men coffee. All accepted, and Mrs. James, regaining her composure, went off to fill three cups. She was wearing the pink glasses today and rolled her eyes behind them when she looked at me.

Raymond Smith, the youngest of the visitors, made the introductions. "You've met the Reverend Harry Simmons. He is the pastor of the Antioch Baptist Church. And this gentleman, you probably also know. He is Deacon Jimmy Marshall, who was fortunate enough to live through the bomb blast at the church. He was sitting on the front row."

I had not met Marshall before, but knew a lot about him. Since surviving the blast, he had become a minor celebrity. We had written an article on him, so had the *Examiner,* and several television stations had interviewed him. A local leader from the civil rights protest era, who had walked away from the second church bombing, made good copy. Marshall was smaller than I expected. He was dressed in a black suit, at least one size too big for him and several years past its prime, a blue shirt and a thin Navy blue tie. He sat smiling and nodding at me.

Simmons was a sharp contrast. The pastor of the largest black church in the city with a Sunday congregation of eight hundred to a thousand people was a large man whose neck spilled over a white collar. His clothes were expensive and his tie was a fashionable tapestry of greens, reds and grays. He was not smiling. He did not look like a man who smiled often.

Smith was a good-looking man, tall with an athletic build and well dressed in a black pin-striped suit. He had worked for Grey as his chief of staff and had been involved in local political campaigns for years. He owned a small title company and several buildings near the church that were rented to doctors and accountants. I expected he would be a formidable campaigner for Grey's seat, particularly if Simmons and the other ministers backed him.

With the coffee passed around, Smith came to the point. "As you know, the Iron City chapter of the NAACP voted last month to honor you, the editor of the *Post*, as its man of the year."

"Yes, and I am honored that we were chosen," I said. I had actually forgotten about the letter telling me that I was this year's recipient and featured speaker.

"Well, the three of us served as the executive committee of the Iron City chapter for the NAACP," Smith said. "And we, uh, we would like to give you your award today. We are thinking about postponing the dinner with everything going on."

It took me a minute to realize what they were really saying. "Yes. Of course, that would be fine."

They relaxed. They had been as uptight as Mrs. James, worrying that I would be offended. I was a natural choice for the award a few days ago. But after saving four white cops from being attacked, the NAACP could not give me an award and let me make the keynote address at its annual banquet without creating a controversy and drying up ticket sales. Yet to withdraw the award would draw even more attention to it and cause more difficulty for Smith and Simmons in the middle of a political campaign. Smith and his supporters might also worry that withdrawing the award would embarrass the *Post* and end up costing him our endorsement for the election.

"It is a great honor to give it to you personally," Smith said. He slowly unwrapped the framed award from brown paper. The *Post* received dozens like it every year from civic and charitable organizations in the city. We write about their events and help them raise money. They give us plaques.

"The community is just real uptight right now. Any little old thing is blown way out of proportion," Simmons said. His voice seemed to originate deep in a barrel-like chest. I wondered if he even bothered with a microphone on Sundays.

It would have been interesting to be a fly on the wall for their discussion on how to handle what could well have turned into a major political blunder that could hurt Smith. Other candidates, even my friend H.T., would have painted the executive committee of the NAACP as being soft.

"It might have been all right, you understand, but helping those cops, well, that's got a lot of folks upset," Simmons said.

Smith's face contorted as he gritted his teeth and shook his head. "Now don't misunderstand us. Reverend Simmons is not saying we feel that what you did was wrong. He's just saying some folks are upset with it."

Simmons nodded. Marshall just sat in his chair smiling, his legs crossed.

I felt that knot growing again in the pit of my stomach.

"Well, thank you, gentlemen. If you'll wait here, I'll find a photographer. He can shoot your picture giving me the award. That way we can run the photo in the paper and frame you a copy for the NAACP office," I said.

A new wave of anxiety swept across their faces. I shouldn't do that to people. It was my bit of mischief, but still fun. The bad, little boy my father often called me would come out sometimes. I stood in the doorway looking for a photographer. "Oh, I'm sorry. I'm afraid that all our photographers are out on assignment," I lied. "Maybe we can postpone taking that photo until another time."

They relaxed again. Then they moved to the other reason for their visit. Smith was looking for some help with his campaign and turned the conversation in that direction.

"How do you see the race shaping up?" he asked.

Not knowing much about the campaign, I kicked the question back to the group.

"Well, there is a lot of interest in this race. There are a couple of white candidates, but more are black. With the population of the district, a black candidate should win, but so many are running probably not without a runoff," Smith said.

"Who are the strongest black candidates?"

He looked down at the brown, well-worn carpet on my office floor. "There are several," Smith said. He mentioned a minister in Bessemer and Jerry Franklin, a city council member. "Then there is Henry Jones. He's a tough street organizer, I guess you would call him."

"What he ain't tellin' you is that this race is really between that small-time hustler H.T. Jones and our man Smith here," Simmons said. "Both are likely to get into the runoff. Then we'll see."

"So H.T. is your primary competition? What do you plan to do to beat him?" I asked.

"Run that muscle-bound little jerk all around the district," Simmons said sharply.

Smith leaned over and put his hand on Simmons arm. "You'll have to forgive my good friend. In the heat of battle, and let me tell you this is a battle, good folks can say things they don't mean."

I nodded, then asked which candidate the business community was supporting.

"That's a question we are trying to figure out ourselves," Smith said. "We think we should be getting a good deal more support than we are. But either they are not backing any candidate yet or something is going on that we don't understand."

Simmons chimed in, "Most of these so-called corporate leaders sitting up in those tall buildings are either too scared to get in this race behind the best candidate or they are being conned into backing one of the other candidates."

"You know which one?" I asked.

"No, we don't," Smith said, getting upset with Simmons' candor. "I would like to think that it does not really matter. We are out among the people. That's what counts."

"The community leaders, besides yourselves, who are they backing?" I asked.

Smith smiled. "The black leadership in Iron City today is not as together as it once was. We feel that most of the leaders believe I will make the best commissioner."

I nodded and told him that Mike Rose would call him for an interview. As we left the office and walked by the newsroom toward the elevator, I told Marshall, who had said nothing during our meeting, that I was glad he was still with us. It was idle chatter, but it clearly pleased the old man. Stooped and coming barely up to my shoulder as he shuffled along beside me, he patted my arm. As a young man, he had been thrown into jail for twenty days, I remembered reading about him. When he was released, he started the protests all over again, undeterred by jail. Sometimes size and character don't always match. He couldn't weigh more than hundred and forty pounds. But he projected a presence that was much greater.

"You be careful, young man," he said to me, "There are bad men in the world. Some of them would like to dance on your grave."

I smiled at the memory of the old Irish blessing that his comments evoked. When my grandfather or one of his Irish buddies had said it, they would laugh, toast one another's health and hope they would still be around to dance as old men on their enemies' graves.

As I watched the elevator doors close, a wave of my own anxiety crashed over me. Maybe I had taken on more than I should.

It was not a visit I looked forward to. I had postponed it as long as I could. Mark's wife, Peggy, and I had never been close. She seemed to resent her husband's friends and blamed me for leading him astray, encouraging him to pursue his reporting career rather than getting a job she considered respectable or at least one that paid better.

I hadn't talked to her since the funeral. Her face in the doorway looked like she was in an ad for depression relief medication. Her eyes were red, like she had been crying for days. I doubted it was for Mark. It was four thirty in the afternoon, and she was still in a bathrobe. I knew a lot about grieving and the feelings of hopelessness it brings. Maybe I had it easier. I had Chris and my newspaper family. Peggy had neither.

"I wanted to stop by to see if you were all right," I said. She nodded and opened the door. Ms. James had called to make sure she was still home on leave. Peggy, when she tried, looked good. She was thirty eight, but looked younger. She took her diet and exercise seriously. But it was done obsessively, without love. She harped on Mark's love for French fries, grits and country fried steaks. Mark never found much joy in doing sit ups or riding a stationary bike. He joked that he liked to get somewhere if he was going to sweat.

She seemed to accept my visit, as she did the rest of life, with resignation. We sat in the living room, saying little. The house was a two bedroom near Ramsey High School, a fortress of an old school halfway up the mountain. Mark and I had both graduated there. Seeing the school always brought back fond memories. Their house had a small yard in the back with a lone azalea bush growing there. The living room was spotless, almost sterile. I didn't feel Mark's presence there.

Peggy told me she had no real plans. She had taken time off from her job at General Insurance, but would go back in a few days. She said she would have to. They had taken out a small life insurance policy on Mark, but the funeral had eaten most of it. She thought she might move into a small apartment. With Mark gone she didn't need the house and yard.

She looked up at me through deep red eyes. I read how unhappy she was. She looked away and said, "I don't like for you to see me this way."

I told her about the article Mark had been working on, that it was important, but unfinished. It did not seem to matter to her. But then she had never been interested in Mark's work. She smiled wanly when I told her I wanted to pay her for the article. It wouldn't solve her financial problems, but it would help pay the rent this month.

"Did Mark talk about this article? Was he excited about it?" I asked.

She shook her head, brown stringy hair hung in clumps around her face. "No. He kept all that to himself. I didn't know he was working on anything important." She thought a minute. "I guess he was pretty tense the last few weeks. I did notice that. But I didn't know why."

I asked if I could look in the small bedroom Mark used as an office to see if he left any notes. She waved her hand at the door to a side room. When I stepped through the door, I felt it. That is where Mark's soul lived. As I sat in his chair and looked at his desk, the sadness I felt in the cemetery engulfed me again. Like the pain of losing my mother, grandfather and wife, a bottomless pit of loss and loneliness swallowed me. I sat for a long time just staring at the top of his desk, choking back tears. I wasn't sure I could move. A great flat rock sat on my shoulders.

The desk I stared at was a mirror of his life. There were stacks of papers, old newspapers, notebooks filled with his scratchings, old bills and receipts crammed in a file folder marked bills and another labeled taxes. Mark had kept scrapbooks of articles he had written over the years. I counted about fifteen books, a chronology of his career. Looking at the articles helped me connect with him again, as we were when he was alive. I spent a soothing half hour paging through them, walking down memory lane. Some articles had been written for the *Post*. Others were published by several newspapers he had worked for off and on through the years. There were a couple of dozen longer pieces printed in magazines.

He specialized in profiles on political officeholders and union officials. He treated them like celebrities and played a no-holds-barred game. Some of the magazines like *Rolling Stone* and *Ramparts* appreciated his style and approach. They printed some of Mark's most scathing pieces. A few had brought him fleeting fame.

I went through each stack of papers on Mark's desk hunting for his notes on the Crenshaw story, hoping for an organized file. No such luck. Mark knew where everything was. No one else could make sense of his filing system.

"Just think of it as my own security system," he joked once when an assistant city editor at the *Post* chastised him for the mess on his desk.

What I found was a stack of clippings from several newspapers on the bombing and a photo of the church before the bombing. There was a copy of Crenshaw's Army record. I wondered how Mark got that. Thrown on the floor was an early draft of the article he had given me with bomber's name blacked out. Beneath it, I found a notebook with several pages of notes. The first pages looked like his notes after his conversation with Crenshaw. There was also Crenshaw's home number. I wondered if Mark had called him back after their bar interview. If he did, did it spook him? On the next to the last page there were two other phone numbers. I dialed both numbers, but they just rang. I called Clay and asked him to run the numbers to see whom they belonged to.

I turned on his computer. It asked for a password. It took six guesses, but the words hamburger&beer let me in.

The computer files were no more organized than his desk. In one entitled New Stuff, I found the article. There was also a file with a list of names. My heart almost stopped. There on the page were the names of seven men. The fourth on the list was Lonnie Crenshaw. I didn't recognize any of the others. Were these the names of the conspirators in the bombing with Crenshaw? But if so, why didn't Mark identify them in the article? None of the names were prominent Iron City businessmen, who might be members of the Jackson Group.

In one file, Mark had written: "Who gains most from Grey's death?" I smiled. I had done the same thing. He had more answers than I did. He listed the sheriff first, then the mayor, then the white members of the county commission, white businessmen and several Klan members. Last there were black politicians. Under the last category, he wrote Ray Smith's name and phone number. Did he really think Smith had something to do the bombing? Did his feud with Grey run that deep? Or was it just his ambition?

I printed the list and in a reflex action slid the sheet of paper along with two of his notebooks into my right coat pocket where I had always carried my notebooks when I was reporter. It felt right to have the weight in that pocket again. I was back in the hunt.

Peggy knocked on the door and stood in the doorway. She had combed her hair and put on makeup. She was wearing a dress that showed off her slim waist. In a bar she would have gotten attention.

"Find anything?" she asked, not really expecting an answer. "Mark talked some on the phone to a guy who called a few times just, well, you know, before he died."

"Do you know who it was?" I asked.

"No. He asked for Mark. I told him I would take a message, but the man just wanted to know where he was. He said he needed to find Mark and give him something. I think he said it was important."

"Do you remember when that was?" I asked.

Peggy thought for a minute. "That's weird that I didn't think of it before, but it was just a couple of hours before .... I was watching that movie, *Father of the Bride*, on the cable when the police came and told me about Mark."

"This guy was looking for Mark just before he died?" I asked.

She nodded.

"Did you tell him where Mark was?" I asked.

"I didn't know. I never know where he is, was. But I told him he liked to go to Fergie's on Highland Avenue sometimes. He might try there," she said. "Does it mean anything?"

I shook my head. "Just a coincidence. Mark knew a lot of people. Probably didn't find him anyway. It's nothing. The voice on the phone, did you recognize it?"

She shook her head.

"Black, white? Could you tell?" I asked.

Again she shook her head. "Probably white. But then you sound white to me, on the phone."

She crossed her arms and watched me as I sorted through the rest of the desk. She seemed to be trying to get up the courage to say something. I stopped messing with the stacks of papers on his desk and looked at her.

"I probably shouldn't ask this, but I just kind of wondered if maybe...well, maybe if you'd know anyone you might introduce me too. It's kind of hard getting back into dating and all."

I didn't know what to say. I stood up and walked over to her and put my hands on her shoulders and then pulled her close. She was trembling. I thought what she needed more was just someone to hold her. Another time I had been just as needy. My grandfather once told me: "Loneliness is all it is cracked up to be." When Sheila was dying, I mistook sex for intimacy and security. It proved to be neither and almost cost me everything.

"Don't worry, Peggy. You'll be all right. You're young, good looking. You'll find somebody, who'll love you and make you happy, better than you've been. It happens all the time," I said with my arms still around her.

She turned away and left the doorway. Tears rolled down her cheeks. I saw her go into her bedroom leaving me alone to finish looking through Mark's desk. I sat for a few more minutes in his desk chair and stared at the one photo he had in the room. It was of the two of us when we were rookies. He and I were outside the county courthouse, working on a story about a multi-million dollar real estate swindle. Being the day before payday, we had three dollars and a few coins between us, enough to share a hot dog and a coke. We had laughed ourselves silly over the irony. While we were fighting off poverty, we were about to expose how some guy had made millions and skipped the country. A *Post* photographer came out of the courthouse where he was shooting photos of a guy standing trial. He saw us on the street and stopped to take our picture, each holding onto the Coke can and our halves of the hot dog. I had a copy of the same photo on my desk at home.

I picked up the file with his tax receipts. I hoped it might tell me something. I put a check for Mark's article on the hall table and let myself out the front door.

6

The bar at the Monteagle Hotel just wasn't the same. When I was a young reporter, it was one of the sleaziest downtown watering holes, where run-down bars were the norm. Threadbare carpet was now replaced by padded carpet with a red and gray pattern. Ferns hung in the windows. The bar's brass rail gleamed, and long-stemmed wine glasses hung from an overhead rack above the heads of two well-dressed bartenders. The waitresses were young and well dressed in black pants and pale yellow shirts. Gone were the old floozies waiting tables to pay for their next drink.

"I can remember when you could get a hand job under the table here for ten bucks," Walt Simpson said, after I noted the impact the young professionals living and working downtown had on the bar. We sat at a corner table that looked out on Fifth Street. Walt and I had first met when I volunteered to work in a U.S. Senate campaign where he was the Iron City campaign manager. I nailed up posters with him for a four-term U.S. senator when I was a sophomore in college and just learning about politics. That made Walt my oldest friend that I still saw regularly. I liked him for a lot of reasons, but mostly he was probably the savviest person I knew.

"Now it would take a hundred dollar dinner and a bunch of sophisticated conversation to get anywhere with the women who come in here," he lamented. "Progress ain't always good."

Walt's cynicism was one of his most endearing traits. He had seen and done a lot, and little of it would make you an optimist about the human race. When we had been hanging signs and planting yard signs for the old senator, he had been a lot slimmer. Jumping in and out of a truck, climbing telephone poles with a sign and hand stapler would now be out of the question. His mustache and goatee had turned to a distinguished white, and he weighed close to two hundred and sixty pounds on a five-foot, ten-inch frame. He had diabetes and an arthritic knee, which he loved to complain about.

Walt's value to political candidates these days had little to do with his knees. He was paid for his brains and contacts. Walt would work for Democrats, but Republicans, he said, paid better and had a much better chance of winning in Alabama. A white man, Walt did not care what the candidate's skin color was and had gotten a few black candidates elected. Nor did he care whether the candidate was male or female, although he said working for women candidates presented different challenges. He liked candidates who understood the game. The only candidate I ever heard Walt refuse to work for was a man who forgot to take care of his friends once he was elected. When he ran again, Walt worked for his opponent, discounting his fees to prove a point. The man was not re-elected.

The waitress showed up at his shoulder. "Give me another one of the bourbon and Diet Cokes, honey. My wife's got me on a diet." I was working on my second Coors Light. "I don't know why you drink that lightweight beer. Now that you're the big editor-in-chief, you should drink bourbon or scotch or at least one of those Belgian brews."

It was comfortable banter. He had already commented on the article about the rescue of the policemen and said he thought I was a "damn fool," but didn't mean it.

"It's not getting better out there," he said waving his hand at the street outside large windows. "The governor's talking about declaring martial law and send in some soldier boys. He's worried about getting elected again next year and can't decide which side to piss off, whites or blacks."

The waitress brought the drinks. Walt watched her walk away. "Chief Bates never bargained for this heat, keeps swearing he's gonna put the bomber away. Shit, he can't put his pecker away after pissing. And the mayor, well...you know the mayor, he's scared shitless. He's stopped listening to good advice. Never was too smart. But always before, he knew how to listen."

"Listen to whom?" I asked.

"You know. To those who got him elected - them who put him dere." He smiled.

The mayor was often compared to Ronald Reagan, a comparison Mayor Marsh promoted. He was tall with movie-star looks and often radiated a vacuous expression when asked a question that went beyond the state of the weather. President Reagan had been a pragmatist with an agenda. Mayor Marsh blew in the wind. His real advantage was that he was white and had enough income from a chain of florist shops that made it less likely he would steal as much as his predecessor had.

"My business editor says lots of businesses are moving to the suburbs, packing up and leaving before they are forced out."

He nodded. "Can't blame them, can you? Those businesses are all they've got. If they get burnt out, can they afford to rebuild? Will the insurance pay what they are worth?"

Taking sips of his bourbon, he stroked his goatee. After a thoughtful minute, he said, "I figured by now it would have run out of steam. Black folks don't usually have this much stamina. Good at the forty-yard dash, not the mile." Walt was a benign racist. There was no hate in it. He thought of himself as a realist, and I knew he cherished our friendship. He never seemed to notice I was black or if he did, it didn't matter.

"Without the commissioner and his preacher buddy I am surprised it has continued, maybe even escalated." He paused to look out at the street. "Now it's like one of those dragons the Greek heroes were always fighting. You cut off its head and lots of little ones spring up."

"You mean the community is getting some new leaders?" I asked.

He waggled his head. "A lot of wannabes competing to be the next king fish." He sipped his drink and stared over my shoulder at a couple who sat down at the table near us. "The primary election in a few weeks will narrow the field some. None has the juice Grey had. But what they lack in style, they make up for in volume. It's one-upmanship. They are beginning to talk about burning more stuff downtown and moving south. They aren't brave enough yet to go over the mountain. That really would bring on the Guard."

In Iron City the often-heard phrase over the mountain referred to the nearly all white suburbs to the south where the wealthy and would-be wealthy lived. Most eastern cities grew north or west, because rich folks moved upriver to avoid the stench caused by untreated sewage, meat carcasses and chemicals. Poorer people, new immigrants and particularly black people, always settled on the cheaper land downriver. Iron City had no river. The mountain set the housing patterns. Those who could afford it moved over the mountain to escape the dirty air belched from the old steel mills. Whites also liked having a mountain between them and blacks.

"A bunch of outsiders are pouring in. The Atlanta boys can smell a good show a hundred and fifty miles away. You saw Reverend Sharpton was in town. He flew in from New York City to record his TV show. I expect to see the good Jesse Jackson on a plane from Chicago any minute. Grey and Smallwood have become martyrs. It's a good time for passing the plate in Iron City. Bunch of them were here Sunday talking about the need to make the city a symbol once again of how black folks won't stand for any more abuse. They'll be back this weekend. Count on it," Walt said.

"The Southern Christian Leadership Council? NAACP?" I asked.

"Oh, yeah." Walt's voice was getting louder. I looked around to see if anyone was listening. Walt read my mind and leaned a little closer. "Not just the Slick boys and the N, double A, C and P boys, but also the Urban League girls and boys, you name it, they're here strutting their stuff. I heard that Spike Lee may make another movie about the streets of Iron City or some damn fool thing. Nothing like it to open those corporate checkbooks."

He stared into his glass. "Just like the old days?" I asked.

Walt shook his head. "Different now. Something's different. There is more meanspiritedness – is that a word Mr. Editor?" He sat back smiling at me. "It used to be just the whites, the police commissioner, the Klan boys, the rednecks, who were full of hate. Now it feels like both sides are full of it." He laughed. "In more ways than one."

I thought the conversation had gone long enough and Walt had downed enough booze. Although it was not unusual to meet Walt for a drink, I had called him because I wanted to know more about the mysterious Jackson Group. I took a deep breath and asked him who was in it and what was it up to.

Walt looked at me for a moment, sizing up my questions. "This just between us? What do you call it, off the record?"

I nodded.

He cocked his head and looked at me. "Why you asking anyway?"

"Heard some talk about the group, behind the scenes, the rich and powerful, all that. Thought you would know," I said.

He paused, took a long sip and smiled. "Hell, yeah, I know. But I am not sure you should know about my boys."

"Why not?" I asked.

"Don't need the heat, especially right now," he said.

"Heat?"

"You know what I mean, publicity. If you spread them across the front page of your newspaper, who knows what happens? Maybe somebody wants to start an investigation. Maybe some outraged black citizen takes a shot at one of them or their businesses get burned, blowed up. Out in the open, they lose power, that's for sure. That's my job. Work behind the scenes."

I was quiet for a few minutes. I needed to know more about the group, but was not sure what I had to give up to get the information. "Okay, here is the deal. I will never quote you."

"That's no deal. My guys know we're friends. I want to know why you need to know. It's more than curiosity. I know you. Why do you want to know?"

I nodded. "You're right. It is more. It could be a lot more. But I can't tell you why, right now. I promise to tell you before I use it in any story, and I won't use the information unless it is critical to a major story."

We both sat thinking for a while. Finally I said, "You'll have to trust me on that."

"Oh, I trust you, all right. That is not the problem. I just think we are all on a cliff, could fall off one way or the other. Anything, everything is being blown out of proportion," he said.

Then he shrugged. He decided to take a chance. I didn't know why he was willing to tell me all he knew about the Jackson Group, but he did. And I had to keep my promise.

Legally there was no Jackson Group, Walt told me. There were no incorporation papers at the Secretary of State's office. It had no office, no name on a door anywhere in town. There was no payroll for Walt or anyone else. It was not clear how he got paid, but apparently from the new Cadillac that sat on Fifth Street, it was a more than a small retainer. The group, named either for General Stonewall Jackson or President Andrew Jackson, depending on who you talked to, was made up of the business power structure. All white, all male, it included the chairmen or presidents of most of the major businesses, banks, pipe manufacturers and steel fabricators in the city, plus a few insurance companies and the managing partners of the largest law firms. He named a few. It also included Robert Daniels, Jr.

The men who made up the group were nowhere near as powerful as their predecessors in the corporate suites twenty years ago, he said. But they could still leverage contributions to get government contracts and favorable laws and regulations for themselves and their friends. They could also stop others from benefiting from the largess of city and county coffers. It was an old game, one that thanks to Walt's brains and skills, they still played well.

Jenkins, my predecessor as editor, had been allowed in the group. He wanted it badly, his badge of acceptance. Over a tepid objection from Daniels, he had been let in. But Walt said it never really took. The guys with power knew Jenkins was too afraid to take risks. He was too scared of losing his title, his acceptance in the business community, to be glad-handed at the clubs and restaurants where the rich and powerful congregated. The group kept him in it just to make sure the *Post* wrote only articles the members wanted to see in print.

With his third bourbon loosening his tongue, Walt said they didn't know what to make of me. "I wouldn't count on an invitation to join," he teased.

"So how is the Jackson Group taking the riots?" I asked.

"They're pissed and scared. Mostly they're pissed. Before the church was bombed, things were going well in Iron City. The economy was rebounding from the last recession. People had money to spend. They never thought this would happen." He shook his head in frustration and swirled his glass before draining it. "They meet several afternoons a week. Half of them are ready to pull up stakes, move south, leave every thing north of Vulcan to the blacks. One guy actually said that. Iron City would be worse than Detroit, the donut hole surrounded by the suburbs. The others want the governor to send in the soldier boys and show everybody who's in charge."

"The mayor meeting with the Jackson Group?" I asked.

"Yeah, governor's guy too. The mayor was meeting with them a lot at first. But he's lost his nerve. Now Harden has to call two or three times even to get Marsh to call him back. He's the most pissed of all. You know how he gets. Talking about getting somebody else to be mayor," Walt said.

Harden, I guessed, was Harden Braddock, who owned a couple of car dealerships, a bunch of apartments on the Southside and a lot of land up north. He wouldn't be in favor of abandoning Iron City. He had too much of an investment in the city.

"Who would they back for mayor?"

"Doesn't matter right now. Long way to the election. Idle threat. They'll patch things up with the florist before the next election. There's nobody much out there my guys could work with better. Besides, it is usually too risky to abandon the incumbent," Walt said.

He stopped and looked at me. "It's kinda funny really, watching all this blow up in their faces. They think they are so damn smart. Won't listen to good advice, even when they're paying for it. But no, would they let me buy off the late, great commissioner, get him and his buddy off their soap boxes?" Walt shook his head in disgust. "No way. They refused. Fools."

Walt ordered another drink. He was going to have trouble driving home with the amount of bourbon he was drinking, but I wasn't interrupting him. He was so close to telling me everything he knew.

"Would Grey and Smallwood have taken their money?"

He laughed. "Money has a funny way of getting attention. But maybe you are right. They believed they were on a crusade, on the side of the angels, much like King and Shuttlesworth years ago." He finished his drink and smiled at me. "But there are other things than money. Maybe my boys would get rid of the sheriff, make the jail a bit safer for black folks, get a few more black judges elected, that sort of thing. Then Grey can declare victory, build bridges with the white power structure. Something good for everybody, but no, my guys wouldn't see it. Thought I was whistling Dixie."

"So did they kill Grey and Smallwood?" I asked and held my breath.

He stared at me. I knew I had asked the wrong question even if he was getting drunk.

"I don't know who did the bombing. And that's the truth. I hear rumors. I even hear you may be getting close to something." He was suddenly surprisingly lucid. "But understand something: whoever did it enjoyed it. He ain't got no guilty conscience, Mr. Editor. If you get too close, he'll either run, if he can, or kill again. He wouldn't think nothing of digging a hole for your big ass."

"I've been there before," I said, trying to sound more macho than I felt.

"I know. You got a gun pulled on you by Hawkins in his office up at city hall." It never ceased to amaze me what Walt knew. "That was the minor leagues compared to this. These guys drive around with dynamite or whatever in the trunk. They see your car at your house or outside your girlfriend's place, they'll tie a few sticks to your ignition and you won't know what hit you."

I shook my head, marveling at how he knew about Nicki. He downed his glass, stood up and put his hand on my shoulder. "Just be careful, buddy. Remember, it is our favorite sins that do us in. Watch your back. These are troubled times, not just in the streets, but in a lot of places. We can't afford to lose you or your newspaper right now," he said, moving away slowly and turning to smile at me.

He gave the waitress a bear-like hug and handed her some large bills before weaving his way out the door and into his car. That was the second warning today that I was putting myself and my newspaper in someone's cross-hairs.

Clay jumped up from his computer terminal on the city desk and met me as I came into the newsroom. It was late. The first edition, which rolled off the presses in the early evening, was already in the racks and on the trucks headed out of the city. The next edition went upstairs in an hour. Usually, at this time, Clay was doing his octopus imitation, talking on the phone to reporters, editing copy on the computer and fielding questions from the layout and copy desks.

He looked worried as he fell in step with me. "Mike Rose is on the line. He's been asking questions around city hall and may have has stirred up some folks. Jack Grisham, that weasel of an aide to the mayor, dropped down to the press room to see him. You know that prick never goes to see any reporter unless the mayor wants something."

Clay was right to worry. We were walking a tightrope. There was always a danger of tipping off someone about Crenshaw, while we searched for him. Mike was good, but might have asked one question too many or of the wrong person.

"Grisham just wanted to know what he was working on about the bombing, real friendly and all. Mike couldn't get him to admit he or the mayor knew anything. It was a standoff, but he figures if the mayor sent him to ask the question, there's gotta be some heat somewhere."

This was getting frustrating. Why couldn't we track this guy down? He was probably hiding in plain sight.

"Look, you know this, but let's make sure we are all on the same page. We have to treat the story like it's a tip. It's one source. We need confirmation from at least one other source, maybe two, on all points that we plan to print. Let's find the guy. This is way too big for us to take any chances," I said.

"Right, right. But if Mike stirs things up too much, the *Examiner* guys could get on it. Their city hall reporter already asked why Grisham came by for a chat. None of us want to blow this." Clay was uncharacteristically wringing his hands.

"Okay. Tell Mike to cool it around city hall. I don't think those guys will get us very far anyway. Get Pat moving. He has more connections and people who owe him, big time."

If any of us could, Pat Galloway with all his years working the police beat, could find and interview this constable. Clay assured me that Pat was looking for Crenshaw, but the staff in the sheriff's office claimed they did not know where he was. Suddenly the guy took a vacation. Nobody seemed to know when he would be back.

That was my worst nightmare. Crenshaw would just disappear into the ozone. I called Pat from an office I regularly had swept for listening devices. Howard had found a bug once. He couldn't trace its origin and became mildly paranoid on the subject. I waved to Clay to stand in the doorway. I couldn't shut the door. Things would be too close in the small space, but I didn't want anyone listening.

"Has our boy disappeared?" I asked Pat.

"Yeah, Joe. He's gone. Nobody's talking either. People that would tell me their mother's bank account number are clamming up or just don't know," he said.

Had something spooked him or had someone told him to get out of town? If Crenshaw had hung around town for weeks since the bombing, was it just a coincidence that he would leave now? A regularly scheduled vacation? Not likely.

"Okay, keep looking, but let's don't bring an avalanche down on us. Okay?" I said.

"Right. I do hear rumblings in the distance," Pat said.

"How do you mean?"

"The sheriff pulled me into his office. He was not happy, asked why I was looking for one of his constables. I told him it was just routine, that I heard he was involved in rescuing some little girl in one of the looted buildings. It was all bull, but it was the best I could do on the spur of the moment."

"Did the sheriff buy it?" Clay asked.

"Yeah, sort of. He said that sounded like Crenshaw. He told me Lonnie's big and dumb, but has a heart for kids."

I wondered if old Lonnie had worried about kids in the church when he placed the bomb.

"The sheriff let me go, all smiles and said Lonnie was just on a short vacation," Pat said. "He promised to have Crenshaw give me a call when he came back to town. I told him that old news wasn't worth much and asked for Crenshaw's cell number or where he went on vacation. He just stood there smiling, saying Lonnie wasn't family or even a real good friend and that he doesn't keep tabs that closely on the constables. Crap. I bet old Ned knows right where he is so he can lay his hands on him when he wants to."

"Okay. If it is getting a little too hot over there for you, if you need to come in the newsroom for a few days, do it. We can send somebody else over to cover the cops."

"Nawh. I'm all right. We've got a better shot if I stay here. Maybe somebody will call me when things cool down a bit. Besides they know where I live, what I drive. If they want to find me, they will."

I never thought it was going to be this hard. When I hung up, I was more frustrated than ever. "Clay, find him. We've got to have him alive and talking."

"What about the expense?" Clay knew I was always under pressure to keep costs down. The owners of the Babcock News Syndicate seemed less concerned with good news coverage than in maximizing the return on their investment. Weitzman and I had a monthly fight on the phone over expenses.

"Damn it, Clay. Spend what you have to." The beers with Walt had made me tired. We weren't making progress. I felt the story slipping away. "This is the biggest story we've ever worked on. Do it."

"Can I bring in that private detective Nicki?"

"If you have to. But let's do as much of this as we can ourselves. If we really believe by tomorrow that he is hiding, then we'll have to use Nicki to find him."

Nicole (Nicki) Fabrini worked for one of the best private detective firms in the city. I was sure she could find anybody, anything, anytime, anywhere. She hacked her way through a universe of databases. When the computer failed her, she was good at disguise. One day she posed as a biker's mom to track a deadbeat father and collect years of overdue child support. She rode for a weekend on the back of another biker's cycle and called in the police when she found the deadbeat camping out. The next week she was an over-the-mountain socialite, helping a wealthy Louisiana family find their son, who had stolen millions of dollars in family art and was trying to sell it off. While hanging out in the bar at one of the country clubs, waiting for her target to finish his daily eighteen holes, a middle-aged doctor bought her a drink and a half hour later offered her an apartment and a Mercedes. She declined, set her drink down when she saw her target coming off the green, doffed her high heels, chased him across the parking lot and tackled him on the practice green amid a dozen stunned putters.

If I were lost, I would want Nicki looking for me. Fortunately for me, she would. We had started dating several months ago, but for reasons, mostly related to our jobs, we had decided to keep us a secret. Dating Nicki was a whole new world for me. Unlike Sheila, she was tough mentally and physically. A self-assured person who loved being playful, particularly in bed, she showed her soft side at unexpected moments. Happy in herself and her work, she sounded glad when I called, but she loved her hobbies, riding motorcycles and shooting handguns at targets, and had several crazy friends to hang with when she wasn't with me or working around the clock. I flattered myself that I could live without her, but knew I was deluding myself. I was growing more attached every time we were together.

Sleeping together had not given the *Post* any break on her fees. My boss would have frowned on paying for her work if he knew I left her apartment some mornings at three. So not even Clay knew about Nicki. It made conversations about her a bit humorous.

Of the papers I had brought from Mark's house, his notebook was the most intriguing. I wanted to know who the other guys on the list were. Could they be other bombers? Were they part of the conspiracy?

Ed limped across the newsroom. He held his palms up to ask wordlessly if there was anything happening. I handed him the list of names. "Anyone you know?" He looked at them, shook his head and shrugged. I told him where I had found the list and why I thought they might be important.

"I'll show it to Amanda," he said, obviously uncomfortable talking about Mark. Our society and community section editor had an encyclopedic knowledge of the local rich and famous. If she didn't know them, they were probably low-lifes. He was back in a couple of minutes shaking his head.

"Are these the names of other bombers? Conspirators?" I whispered to Ed.

Ed leaned forward and put his elbows on the desk. "Maybe they were suspects that Mark cleared."

That seemed right. We sat at an empty desk, the newsroom swirled around us as reporters and editors worked on routine stories. "You remember that Mark's story speculates about a conspiracy, members of the Jackson group, who may have paid our bomber, right?" I said.

Ed nodded. Clay joined us, curious at what we were working on.

"Since we know the Jackson Group is composed of powerful business executives in town, none of these names fit. So you're probably right. These must be the names of the men Mark suspected of being the bomber. He talked to several of them. Then he got to Lonnie Crenshaw, and that was where he stopped," I said. "So the chances of any of these guys knowing any more about the bombing or where Crenshaw is or anything we need to know are pretty slim. Damn, I was hoping this would get us somewhere."

I told Clay to read the list to Pat. "See if he recognized any of these names from his coverage of the police." It might be a wild goose chase, but I wanted to know how Mark found Crenshaw. Maybe we could find him the same way. Did he look for people who knew how to blow up things? Did he try to spot guys with a real hatred of black people? Or was it something else?

The rest of the stuff from Mark's office showed he took a round-trip flight on American Airlines to Kansas City, an Enterprise rental car receipt for two days, a night in a Holiday Inn Express. I went through his phone bills to check his long distance calls since the bombing. Most were to newspapers and magazines. Others were to the FBI and Justice Department in Washington. A couple of calls were to Fort Leavenwood in Kansas. And there were four calls one morning to a town on the Florida border near Dothan. I looked it up.

Clay's assistant told him that she had finished editing a story about the latest round of arsons. The article, which reported fewer buildings burned than in the last few days, was in his computer. No one was excited that a half dozen business had been torched. Maybe this was just the new norm in the streets of Iron City.

I asked Clay about the phone numbers I had given him.

"Yep. But don't get your hopes up. They were two pay phones up on the northside," he said.

Why had Mark written down two different pay phone numbers in the black neighborhoods of Iron City? Clay looked at my puzzled expression. "Does that mean something? Where'd you get these numbers?"

I shook my head. "Probably nothing."

When I got back to my office after making my daily rounds to watch the page designers put the finishing touches on the layout for the final edition, a sad little rich girl sat in my office. Sandra Galloway, Pat's wife, dropped in every six months, always at night while Pat was working at the police station and usually after being at a reception for some charity where the wine flowed. I knew why she was there. Always desperate for money, she was as persistent as she was dignified. She wanted me to give Pat a raise. Shortly after taking over as editor I made the mistake of agreeing to a hundred dollar-a-month raise for Pat when she came to ask. I didn't tell him she had asked me for it, but she told him. It had embarrassed him, and we both felt like fools. As the old saying goes: No good deed goes unpunished.

Pat and I had known each other a long time. He was thirty and a veteran reporter and a mentor of sorts when I joined the paper. We had become friends. He was the person who called to tell me the police had found Mark and his car in the ravine.

"Well, Joe, I hope you don't mind me just dropping in like this, but I need your help," she said.

She smoothed out her dress with her hands as she sat overly straight in the chair across the desk. Wine had given her courage, but she didn't want me to know.

Pat and Sandra had married after graduating from Auburn University. He was four years older, having been in the Army before using the government's money for college. She had been born to money, the granddaughter of one of the old Montgomery cotton gin owners when cotton was king in Alabama, and had grown up in a standard of living that few could match. She had fallen for Pat, an older, more worldly man, never giving a thought to whether he could afford the lifestyle she was used to. Or maybe she married him in her youthful rebellion against that lifestyle.

Pat had never aspired to be anything but a newspaper reporter. At first, she liked to read his name on stories he wrote. But then she learned that it meant working late nights and little pay. He refused to let her father supplement his income, at least overtly. His independence was admirable, but to pay the mortgage on a house he couldn't afford, the cars, parties, dresses, shoes, their own boat for the parents' house on Lake Martin put a tremendous strain on him, and I thought, on their marriage.

She was a regular in the social swirl. There were few parties for the museum or the theater or the cancer society that she missed. Pat once joked about a party. "I'm not sure what disease we were dancing to, but we all looked good."

We talked a few minutes about irrelevant things. They had no children. She would never risk spoiling her waistline to get pregnant. That was a mixed blessing. Children are expensive, but they might have given her a purpose and brought her maturity. Pat told me that both sets of parents wanted grandchildren, but none had come.

"I came to ask you to help out my Pat. He works so hard for this damned old newspaper, and you and him being good friends and all. You can give him some more money. And I can pay off some of those old credit cards that keep calling me," she whined.

The Scarlett O'Hara routine did not play well. She had grown up getting her way with men with a wag of the head, a flutter of the eyelashes and a smile. It must have worked on her father and might still work on Pat. I tried once again to explain about the union and how we had a contract with the employees of the *Post*, and we couldn't make any exceptions, including Pat.

"But Pat never joined that damned old union. He wouldn't do that. My Daddy wouldn't like that. So it doesn't matter what the union does. You can still give him a raise."

I shook my head and tried to make her see that things didn't work that way. She wasn't interested in my explanation.

"Well, just, maybe you could slip him some money, you know, under the table."

I told her that I already stretched the rules for Pat by allowing him to freelance for other newspapers on crime stories. It didn't bring in a lot of money, but it was income others didn't get. From time to time it came up as an issue in the newsroom.

Finally accepting defeat, she stood. She wanted to make a grand exit, unbowed. But the alcohol made her pay. Light-headed, she had to sit back down hard in the chair. I stood up and grabbed her arm to steady her. She yanked her elbow out of my hand.

"Damn you, Joe Riordan. I thought you would help me. You'll be sorry. I know a lot more than you think." She tilted her chin in the air, stared at me for a second, just long enough for me to see the real person under the makeup. It was not pretty.

As she marched out of my office, I wondered what Pat saw in her. Her visit made me uncomfortable, though I didn't know why.

7

Rachel Stanton was waiting when I arrived the next morning. The earrings she wore always amazed me. She wore big looped ones that had what I expect was the desired effect of widening her thin face. They certainly caught the eye.

While I perched on the edge of the city desk, she sat very straight in a chair and asked about Chris, the unofficial godson to all the women who worked at the *Post*. They worried about him, not having a mother. Chris loved to come with me to the newspaper and be thoroughly pampered by them. He and I had just finished breakfast and our hour of cartoons, so I regaled her with Chris stories.

She wanted to report on her progress, or rather her lack of progress in finding out more on the Jackson Group. A search of the *Post*'s archives for any articles on the shadowy power group showed little. There was nothing in the *Examiner*. We had carried a story that briefly mentioned the group when a candidate for mayor announced that he had the backing of the group during a campaign. But there was no follow up. We'd carried no substantive piece, which made me wonder how we had missed this story.

There was a lot of articles on those we assumed were members, although we were only guessing who might actually be a member. "I looked up Phil Dingle, chairman of SouthBank, and Harold Smith, head of the electric and gas company. I assume they are members. I

don't know about some of these others: Jim Henderson, the managing partner at Lang, Dickens and Holt; maybe Bob Devine, chairman of Raleigh's, the department store chain, and John Higgins at
Alabama Iron & Steel. What do you think?" she asked.

"I would be surprised if they weren't members. Who else?"

She named three other men, all heads of major corporations in
the city. Then she paused. "I don't know about Robert Daniels. You
know him better than anyone around here. What do you think?"

"Yes. He is in the group." My off-the-record talk with Walt gave
me good information, but none of it was printable yet. Useful, but a
long way from where we needed to be on a story like this.

"There are a lot of stories on Daniels, of course. He isn't media
shy, for sure. But most of it is junk; awards he's gotten when he was
named publisher, the legacy of his father, and so forth. Not much
to link him to either the Jackson Group or the bombing. From the
Examiner's editorial policy, he is conservative, and the *Examiner* certainly did not like Commissioner Grey. But that doesn't make him a
bomber, does it?" she said.

No, this wasn't getting us very far.

"Is Amanda in? This is her turf. And get Bob too," I said.

Bob Karem, the business editor, was kind of a nerd who idolized
business executives. If the rap on sports writers was that they were
jock sniffers, Bob was a leather briefcase sniffer. He knew all the
CEOs and their public relations staff and thought they all walked
on water. Amanda saw them more clearly and liked most of them,
warts and all. Bob couldn't see they had any warts.

We walked over to Amanda's desk and pulled up a couple of
chairs. I waved at Bob to join us. He rolled his desk chair rapidly,
excitedly across the newsroom.

"What's up?" Amanda said, always informal in her approach to
life. I told them we wanted to do an in-depth feature on the Jackson
Group. I explained that the membership is secret, so we are trying to figure out who the members are. Rachel went through the
list again. Bob's body language said he was not comfortable with

this story. He could envision being chewed out by several corporate public relations people if we wrote a story mentioning their boss as a member of the group.

"Who else do you think is involved?" I asked, feeling more frustrated by the day on the slow progress we were making on this story.

"I really did not focus on him at first. I was looking for heads of large corporations. The guy who has come up repeatedly in my interviews is Harden Braddock," she said.

Amanda agreed. "I would think we can put him on the list. He and his wife, Lori, are everywhere. They chaired several charity balls. And you know, that he is the largest contributor to the University of Alabama athletic program?"

The athletic program? I asked.

"He gives to the university in general, but mostly he supports the athletic programs. He's real tight with the athletic director and the coaches. Didn't he play football or something? And Lori was like the head cheerleader."

Bob chimed in, proud he could contribute, telling us Braddock graduated from the University of Alabama in Tuscaloosa, a big fraternity man, played second team quarterback, then married the daughter of one of the coal kings in Jasper and shortly inherited all his money when his father-in-law went hunting one fall morning and didn't come back. They found his body a few days later. He had been hunting alone and apparently fell off a cliff. Braddock never looked back. The Braddocks had taken Iron City by storm.

"He likes high-risk, high-reward businesses, automobiles and real estate," Bob said, sounding like he was quoting a public relations associate.

It was hard to stifle a laugh.

"Sounds like a couple in a bad Harlequin novel," Rachel said, smirking. Amanda laughed loudly.

"President Schremp comes up from Tuscaloosa for one or two of his parties every year," the business editor said, trying to regain face.

Amanda giggled, her bracelets jingled. "Have you seen the den in Braddock's house? It's incredible. There are, I guess, a couple of hundred Crimson Tide pieces of junk in that room. It is like a museum to tacky Tide,"

I smiled, trying not to laugh myself. Rachel scribbled notes. Bob was not happy with our disrespect for a major business owner he had profiled in glowing terms.

"What else do we know about Braddock?" I asked.

Bob talked about his businesses, his car dealerships, apartment complexes and other real estate he had inherited from his wife's father. "He is a real entrepreneur, shrewd, knows his business, gets in, gets out at the right time. He rolls the dice and so far has come up winning."

"Oh, Bob, he married his money. He didn't make it," Amanda snapped. "When you get it handed to you like he did, all you got to do is not be stupid. And the one thing Braddock's not is stupid. His ego may be getting the best of him these days. He's a little eaten up with himself. But he is smart."

Bob drew back, not strong enough to take on Amanda. He turned to me, deciding that he needed to join in the conspiracy. "You might want to talk to Mike Rose about Mr. Braddock. There's been a lot of rumors that the highway department built the extension of the loop up north to go through some of his coal mining properties. I don't know the details, but there's been a lot of talk."

I nodded. "What else?"

"Well, you know he is very close with your good friend, Bob Daniels," Amanda said, her sarcasm dripping. I looked up surprised. Braddock did not seem like Daniels' type.

Rachel said, "One of the better photos I found in the files was Braddock and Daniels standing together, collecting some award. They looked like great friends."

She handed me a copy of the photo. I wondered if this was what Mark was chasing. Was fingering Daniels for the bombing too hot even for Mark to handle? Were they even capable of such a conspiracy? Maybe I have been reading too many books by conspiracy theorists lately.

"Who've you interviewed?" Amanda asked Rachel.

"Well, I didn't get very far at first. I talked to a guy at the chamber of commerce." Bob looked hurt. He saw the chamber as his exclusive turf. "Then I made an appointment with the general manager of the country club and a few of the other clubs. I called up the development director at Southern College and the art museum manager. I think that's all so far. I wanted to talk with people who work with these men and see what they observe."

"Did they tell you what you needed? Maybe I can help," Bob said.

Rachel thanked him. "Mostly I learned a whole bunch of gossip and general crap about how things get done around here. Who they are married to, who they are having affairs with, how much they drink and with whom, how their businesses are going, do they golf or play poker, whether or not they are coughing up much to support the arts or universities. That sort of thing."

"Oh, I love that stuff," Amanda said rubbing her fingers together in delight. "As Eleanor Roosevelt once said, if you can't say something nice about somebody, come sit by me." We broke out laughing. It felt good to laugh after all the tension of the last few days.

"What kind of story did you tell all these people you were working on?" I asked.

"Oh, a different story for each person. Mostly I told them I was working on a feature story on the rich and famous of Iron City," she said.

Of course, being young, female and good looking never hurt getting people to talk.

She checked her notes and said, "I got stuff like who the power boys are. It used to be that the steel companies and coal companies ran everything. If they didn't want something to happen, it didn't. That's why Iron City didn't grow as fast as Atlanta."

Things had changed a lot. The city fathers encouraged growth now to increase tax revenues, which have sagged badly in recent years. And a number of new businesses were showing up. Iron City had been growing again, at least before the riots started. But there was still a lot of people who believed that bringing in a bunch of outsiders eroded their control and would change the city, especially between blacks and whites.

Amanda joined in. "Mostly the city is run by the utilities, banks and lawyers. A few of the pipe companies are still important. And then there's our friend Braddock and your good friend, Mr. Daniels."

"The *Examiner* has always wielded a ton of power. What else, Rachel?"

She said her best interview was at the country club. Flipping through her notebook, she said the manager told her that the Jackson Group meets in the poker room off the men's locker room. He never goes in there when they are meeting, so he didn't know who attends regularly or what they are talking about. He let me talk to the waiter and bartender who have been serving them regularly. I sat up, my frustration drained away in a rush.

"The bartender said he didn't know much. The waiter, though, was good. The manager left us alone to take care of a woman who was upset about her daughter's wedding reception. The waiter told me that they have been meeting almost every day, about five o'clock, and drink a lot."

"Is the waiter black?" I asked.

"Yes. An older guy. They probably never noticed he was there, at first, anyway. He said once last week when they were shouting at each other, one of the men stood up and pointed a finger at another man and yelled it was his fault this is happening, that he had it in for Grey."

Now we were getting somewhere, if we could just nail that conversation down.

"The guy he was pointing at told him to shut up and that he didn't know what he was talking about. Then the man seemed to notice the waiter was there and waved him out. The waiter couldn't hear any more from outside the room. But pretty soon the first man came stomping out through the door, muttering what sounded like 'ain't half the man his father was.'"

I must have smiled because Rachel looked at me a second, then said, "You think they are talking about Daniels?"

"God should love me that much."

Amanda laughed. Bob looked confused and pained at the same time. I wondered who he would call first after our meeting.

I asked Rachel if she could talk with the waiter again. She thought she could, although she was not sure how much more he knew. The country club manager would not want to offend the morning newspaper, but his loyalties would be to the members. He might earn points by telling someone that we were interviewing the waiter again.

"Get as many photos of the guys we think are in the Jackson Group and see if you can find an excuse to show them to the waiter. We need to know who was upset and who that guy was pointing at. This is a great lead, but move carefully, understand?"

Rachel asked how she was expected to go back to the club without stirring up things.

"Since nobody here has a membership, we will need to ask a friend. Now, who has the most friends of anyone who hangs out at country clubs?" I asked.

We each turned to look at Amanda.

She laughed. "Of course. Amanda to the rescue, right? I can think of a couple of possibilities. What do you want them to do?"

"Just get Rachel in, then she can play it by ear, when she talks with, what's the waiter's name?" I said.

She looked at me somewhat indignantly. "Jerome."

"What time of day did you see him?" I asked.

"About 4:30."

"Well, if he has been serving the Jackson Group at five, he clearly works the afternoon shift. So..."

"So," Rachel said, finishing my thought, "I should go about four and see if I can get him to wait on me and Amanda's friend, right?"

Rachel, Amanda and Bob spent a few more minutes going over the names of the Jackson Group again, fleshing out the sketch of each. Amanda called a friend and nodded at me that I took to mean the woman would play along with us. I told Amanda to try not to get Jerome fired and enjoyed a few minutes harboring evil thoughts of what the headlines might read if my fondest dreams came true and we nailed Daniels for conspiracy in the bombing. Bob interrupted my daydream. "What's this really about. It seems more investigative than a feature piece."

I nodded. "Could turn into that. But let's just see where it takes us right now. You can be a lot of help on this, maybe the lead by-line. We might put it up for an Alabama Press Award, who knows?"

Bob smiled, his anxieties abated for the moment.

"Just keep it all among us. Can I trust you?"

"Yes, sir," he said.

Pat Galloway came from his usual haunts at police headquarters to talk to Ed, Clay and me about the results he had in tracking down Crenshaw. Before the meeting, he stopped me for a chat. That was not unusual. Besides being friends for a long time, he worked out of the office so much he liked to catch up. But today he also wanted to test my reaction to his wife's visit. I told him not to worry. We did not need him distracted from the hunt for Crenshaw.

I asked him about the names from Mark's notebook. He recognized two of them. One was a sergeant in the Iron City Police Department, a fat, good old boy. He didn't know him well and could find out more, if we needed it. It made me recall my conversation with H.T. about the community's belief that a policeman was involved.

The other name Pat knew was a guy he described as a "mean fucker" who lives up in Oneonta. "He's been in and out of trouble for years. He may have served some time." Pat smiled and asked why

I was looking for these "lovelies." I decided not to tell him where the names came from.

"We think they could be involved in the bombing. Crenshaw is probably our man, but these guys may have done it or helped. We have to find Crenshaw."

Pat and I talked for a few minutes about his efforts to track Crenshaw. Ed and Clay joined us in my office to hear his report. In a few minutes Mike Rose came in to tell us he had talked with the women at the church, but none of them could recall much about anyone coming in on the afternoon of the bombing. They said the FBI had asked the same question and got the same answer.

Pat said he had found the mail at Crenshaw's piling up. He used to take the *Examiner,* but stopped it two days ago. According to a talkative neighbor lady, Crenshaw was divorced. His wife lives in Tennessee, up in the mountains, north of Knoxville.

"Maybe he went to see her. Any children?" Clay asked.

"No, they were not together long. Lonnie wasn't much as a husband. His wife took off soon after the honeymoon. I can't find much trace of family. On his personnel records at the sheriff's office an aunt was listed as his next of kin, not parents or brothers or sisters. When I called the aunt, she claimed she had not heard from dear Lonnie in months. I gather his mother and the aunt raised him. The mother's not in the picture anymore."

I asked him for the aunt's number so I could check it against a phone number on Mark's phone bill. We discussed other options of how to find our missing constable. But no new ideas surfaced. I asked Clay to have someone try to get what they could from the Army. I was pretty sure that Mark had gone to Kansas City to check out Crenshaw's record when he was stationed at Fort Leavenwood. But I wanted it confirmed.

Pat said, "I think he is hiding. And I think the sheriff's department okayed it."

"Why?" Clay asked.

"The woman in personnel I know told me the first day he was gone there was some talk about it. Several of the guys, including a deputy sheriff, said he was probably just drunk or shacked up somewhere. He said he has done that before. But then when she asked the second day how to record his absence, she was told it was an extended absence with permission. The sheriff has assigned a deputy to cover for him. She thinks the whole deal is a bit odd."

Clay asked the question we were all thinking. "Do you think the sheriff's behind all this?"

Sheriff Peebles was irascible and cantankerous on his good days. He ran a county-wide political organization that was unbeatable every four years. Made up of mostly white men and women, frequently referred to as the Redneck Mafia, Peebles' organization was fiercely loyal. Rumors were that Peebles' posse was funded by protection money paid by bars that ran gambling rooms and sold cheap cigarettes and liquor smuggled in from North Carolina. But nothing had ever been proven. The posse did not get involved in other county races. The sheriff and his posse seemed content just to keep re-electing Peebles. He put as many of his supporters to work as deputies, jailers and a couple like Crenshaw he got elected constables. Pat said he had heard he leaned on the utilities, banks and other large employers to put his people on their payroll.

Pat said, "Ned doesn't like black folks much, and he and Grey tied it on over the treatment of blacks in the jail and the number of black deputies and jailers. But that seemed like it was just politics. The church bombing seemed personal. And I'm not sure what would be in it for Peebles. Who knows? Maybe he was doing someone a big favor or paying off a very, big debt."

Clay asked about Crenshaw's job with the sheriff's department. "What exactly is a constable? What does he do?"

Pat explained that constables were elected positions who worked closely with the sheriff. "They can arrest people. They carry a badge and gun. That's why they work out of the sheriff's office. But mostly what they do is deliver court summonses and legal documents."

"You mean we elect guys to be gun-toting delivery people?" Clay asked.

Pat laughed. "Well, sort of. But they have to be able to get signatures for receipt of the documents. They go to court a lot. It isn't much of a job really, kind of a holdover from the old days. But you know the legislature. Things change pretty slowly down in Montgomery."

That was an understatement.

"One story I did hear on Crenshaw makes me think he is pretty lazy," Pat said. "A few months back he started mailing the summonses and asking people to sign the papers and mail them back. He didn't even get in his car and deliver the papers. Just cashed the checks for his gasoline vouchers and bought postage stamps."

We broke up in laughter.

"He got caught when a judge started asking why some documents hadn't being delivered. Peebles really hit the roof, chewed old Lonnie out something good."

"Okay, so he's lazy and carries a badge and a gun. How do we find this son-of-a-bitch?" I asked, growing even more anxious at the slow pace of our investigation. "Does he have a trailer on a lake where he might hold up? Does he like Gulf Shores? Panama City? Where does this guy feel at home? If frightened, would he run to his ex-wife?"

My outburst launched a lively discussion. Pat had the license plate of the Corvette he drove.

"Check the airport, see if it is parked out there," Clay said, now in high gear. "We need somebody to check the tax roles. See if he's got a river or lake place. Pat, where does he like to drink?" That was where Mark found him. "Does he have any buddies, girl friends? Be discreet, if that is possible for you."

Pat stood up. "Oh, I feel a pub crawl coming on. For the sake of this fine newspaper, I pledge my body, and specifically my liver, to the cause. On the paper's expense account, I assume?"

He looked at me, and I nodded. He walked out singing.

"Just come back with something besides a headache," Clay called after him. Pat stopped at a desk and made a phone call.

Clay walked over and sat beside me. "What about Nicki? If Crenshaw's out of town, we need her. She can track him."

Before I could answer him, Pat ran back into the room. "The FBI has called a press conference in twenty minutes. It sounds like they've got something. I'm going over. It'll probably be on the TV if y'all want to watch."

"Oh, shit," Clay said. "They've got him. That's why they put him on extended absence. They know where he is, in custody with the Fibbies. Damn. I thought we would get him."

The television set that hung from a column in the newsroom was turned on.

"They timed it well," Ed barked, his cynicism gushing. "Just in time for the national news, hot breaking story, no time for reactions, but certainly the top story for the TV network news shows."

"If they have him," I said.

"If ...You don't think they do?" Ed asked.

"Maybe, but if they do, we've got the break over the *Examiner.* And we know a lot about him that we can use. If they have him."

A local television anchor came on as the station interrupted an afternoon talk show. Beside a flashing sign on the screen that said Breaking News, the woman anchor reported that the FBI had called a "hasty" press conference at the federal courthouse. The camera panned to a lectern full of microphones. Reporters scurried about, positioning cameras and recorders, finding chairs and making noise as Wayman Wright came into view and stood behind the lectern. Pitts stood just behind him in clear view of the cameras.

"I am Assistant Attorney General Wayman Wright. With me is Harrison Pitts, the special agent in charge of FBI's Iron City division. We have a brief announcement today. In the ongoing investigation of the bombing of the Sixteenth Street Baptist Church, we have determined through extensive field work that the explosive, five pounds of C-4 explosives, and a detonator used in that incident was purchased in Dothan, Alabama."

There was a murmur in the ranks of reporters on the television.

"I'll be damned," Ed yelled, "they don't have him." A competitive newsman through and through, Ed did not want the bomber caught, at least by anyone but us. I felt exactly the same way.

"The individual who sold the explosive, an illegal transaction, is now assisting in the investigation. He has described the man who bought the explosives." Wright paused for effect. "Working with the FBI's computer technology, we have been able to create a photograph of the man we are seeking."

Pitts directed another FBI agent to pass out copies of the sketch. "He is a white male, about thirty five years old," Wright continued. "We have copies of this photograph for the news media. We believe that with the help of the public, we can identify the man who planted the explosives and bring him into custody."

The photo appeared on the television screen.

Wright began to take questions from the reporters and was barraged with seemingly endless and repetitive questions. But there was little new information. The phone rang in the conference room. Pat was on the line. "Hey, guys, you know they don't have him. I've seen a head shot of Crenshaw in his file. That sketch is pretty far off. His aunt probably wouldn't even recognize him."

Pat went back to the news conference. We decided we would run the FBI announcement as the lead story with the photo. "Okay, they don't have him. They don't know his name, yet. But they are getting close. The guy in Dothan may know his name and give it up. Somebody might recognize him from the sketch. So let's find him, now," I said.

I whispered to Clay to get Nicki tracking Crenshaw and fast. "And if she gets caught, we'll try to keep her out of the federal pen," I said, smiling a smile that puzzled Clay. How much would it piss her off with her independent streak for me to rescue her, I thought.

We discussed the possibility of running a modified version of Mark's story and tie it in with the FBI's drawing. Clay was for it, worrying that we were going to get beat on the story. I decided to wait, hoping it was worth the risk. I wasn't ready to give up on the hunt for him ourselves. If the photograph had been better, we probably would have run it, naming Crenshaw, based on Mark's story and the tape. I would have called Wright and Pitts to let them know after our city editions went to press and the local television stations were talking about the weather and sports. We'd held stories out of the early state editions and off the web site before just to keep the television and Internet news sites from scooping our story.

But with such a bad likeness of Crenshaw, we still had a chance to find the man ourselves. I hope we wouldn't regret my decision.

8

The FBI's decision to release a computer-generated sketch of a white man as the probable church bomber was like opening a window to put out a fire. The riots spread through the streets, engulfing buildings, people, everything in their path. The violence, carnage and destruction moved southward toward the traditional white sanctuaries. The city-owned golf and tennis center at the base of the mountain was engulfed in flames. More stores and restaurants were looted and burned. The fires burned what was left after the rioters left. On the northside, Sammy's Barbecue didn't survive this time. Fire trucks worked only the worst fires; many burned without any attention. Whole blocks were in flames. The police were spread too thin even to cordon off some of the buildings that were ablaze.

The photo confirmed what most had suspected, that a white man had blown up the beloved church, killing Commissioner Grey, Reverend Smallwood and ten deacons. That no one had been arrested for bombing the church seemed almost a replay of the 1960s when it took so long to make an arrest, when klansmen could lynch and bomb almost with impunity. It made many doubt if the FBI and police were serious about pursuing their leads. I almost felt sorry for Pitts and Wayman.

"Clay, we need everybody we've got to cover the streets, hospitals and jails. Call Pat and tell him to postpone his pub crawl, and get our freelancers out on the streets. You know the usual places. Put our people in cars around downtown, have them call in any signs of activity. Dispatch the photographers where you need them."

The newsroom was abuzz. "We're getting some good quotes on the FBI's photo. We'll have a strong first edition. Then we'll see what happens tonight," Clay said.

I stood up on a chair and whistled for attention. "Listen up, folks. The FBI broke this story on our time. Let's show the *Examiner* what an understaffed, underpaid bunch of newspaper people can really do. This is why we became newspaper reporters. Go get 'em."

Editors and reporters laughed and whooped. It was not hard to motivate this group. Most were self-starters. We occasionally duked it out over wage packages that came down from Alexandria. Most of the reporters belonged, at least nominally, to the union, but there was less animosity between management and staff than in many newspapers. Most who worked at the *Post* was there because they wanted to work for a newspaper. Some aspired to be at a larger, better-paying newspaper, television station, news site or public relations firm some day, but most knew the *Post* was the best news organization they would ever work for and took pride in it. For the moment, we were in a city with the hottest story of the year.

I called the director of the black business association. He was always good for a few provocative quotations. I left a message for my friend, H.T., to get his reaction. I thought it was worth a chat with Jimmy Marshall to see what he thought of the FBI's photo of the man who almost killed him. I only reached Marshall. He said he harbored no bitterness toward the man. "If it was my time to go, then I was ready. But I'm still here."

To have such faith must be comforting. I doubted few others would.

Hoyt Williams, the president of the black business association, called back to say, "Tell us something we don't know. We all knew it was some dumb ass, white thug who planted the bomb. But how come the great and glorious FBI has been on the case for weeks, and all they got is a drawing of some redneck? What do they think we are? We know what's going on here. They're stalling. This son-of-a-bitch has already hightailed it out of the country."

I hoped he was wrong about Crenshaw's whereabouts, but feared he might be right.

"There is a lot of frustration out there. I'm afraid that some black folks are gonna get justice the only way they can. I don't condone it, but I can't blame them. All the promises we've heard. We don't see a whole lot of progress, now do we?" It was a rhetorical question, and he barely paused long enough to take a breath. He certainly didn't expect an answer.

He was just getting wound up, and I had heard it all before. So I handed the phone to a young reporter who took down the quotations that would run in the first editions before the street battle stories push them to the inside pages.

Clay yelled at me that Reverend Webster was on television. I changed the channel and turned up the volume. There was the man of God in his television studio, every hair in place, his fat face red from excitement, arms flailing, calling on his latter-day crusaders to bear arms and prepare for war.

"Armageddon is upon us. The Devil is loose in the streets of our city tonight. These Negroid people, those of weak minds who are easily influenced by Satan, are out to destroy the God-fearing souls in our city."

Webster stood behind a pulpit, his logo with his photo behind his head. If it were not so dangerous, it would be a laughable cliche.

"Defend yourselves, defend your homes. These devils will continue to destroy, burn and ravage until they are stopped. And stopped they must be. There is no other answer. The white police officers, God bless them, are doing their best. But it is not enough.

There are too many of these heathens. The police need our help."
He raised his arms with clenched fists. "Stand guard tonight. Turn
on the lights in your house and in your yard. Let them know if they
set foot on your property, they will be shot. Remember, an eye for
an eye. If they are willing to destroy you or your home, you have the
right to defend yourself, your family, your property."

I turned him off. Wrapped in the false cloak of Jesus, he was
calling for armed violence. Full-scale riots were starting again.
With him egging them on, Webster's white followers would launch
their own attack squads. And the blacks and whites would make
the streets of Iron City a war zone. I hoped Walt Simpson was right.
Maybe the steam would run out of this crisis, and everybody would
take a break.

Wishful thinking. By sunset, white gangs in cars and trucks began attacking black people, armed or not. They inflicted scores of
casualties; people of all colors, black, white and police blue, were
dying.

By ten o'clock we got out the first city edition. One front page
story reported that five policemen were dead and twenty two hos-
pitalized. We couldn't get a good count of the civilian dead and
wounded. The gangs, black and white, were taking their dead and
injured away, not stopping to be counted. Hospitals reported more
than seventy people had checked in at the emergency rooms with
riot-related injuries. Reporters from around the country were interviewing them. Television broadcast trucks lined the streets in front
of the large University Hospital, where many were taken. As the
night progressed, the toll worsened, the hospitals got even busier.

After the first city edition rolled out on the trucks, Clay and I
left the building to see what was happening. We told ourselves we
were out looking for "color" to augment what we were getting from
the reporters and stringers. The truth was we knew this was a night
for the history books, and we wanted to see it first hand.

In one of the old Ford vans used by the circulation department,
we drove across the Twenty-six Street viaduct to the north. It was

one of the first cool nights of the season. Perfect football weather, but the games being played tonight had no rules, no referees.

We passed several cars in the area. A few had three and four black men riding in them, looking like they were on patrol. Other drivers were just trying to get home. Several police cars went by. One pulled us over and told us to go home, not caring who we were. He barked that it was not safe to be in the area.

An old dented Chevy passed us with five white men inside. They looked more out of place in this neighborhood than we did. "Webster's disciples," I said and reversed direction to see what trouble they would get into. They turned on a side street and drove through quiet neighborhoods of houses owned by middle class blacks. The guy in the front seat was on his phone. A few blocks east they pulled over and parked. They opened the trunk and took out a crowbar and a couple of baseball bats. Each put on what looked like Kevlar flak jackets over their t-shirts.

Clay grunted, "Bubba been shopping," as he hung up from talking with the assistant city editor.

The guys got back in the car and resumed cruising the neighborhood. They spotted a small group of black men standing on a corner. They pulled the Chevy to the curb and stepped out of the car to face the group of eight black men. A few of the black men were armed with bats, one had a hockey stick. A white guy started hitting a metal light pole with his bat, making a gong-like sound that reverberated off the houses, the ancient warrior beating a drum to bring on the testosterone. The white men were all in their twenties and thirties, one fat with little hair, the others younger, thinner, some with scraggly goatees and mustaches. A couple with mullet-style hair cuts under ball caps lit cigarettes. All wore jeans and boots.

The black guys looked like they were dressed to go to a college basketball game. Wearing high-top tennis shoes, jeans, t-shirts and ball caps turned backwards or cocked on their heads at an angle, they looked ill prepared for a fight.

Then around the corner came reinforcements, about fifteen well-armed black men striding with confidence that they had the upper hand in this fight. The small band of younger black guys were just bait, like a teetered goat hunters used to lure in a lion. The white guys, slow to react, were suddenly outnumbered. They should have run, but their hormones made them stupid.

"No heroics this time. Okay, Joe?" Clay said. I hadn't meant to be heroic before. Clay telephoned the police department and reported the ensuing battle, but the police had bigger battles. Clay aimed a camera and started shooting. I took notes, although it was unlikely I would forget anything I was seeing.

In seconds the fight started. The white men charged across the asphalt waving their bats at the blacks. I looked at my watch. It was over in three minutes. Two of the five Bubbas were dead, knocked to the ground, their throats cut, their t-shirts under the flak jackets turning black from the blood. They lay in the street, pale lumps in the florescent street light.

A third man was beaten with a bat. Two men hit him five or six times. He tried to ward off the blows with his arms over his head, but had no chance. As he knelt in the gutter, his arms were broken into weird angles. Two blows to his head and neck, and he lay with his battered face against the curb. Two men with the bats looked down at the mangled body and laughed. One tossed his head back and screamed in victory. They gave each other low fives and danced around the body before turning to find other targets.

Clay whispered "damn" several times as he snapped the photos. I called 911 and asked the operator to send several ambulances. She said she would try when they were done with other calls. We watched as the two other white guys crawled toward their car. They didn't make it. Their attackers took turns kicking them. A group of the attackers up-ended the Chevy, then lit some rags and threw it into the trunk. In seconds the car was fully engulfed. The black men left the dead and near dead white men in the street and headed north.

I told myself the white guys had asked for it, egged on by Webster. I wished the good reverend were here to see his handiwork, although he would find a way to rationalize it. He thought so highly of himself, he would never admit he was responsible for this tragedy.

The police arrived in force several blocks in front of the advancing gang. Even several blocks away we could hear pistol shots and shouts in the air as the battle began. We pulled the van forward a block and from the top of a rise sat watching the battle unfold. It was hand-to-hand combat with heavier weapons. The police wore helmets and layers of protective gear. Most of the black men had on only ball caps. One man ran past us wearing a baseball catcher's mask and chest protector.

"He forgot his shin guards," Clay said.

My phone rang. H.T. was calling. I put down my notepad. Clay picked it up and started scribbling.

"Hey, big man, big-time editor. You want to know what's going on out there on our streets?"

"Sure, we're sitting here watching one battle going on. You might hear some of it if I hang the phone out the window."

There was a long cackle of a laugh on the line. "You thought we were just flapping our gums, didn't ya? You didn't think we really meant to have a war?"

"You're right. Now how we going to stop this?"

"We ain't. It's to the death," he said.

"How's this going to get you elected county commissioner?" I asked, trying to find something that would appeal to his saner side.

"When we're finished, white folks gonna be begging us to stop. Then we'll have all the leverage we need. If we want money, we got it. If we want power, we got that too. If I want to be commissioner, I will have it. White folks be saying, just don't hurt us no more."

I told him he was wrong. White folks, the police, the governor were being pushed against the wall with no place to go, but back at the rioters. "They're losing face." He understood the importance of losing face. "You think this isn't going to be on the front page of every newspaper in the country tomorrow. CNN, *Fox News*, *Good Morning America* will be all over us."

"Yeah. And they're wanting to talk to me. I'm in charge now. I am the man," he said.

"You may be, but soon you and your friends could be looking out from behind bars. If you stop now, maybe you can make a deal. But you keep killing policemen, nothing's going to save you," I said.

"Hey, listen up. This here is the revolution talking. You write this down: Tonight black folks killed a bunch of pigs and hurt a lot more. They burned down white folks' businesses and are moving to where it really hurts, Southside and over the mountain. Whitey, look out. Nobody sleeps tonight." He hung up.

We sat staring at the phone. Clay had heard H.T.'s rant and was writing down what he said. Neither one of us spoke for a few minutes. I tried to make sense of it. Was he crazy? Or had the riots and violence in our city made us all crazy? Clay refrained from stating the obvious because he knew H.T. was an old friend. The war moved down the street, each side picking up its wounded and dead. The police had cars and ambulances. The black men used vans and pickup trucks. The moans and cries of the wounded floated on the wind. I put the van in gear and moved down the street, following the sporadic fighting. Clay used his tablet to upload the photos and paragraphs of inserts from the battles, including H.T.'s comments. We needed to get back to the newspaper to work on the last edition. So I turned south toward downtown.

I called home and told my mother-in-law to make sure all the doors were locked. She was almost frantic and said they were watching the fires from the balcony. I tried to reassure her that the battle would not go as far as our house, but she said she would wait up until I got home in case anyone came to burn it down. A random thought: it was probably time to change the batteries in the smoke alarms.

As we drove downtown, the battle moved south. The police, outnumbered, used tear gas to disburse crowds, but people carrying guns, bats and axes ran in every direction. When we drove by the police precinct office, the officers inside were being pelted from the street. Small fires burned on the roof and in trash cans outside. Gunfire was coming from inside and from the street in front. It looked like a standoff. Clay shot more photos. When one of the attackers saw us and started toward us, we knew we had pushed our luck far enough. I turned the corner and headed to safety.

Delivery truck drivers are the Achilles' heel of any newspaper. The Internet may soon make home delivery obsolete, but not yet. We still had to print, fold and stack the daily papers on trucks with routes around the city.

Most of the time the system works well. Tonight the drivers were balking at delivering the newspapers. The circulation supervisor stood in the middle of a circle of angry, frightened drivers. Failure to deliver the newspapers meant a major financial loss, ironically not for the *Post*, but the *Examiner*, which was responsible under our operating agreement for placing them in boxes and throwing them on each subscriber's lawn.

After what Clay and I had seen, I knew the drivers were right. I stepped into the middle of the gaggle.

"It is too dangerous to deliver to routes north of downtown. I've been out there tonight. We don't want to lose any of you or any trucks," I said to the supervisor and the drivers who surrounded us. "But the routes south are still safe, if you hurry. Take all the papers south. We'll sell every one of them. Double the number you usually put in the boxes. And throw the extras at every house you can. Maybe we'll pick up a few new customers."

The supervisor did not seem to know whether to be mad or relieved that I had intervened. "I don't think the advertisers will care, do you?" He shook his head and looked down at a clipboard before he started redirecting the drivers. The drivers raced to their trucks and cleared the parking lot in minutes.

Upstairs on the second floor the newsroom was full of reporters, editors, photographers, each looking like he or she was on a mission. Except for Friday nights during high school football season or on election day, I had never seen the newsroom so busy, so late. People who worked days were still there. A part-time reporter who wrote movie and restaurant reviews was taking dictation from stringers and filing copy. Copy desk people were merging and blending stories, inserting new information on the fly. A columnist who rarely got involved in day-to-day news helped the photo editor select the best shots.

The editorial page editor handed me a printout of the lead editorial he had written. It called for calm and for negotiations between city officials and the rioters.

"Let's pose a question in the editorial and promo it on page one," I said.

"What question?" he asked.

I sat down at a computer and typed my thoughts. "We want to know why, after six weeks and all the manpower, has the FBI and police come up with so little? This riot is fueled by frustration. And that frustration is aimed at law enforcement, because people have nowhere else to direct it. If the FBI had announced an arrest today, we might have had some rioting, but nothing like this war."

I felt a bit guilty sticking the knife in Pitts' back, when we could have given him Crenshaw's name. Maybe the FBI would have found him, when we had not been able to.

"Hey, Joe. Come look. They've moved onto Fourth Avenue," Clay yelled.

Below our second floor row of windows, we watched as a group of black men, armed mostly with bats, rocks and bricks, advanced on a line of police. A few black men had guns, mostly pistols now. There were a few young white men and women, probably students at the university, who identified with the blacks. They looked awkward and out of place.

The police were wearing full riot gear, carrying guns and batons. Behind them were fire trucks. I knew what was coming. The riots were looking like a replay of the protests half a century ago in the streets of Iron City. When my father was a young banker, black protestors squared off with police in a mostly passive demonstration that turned violent. Documented in black and white films and television, fire trucks turned their hoses and police unleashed German shepherds on the protestors. Adults and teenagers were knocked down and pushed like trash across the grass and pavement. Some grabbed for utility poles and trees to keep from being pushed out of the park. Those strong enough to hold on had their clothes peeled off by the water pressure. Others were badly bitten, their arms torn to shreds as they tried to fight off the attacking dogs.

"Stop," I shouted behind the closed windows. My shout startled my staff standing at the windows. It brought me back to the present. Instead of the King-inspired largely passive protestors of the past, these black men and women in the street were heavily armed, bent on violence. Clay and I had just watched three men killed and two more beaten close to death. The world of the old Civil Rights era seemed almost innocent.

The group lining up for battle on Fourth Street knew more about tactics. They were not relying on political pressure from Washington to end segregation. The demonstrators were not waiting to be blinded by tear gas or knocked down and their clothes ripped off by firehouses. They stood ready to use force to win justice for Grey, the others killed at the church and themselves. Opposite them were rows of well-armed police, who marched ahead in lock step, tapping their batons on the asphalt as they moved forward.

One of our veteran photographers came running into the newsroom. "Guys, you gotta come out and see this. It's war right here in front of the building."

I felt the need to be out there. I grabbed a notepad and pen and started to follow the photographer and a pair of young reporters as they headed downstairs. Ed grabbed my arm and pulled me back. "Joe, you're the editor. You don't need to be out in that. It's dangerous." He didn't have to tell me that with my skin color, even in a shirt and tie, I could be mistaken for one of the demonstrators. "You could be hurt or shot. They have tear gas, fire hoses and guns."

Ed often mothered me, probably because he still saw me as a rookie reporter. He did not understand because he was a reporter for only a short stint before joining the copy desk. He could not know how much I missed being in the fray, being a reporter. That is why I related to Mark and other reporters, who never wanted to sit at a desk. It was a lot more fun to be in the middle of the story, even if it paid a lot less.

I told Ed to keep things moving, while I joined the photographer and two reporters at the elevator. We made our way passed the guards at the backdoor, who also told us we should not go out. We went anyway.

Outside in the pale white wash of the television camera lights, black men and women spread out in a wide attack formation and charged. A whistle blew and suddenly they hurled plastic shopping bags through the air in the direction of the police lines. The bags were the large ones with handles that department stores use to send you home with your latest shopping treasures. What the demonstrators had packed in these bags would hardly be considered gifts.

"It's shit," yelled one of the officers who had been hit by one of the flying bags. "They are throwing bags of shit at us."

The officers tried to dodge the bags, but a few found their mark, excrement covering the helmets, uniforms and bulletproof vests. After the bags, the demonstrators hurled rolls of toilet paper that unrolled in an arch above the police. Suddenly the street was covered in white streaming toilet paper. It looked like the front yard of a teenager who was a victim of a high school prank.

The demonstrators cheered, yelling, "Wipe your white asses, pigs."

The police officers cursed and tried to clean off their uniforms, but otherwise there was no response. On an order, the police lines parted to let a fire truck pull forward. Firemen jumped down and pulled out hoses. They turned the levers and in seconds jet streams of water spewed at the demonstrators. The water found its marks, knocking men and women backwards. Other demonstrators, untouched, raced in and attacked the police in hand-to-hand combat. Officers swung batons. Demonstrators wielded axes, knives and bats.

From behind a parked pickup truck, I watched as a white policeman hit a black man a half dozen times, his stick striking him from high above his head and cracking down on the man's head, shoulders and back. Twenty yards away two men held a cop and kicked him repeatedly in the groin until he was a mass of writhing flesh on the ground. A black policeman was hit with an ax between his shoulder blades. He fell forward and didn't move. His attacker did not seem to care about his skin color, just his uniform. A white policeman without his helmet was holding the side of his head with blood flowing through his fingers. He had lost an ear and was desperately looking for it on the ground.

Our photographer shot photos in every direction, capturing the carnage for the next edition. One reporter, Janice Barkley, scribbled notes, while Jason Webb, the other young reporter, knelt over an injured man. He was taking down the man's comments while he lay bleeding on the street.

I stood up to get a better look, only to be hit with a powerful stream of water from a fire hose. The blast of water soaked my chest and head. It felt like I had been tackled by a linebacker. Knocked to the curb, I saw it had torn my shirt. My elbow hit the pavement and ripped another hole in my sleeve. I crawled behind a car. My soaked clothes hung on me. I laughed at the thought that Ed would so love to tell me "I told you so" over and over.

Shots rang out. The gangs had traded bats for guns. The cops, protected by vests and helmets, fired back. The black men fared poorly in the gun battle, but outnumbering and outflanking the copes, they forced them down the street until the whole battle moved out of our sight. The group of newspaper and television reporters, photographers and cameramen, including my reporters and photographer, some with soaked and torn clothes like mine, followed in the wake of the battle. The media recorded the event for broadcast around the world. Any hope for a peaceful resolution that would save Iron City's already tarnished image vanished.

The battles raged all night with the black gangs slowly gaining ground, pushing through the heart of downtown and then south toward the middle and upper-income white neighborhoods.

The headline on our first editions ran, *War in the Streets*. The subhead said, *Police Battle Rioters in Deadly Skirmishes*.

The story led with:

> *War erupted in the streets of Iron City Monday night as police battled with rioters, using tear gas and water from fire hoses to quell the riots. Black and white gangs attacked one another and the police.*
>
> *The outbreak of violence followed the announcement by the FBI that it believes a white man placed the bomb in the 16th Street Baptist Church which killed County Commissioner Samuel Grey and 11 others.*
>
> *According to a Iron City Police Department spokesman, 12 policemen have been killed and 63 injured in the rioting. More than 150 civilians were hospitalized. At least a dozen black men were believed to have been killed by police and white rioters. Several white men were killed in clashes with black rioters across the northern tier of the city. These numbers, which were based on eye-witness accounts and police estimates, were unconfirmed.*

Mayor Jason Martin called for a cease fire. "I urge all citizens of Iron City to lay down their weapons and return to their homes. Allow the authorities to do their work and bring the man responsible for the bombing of the 16th Street Baptist Church to justice," he said.

Gov. Sam Kitterage threatened to call up the National Guard troops to quell the violence in Iron City. "We will not tolerate lawlessness to run rampant in our streets. If we have to, I will send the National Guard to augment the forces of the Iron City Police Department and the state police. Tanks will roll through the streets to bring peace so the residents of Iron City can resume their lives."

The violence raged into the night and showed no signs of abating. In numerous clashes across the city, black and white gangs used guns and other weapons to injure and kill one another.

Blame for the riots was laid on the FBI, state troopers and the Iron City police. Black leaders accused the authorities of stalling in arresting the man identified in the drawing.

"Do they think we are stupid? We know they could have arrested this bomber by now if they wanted to. They are just stalling to let him escape," said Iron City Councilman Jerry Franklin.

Other African-American leaders echoed Franklin's comments. Hoyt Williams, the president of the Iron City Black Chamber of Commerce, said, "We all knew it was some white thug who planted the bomb. How come the FBI has been on the case for weeks, and all they got is a drawing of some redneck? What do they think we are? We know what's going on here. They're stalling. This son-of-a-bitch has already hightailed it out of the country."

The war story and several sidebars, describing the street battles in detail, with photos covered much of the front page and jumped to two inside pages with more sidebars and a double-page of more photos that captured the warfare across the city. I had demanded additional pages. Jensen initially said no, but finally relented when Daniels approved an increase in space. I pulled together a poignant piece comparing the battle a half century ago where the police and fire crews used fire hoses and dogs to what we saw on Fourth Street. We dug up an old photo of the battle in the park and ran it next to one our photographer shot.

The FBI's computer-generated photo dropped below the fold on the front page. It was almost an after-thought. We carried little international or national news and none on page one. It was all local. The coverage was extensive and well written, given the crunch of time.

The last edition ran at one thirty in the morning. With my clothes still damp and my ego a bit bruised from the kidding I took in the newsroom, I followed one of the delivery trucks halfway home. The battles were still raging around town, but they hadn't touched the neighborhoods up the mountain.

All was quiet in the house. My mother-in-law sat in the living room. She followed me out on the balcony where I could breathe easier. We could see the fires burning across the city. A lone dog barked somewhere in the neighborhood. As tired as I was, it was hard to hold back the tears. The smoke from the fires below was so thick, it almost blocked out the moon.

"Bad moon's rising tonight," my superstitious mother-in-law said. "And bad moons bring out the evil in people."

I try to stay grounded, but being a son of the South, it is hard not to see the hand of evil in things. Tonight as I watched the moon high above my balcony, I feared she was right. The bad moon rose over my city as fires raged below.

When I was a boy, one of my most exciting adventures was going with my grandfather to the mills where he worked. The huge blast furnaces dwarfed the giant men, like my grandfather, who kept them ablaze. They forged the steel out of the raw iron ore that was mined from the mountain. I was mesmerized watching the liquid fire turn into solid sheets of metal. The city, burning below, was like those giant furnaces, the city burning in Vulcan's forge. The raw materials of hate and fear were being made into something new, a new Iron City being formed. At least, that is what I hoped.

9

"Our scam worked like a charm," Rachel Stanton said the next morning about her second trip to the country club. "Amanda's friend was great. It was like a spy operation to her. I think she's a little bored. Cute though. Maybe Amanda should introduce you."

Why is it that every woman loves to play matchmaker? "Right. Just what I need right now, matchmakers." I had slept badly. I was as tense as the streets outside, which remained highly charged even as the dawn broke and rains came to quell some of the fires.

"We got there before all the mayhem broke out. The club was quiet, and it was easy for me to play the role of the ditzy socialite who only wanted her special waiter. I just asked if Jerome was working today." Rachel flipped her head and hair and made her earrings dance in a dead-on imitation of a wealthy Iron City woman with too many credit cards, a busy husband and empty hours to fill. "Jill, that's Amanda's friend, played right along."

I waggled my hand to tell her to get on with what she found out.

"Jerome recognized me and looked a little worried, at first. He took our drink orders. Oh, I've got to remember to send Jill some money." She pulled out a small notebook from her purse and wrote herself a note. "And then when he came back with the drinks, Jill took hers and walked over to talk with some people at another table. That left me alone with Jerome, just like we planned."

She sat back down at a desk and crossed her legs. I sat in the chair beside the desk. "I told Jerome how much help he had been, and I wanted to see if he remembered any of the men in the room who were yelling at each other. That scared him even more, but I did a lot of cooing to reassure him that he wouldn't get in any trouble. Then I just smiled real big at him. He stopped fidgeting."

She opened a large envelope and slid the photos out on the desk. "He recognized almost all of them as men who had been attending the meeting. I made a list. Then I asked him who was yelling at whom. At first, he shook his head. I asked him to look at the photos again. He shuffled through them and picked out the photo of Herman McGee, head of Southern National, as the man who stomped out mad. Then he picked out Mr. Daniels' photo." She held up a photo of Daniels taken at an awards banquet. "Jerome said he believed he was the one Mr. McGee was yelling at. But he said he wasn't a hundred percent sure. He thought it was this man, Mr. Braddock, who yelled at Mr. McGee to shut up."

My heart may have stopped for a few seconds. Would I dare? Would the owners of the *Post*, sitting detached in their office building overlooking the Potomac River, let me print a story naming Robert Daniels, publisher of the *Examiner* and our partner in the joint operating agreement, as the man who conspired to have a historic church bombed? I knew the answer and didn't like it.

"Who else was there? Let me see the list," I said. Most were predictable: the bankers, real estate brokers, lawyers, car dealers, a couple of big manufacturers and the utility executives. "Just about everybody we thought. Anyone there we didn't expect?"

Rachel shook her head. "There were a couple of men there I didn't have photos on. Jerome said there was one guy who sat in the back of the room and didn't say much. Except every once and a while, the others would turn and ask him something. Jerome said he looked like a lawyer. He drank Scotch and wouldn't eat anything.

Once he stood up and whispered something to Mr. Daniels. Then he left."

I was tempted to send her back to the club with a local Bar Association directory with the photos of every attorney in the city and have Jerome to pick him out. But that probably would get him fired. We could always do that later, if it became important. I had a feeling we would run into this mystery man if we kept asking questions about the Jackson Group. I could also ask Walt if the group had an attorney on retainer.

"Pull together your notes and start working on a feature on this group. We're not ready to print anything yet. But get it ready," I said.

"Are you thinking we might run a feature on the group as a sidebar to the bombing story?" she asked, her excitement showing.

"Don't know yet. Everything depends on what we get from the bomber. But who knows?" I could hear my boss saying, drop it, don't embarrass Daniels, turn it over to the FBI.

Clay stuck his head in the door. It was shortly before noon. The newsroom was filling up. "National Guard's on the way," Clay said. "Governor mobilized them this morning. They will be camped out at Veterans Field. I've got a photographer headed out there. Then we'll see what the *Examiner* has. Okay?"

Rachel asked if I still wanted her to work on the feature story or help out with the riot coverage. "Both. We're short-handed." Clay could use the help, but I told her to get the feature on the Jackson Group ready. "We might run that piece before the end of the week."

We spent the rest of the day watching the Army roll into the city. Helicopters circled overhead as the rain stopped and the clouds moved east. A convoy of flatbed trucks brought in a half dozen tanks, about twenty armored personnel carriers and dozens of jeeps. They used the jeeps and armored personnel carriers to patrol the streets and alleys. The tanks, which hopefully were there more for intimidation than actual firepower, were positioned at strategic intersections. City council members who represented neighborhoods to the south were screaming that more troops were needed in their districts or the war would simply move south. That seemed to be the direction it was headed anyway.

"Damn if it don't look like Kuwait City," Clay said.

The afternoon passed quickly. The newsroom churned with activity as reporters chased story angles and got reactions from various people throughout the city about the occupation by the National Guard. We found and interviewed old civil rights activists in Mississippi and Arkansas.

On the surface there were many similarities to the old Civil Rights days. But hidden below were new currents, more violent and less predictable. In the 1960s, there had been a raging debate in the black community about the use of violence. Martin Luther King and his doctrine of non-violent disobedience versus Malcolm X and Bobby Seale who believed that only through violence could blacks win equal rights. Today the advocates for peaceful protests seemed anachronistic. Deals were made in back rooms or fights erupted in the streets.

Mike Rose came into the newsroom and walked to where I was sitting at an empty desk, finishing a call from Maury Weitzman in Virginia. We were now covering the story for all the papers in the Babcock chain of newspapers. That was a strength of being part of a newspaper chain, which gave the other newspapers something different than they could get from the wire services.

"Mike, what do you know about some land developments that Harden Braddock's doing up north around the highway loop extension?"

Reporting on city and county governments meant he heard a lot, only a small portion made it to print.

He laughed. "That's interesting stuff. It's something I've been trying to get into for weeks. Wild rumors, people bitching. Not enough to go to print with yet. Braddock, I hear, paid some state guys to reroute the highway through his property. As I understand it, Braddock owns land north of town where his father or father-in-law used to do a lot of strip mining. The land wasn't worth much. It's all been worked to death and pretty tough to get to. So he's just been letting poor folks live on it and pay a little. He was sort of banking the land until he could find a good use for it. Then the state started planning the highway up north to connect with the southern loop. The rumor was that Braddock saw an opportunity to turn his worthless land into high-priced homes and shopping centers. He gave the state the land it needed so the engineers redrew the highway through his property. At one point they had to create a sharp turn south to make it work. People are saying it will be dangerous, but the state is going forward with it."

"Do these developments have a name?" I asked.

"I need to double check, but its something like Highland Shores or Lakes. There was to be some big shopping center there too, North Lake Mall, I think. I'll get it for you tomorrow."

I asked how he had heard about it.

"Commissioner Grey told me about it. He was really pissed about it after a commissioners' meeting. He was saying that black folks were going to be run out of their homes so rich white people could move in. He was going to ask the state attorney general to investigate how the highway got rerouted. He also said he would vote against any extension of sewer lines or streets to that property that the county had to build."

Mike said he asked other county commissioners about it. They told him it was a non-story, that Grey didn't understand the economic potential of that land and how these developments were good for the whole county, raise property values and increase tax revenues.

"When was all this?" I asked.

"Oh, I guess it was probably a couple of weeks before he died."

Having covered that beat for several years before I went to D.C., I understood the challenges and read more closely the stories he wrote. That was probably why Clay had run off the two previous reporters on that beat. He grew tired of my bitching about the lousy stories, or worse, getting beat by the *Examiner*'s reporter. When he needed to find a replacement for that beat, Clay asked me to pick someone. At least, that way I would only have myself to blame if the stories did not measure up. I gambled on Mike because I liked his writing and reporting on general assignments. It didn't hurt that he was black. He had not disappointed.

When I asked him what he had thought about Grey, he didn't respond right away. He looked at me with a puzzled expression, like he wanted to ask why I wanted to know about a man who was dead. I just smiled.

"I guess I've thought a lot about him since he was killed, maybe more than when he was alive. It seems so final. He walked into the church to make an important speech and was gone from this Earth. What did I think of him?" he mused. "I guess I thought he was a pretty good man, for a politician. He didn't deserve to be killed. I liked him. There was a dark side to him, he was not happy. I don't know why. He lived hard, he loved his scotch. Rumors were that he gave in easily to temptations, women, private parties. But I don't think he was corrupt."

"How was he as a politician?" I asked.

"Better than most. Conscientious, worked hard, lots of energy, worried about the details. And he had a vision for the African-American community in Iron City. In that way he was a leader. But he got hung up in the crap of being commissioner and the petty politics that goes with that."

He paused to gauge my reaction to his comments. I just nodded to encourage him to continue.

"That's why I think the Reverend Smallwood wanted him to run for Congress when the new districts were drawn after last year's census came out. Smallwood thought he would be better on the national stage. Grey could have been elected, even though it is not a majority black district. He had the charisma."

"So why didn't he run?"

Mike thought for a minute. "He didn't want it. Maybe the insecurities inside his head got the better of him. Maybe he knew his dark side would do him in if he got away from his roots. He also believed he had more power over the lives of his people here as commissioner than he would have had as one of several hundred members of Congress. And, you know, he may have been right. Do you think we would have the riots in the streets over a congressman being killed?"

I laughed at the thought. With the popularity of Congress in the dumpster, no one would take to the streets to avenge a congressmen.

"What else? Was he honest? Did he have enemies? What was he working on that might have gotten him killed?" I asked.

Mike cocked his head and looked at me. He now understood why I was asking about Grey. "Wow. That's cool. I kind of dismissed all those ideas when the church got bombed. I figured the bomb was the work of some klansmen out to recreate white folks' glory days."

He looked down at one of the many spots of worn out linoleum.

"Enemies? He had a few. Peebles mainly. He and the sheriff tied up a bunch of times. Blacks get messed with in jail, and Grey was always going after the sheriff for it. He wanted more black guards and black deputies. You know the sheriff wants all those jobs for his boys. Peebles hated him. So Grey made the sheriff explain every nickel, put his budget through the ringer."

"Who else hated him?"

He chuckled as he thought about the question. He shook his head and giggled a low soft laugh. "You know who really hated him? Some of the most rabid supporters of Bama football."

I thought he had lost his mind.

"You know how the Crimson Tide is sacred, more to some, than others. For the loyal Tide fans when Grey called on the university trustees to name a black head football coach, it was like telling Catholics they had to elect a black Pope. It really stirred them up.

Other colleges can have a black coach, but Bama, they wouldn't like that."

The passion for college football in Alabama was stronger than in most cities with a professional team. The fans for each team far exceeded the alumni who had graduated from either university. The supporters of the team which lost the annual Iron Bowl game seem to go into a blue funk through at least Christmas. Players and coaches who had a bad game could get death threats. Two middle-aged, normal-looking guys once got into a fist fight in a grocery store right in front of a bunch of school children because one man had on an Alabama sweatshirt with the score of the latest Alabama victory over Auburn.

"But your real question is: Did anyone hate or fear Grey enough to have him killed? I find it hard to believe that anyone would bomb a church, any church, just to kill Grey. He wasn't that powerful."

The conversation drifted to the special election to fill Grey's seat. Mike felt there were only three viable candidates. Jerry Franklin, the most prominent of the black city council members, was campaigning hard and had a strong following.

"The preachers, undertakers, lawyers, they all seem to be lining up behind Ray Smith. I would have thought the traditional powers would back Franklin," Mike said.

"Tell me about Franklin," I said.

"Jerry's okay. Level headed, pretty smart. He votes often with the mayor and the establishment. The riots have pushed him into a corner. You know, he's got to say things to make sure his folks think he is not a sell-out to the whites. It's pretty hard to be a moderate black politician right now."

I nodded. Being called a sell-out, an Uncle Tom or an Oreo was tough to overcome. With so much anger, a candidate had to work hard not to sound even slightly conciliatory. I asked him about Ray Smith. I didn't know much about him except that he worked for Grey.

"Smith's a political junkie. Grew up handing out fliers, taking old ladies to vote, mostly for Grey. The last couple of years he was expanding his base and made new friends. I heard there was a bit of a falling out with Grey. Nothing big. I think Smith got ambitious and wanted to get elected on his own. Grey had other ideas for him. And the commissioner didn't care much for his personal life."

I shook my head, looking puzzled.

"Oh, I figured you knew. Well, maybe I shouldn't talk about that. It's nothing I can prove."

"Does he dress up in pantyhose, chase little boys?"

Mike laughed. "No, nothing twisted about Ray. He likes women and women like him, especially white women. For the last year or so, he's been dating a nice-looking blonde. I've met her. They go out to dinner in public. He likes to show her off."

"I thought he was married."

He nodded. "Wife and three boys. But that doesn't stop him from keeping the blonde in style in one of those new condominium towers off Highland." Mike suddenly looked uncomfortable. He remembered that Sheila was white. I guess the brothers talked about me the same way. "I haven't written about his private life because I can't prove it, and as long as none of the candidates are talking about it, I didn't think it was relevant to the election."

I asked about Smith as a politician.

"Not as good as Grey, but Smith has worked in the trenches. He knows everyone, all the preachers and funeral home owners. I think maybe they're more comfortable with him, than anyone else who is running. A vote for him is a vote to keep the traditional power structure in place."

"Do you think Smith or Franklin can win?" I asked.

"Don't know. Normal year with no incumbent, yeah, probably. But this isn't a normal election. Being a special election, you know, not many people will vote. It's more about who is better organized," he said.

It was tough enough to get people to vote when there were major national elections on the ballot. It was almost impossible for special elections.

"Who should we endorse?" I asked.

He smiled. "I'm not sure I should say. It might influence the way I write about the campaign. A vote for either Franklin or Smith is a safe vote, not as charismatic as Grey, but probably would vote the same way he did. I doubt much would change."

Mike clasped his fingers together and leaned forward in the desk chair. He looked me straight in the face and said, "H.T. Jones, on the other hand, is the third candidate who has a chance in this race. He is really stirring things up. He is not liked by the preachers. He's got his own following, different from folks you normally expect to get involved."

"H.T. really? I never would have thought he had any chance."

"Jones has mobilized a lot of folks that didn't care much before. More extreme. People who are likely to drop out or want to change the system. Not your ordinary voters," Mike said.

That fit with H.T.'s personality. He was anything but conventional. And it would not set well with him to have the support of the old power structure. It would please him to put them on their rear ends and try to create a whole new power structure.

"Can Jones win?" I asked.

"I would say no. Jones scares the money boys. He should not be able to raise much money to counter the establishment's money. But that is not what's happening," Mike said.

"What?"

"Jones suddenly seems to have lots of money. I don't know where he is getting it. He doesn't have to report any of it until after the first primary. He isn't talking about it, but he's got money and he's spreading it around pretty good."

"Do you think it is outside money? Some of the black power money from up north?" I asked.

Mike shook his head. "Maybe. There's a lot of outside interest in Iron City, but I just don't know."

H.T. having money seemed odd. He was the rebel, the outlaw. Who would back him with money? I would ask H.T. about his money sources.

"Forget your objectivity for a minute. It's my responsibility whom we endorse. I just want your personal opinion," I said.

He thought for a minute, then proposed that we back Franklin. "That avoids either Ray Smith and his problems or Jones and his. If you want the paper to be on safe ground, back Franklin. I have to live with him anyway since he will either be a city council member or county commissioner after this election."

"Is that what you're heart says?"

He broke into a big smile and leaned way back in the chair. "No. I know it is kind of irresponsible, but it would be fun and make good stories for Jones to be elected and kick the crap out of the old boys at the courthouse."

The phone rang in my office. Mrs. James looked at me and I stood up from the desk where I had been talking with Mike. She was wearing an exasperated look behind her green glasses.

"It is that FBI Agent, Mr. Pitts, for you," she said formally, her distaste for the man dripped from her lips. Mrs. James either really liked or disliked a person. In her world, there was little room for gray.

"Special Agent in Charge Pitts, how are you?" I said sitting on the edge of her desk.

"Cut the crap, would you? I've had better days," Pitts said, sounding more down than I thought possible for a guy like him. "Thanks to you, Wayman and I just got our butts chewed out. Deputy Attorney General Keene saw your editorial and was not happy at your accusation that we caused the riots yesterday."

"Well, sorry about that. We can't be making the future Supreme Court justice angry, now can we?" I teased.

"Damn it, Joe. I'm serious. My career's on the line here. And Wright's too. You wouldn't believe the pressure we are under. You know what's happening in D.C. The Hill, the Republicans are looking for any crack in the President's armor. The longer we don't have a bomber in custody, well you know what's being said. He may have gotten Bin Laden in Pakistan, but he can't catch a church bomber in Alabama."

He sighed down the phone line, his frustration showing. "We know you're working some leads over there. We've got our sources too. Cooperate with us. We can bring this guy in. And we'll do it on the afternoon cycle so the *Post* can break the story. We won't let the *Examiner* beat you to your own tip," Pitts said.

At least he understood the competitive side of my business, even if he did not understand some of the ethical issues he was asking me to violate. The White House, the Attorney General, Keene and Wright all needed the bomber behind bars for political reasons. Because that hadn't happened, they wanted to pass their failure off on someone else. We were a good target. We were withholding information.

"I told you before, Harrison, once we have something solid, something we can print, we'll call you."

"We don't need anything solid. If you've got anything, names of guys who might be involved, that would be a lead. We can run it down better and faster than you can. Let's work together, okay?"

My stomach churned. Maybe he was right. We weren't finding Crenshaw. Maybe we were out of our league. Should we let the FBI handle this?

No. Not yet. "I understand. As soon as we have something I'll call you personally. Give me your home number. It might be late."

"You shit. If we have to, we can get a judge to compel you to cooperate," he said.

"Good luck with that," I said, knowing he was bluffing. Getting even a law-and-order federal judge to sign an order compelling a newspaper to disclose information would be hard. And we would tie it up in appeals for months. It was an idle threat, but no less annoying.

"You're going to call after your story is running on the presses, right?"

I didn't respond. Tense silence on both ends of the phone line.

"We know all about you, Joe Riordan. We know about all those nights in sleazy motels, some of them even before your wife was in the grave. You feel good about that, Joe?" Pitts said.

I squeezed my right thigh, an old habit when I was really angry. It distracted me while I tried to get my emotions under control. The worst thing I could do was to let him think he was getting to me. The skeletons in my closet may once have been of interest to J. Edgar Hoover, but today they weren't something that the FBI would investigate. He was bluffing. It would only get worse if I let him know he had hit a raw spot.

"Oh, excuse me, Harrison, somebody came in my office. What were you saying?" I heard a curse word on the other end of the phone, then just the dial tone.

Mrs. James brought me a Diet Coke. I swear she could read my mind. "I don't like that man very much, and it is not because he is black," she said.

"I can't disagree with you." She smiled and left.

Clay popped in a dozen times with new developments. Like most former reporters who took a desk job, Clay itched to be out on the street, covering the breaking news.

About two thirty, he stuck his head in my door, "Nicki's on my line. I think you want to hear this."

When the call was transferred, she said, "You were right. Our boy headed south."

Crenshaw's aunt lived in Dothan, where he had grown up on the Florida border. One of Mark's calls had been to this aunt. And despite her telling Pat she hadn't seen her nephew, I figured he might head home. When the FBI found that the C-4 and the detonator were bought in Dothan, I was sure that's where he had gone.

"He used a card to buy gas and groceries in a town north of Panama City. That was two days ago. The records sometime lag a few days. I'll keep looking. Maybe we'll get lucky and find a motel charge," she said.

"That's great, Nicki. Thanks. Clay and I will be here if you get anything else. Let us know."

"Anything else you want to say to me?" she asked.

I smiled inside. "Yes, but not right now. Thank you for the work."

With Clay hovering over my desk, the conversation I would like to have with Nicki was impossible. I wanted to call her sweetheart and tell her she was wonderful. But I couldn't right now, not without stirring up a lot of talk in the newsroom.

Nicki whispered in the phone. "I sure enjoyed being with you last night."

She was making me uncomfortable. She knew it and was probably laughing silently on her end of the phone. "Call me when you have something new. Thank you," I said and hung up the phone.

"Good move to bring her in," I told Clay. We've got to find Crenshaw, and she may be the only way."

Clay smiled and said, "You're paying her fee."

I stared out the window onto the street below, thinking about Crenshaw being in Florida. How would we get him back to Iron City? Did we want him back? Should we just interview him there? The most disturbing thought was that he might have bought enough groceries to rent a condo on the gulf. He might pay cash, particularly since he told Mark he was paid for the bombing in cash. Or he could be borrowing a place from a friend or someone involved in the bombing. If so, we would have to hope for a restaurant or bar charge to narrow the area, then launch a full-scale search. We didn't have the manpower for that.

The daily news meeting had started. The focus was on the National Guard and the aftermath of the battles. The Iron City Vulcans were screaming that they had not been added as a new NFL team to pair with returning a team to Los Angeles. Could we speculate that the bombing and the riots cost us an NFL team? The commissioner had declined to say why Iron City did not get a franchise. Our city was larger than Charlotte or New Orleans or certainly Green Bay. And it was unlikely that the NFL could find a base of more football crazy fans than in Iron City. So Bud Shaw, the sports editor, was asked to write a front-page column suggesting that the riots had cost the city the chance to watch the Vulcans play in the big leagues.

The rest of the stories were routine. A tropical storm in the Atlantic had taken a right turn off Cuba and looked like it was headed for the Gulf of Mexico. But with the National Guard in the streets it would take a major hurricane headed straight inland to make it above the fold on page one.

I dealt with several pressing issues. The thorniest was again home delivery. The truck drivers still did not want to haul newspapers to neighborhoods just north of downtown. One truck had been shot at while driving the *Examiners* just north of downtown. Another had been spray painted with a man hanging from a noose. The *Examiner* had decided not to deliver papers to the northern neighborhoods just like we had. We would do the same again tonight.

We were also losing space. The *Examiner* cut back on the size of our news hole. The advertising department claimed the grocery stores, department stores and car dealers, the lifeblood of newspapers, were waiting for the riots to stop. "Nobody's calling attention to themselves until this mess is over," Joiner told me. I called Weitzman in Virginia to ask the owners to authorize more pages without ads, an expensive move, but one that I believed had to happen if the *Post* was to survive this crisis.

"If we can't tell our readers about the worst crisis in the city's history, why would they need or want to read what we have to write after the crisis is over?" I asked.

He said yes. We got the additional space, but he was not happy. There would be a price to pay.

10

An excited Nicki called back a few minutes after six o'clock. Crenshaw had used a credit card to charge two nights at the Pelican Seaside Hotel and Resort. The hotel said he was still checked in and was about to forward her call to his room, but she hung up. Clay was out for his usual greasy cheeseburger. Ed was in the newsroom talking with two sports reporters. So I could talk to her openly. She confessed that she liked teasing me earlier. I joked that I would deduct a portion of her fee for the discomfort.

By the time Clay strolled back from dinner at the Elite Grill, Nicki had chartered a airplane out of a suburban air park for the three of us. We both thought there might be more eyes on the Iron City airport. Panama City is only a few hours drive south and most residents of Iron City seemed to make that trip at least once a year. But I wanted to get there before Crenshaw got spooked and disappeared again. And I wanted to try to bring him back to Iron City tonight or early tomorrow. It was Thursday. At the earliest we couldn't get a story in until Saturday's paper, usually our smallest paper. I was not about to risk holding the story until Monday. It had taken too long already.

Nicki met us at the air park off the interstate south of Iron City. Clay and I had stopped to pick up clothes and toothbrushes. I kissed Chris and told him I would see him in a couple of days. He cried, held on to my leg and looked like I had just told him Santa was skipping the house this year. His grandmother came in and rescued me, taking him away to play a new game.

At the air park, Nicki was talking with the pilot. She told him we were headed for the casinos in Biloxi. The pilot was shaking his head. With the storm threatening, although it was still a long way out in the gulf, the strong winds would push any plane around.

Nicki had chartered a small Cessna Citation in her name. She whispered that it might slow down the FBI and maybe others who could be watching for us to make a move toward the bomber. She was not the only person who had the ability to track credit card usage, she said, smiling at me.

The pilot overcame his fears when Nicki handed him another five hundred dollar bills in cash. He filed his flight plan, and we were off the ground in minutes. The Citation accommodated five passengers. I sat behind the pilot, while Nicki and Clay in the seats behind me talked solidly for the next hour. I sat thinking about everything that could go wrong. Was Crenshaw still at the Pelican? Was he hiding? Did he know people were looking for him? Would he come with us? Would he shoot us when we tried to get him to go back to Iron City? How far could I go to bring him in? Should I find him and call the FBI who had handcuffs and the authority to arrest him? Could we be charged with kidnapping?

I looked back at Nicki and Clay. I envied him talking with her during the flight. But we live in a world of perceptions, and keeping up appearances right now was important. As we flew out over the Alabama plains, I thought how strange that I should be so attracted to her. She was the polar opposite from Sheila. Where Nicki was short and muscular and worked out with weights, Sheila had avoided any form of exercise even after Chris was born. Tall, willowy and blonde, Sheila preferred reading and laying in the sun. Nicki enjoyed movies, though she was well read and could talk about almost any subject from football to Renaissance artists. Sheila was subtle in her efforts to change me. Nicki hit it head on. Her current project was trying to talk me into juicing vegetables and riding a stationary bike. I turned again to look at her. She was a taut spring. Even when asleep, she radiated energy. She was a generous and inventive lover. Soft was a word I associated with Sheila, not Nicki. She smiled at me when I turned my head to look at her.

Nicki had walked into my life abruptly. There was a knock on the door in the middle of the night about a year after we had buried Sheila. It was in a second-floor room of a motel that would never be on the Zagat guide to Iron City. Nicki was there to rescue me. Ultimately she was there to restore order to my chaotic life.

The small plane hit the first of the headwinds coming from the approaching storm. We bounced around, until the pilot dropped a few hundred feet and found smoother air.

"I've heard of compulsive gamblers, but this is ridiculous," he muttered into the windshield.

"Just think what it will feel like to hit a big jackpot just as the storm comes inland," I said. He grunted, stared straight ahead and held on tighter as the wind battered the plane.

Nicki's entrance into my life brought an end to a bad period. Sheila's death had left me feeling empty and alone. My grandfather had died. Howard and my mother were dead. Only my father was still alive, and we were far from close. I was trying to fill the large hole in my life by screwing as many women as I could. Screwing was the right word. It certainly was not making love. The sex was much coarser than that. It didn't matter much who the women were. Black, white, Hispanic, Asian, tall and skinny, short and plump, if they had most of their teeth and I had enough to drink, we headed for their place, a motel or the backseat of the car. I don't remember most of them. Sometimes I feared they might remember me. When a woman across a restaurant would look up and smile at me, panic bubbled up in my throat. It might be one I had been with.

I had never strayed until Sheila lay dying in the hospital, tubes attached, drifting in and out drug-induced sleep. It was like seeing my grandfather and mother dying all over again. Watching my wife die by inches cut me open and left what remained raw and exposed. It was late and I was leaving the hospital. I stepped out of the elevator and almost collided with a woman I had dated as a young reporter out of college, long before I met Sheila. She was visiting her father who was dying of colon cancer. I met her an hour later in a bar near the hospital. We held each other together with alcohol and intimacy. When we dated, we had never been close to marrying. Her white, over-the-mountain friends would not have accepted her marrying a black man, even one with a Princeton diploma. We had fun, but I couldn't compete with an older guy, who owned a chain of pet stores and wanted to share a fat bank account. He and his money were still around, but it didn't take much for us to end up in a room. I felt supremely guilty, but I wasn't alone, at least for a few minutes.

That evening launched a bizarre pattern of behavior for me that extended for months after I buried Sheila. I was the second in command at the newspaper then, the *Post*'s managing editor. Once I saw the last edition roll off the press near midnight, I could not turn off the rush of running the newspaper. I would head for any of several bars in town where available women hung out. My mother-in-law watched over Chris and never reproached me. I did enough of that myself.

"People grieve in different ways," she told me.

As much as I kicked myself every morning, by midnight, like an addict, I was off the wagon again. The night I met Nicki I was in the Downtowner, a motel just north of the convention center. It was now rubble in the wake of the riots, not much of a loss. It was the kind of place you felt you needed to bring two sticks with you, one to beat off the rats and roaches, the other to prop up the bed. The girl I was with was goofy, thin with small breasts, but pretty and into sex. I fell exhausted into sleep, swearing to stick to older women.

About three in the morning. I woke up and saw a light on in the bath. The girl wasn't in the bed. When I pushed open the door, she turned and looked at me. On top of the toilet were two lines of white powder. She handed me a cut straw, "You ever done it when you're high?" I shook my head. "Try it. You'll like it."

She bent down and snorted one of the lines. She turned to me and smiled. She reached down and fondled my penis. It stiffened. I stared at the line of powder and shivered with excitement. She knelt down and kissed my penis. She licked it, then swallowed it deep.

I realize now how close I was to stepping on the path of destruction, one of those forks in the road of life that poets, preachers and philosophers wax on about. Take one path and life is good. Step out on the other and you find out what hell on Earth is all about. If I had bent over that toilet, given in to the temptation of forbidden pleasure, getting higher than I had ever been and going for another round with this young, sexy girl, I might have found myself on that second path.

Nicki saved me.

A knock on the door startled us. Dazed with the pleasure of the girl's lips, I pulled away. I was scared. The girl wrapped her arms around my legs.

"Don't open it. It's the cops. I can't go to jail. I can't."

I told her to stay behind the bathroom door. She shut it, and I heard the toilet flushing. I went to the door and looked through the peephole. "I don't think it's the police," I called back to the girl. I pulled on my pants and slipped my arms in my shirt sleeves. The knock came louder and faster. I opened the door. In front of me stood a woman with dark hair and olive skin. She wore a ball cap turned backwards. Inside a tight-fitting black uniform-style shirt, black pants and black running shoes, she had a tight waist, small hips and larger than average breasts.

"Mr. Riordan, please come with me. You are in danger," she said and stepped into the room. The girl peaked around the bathroom door. The woman looked at her, then she picked up my jacket, tie and shoes and started pulling me out the door.

"What?"

"Trust me, sir. We have to get out of here."

"But why?"

"Please come with me now. I will explain," she said.

Her tone left no room for argument. She was strong and had little trouble pulling me out of the room and along the concrete walkway that led to the steps. I was mumbling, but not really able to form a question as I stumbled along. I looked back at the room, vaguely thinking I should help the girl. I saw an older man, also in black, leaning on two metal canes waiting at the other end of the building. A tall, younger man, with muscles bulging under his black shirt, stepped along the walkway and went in the room.

"Don't worry about your friend. We've got her too. She'll be all right. Wouldn't want her to talk to anyone about who she was banging tonight, now would we?" the woman said.

I thought I saw a smirk on her face. I guessed I was the target of some joke. She guided me toward a van. I stopped to put on my shoes. She tugged at my arm. "Do it in the truck. We need to be gone." She unlocked the door of a black Chevy Tahoe and motioned for me to get in the front seat, then went around and opened the driver's door and got in. "Don't worry about your car. We've already moved it," she said.

"How?" I took my jacket from her and felt in the pocket for my keys. They were there.

"It's okay. Don't worry. Anything you left, we will bring along." I realized that I had left my underwear in the room. I had put on my pants, without bothering with the shorts.

We rode through downtown in the giant truck the folks in Detroit had made into a car. Up Twentieth Avenue, then east on First Street. She drove by the old iron-making furnace that was now a tourist attraction, through the neighborhood where I had grown up and continued east passed old shopping centers, churches and schools. We rode without talking. I was trying to understand what was happening. Who was this woman? Why had she pulled me out of that room? Who were those other guys? And what danger had

I been in? Or was I still in? I thought about the girl and the coke. Wow, can my little head get me in trouble?

She kept her eyes on the road. It was starting to mist and the streets were getting slippery. "What danger?" I asked.

She looked at me and smiled. "He speaks."

The woman drove on for several blocks before answering the question. "Police were going through the rooms, pulling out anyone they could arrest. It is that time of the month. Arrest quotas have to be met. Law abiding citizens want to read in newspapers like yours that the police are doing their jobs, cleaning up crime havens like the Downtowner. Mostly it is for drugs, but they usually find somebody selling guns, fencing stolen stuff. The Downtowner is a hotbed of local crime."

I was stunned. She obviously knew who I was. This was not some random rescue. Who else knew what I was doing? That was when I had a small anxiety attack. My breathing got shallow as I thought about what could have happened. The girl and I would have been arrested. I might have lost my job. For sure, I would never have been editor, something I guess I took for granted, and something I wanted very badly.

"You can really pick 'em," she said as the Tahoe went east.

I looked at my mystery woman. How had she known that tonight the police would be raiding the motel I picked? She must have read my mind because a trace of a smile crossed her lips. "Yes, I have been following you for several nights. You really do get around. But it wasn't tough duty until tonight."

I heard a trace of a northern accent, something familiar from my college years. But I couldn't place it. It certainly wasn't an Alabama drawl.

"Why were you following me?"

"It's a job," she said.

"Who are you?" I asked.

"I was wondering when you would ask that. You must be getting a bit rusty. I bet you used to ask the most important question first. Maybe it's all that booze and sex muddling up your brain." She paused to look at me briefly before she turned to look ahead at the street again. We seemed to be riding around in a large circle. I had no idea where she was taking me.

"My name is Nicki Fabrini. I'm a private detective. The man on the sticks is my boss. And the guy with him works for us sometimes."

So watching after me was an assignment. It made no sense. "Someone paid you to do that? Who asked you to watch over me?" I asked.

"Can't say. Never divulge a client's identity. That would be unprofessional, violate our code of ethics, lousy for business. Don't you ever watch television?"

I shook my head.

"I know, you work nights. And you party hardy. I'll give you one thing, you do have stamina."

Her opinion of me must have been a few inches above the gutter. I never thought anyone, other than my in-laws, knew what I was doing. It was supposed to be my little secret. I never told anyone where I went. Most guys like to brag about who they bang. I didn't need that. Truthfully, I was not particularly proud of my weakness. It was just filling a hole. But now Nicki knew, so did her boss and the guy who worked for them. And whoever was paying them.

The headwinds from the Gulf were getting stronger, bouncing the little plane like a feather on a breeze. The pilot was frowning even more and talked frequently on the radio to get weather reports and search for calmer air. There apparently wasn't any. Nicki leaned forward, tapped the pilot on the shoulder and told him to put us down at an airport just north of Panama City.

"It's closer," she told him.

"Not a lot," the pilot said. "We might get in, but I don't think we'll be coming out. What y'all going to do, drive over to Biloxi? You won't be back until tomorrow. An overnight will be extra."

Nicki shrugged. "Maybe we'll just be a few hours. Who knows?"

The pilot looked unnerved, but made the course correction.

Nicki looked very nice in tight brown pants. The first night we met she had parked the van at a donut shop by a mall. We drank several cups of coffee while the police were finishing cleaning out the Downtowner Motel. After she got through needling me about my tastes in women, she took off her baseball hat and shook her head. Soft, dark curls cascaded down her back. She turned and smiled at me. I wonder if she knew then the effect she was having on me. Two hours later, she let me off at a parking lot where someone had moved my Blazer. My underwear was folded on the front seat.

The pilot radioed the tower at Panama City. We landed as the winds bounced the little plane around the runway. I looked back at the woman I had fallen in love with. She was holding on tight, but still chatting happily with Clay. While we taxied toward the small terminal, she checked the revolver while the pilot was not looking. She carried it next to her laptop.

A walking contradiction, Nicki had come to Iron City from Philadelphia, the only daughter of a wealthy Italian family. She had grown up on the Main Line in Radnor, a town I knew from a couple of college friends who grown up there. That was where I had knew the accent. She graduated from Smith College and spent a year in Switzerland. Besides her very proper English, she could speak three other languages besides English: French, Italian and what she called Philadelphia street slang. Her knowledge of European art approached that of some museum curators. She had been groomed to spend her life in art galleries and working for charities. Her mother had planned since she was born for her to take her place one day raising money for a hospital in Philadelphia. It was what was expected of many daughters of wealthy lawyers, doctors and merchants in Pennsylvania's Delaware County.

She rebelled, bought a Harley and at twenty-three, drove down a long driveway to seek a new life, grateful for the education her parents had given her, but needing more than a bird-cage existence. The bike had broken down in Iron City after four hard months on the road. Instead of calling home for money, she answered an ad in the *Examiner* and found herself handling the phones and visitors for a local private detective. She told me she liked the look of Iron City, its mountainous terrain and Southern hospitality. She also found she liked the private detective work and got her license. Even after the bike was fixed, she stayed.

That night we drank coffee, and I ate donuts while she talked. I was afraid to like her. This was one tough woman, intriguing, but hardly my type. Clay had filled in some of the gaps about her. The guy on the canes owned the detective business. His canes were the result of a high-speed car chase that had ended badly for him. The impact with the rear end of a bus had crushed several vertebrae. He woke up from nine-hours of surgery without the use of his legs. He bought a wheelchair and went back to work. He started looking for someone with brains and two working legs. He had not planned on a woman to fill that role. But Nicki turned out to be everything he wanted. She was good looking and could make a computer do more than most. She helped him with his rehab and got him walking with the canes. They made a good team.

Nicki didn't talk much about her work. I often wondered how dangerous it was, action packed like in novels or more mundane surveillance jobs like following me. I teased her that she was probably the first Smith College grad to become a private detective.

Until Nicki came along, I had tried cocooning myself with work and women. No personal commitment, no risk, I thought. Now I was feeling things again, caring about something other than Chris and the *Post*. It felt good, like the high an acrobat must get, letting go of the swing, falling toward the net. I just wanted to make sure that strong hands were there to pull me back up.

The Pelican was a walled complex, almost a city in itself, complete with guards manning the entrance, two golf courses, tennis courts and three pools. The rooms and condos were in four high-rise concrete towers that offered views of either the gulf or the golf courses. There were two restaurants, a half dozen bars and waiters darting about refilling glasses and plates. The spas and exercise gyms with personal trainers on call, three salt-water pools, two spas for massages and lush landscaping catered to the elite of the South. I had heard about the Pelican for years. Even if we didn't catch Crenshaw, at least, I could now say I had been to the Pelican.

"Our boy's going first class," Clay said. "I think the suites, and it only has suites, run about three fifty a night."

"Yeah," Nicki said. "His room charge was over seven hundred dollars. He's getting near the limit on his card, but Visa'll probably extend him. The rooms I booked for us will cost you about three seventy five each for tonight."

I hoped we got our bomber quickly. Weitzman would not like paying for a pricey room in Florida.

"Crenshaw may be a bit out of his league here," Clay said. "After my first wife left me, I used to come down to Panama City a lot. I stayed at the Pelican once. It is great, lots of single and soon-to-be single women come there. Most want guys with a thick wallet. I couldn't compete, but had fun."

We had left the pilot at the Panama City airport. He was still shaking his head at the "idiot gamblers" and warned us that if the storm got any worse, we were staying on the ground.

Nicki had a Chevy van waiting for us. I hoped we wouldn't need it, but if we had to drive Crenshaw back to Iron City, I didn't relish the thought of being stuck for hours in a Ford Focus with that redneck.

We drove in darkness along the Gulf Highway toward the Pelican. As a child my family used to spend a week each summer on Florida beaches. Sand and salty air, lapping waves brought back fun memories. Coming to Florida with my family was always a glorious time, a week of running along the beach, building sand castles, pretending to body surf and taking long walks in quest of the perfect shell. My grandfather went with us one year after my grandmother died. My father didn't really want to include him, but I heard my mother telling him it was the right thing to do. I loved it. My grandfather told great stories. I'm sure my father had heard them all many times, but did not interrupt. Stories about growing up in Ireland and coming to America as a boy. My favorites were about the two seasons he pitched for a semi-pro team in Pennsylvania. My father asked him if he missed living in Pennsylvania, had he regretted moving to Alabama. "Nope. I met your mother here," my grandfather said. "She wouldn't have been happy there. She always thought northern cities would be too hard on us, her being black and me white. I told her it couldn't be any worse than than us being here, a mixed couple in Iron City. But she wouldn't have it," he said.

The years had brought change to the area, the growth nothing short of phenomenal. Resorts like the Pelican had not existed when I was a child. In those days it was not the Redneck Riviera. It was just Redneckville, a place of cheap motels, seafood restaurants, bars, pine trees and alligators. Convenience stores had replaced bait shops as the place to buy beer. But you don't sit around convenience stores telling stories. I don't think my grandfather would have found much reason to hang out at a 7-11 store.

At the Pelican, the guards at the front gate waved us through. Had they known we wanted to haul one of their guests back to Iron City to stand trial for mass murder, they might not have been so welcoming. When we checked in, an impatient Clay asked the desk clerk for Crenshaw. Nicki had suggested we wait until we got into our suite and then call for his room number. So much for advanced planning. Clay told the clerk we were supposed to meet Crenshaw. The desk clerk checked the registration cards and told us he was still registered, but then shook his head, "Oh, no, wait. He checked out a few hours ago. That's weird. He was supposed to be with us for another night." He punched several keys on the computer and said, "Yep, he checked out. I guess maybe the storm spooked him, huh?"

Clay showed him a photo of Crenshaw that Pat had copied out of his employment file. The clerk, a young man in his late twenties, was pretty sure that we were talking about the same guy.

"It must have been some emergency," Nicki said, thinking fast. "Did he have any phone calls before he left?"

"Well, we, uh, we only track out-going calls," the clerk stammered. But Nicki's smile seemed to calm him. "We just don't have any way to know if he got some in-coming calls."

"Could you check his out-going calls for us? Maybe if we knew who he called before he checked out so suddenly, then we might know what happened to him and we could find our friend," she said.

Clay jumped in and said, "While you check that, Joe and I'll go on and get us settled, all right?"

From her invoice, which I happily paid, I learned that she had given the clerk forty dollars, no receipt, of course, for a copy of Crenshaw's bill. It did not tell us where he had gone. But it did tell us whom he had called. There were two calls to Iron City. One was to the sheriff's office, made shortly after the FBI released the photo. The other was to the main number of the *Examiner.*

The *Examiner?* Why the *Examiner?* Who did he talk to there? My heart was pumping faster. Could it be that he talked to Daniels? Maybe, maybe we had found the conspiracy. Whatever, it was one hell of a story. And I got that queasy feeling in my gut. If Daniels was involved, it would get complicated. It would really piss off my bosses. They liked the money the partnership with Daniels generated.

The Pelican suite was everything Clay had described. Elegant from the thick pile of the carpeting to the floor-to-ceiling drapes that framed one of the best views on the Gulf, it seemed too good for people who came down just to relive memories of college spring break. Whitecaps crashed onto the white beach, barely visible in the dark overcast night. Too bad that Nicki and I couldn't stay a few days. It would be fun to watch the storm roll in from this vantage point.

I called the *Post* to report in and find out what was happening on the streets of Iron City. With the National Guard on patrol, the city was quieter. There was not even the random incident of burnings or rock throwing that had been going on for weeks. Were the rioters intimidated by the Guard?

While on the phone with Ed, I asked him to get Rachel to sweet talk a friend of hers at the phone company and hopefully get a copy of what calls had been placed to the resort from the *Examiner's* phones. Then we went looking for Crenshaw, Nicki with her computer, Clay and I with shoe leather. Nicki sat in the suite with a glass of wine from the mini-bar tapping into the Pelican's wireless connection. Clay and I started the rounds of nearby bars.

I had once asked Nicki how she had access to other people's charge cards. On television, it looked so easy. She told me first that I didn't need to know. But when I pressed her, she said it was not so easy and required connections to the credit card companies. The man on the sticks had several contacts that proved very useful.

For Clay and me, finding Crenshaw was the classic hunt for a needle in a haystack, one drunk redneck among thousands in bars and restaurants spread out along the beach. Our hope was that his large size and crude personality might stand out. With the storm approaching and the barometer falling fast, I felt more pressure to find our quarry fast. In most of the places we went there was an intense level of excitement. The approaching storm and heavy alcohol consumption seemed to be revving up everyone's adrenalin. I had heard about hurricane parties along the gulf. We stumbled into several.

Dressed in raincoats over blazers and open-necked shirts, Clay and I worked the bars. We showed Crenshaw's photo to bartenders and waitresses, explaining we had lost our friend. Everyone shook their heads and went back to the frenzy of handing out drinks and grabbing fists of money. One waitress thought she may have seen him, but didn't know where to find him now. I asked if he had paid her with a credit card, but she did not volunteer to check her records.

With the wind blowing harder each time we left a bar to find another, I was about to suggest we head back to the Pelican, when Clay pointed the van into the parking lot of a strip club. Compared to the other clubs we had been in, the Foxy Lady was a step above. BMWs, Cadillacs, Big SUVs with license plates from Alabama, Georgia, Florida and even one from Texas filled the parking lot. There was one Corvette, but its license plate did not match Crenshaw's. Clay pointed out a large pickup truck that had a fish/Jesus magnet attached to the trunk.

"We may not find Crenshaw in here, but at least we will be among Christians," Clay joked.

Big guys in tuxedos welcomed us inside the door and took twenty dollars each. When we held up Crenshaw's photo, they shook their heads without even looking at it. Inside beveled glass double doors, the club had faux marble painted walls and rich paneling that could have decorated a law firm. Two long bars took up the back and a side wall, each with every stool filled with a man watching the show on the stages. Small tables with well-padded chairs filled the center of the large room. A VIP area was upstairs with even larger chairs and small sofas. A long stage was against the front wall with three smaller stages scattered around the room. A girl danced on each stage, collecting ones, fives and ten dollar bills that were spread out on the floor beneath her high heels. The girls working the floor were dressed like they were going to a charity ball with long flowing gowns, tightly fitted and cut low to show off their assets as they leaned over men sitting deep in the chairs. No hot pants, t-shirts, jeans or ball caps here. I did not feel overdressed.

"If Crenshaw's down here, he's been in here," Clay said.

"This place looks a bit too upscale for him," I said.

"Probably is. There are other strip clubs down here, but this is the best. Look at that girl on stage. Wow! Even a neck like Crenshaw would come in here. Maybe somebody'll remember him."

Clay took the lead. Since he was dating a stripper, who would know strip club etiquette better? We showed the photo to the bartenders and several waitresses. Then we started talking with the girls. Amazing what a fist full of fives and tens will do. The fourth girl we tried started nodding her head as Clay talked to her. I walked over and joined them.

"Yeah, that big son-of-a-bitch was here. Last night. Real jerk. Kept asking me to go out in the parking lot with him. Said he had a real sweet vette. Do you know how many guys tell me stuff like that? It probably was just a pickup. Besides you ever tried to do more than a handjob in a vette?"

I could see why Crenshaw was interested. Her long blond hair ran down her back, beautiful eyes and lips and a cleavage that would make most men shiver. She wore a long black evening gown with black gloves that came up over her elbows.

"You're right, Lonnie is a real jerk sometimes," Clay was telling her. "Specially when he's drunk. We need to find him, you know what I mean?"

She nodded.

"You know where we might find him? Where he might have gone?" Clay said.

"No. He was with several of the girls. I'll ask around. Try that waitress over there, Joanie. She waited on him. Maybe he told her where he was headed. I'm just glad the jerk's out of here, you know. While you're hear, you handsome guys want a dance?"

Crenshaw had not made any better impression on Joanie. He had told her about his Corvette too and asked if there was some-place he could go where the girls were a little more "understand-ing," she said, rolling her eyes. She had suggested that he try the Blue Lagoon two miles down the beach. "I will say one thing for him, he ain't afraid to spend money. He tipped me pretty good."

I asked if he might be in the VIP room. She shook her head. "That costs more than even he had to spend," she said.

Halfway back to the van, my phone rang. "Find him?" Nicki asked.

I told her we were striking out. When I said we were headed to the Blue Lagoon, there was a pause in the conversation. I asked if there was anything else. "Just don't you be looking at any of those girls. Let Clay do that. You're the editor, and remember, you're mine." The phone went dead without giving me the chance to tell her she was better looking than any of these girls.

The Blue Lagoon was way down the economic scale from the Foxy Lady. Next to a bowling alley, the bar door was open with just strips of plastic blowing wildly in the wind. The music, smoke and the smell of fried food hit us when we stepped out of the van. To avoid looking out of place, we left our raincoats and jackets in the van.

"This is more like it," I shouted over the wind and the noise.

The Foxy Lady was one large open room with beer stations around the room. It was packed. Men and women danced to very loud music on a small dance floor, surrounded by low tables and straight-backed chairs. Most of the men were dressed in short-sleeve shirts and jeans. A few sported well-worn ball caps. The women were better dressed in tight dresses and skirts. The Blue Lagoon was a meat market, a place men and women met and groped one another, drank a lot and went home, sometimes together. I had been in a lot of similar joints.

Clay stopped a waitress carrying a tray of beers and showed her the photo, making hand signals to explain who we were looking for. She shook her head, looked at him like he was nuts and hurried off to deliver drinks. We tried three others with no luck. Crenshaw could have been their last customer, and they still would not re-member him. Clay took one side of the room, while I worked the other. I just hoped he was still here. It was late, and if our boy was feeling frisky, he had probably already found a new friend. Or if he had been spooked, he could be halfway back to Iron City or South America by now.

We gave up after another twenty minutes. Halfway across the large parking lot passed pickup trucks and small Japanese-made cars my phone rang. "Call me at the room from a land line." Nicki gave me the number and hung up. We drove for about a half mile before we found a phone on the wall of a grocery store that was packed with people clearing the shelves ahead of the coming storm.

The phone, one of what once was a bank of three phones, looked like it had been hit with a bat, but it still worked.

"You want the good news or the better news first?" she asked, when she picked up.

"Either. Both sound good after the frustrating night we've had."

Rachel called. The phone company guy had asked her to dinner. "You allow that sort of thing to go on with your reporters?" Nicki teased.

I thought it was a good deal for everyone. "Rachel's a grown-up. What'd she learn?"

"Impatient, aren't we?" She laughed.

"Yes, and why did I have to call you from a pay phone?"

She laughed. "For all your Ivy League education, you don't know much. Some people, some you know well, have the ability to listen to calls. Certain words trigger the recorders. Do you think they, whoever they are, haven't been listening to your phone?"

I did know that. I just didn't think we qualified for an National Security Agency phone tap. But she was probably right, and I knew who might be listening.

"It is a good thing you have me, right?" she said. I could see her sitting there on the phone smiling, tossing her long brunette curls with a shake of her head. I wanted a hug.

"A call was made from the *Examiner* to the Pelican yesterday. And guess whose phone the call was made from?"

"No, it can't be," I whispered in my excitement. "From Daniels' office?" I was feeling like a kid just before the birthday party starts.

"The one and only. That was the good news. Now do you want the better news?"

I was so excited I couldn't speak.

"Go check the Bayou Inn. Our boy charged something, probably a room, there." She gave me the address.

"You're the best," I whispered.

Someone watching me leave the parking lot would have thought I was qualifying for the race in Talladega.

11

As the van rolled down the beach road, rapidly moving clouds blocked out the moon and stars, making it really dark along the highway. I was beginning to think we had missed the Bayou Inn when its lights flickered ahead. The exotically named motel was a one-story concrete block building, badly in need of painting, sandwiched between a Shell gas station and a small restaurant on the north side of the Gulf Highway. Because it was on the far side of the highway from the beach, it was not a place for families with kids. On summer days the highway was too busy for pedestrians to run across carrying coolers, umbrellas, bags of towels and suntan lotion. So even in the height of vacation season the rooms at the Bayou were cheap. Even cheaper now in the fall with a storm blowing in.

When we pulled into the parking lot, there was a white Corvette. The tag number matched the one Pat had given us for Crenshaw's car. It didn't look like he was trying to hide. The car was a beacon in the dark. A faded bumper sticker read: "If I don't get laid soon, someone is going to get hurt."

We stood reading the sticker. "Classy guy," Clay said.

The hood was cool, glistening with moisture in the motel lights. Crenshaw had been there for at least a few hours. I called Nicki from a phone at the gas station and asked her to join us.

We would need her talents at persuasion to get Crenshaw to come with us. She said she would grab a taxi and join us. I gave her directions, even though every cab driver on the coast would know the Bayou Inn.

At the registration desk Clay was talking to an old man behind the desk. I was still a little light-headed thinking that Daniels could really be the guy. Clay was telling the old man we were looking for a friend. Because of the storm we needed to find him and make sure he was all right. Behind the desk, the man wore only a robe over a pair of tighty whities and an undershirt. He smelled of Ben Gay, and while Clay went through our rehearsed routine, he scratched his backside under his robe.

"His name's Lonnie Crenshaw, but sometimes he likes to play games and register as somebody else. Maybe you've seen him?" He showed him the photo.

"We may have a Crenshaw. I'm not sure. I'll have to look at our database," he said smirking at us. There was no computer in sight. "Yeah, I think a guy that looks like that checked in here, maybe yesterday. I'm not sure."

He tossed the photo back to Clay.

"Could you tell us what room he's in? We want to surprise him," Clay said.

The man sized up Clay and looked at me over glasses halfway down his nose and said sarcastically that we were asking him to violate motel policy, but he picked up an old black phone and said he could call him.

"No, no," Clay said, waving his arms to stop the man from dialing Crenshaw's room. "As I said, we'd like to surprise him." Clay pulled out some cash from his wallet. "Would twenty bucks make you forget company policy?"

"Nawh, but fifty would, maybe."

Clay looked at me, then said, "I tell you what, I'll go fifty if you tell us his room number and if he's made any phone calls and to what number."

All pretense that we were looking for our friend evaporated. The old man only carried about the bills in Clay's hand. He leaned across the counter and held out a gnarled hand. Clay gave him two twenties and two fives. The man told him Crenshaw was in room number twelve, but had registered under the name Virgil Griffin. I smiled. Lonnie may be dumb, but he knew his Ku Klux Klan history. Virgil Lee Griffin was the imperial wizard of the North Carolina klan who went to war with leftist workers in Greensboro. Several people died, because he claimed "God guided their bullets." Maybe Crenshaw thought God told him to plant the bomb in the church.

"He's only been here one night. And no, he ain't made no calls from his room. If I had that little honey I saw git out of that there fancy sports car, I wouldn't be phoning nobody," he laughed, showing off several spaces between his teeth.

"But I did see him make a phone call."

"What'd you mean?" Clay asked.

"Well, he comes in here and gets five bucks in quarters from me. Then I see'd him go out to the pay phone at the filling station and talk a bit. Maybe he doesn't want the woman to hear him call his wife and lie about where he is."

Clay laughed and winked at the old man. "You're pretty smart, old man."

"Who you calling old?"

By the time Nicki arrived, we knew Crenshaw was inside the room. I jotted down the pay phone number for Rachel's friend at the phone company, while Clay slipped up to the door and listened. He reminded me for the umpteenth time that he was a trained sniper.

"Our boy is entertaining. I heard a woman's voice, and I don't think they were discussing Plato," he whispered.

The curtains were drawn. No one came out while we waited in the van. Nicki came armed with more than her computer. I don't like guns, and I hoped we weren't going to need it. But Crenshaw might have a gun inside the room. Taking him by force, even in self defense, could be interpreted wrongly by the FBI. We discussed our options and decided to try subtlety. Nicki walked to the room door and knocked just below the painted number twelve. I hoped he would not shoot her through the door. Using her sultriest voice, Nicki asked Lonnie to open the door. Crenshaw yelled, "Go away. We don't need no room service." We could hear him laughing.

Nicki came back where we stood by the van and proposed that she break down the door. I told her she'd been watching too much television and suggested that she try again. She smirked at me, which made me think she had broken down a few doors. She and Clay went back to the door and she knocked again. She called out, "Lonnie, honey, please open the door."

It took about two minutes, which seemed like a year, for him to open the door. He had only pants on. "Yeah, what'd ya want? Do I know you?" he said. Crenshaw was even bigger than I expected, his bare torso was hairy and sagging. He was taller than six feet and must have weighed close to three hundred. He had a small goatee, no mustache. No one had mentioned facial hair. I wondered if he had grown it in a poor attempt at a disguise.

"Oh, Lonnie, darling, you've forgotten me already?" Nicki cooed.

From behind him, I heard a woman ask what was going on. "Is that your wife?" she barked. Crenshaw, leaning on the open door, turned and told her to shut up, that he didn't have a wife. I couldn't see any gun. At that moment, Clay stepped quickly to the door and pushed it open. Crenshaw, holding the inside door handle, stepped backwards into the room. I stayed outside, not wanting to frighten him with too many people or worse a black face.

The glass in the framed picture on the far wall popped and fell to the floor with a crash. Nicki looked back, then bolted through the doorway and tackled Crenshaw mid-torso. She hit him like a linebacker plants a quarterback on the turf. Crenshaw cried out as they sprawled on the carpet. Clay, still standing in the doorway, turned to look across the parking lot. Then he yelled, grabbed his leg and went down. He writhed on the ground.

"Get down, Joe. Somebody's shooting," Nicki yelled as she kicked the door closed. She was inside the room with Crenshaw and the woman.

Clay on the concrete walk outside yelled that he had been shot. I was slow to react, my mind and legs were not working together. Another bullet whooshed passed me and hit the door, splintering the thin wood. Clay dragged himself under the roof over the sidewalk in front of the rooms. I ducked behind a car, then crawled onto the concrete with him. Nicki yelled through the door, "You want the police?"

There was a muffled response from inside. It sounded like Crenshaw talking. The woman was bitching. I ran to the door, bending over as far as I could, hoping I wouldn't get shot. I looked at Clay. Blood flowed through his hand holding his leg. I yelled to Nicki, "Not if we can help it." The discussion inside continued, but I couldn't make out the words. Crenshaw was probably getting the short version on us. The woman bitched louder. Kneeling over Clay, I felt helpless. The man with the gun was probably on a dune across the highway. Being dark and late and a storm coming, nobody was likely to walk down the beach. He could stay there as long as he didn't mind getting wet.

Clay groaned and grimaced, his eyes shut, his face contorted. He told me to take off my belt and tie it around his thigh. The bullet hole was in the back of his leg a few inches above the knee. I couldn't see an exit wound.

"God dammit, shit fire, fuckin' A," Clay barked. "I spend a year in Iraq and get in several firefights, but never get hit. Back home I get shot. What the hell?"

I told him we would get him to a hospital, just as soon as we lost the sniper. Who was shooting at us? Who knew we had found Crenshaw and where to look for us? Maybe Nicki had been right. Someone was tracking us. But who? And why?

"You didn't tell anybody where we were going?" I asked Clay.

"Shit, not even my girlfriend knows where I am. I just told her I'd be working all night," he said, wincing with the pain.

My mind flooded with questions. Had someone followed Crenshaw down here? He had called someone. Why would he use the pay phone and change rooms so abruptly? Had he known we were on our way? Or was he more afraid of someone else? If he was hiding, why had he not covered his tracks? If we could find him, anyone could.

The van was parked at least twenty-five yards away. I hadn't sprinted that far in years. If the sniper was still there, there was no way I would make it.

"You going to try to make it to the van?" Clay asked, reading my mind.

I nodded. He told me to crawl, not run. "It will be slow and you will feel stupid, but you will get there with no new holes."

Where could I find a weapon? The only thing I had was my phone. Should I call the police? If I did, I'd lose Crenshaw, and by tomorrow afternoon the *Examiner* would have his arrest in Florida on page one with no mention of the *Post* finding him.

The old man in the registration office had been watching us. He came out of the lobby and stood staring at us, his robe billowing in the wind and rain, showing off pair of pencil legs.

"What's going on out here? I'm calling the cops," he yelled. As he turned back toward the office door, a bullet crashed through the glass door. He stopped and turned to look across the highway. Then he darted into the office. In a minute he came out carrying a shotgun.

"All right, whoever you are, you better get out of here or I'll blast you to kingdom come." He pulled off a shot that echoed across the parking lot. Then the sniper hit him in the chest. I watched him stagger and fall flat on his back. He didn't move or make a sound. Blood pooled on his undershirt. He looked dead. I thought about going for his shotgun, but it was too far to run and I didn't know much about firing a shotgun. As it was, the sniper could just walk over and shoot us. We couldn't stay where we were, but we couldn't run. We were sitting ducks, I told Clay.

Clay reached down into his right boot and pulled out a small handgun. I don't know one gun from another, but it looked like one of those in the movies that women carried in their handbags and gamblers kept up their sleeve. I doubted it would shoot anything more than three feet away. My best chance was probably to point it at the sniper and hope he would fall down laughing.

"I thought we might need it. It's my girlfriend's. She keeps it in case some guy hassles her outside the club. I never thought I would want to be carrying my gun again. But I sure miss my old rifle right now."

The minutes seemed like hours. Clay's leg was bleeding bad. We needed to get someone to stop that bleeding. But nobody was coming to rescue us.

"Did I tell ever you about the time we were pinned down like this for hours just outside of Kuwait City?" Clay said.

I must have looked at him like he was crazy. "No, and I don't think right now is the time."

"My point is that sometimes it's best just to wait. Wait for help, wait for the conditions to change. That's what they preached at us in sniper school all the time, patience, learn to wait. We had to repeat that phrase over and over." Clay winched in pain, but nothing was going to keep him from telling his story.

"Hussein's boys had taken over this building. We were supposed to sneak up, take out the Iraqis and try not to hurt the civilians. It turns out that there were about thirty Kuwaiti civilians and seventeen Iraqi soldiers in this seven-story concrete building, a command headquarters with lots of computers Hussein was dismantling and trucking out of there. That's why we couldn't just use a missile to take out the whole building. We wanted to save the computers and the civilians."

I peered around the car bumper afraid I would see someone walking towards us.

"So we asked the guys back at the base to play some Arab music over the radio. Then we waited. First one of the soldiers, then two more came out to see what was happening. We took them out. Pretty soon three more came looking to see if there was a party. The odds were moving in our favor. By morning, we had killed twelve. So at dawn we took the building. We saved the civilians and the computers and didn't lose even one."

We could not wait until morning. Clay was bleeding too much. But I got the message. We needed a distraction, change the odds, which were clearly in the sniper's favor at the moment. I dialed 911 and hoped the Panama City Police Department was not too busy with the storm to answer. When the operator answered, I told her there was a robbery going on at the Shell station next to the Bayou Inn. One man had already been shot. "Tell your guys to hurry."

"What is your name, sir?" came the inevitable question.

"Clay Josephson. I'm on my cell. I'm watching this thing go down. Hurry." I disconnected.   A guy in room eleven peeked out the window, so I knocked on it. The curtain moved an inch, and I could see the top of his head. "Hey, we could use some help," I said in a loud whisper.

"What's going on out there?" he asked.

"Somebody's shooting at us. We're just lying low," I said.

"So what'd you want? I ain't getting killed for you," the voice came back.

"No, no. Do you have a gun?"

"Hell, no. And I wouldn't give it to you, if I did. I don't know who you are. I'm calling the police."

"I already did that. They're on the way. Just stay down."

I texted Nicki to get ready to move.

It took the police another four minutes to arrive, but then they came in force, sirens blaring and lights flashing. Two cars converged on the Shell station. I am not very religious, but as the saying goes: there are no atheists in a foxhole. I whispered a little prayer for protection, then jumped out into the open and ran bent over toward the van. I hoped that the sniper had been scared off, or at least was too concerned with the cops to shoot at me.

At forty three, I had given up taking the steps two at a time years ago. I could still play a couple of sets of tennis, but sprinting twenty five yards against a hurricane-force wind was out of my league. I ran as best I could, hoping not to take a bullet myself. Nothing happened for the first fifteen, the last ten seemed to take forever. I reached the van out of breath, partly from running, more from fear. If we got home again, I promised myself I would follow Nicki's advice and take up biking or running steps at the high school stadium. I opened the van door and ducked inside, no new holes in me.

Nicki's renting the Chevy van now seemed a stroke of genius. It would serve as an ambulance and a transport vehicle. Staying low in the driver's seat, I backed close to the door at an angle that gave us a little protection as I pulled Clay onto one of the bench seats. Then I yelled for Nicki to bring out Crenshaw and the woman. She had them walking under a blanket. Nicki's dark curls showed in the clear, which could make her a target if the sniper took another shot. Crenshaw and the woman moved slow, dragging their feet. He pulled off the blanket and threw it on the asphalt, giving me my first close look at the man we had been hunting for more than a week and who had occupied most of my waking moments and even invaded my nightmares. Crenshaw looked much like I expected. Now wearing a white t-shirt that said Born to Rumble, he carried most of his weight above his belt with skinny legs and little butt. He walked slew footed. On each step he kicked out his legs and large feet away from the bulk of his belly. In his right hand he carried a twelve-pack of Pabst Blue Ribbon. He spit on the pavement before he stepped into the backseat. The woman followed him. Whatever Nicki had told them, it had not scared them enough to run. She seemed to be making a career out of dragging people out of cheap motels.

I jumped in behind the wheel as Crenshaw and the woman sat on the third seat. Nicki sat blocking their escape. Crenshaw looked over at Clay on the bench seat as he held his leg and groaned. In the rear view mirror I could see a shadow of fear cross Crenshaw's features. He opened his mouth, but no words came. I turned on the car, put it in gear and stomped the accelerator as we raced out of the parking lot. Any second I expected a bullet through the window. I didn't breathe until we pulled out on the highway and sped off down the highway. Crenshaw sat back in the seat and looked around. He opened the twelve pack, pulled out a beer and twisted the top off it. The woman held out her hand, and he gave her an unopened beer. In the mirror, I could see her look of disdain at her date.

After he drank half his beer, his gaze landed on me. "You the driver for these folks?"

"Yes. I am the driver," I said, smiling inside. Clay groaned and Nicki chuckled. It was going to be a long trip back.

"That's good, boy. We'll come back for my vette later. My stuff's in the trunk, my badge and gun."

That was a relief. He was not carrying his gun, but he wanted us to know he had it and he was in law enforcement. In the side mirror, I watched the police get out of their cars at the gas station and crouch with guns drawn behind open car doors. Not far away the motel clerk's body was lying in the rain on the asphalt. I asked Nicki to call the police again and tell the operator there was a dead man lying outside the Bayou Inn.

Nicki's breathless performance was convincing. She whispered that she had just come upon this poor dead man as she tried to check in. "I'm not staying here. Dead people give me the willies," she told the operator.

Crenshaw's date coughed twice as she lit up a cigarette to go with her beer. Her hands were shaking. Crenshaw didn't offer to light her cigarette. He barely seemed to know she was still there. I wondered what she would think when she learned that her tempo-rary sex partner was a mass murderer.

"How come you care if they find that old man? I'd just let him lay there." Crenshaw smirked, trying to sound tough. Hearing his voice in the van I knew he was the same man talking to Mark on the tape. I studied him closer in the mirror. I saw a big redneck, his blond hair trimmed so short the ruddy skin showed through, which gave the impression that he was bald. His big nose and lips rose out of a reddish blonde goatee. A large wart was on the side of his nose.

"Probably no reason," I said. "But maybe it will keep the police there a while longer and keep our sniper pinned down."

Crenshaw looked straight at me, startled that I had answered his question. I realized he had expected Nicki to answer, or maybe Clay. They were white. Nicki found the address on her phone for a hospital on the highway back to the airport.

"Who do you think was shooting at you?" Nicki asked Crenshaw.

He looked startled again. I wondered if he was often surprised by life.

"I don't know. What do you mean?" he said.

"Who wants you dead?" I said.

He didn't answer, ignoring me as if I did not exist.

Clay groaned loudly every time the van hit a bump. I told him we were getting close to the hospital.

"Right, boss," he said.

I smiled as I saw Crenshaw look puzzled at Clay calling me boss. I wanted to wait until we had him on the airplane headed home before I told him that he had been captured by a black man.

Nicki repeated my question. "Who do you think was out there on the beach in the dark shooting at you?"

"Me? I thought somebody was shooting at you guys, not me." He knew better, and it troubled him. But he did not want us to know. Not much of an actor, but lots of bravado.

"Right, Lonnie," Nicki said, dripping with sarcasm. They had progressed to a first-name basis.

Nicki said later that she had explained to Crenshaw in the motel room who we were and why we had been searching for him. He did not seem surprised that somebody had come looking for him. Instead of running away from us, he seemed resigned to being with us. Maybe he was even a bit pleased.

"Y'all with the newspaper, right?" he asked.

Nicki said yes, but didn't elaborate.

"So what do y'all want with old Lonnie?" he said referring to himself in the third person.

No one answered as we pulled into the emergency room at the Baptist Hospital. I found a gurney, and with the rain and wind getting harder I helped Clay on it. He was fading out as he lay back on the gurney and only grunted. I told him that he would see tapes of the interviews with Crenshaw when he got home. He just smiled weakly and waved. I whispered in his ear, asking him to try to be a bit vague for a few hours, just to give us time to get Crenshaw back to Iron City.

"No worries. Soon I won't even remember my name," he said.

Crenshaw sat in the car, making no attempt to leave. He finished off another beer and stared out the window. His date whined and sobbed, her body shook. A thin woman in her late twenties, she had a raw sex appeal. With long stringy, limp hair and pasty white skin, the closer you looked, the less attractive she was. As the old song goes, "Nice legs, shame about the face." When Crenshaw said nothing to quiet her, Nicki barked at her. The woman shut up and sulked.

At the airport, the winds were strengthening as the outer bands of the storm came on shore. The pilot, awakened from his slumbers on an uncomfortable cot in the basement of the tower, refused to take off. Nicki took him aside and handed him another five hundred-dollars from a money belt she wore under her sweater. Still bitching about the weather and crazy gamblers, he told us to get on board. At least we would have a strong tailwind going home. I paid the lone taxi sitting in front of the terminal to take Crenshaw's girlfriend back where she came from. The rental car office was closed, so I left the van in the lot and pushed the keys through a mail lot. Then we took off, taking the church bomber who headed the FBI's Most Wanted List across the Alabama state line.

Crenshaw looked out the window of the plane, saying nothing. He seemed detached from his surroundings. He leaned over only once to ask how he was going to get "my sweet vette," clearly the most important thing in his life. Nicki said it would be delivered. What she didn't say was that the FBI would impound it in a couple of days. I doubted he would need a car again.

Crenshaw dozed during the flight, his head against the head rest of his seat, drooling across a thick lower lip. The little plane bounced all over the sky, but didn't disturb our sleeping beauty. The pilot swore quietly as he held tightly to the controls. My knuckles turned white as I squeezed the arms on the seat. All I could think of was how many people had gone down in small planes in storms like this. My grandfather had told me about Ryan deGraffenried, who would have been governor, instead of George Wallace's wife, had he not gone down in a small plane like this. Alabama politics, my grandfather said, would have been very different if that plane had not gone down. I hoped we would be on the front page of the *Post* for bringing Crenshaw to justice, not because we crashed in south Alabama.

Landing at the air park shook Crenshaw awake. He got his head together as we taxied to the small terminal. Nicki walked him to my car, while I thanked the pilot and told him he was brave and that he had helped solve the church bombing. He looked at me like I was crazy, one minute we were fanatical gamblers, the next crime fighters. I apologized for lying to him, but told him it was in his own best interests. If he got a visit from the FBI, I told him to tell the agents what happened and refer them to me. I gave him my card. He looked at the printing on the small sliver of white paper with the logo of the *Iron City Post* on it and shook his head in disbelief. "This on the up and up?"

I just smiled at him and told him to watch the *Post* over the next couple of days. He would have a great story to tell.

Crenshaw in the backseat of my car sat next to Nicki. When I started the car, he asked again, "Say, what is it you want with me?" He probably did not really expect an answer. His question was more an expression of his anxiety at heading back to Iron City. But I gave him one. I told him we wanted to interview him. He stared at me and didn't answer. "Why? What have I done?" Crenshaw asked, hoping to bluff his way through.

"You placed the bomb in the Sixteenth Street Baptist Church," I said.

"No, no, not me. You've got the wrong man," he protested.

Fear rose in his wide face, the blood vessels came closer to the skin, making his ruddy face even redder. But his belligerence cracked. He turned quickly and looked out the window, tuning us out. I worried that he might be hard to handle if he ran. Nicki could probably take him, but I didn't want to take the chance.

As we drove north toward downtown Iron City, I concentrated on driving through the rain that pelted the car, trying to crowd out the worries about how the next hours would go. I pulled a recorder out of my briefcase and handed it back to Nicki. She punched the play button and laid it in his lap. It was cued up at the point of his conversation with Mark where he bragged about setting the bomb. He stared at the small recorder as if it was a box of snakes. His recorded voice filled the car. He listened to himself talking with Mark for several minutes. Then he just hung his head and said, "Son of a bitch." I wasn't sure if that was a general commentary on things, or if he meant Mark or us.

As we drove up the mountain, he looked at Nicki and said, "They promised me, you know. They said nothing would ever get written up about me in the newspaper. They will tell you that. I don't want no story about me, you hear?"

"Who were they? Who put you up to this?" I asked.

He sat back and stared out the window. Dawn broke as we drove over the mountain and headed north into downtown, but it was hard to tell through the thickening cloud cover. The car passed through the massive cut the men and machines had made in the mountain for the highway. Water spewed out through cracks in the exposed stone, making our ride seem more like a water park ride. Heading down from the mountain with the city skyline hidden in the clouds, I had an ominous feeling. What could go wrong now that we had Crenshaw? It wouldn't take much to upset this apple cart.

Nicki checked us into a two-bedroom suite at the Tutwiler Hotel, then called Stan, the tough-looking, muscular young man I had seen going into the Downtowner motel room. "He'd be good if there's a fight," she whispered.

I sat thinking about what Crenshaw had said. Was he talking about Daniels? Even Daniels could not promise that no story would be written about him. It was too big a story. The national media would break it if the *Examiner* didn't. And then there was the *Post*, the thorn in Daniels' side. He might control us in some ways, but not in what we printed. But Crenshaw didn't know that.

Stan arrived and sat in the living room of the suite while Crenshaw downed a shot and another beer from the mini-bar, then announced he was taking a nap. He went off to sleep in one of the bedrooms.

I called my mother-in-law to check on Chris and tell her I wouldn't be home this morning. Calling Ed could wait until he came in to work. Stan took a seat in a chair near the door and turned on the television, while Nicki and I adjourned to the bedroom. We were so tired, but the day's excitement fueled our desire. Finding Crenshaw, being shot at, anticipating a story that would expose who was responsible for the church bombing turned on all my juices. We made love hard and fast. Nicki liked me deep inside her, her strong legs wrapped tightly around my hips. She whispered in my ear, "faster," and then suddenly she arched her back and exploded.

That was too much for me. I came quickly. Longer than an eight-second rodeo ride, but shorter than our usual encounter, it left us breathing hard. We laid side by side, touching each other. I loved to caress her skin and nibble on her breasts. I leaned over to kiss her, when she asked, "Isn't there anything you would like to say to me?"

"You're wonderful," I mumbled.

"Yes. And so are you. Isn't there anything else you'd like to tell me?"

"Yeah, you done good today," I said, thinking she might laugh at my attempt to sound like Sylvester Stallone in *Rocky*.

My Philly girl didn't think I was funny.

"Anything else?" she said quietly.

"Get some sleep. Crenshaw's going to be a handful."

I had fallen in love with this tough-on-the-outside, soft-on-the-inside, rich Italian girl. I wanted to be with her forever, but worried that I might be only a passing fancy for her, like her motorbike trip across country and rebellion against her parents' expectations. I might be her dalliance with a black lover she would talk about one day over a latte with her Philadelphia girl friends.

I wanted to tell her I loved her, but that was risky and complicated. I thought I needed to prepare Chris and my in-laws. I had to get used to the idea myself. If I told her I loved her, she might laugh. And then there was no going back. I hoped she understood.

Nicki lay there in the early morning. Her eyes were closed, and she didn't say anything else. I don't think she fell asleep.

12

We started the interview at noon. Crenshaw had slept five hours. While he slept, I called the office and told Ed we had him.

"No shit. You need help? Do you want me to send someone?"

Any skepticism Ed had about the story vanished. I told him about Clay being shot and asked him to check on him, get the hospital bill paid and bring him home as soon as the storm and his leg allowed. I asked him to call his girlfriend so she would not hear from someone else that he had been shot. And I told Ed that I would send a messenger with the car keys I had taken from Clay's pocket and to send a couple of people to bring his car from the air park to the newspaper before the FBI or anyone else decided to impound it.

Crenshaw was totally uncooperative until we fed him coffee and a late breakfast, a double order of eggs, sausage, heavily buttered grits and toast. While he downed the food, Nicki set up two tape recording machines and a video camera that had come with Stan.

The large constable sat in one of the Tutwiler's well-stuffed chairs eating and sulking. The big man with the stupid-looking t-shirt grew surlier by the moment, but was only passively resistant. Stan hung out near the door to the hallway ready to stop Crenshaw from leaving, though legally he could go any time he wanted. I just hoped we could get more out of him about the bombing before he tried to bolt.

Crenshaw looked at the recorders, then at me sitting across from him with a pen and pad of paper. He shook his head and barked, "Uh uh. Ain't no way I'm talking about anything to no damned nigger driver."

We stared at one another, me smiling, him scowling. My heart beat fast. This was a moment I had anticipated since we found him at the motel. How I played it would determine if we got the full story of the church bombing.

"Lonnie, I guess it is time to be formally introduced. I am Joe Riordan, editor of the *Iron City Post*. I am the one who found you with the help of my friends and people who work for me. We have been looking for you. Now we are here." I stopped to let that all sink in. "You might as well tell us your side of the story."

He sighed and frowned at me. "I know 'bout you. I heard there was some Nee-gro working for Mr. Daniels down at the newspaper. You do what he tells you, right?"

I wanted to scream "Hell no," but for once I managed to bury my pride and just nodded.

"Good," he said.

Nicki reached over and patted my arm. She knew how much it took out of me not to tell Crenshaw the truth. He watched her and smiled.

"I bet you think you are something, you fucking this white girl?" He whooped loudly and gyrated his pelvis at us.

Neither of us responded.

"Tell me, honey, is it true what they say, once you go black, you never go back? Maybe you and I could have a nice romp. I bet I could change your mind. Or is his dick that much bigger'n the white guys you had?"

Nicki stood up. I was afraid she was going deck Crenshaw. Instead she walked toward the door, leaned down and whispered something to Stan. They both laughed. I could guess what she said.

Crenshaw could too. She had shamed him. His face turned a dark shade of red and slumped back in the chair. "Yankee bitch. Who'd want her after she been with a nigger anyway?"

He wouldn't look at me when he said it. He stared at his right hand for a few minutes.

"You ready?" I asked.

"What the fuck? Get this over. I got things to do."

I turned on the recorders. Nicki came across the room to focus the video camera on him. Crenshaw watched us. Reality seemed to dawn on him.

"At least everybody'll know it was me, Lonnie Crenshaw, who done blowed up that church. That's worth going to jail for, ain't it?" He tried to smile, but fear twisted his fat lips. He leaned forward and picked up the cigar he had ordered with his room service and lit it. He leaned back in the chair and smiled, a last act of rebellion, lighting up a cigar in a non-smoking hotel room.

"Is this your voice on the tape?" I asked him and replayed part of the tape of his conversation with Mark.

"Yep, that's me." A bit of swagger in his voice now. "I was in the Aces Wild shooting off my mouth. Some guy started buying me drinks. What'd he have a wire on him or something? He working for the FBI?"

"No. Mark was a reporter, one of the best."

I watched Lonnie's face. He did not know about Mark's death. He had used the present tense. There was no point in telling him now. It might scare him.

"Would you mind filling in some details?" I played him the tape. He was like a child listening to his own voice. He laughed at some of his comments or sat smiling as the tape played. "I was getting pretty loaded there, wasn't I?" I stopped the tape in several places to clarify some points. Each time the recording was running, he nodded in agreement with what he had said to Mark.

I then started at the beginning, asking him details that Mark couldn't, about his childhood in a small town in south Alabama, his high school years, which he didn't finish, and a three-year stint with the Army National Guard. He talked at length about how he had been assigned to a demolition unit at Fort Leavenwood and learned how to shape and detonate C-4 to blow up roadside bombs and other enemy targets. That training had earned him a ticket to Afghanistan. After the Army, he and a couple of guys came to Iron City for a weekend of partying during the Alabama-Auburn football game weekend. They didn't have tickets and watched the game in a bar. They just came to party.

"We went and looked at Vulcan up there on the mountain. I'd never seen anything like that. And the women, drunk and ready to do whatever, wow. I never wanted to go home."

He went through several jobs after moving to Iron City and worked his way into the sheriff's reelection campaign. "I like Sheriff Peebles. He's my kinda folks, well, most of the time anyhow."

His reward for helping the sheriff was being elected as a constable, beating the incumbent constable after he had proved disloyal to the sheriff. "Easy job, mostly. Not much money, but enough for some stuff like my sweet 'vette. You 'member you gonna git her back up here, right?" He paused until I assured him again we would take care of the car.

"The sheriff keeps saying if I do well, he'll get me something better to do. Maybe now he'll know how good I am."

He sat back and smiled, showing a mouthful of yellowed and broken teeth. He leaned over, picked up a glass and spit in it. We went through the steps of placing the bomb in the church, how he posed as an air conditioning repair man. From "some ol' boy down in Dothan, a right-thinking guy," he said he had bought the explosives, the detonator and a timing fuse long enough to delay the explosion for several hours. He said he didn't ask, didn't want to know where this right-thinking friend got the explosives. "Probably from some guy at Fort Rucker," he said. "I guess the FBI got to him. That's too bad."

He said he brought the explosives back to Iron City and put it in the church basement. He placed it on top of a metal beam, attached the fuse to go off after seven that night. He added that he had sat in his car waiting until the bomb went off.

"It was great, really sweet. You should've seen it."

We walked him through more details. How he got in and out of the church? Did he know there were no cameras at the church? By mid-afternoon, we were running out of steam. Crenshaw ate a late lunch that included a steak and French fries. He drank two more beers from the mini-bar. I thought it might be the last good meal he would have. Nicki nibbled at a salad. Stan and I had sandwiches. It was time to wrap it up. We had stories to write.

I put off until after he ate asking the question of who else was involved and who had paid him to do the bombing. From Mark's tape I was sure those questions would scare him. "A couple more things before we finish," I said as Crenshaw finished stuffing the last fry in his mouth. "You've told us how you planted the bomb and your reasons for doing it. So who paid you, who thought up the bombing?"

Crenshaw, relaxed and even enjoying the interview, was instantly wary. Over the next few days I replayed this portion of the videotape several times. He looked back over his shoulder unconsciously as if someone might be standing there.

"Somebody put you up to this."

"Nope, nobody. I did it all myself. Nobody helped me."

"Did anyone pay you?"

"No, well, yeah, I guess, some guy gave me some money to get out of town. But that was all," he said.

"How much did he pay you for bombing the church?" I asked.

He hesitated, staring down at his hands in his lap. "Aw, shit. What do I care if you know? It wasn't enough, I'll tell you that. Two thousand dollars, that's what I got paid. Should have got more."

Nicki asked if he had spent it. He nodded.

"That's why you started using your credit cards in Florida?" she said.

Again, he nodded. "I figured I'd come back here and get some more money after I had some fun."

We sat saying nothing for a few heartbeats. Then I asked the big question.

"Who? Who paid you?" I asked.

"Don't remember. Just some guy."

"You don't remember who paid you two thousand dollars?" I asked sarcastically.

He shrugged.

"On the tape, you told Mark that he was some powerful guy. Is he the one who's got you scared?"

"Nawh, what you talkin' about scared? Not me. I'm cool, cool as a watermelon. You know 'bout watermelons, don't ya boy."

Nicki decided to try to get him to talk. "Lonnie, come on, tell the truth, who was the guy who gave you the money?"

"Don't know," he lied.

"He'd probably want everyone to know he helped you, as famous as you are going to be," she said, smiling at him, leaning close to him, making it a personal request.

Crenshaw smiled at her. "You ain't gonna get me to talk about that. It will get me killed, that's for sure."

Nicki and I looked at each other frustrated that Crenshaw was stonewalling. I decided to try another approach. Getting Crenshaw was great, but I wasn't going to be satisfied until we could nail the guys behind the bombing too. I didn't think the community would be happy with just this redneck.

"What about the Jackson Group? Those people tell you to plant this bomb?" I asked.

"What? What's the Jacksons, what'd you call them? That guy asked me about the Jacksons. I don't know nothin' about that."

"You know, you mentioned the Jackson Group at the Aces Up."

"Shit," he said, looking down at the plush plum-colored carpeting. "You know how it is. You get in a bar and start drinkin' and talkin'. You say shit that you shouldn't. Sure, I know about some of them. The sheriff told 'em about me. I picked up some checks from a couple of those guys for the campaign. But no, this was my gig, you know. Nobody else."

He sat back in his chair and folded his arms across his chest.

"Tell, me, Crenshaw. You know Mr. Daniels, right?" I asked.

He nodded. Then he held out his right hand and waggled it.

"What does that mean?" I asked.

"Well, I talked to him one time when he was meeting with the sheriff. I know he is a good guy, thinks right. And some of his friends, well they're my friends." He sat looking at me for a minute. "But y'all know that. Y'all are with the newspaper, right? Not the FBI or somethin'?" he said.

"Yes, I'm the editor of the *Post*."

"So you work for Mr. Daniels, right?" Crenshaw said.

"Well, not exactly. He's the owner and publisher of the *Examiner*. We're with the *Post*," I said.

Crenshaw looked puzzled.

"But they're the same thing, ain't they?" he said, growing concerned.

"We work in the same building. Lots of people get confused. But we are a separate newspaper."

"Shit. I thought y'all was the same." He jumped up and started for the door. Crenshaw was a big guy, but he realized he would have to go through Stan. He sat back down, any semblance of his macho style gone.

I got the last beer out of the minibar and handed it to him. I let him sip it for a few minutes, then asked him again who paid him to bomb the church.

"Nobody," he said. He now seemed even more frightened.

"Then why did someone try to kill you down in Florida?" I said.

"I don't know. Why do you keep asking me these things? Hey, blackie, I'm through talkin' to you. You all can go to hell and say hello to your ol' buddy, Commissioner Grey."

He chuckled, enjoying his own attempt at a joke. We sat for a while, letting the tapes turn. I wanted Crenshaw to think about his answer. He had gone from sprawled in the chair to sitting up and shifting in his chair every few seconds. He was scared, maybe too scared to talk.

"Lonnie, when you were staying over at the Pelican in Florida, why did you call the newspaper?" Nicki asked.

"I didn't call the newspaper. Why would I do that?" he said.

"We have the phone log from your room, and it shows you called the *Examiner* switchboard." She held out the printout of his room bill.

"Maybe I was calling for you, babe, you know," he said, his words laced with sarcasm.

He sat thinking about it for a while. The wheels turned slowly. "Oh, yeah, okay. I may have made one call. It was to some guy who called me after the FBI put out that drawing of what was supposed to look like me. I saw it on the TV. I wanted to know what the FBI was saying. He told me to lay low. I checked out and headed up the strip. Then I tied in with Cheryl Lynn. I thought I'd better let things cool down. That drawing wasn't too good. It didn't look much like me, or nothing. After I got it on with her, well I was thinking things might be all right. I was kinda relaxing when you guys showed up."

I handed Nicki a file folder with the photos of members of the Jackson Group and asked her to put them on the coffee table in front of Crenshaw. He was looking out the window and smoking the cigar. She laid each one out, and I asked him if he knew any of them. He looked down and studied each one. The tension built in him suddenly. His neck arched and he looked away.

"Do you recognize one of these men?" I asked.

"Sure. I told you I got checks from some of them for the sheriff."

"Are any of them the man who paid you to bomb the church?"

He shook his head. "No. He ain't there."

"Who are you afraid of?" I asked.

He slumped in the chair and took a long drag off the cigar. He was through talking. I thought I knew which of the photos he was looking at when he tensed. I picked it up along with the other photos and shuffled them, looking at each one. Then I turned the one I suspected around and held it in front of him. He glanced quickly away.

"He's the one, isn't he?" I almost shouted.

Crenshaw said. "I told you I'm through talking. You can't make me. You ain't the cops. I know my rights. I'm a constable. I work for Sheriff Peebles."

I turned the photo around and looked at the enlarged face looking back at me. It was a photo of a smiling Harden Braddock, Daniels' good friend.

At six o'clock, well fed and a bit buzzed from the beers and a couple of shots, Crenshaw sat in the backseat of my car. Stan sat with him, Nicki in the front, with both watching him as I drove the four blocks to the newspaper. It was getting dark, and we had him in Stan's hat and raincoat as a disguise. It was all we had to work with. Somebody might still try to kill him.

Looking back on it, we should have kept him at the hotel. Was it my ego that wanted him at the newspaper? Did I want to show him off in front of the staff? Did I want him in the newspaper to show off for the FBI? Or did I just want to rub it in the *Examiner*'s face? I would have to live with my decision. I told myself that bringing him to the newspaper might break him down and get him to talk about who paid him. And I thought the staff should share in the glory. They deserved to see the bomber arrested.

We climbed the steps to the side door of the building. The entrance, reserved for employees, faced onto Fourth Street. Crenshaw walked in front with Nicki holding his arm. Stan and I came behind.

A few steps from the door, I heard Nicki cry out. She fell forward on the concrete steps. Crenshaw turned to look down at her. This time I moved faster. I opened the door and shoved Crenshaw through it just as a second bullet bounced off the shatter-proof glass window in the door. Nicki was face down. I knelt on the third step beside her. Blood flowed, staining her shirt and puddling on the concrete. Panic bubbled up in my throat. I was afraid to move her, but I wanted her out of the way in case the sniper fired again. Stan and I knelt over her, shielding her body, while he called the police and told the operator to send a patrol car and an ambulance.

Two guards stood just inside the door, frightened and puzzled by what they saw, Nicki lying a few feet outside unconscious and bleeding. I stood up, opened the door and pulled out the younger guard, the beefier of the two, to add to the human shield over her. He was too frightened to object. He might have refused to stand there had he thought I wouldn't fire him. I hoped no one would tell him I did not have that authority.

"You're gonna git me killed," Crenshaw shouted from behind the other guard. "They want me dead, thanks to you. I was all right, yeah, fine, had me a nice little piece of ass down there in Florida, my vette, all settled to wait out the big blow. What do you do, Negro, you and your Yankee bitch come down and snatch me up and bring me back here, for what? So they can kill me?"

I phoned Ed, who was sitting in for Clay on the city desk, and told him to come down and get Crenshaw and keep him safe in the newsroom. I wasn't in a mood to listen to his redneck rants, and I was no position to stop him from running. It was three hours before the deadline for the first city edition. I needed to get Nicki to a hospital. And then I had to get back to help write the story and turn Crenshaw over to Pitts.

Ed arrived at the door, breathing hard from his dash on his bad knee down the stairs. "Here are the discs of the interview," I said, handing him the innocuous looking pieces of plastic that held so much. "Everything on Mark's tape is true. Have Pat and Rachel start on the main story. I'll write a sidebar and fill in some holes when I get back. And Ed," I whispered, "don't let Crenshaw out of your sight. This is Stan. He is working with us, he can help watch him. Crenshaw's scared. He may try to run."

"No, shit," Ed was looking back and forth between Crenshaw slouched against the wall next to the elevator and at Nicki lying face down on the steps. I tapped Stan on the shoulder and told him to go with Crenshaw. The large young guard stayed in place shielding Nicki. I handed Stan Nicki's car keys I took from her purse and told him where the car was. He nodded, stood up and walked through the door behind Ed and Crenshaw.

A police car pulled into the parking lot at the side of the building. The officers knelt behind their doors as they scanned the tops of the buildings and parking lot across the street for signs of the sniper. He might be on the roof of the Chinese restaurant or by one of the cars across the street, or at least that is where he had been. The arrival of the police may have scared him just like it must have in Florida. I knelt again beside Nicki and felt for a pulse. My heart slowed its pounding when I felt a strong beat. She couldn't die. I couldn't go through losing someone else I loved.

The bullet looked like it had hit her in the upper back, below her shoulder. I put my face down on the concrete step to look under her. Blood flowed from the shoulder and pooled below her. The blood had to be stopped. I rolled her over slowly, taking a chance in moving her, and pulled my jacket off and pressed it against the exit wound.

One of the policemen came up beside me. "How is she?" he asked, crouched as low as possible, still looking up for the sniper.

"Alive, barely. Where is that ambulance, damn it?"

The policeman spoke into the radio and listened for the response. "It's on its way," he said. And true to his word, the ambulance pulled into the driveway and stopped, lights flashing, a few feet away from the steps. Thank God there was no riot somewhere in town that tied up every ambulance. The paramedics took over from my feeble efforts to stop her bleeding. In seconds Nicki was being rolled into the back of the ambulance. She was still out. As I rode to the emergency room at University Hospital, I thought about how important she had become. I knew I should have told her I loved her. I am a jerk.

It was hard to stand in the hallway outside the University Hospital operating room, knowing the doctors were inside the locked double doors stopping the bleeding and extracting the bullet. She had looked so small being rolled into the operating room. I told myself she was strong, maybe the strongest person I knew. I tried to convince myself she would pull through. This was not like the cancer that racked Sheila's body. The bullet hadn't hit a vital organ. The worry was the blood loss, possible infection, maybe some nerve damage. I prayed she would live.

After two hours of surgery, she was moved to a recovery room, where I was still on the outside of the glass looking in. I wanted to hold her hand and tell her everything was going to be right again. Stan brought her boss, who stood on his sticks and looked at her through the glass.

"She's going to be pissed when she wakes up," he said as he turned and shuffled away.

I nodded and said a silent prayer that she would forgive me.

13

Pat and Rachel, with Ed hovering over them, wrote the first draft of the main story. Crenshaw, his mood improved with the attention from Rachel and safe from bullets flying by his head, answered more questions as they wrote the article. Rachel said later that he seemed to be just an overgrown kid, if you didn't think about what he had done. He seemed to feel no guilt, no remorse, she said.

When I walked in from the hospital, they showed me the first draft. It was straight police reporting, Pat's forte.

"Feature it up a bit. Put in some color, more background. Let's dazzle our readers with our writing," I said.

They went back to the computer, both claiming they had wanted to write the article that way in the first place. I sat down at a nearby desk to write some description and perspective, paragraphs we could insert. And I wrote a sidebar about the trip to Florida. I wanted to make sure that Clay, Nicki and Mark were included.

Weitzman, at home in McLean, Virginia, told me to email the stories to him and to the lawyers. The attorneys to my surprise got into the spirit and made only a few suggestions for changes. One attorney was even complimentary.

By eleven the first city edition rolled off the presses and moved to the loading docks. The stories had gone through a lot of editing.

We had redesigned the front page twice to position the stories and the banner headlines.

I dialed the FBI office and asked for Harrison Pitts. I left my name with the agent on duty and told him we had a man who had confessed to the bombing if Pitts wanted to come collect him. In only a couple of minutes Pitts called back to see if it was another of the many nuts who confess to major crimes. I assured him it was no hoax.

"So you did have something the other day," he said.

"You want to come get him, or not?"

"Well, sometime we can discuss the concept of obstruction of justice. But for now, I'll let you have your glory and I'll get my bomber." Pitts was angry.

Wright and Pitts, working with the professional spin masters in Washington, would put the best face on the arrest of Crenshaw. I felt sure they would come out of this as heroes. It had taken less than two months to arrest the church bomber this time, not decades it took to arrest the bombers the first time. They arrived with Iron City Police Chief Billy Bates in less than twenty minutes. In tow was a gaggle of FBI agents and detectives in suits and a few cops in uniform. One the cops knew Crenshaw and looked shocked. They took Crenshaw into my office, read him his rights in a solemn and slow rendition of the Miranda code. Crenshaw recoiled at the sight of Pitts. He yelled that he did not want "no nigger" to arrest him. Pointing at me, he screamed, "I've had to put up with this darkie all day. Give me a break. Do y'all have a white man I can talk to."

Our photographer captured him screaming and pointing at Pitts. It was a classic photo that would run in newspapers across the country.

I gave a copy of our recorded interview with Crenshaw to Pitts. I also handed him a copy of the tape of Mark's interview with Crenshaw. Pitts just glared at me. Wright hardly spoke. Bates, I think, was just glad it was over.

"I'm glad our photo helped you identify the bomber," Pitts said loudly.

The newspaper with the "bomber's" photo on it lay on top of my desk. If anyone could find Crenshaw in that photo, it would be a miracle. I wondered not for the first time if Crenshaw's "right-thinking friend" who sold him the C-4 had deliberately given the FBI bad information. He certainly had not told them his name. But I kept my mouth shut.

Pitts handed Crenshaw off to an agent and turned to me as we walked out into the newsroom. He growled, "You've got some explaining to do about Florida. Do you understand me?"

I started to say something about being a sore loser, but thought better of it. "You and your friends left a dead body down there along with your editor with a bullet in his leg. And there is a little matter of possible kidnapping of this gentleman and crossing state lines.?"

"There was no kidnapping. Crenshaw came willingly. And we didn't shoot anyone. We were shot at," I said.

"Yeah, well, we were just a step behind you. Our guys were waiting in Biloxi for you. We didn't figure out your move in time to get them to Panama City. You outfoxed us with that changed flight plan. That may be a violation of FAA rules that we might have to look into."

Pitts fumed. I smiled. He leaned closer to me, whispered his words through tight lips. "If we had been a little faster, we might have been there to arrest Crenshaw and get that shooter. Think about that, Joe. And who was that woman that got shot outside. Isn't that your girlfriend? She might not be in the hospital right now if you had worked with us."

Pitts had a full head of steam up, frustrated that we had beat him.

I learned later that Pitts had dispatched four agents in two cars from the Mobile bureau to follow us west into Mississippi, the wrong direction. He tried to fly down himself, but the FAA told the FBI pilots not to take off with the storm approaching. The

202

agents were running around the Mississippi Gulf Coast looking for us when they were tipped off by the flurry of police activity at the Shell station and the Bayou Inn. The Panama City police, alerted by the hospital staff about Clay and his gunshot wound, called the FBI. They chased after us to the airport, but we were already in Iron City.

FBI agents in Iron City, including Pitts himself, had staked out the entrances to the *Post* until mid afternoon. We arrived with Crenshaw after they gave up on the surveillance. I could never bring myself to tease Pitts about being so close. He was right that Nicki and Clay might not have been shot if I had allowed the FBI to arrest Crenshaw.

"Girlfriend?" a shocked Rachel said staring at me. I just shook my head and walked away. It wasn't the time to talk about it.

The television cameras, alerted by Pitts' public relations operation, waited outside the building. It was too late for ten o'clock television news, but not too late for the overnight national cable television news networks or the early morning national television news. The crews filmed Crenshaw being put into the back of a police car. By morning it would be the lead story across the country. Wright answered questions, but kept it brief. He promised a detailed news conference Saturday once the FBI and Iron City police had interviewed Crenshaw.

"I'm sure he's not thinking about the Sunday TV news programs, is he?" the ever-cynical Ed joked.

By holding the press conference on Saturday, Wright would follow the breaking news stories on the morning television shows on Saturday with front page stories in the Sunday newspapers. In the Byzantine world of Washington politics, all that really matters is what runs in the Sunday *Washington Post* and *New York Times* and on the major television network news shows. The public affairs staff would work overnight to position the Justice Department to take credit for solving the bombing. Wright would fly to New York to be on the Sunday news talk shows.

The television guys came in the building to interview me or someone on the team who captured Crenshaw. They filmed in the newsroom, put a microphone in the face of anyone they could while I called Weitzman to see how high a profile he wanted us to take. For a guy who rarely got excited about stories, he was ecstatic and told me to milk it for all it was worth. I did the interview in the newsroom with the *Post*'s logo behind my head. I gave a statement, outlining the barest of essentials and bragging on our reporters and on Mark. Asked by a reporter if Crenshaw had confessed, I said, "Yes. He is the bomber."

"Are you saying you caught him?" said a pretty television reporter.

"The *Iron City Post* caught the church bomber," I said.

The questions came in waves. "How did you find the bomber?" "Did this guy Crenshaw act alone?" "Is Crenshaw a member of the Klan?" "Was he trying to kill Commissioner Grey or just blow up the church?"

I answered their questions, giving Mark credit for identifying Crenshaw. I deferred on the question of whether it was a conspiracy by the Klan or anyone else. I told the cameras and notebooks that the target was Grey. The other deaths appeared to be collateral damage. There were more questions about Crenshaw's motive for killing Grey.

"You can ask the Justice Department and FBI what they think, but from our interviews Crenshaw killed Grey because of his role as a black political leader," I said.

Thirty minutes later they wound down, packed up and left the newsroom. I was tired and my thoughts were on Nicki. But we were the news. Maybe we would sell a lot more papers. As I walked away, I couldn't help but smile. A reporter from the *Examiner* had been in the crowd taking notes.

As I turned the corner to push the button for the elevator, Robert Daniels stood in my path. It was unusual for him to be at the *Examiner* late on a Friday night. He was dressed in a tuxedo that fit him perfectly.

"Quite a show," he said, waving his arm toward the reporters who had just caught the elevator. "I hear you brought in the bomber. Congratulations."

I nodded, accepting the kudos, but I was wary. "It was a team effort. My city editor was shot. And a private detective was shot right out here."

Daniels looked calm. "I heard. I'm sorry. I hope they will both be all right." He turned to walk off, but turned back and said, "Again, my congratulations. It should be good for circulation." He smiled broadly, showing perfect teeth, at the irony of our situation. The *Post* breaks a great story and sells a lot more papers. The *Examiner* makes more money.

"You didn't ask me who the bomber was. Did you already know?" I asked.

He paused and stared at me. "One of my reporters told me he is some constable, one of Sheriff Peebles' men, is that right?"

"Yes, a guy named Lonnie Crenshaw. Ever meet him?" I asked.

He shook his head. "No. I don't think so. I don't meet many constables, or at least I try not to." He smiled again and turned to walk away.

The final edition of the *Post* for Saturday morning readers carried six stories on Crenshaw, his capture and arrest. The main story detailed who had bombed the church, how and why it was done.

The headline ran in large type across the front page.

CHURCH BOMBER ARRESTED

The months-long search for the person who bombed the historic 16th Street Baptist Church in downtown Iron City came to an end Friday with the arrest of a county constable who harbored deep animosity toward African Americans.

Lonnie Crenshaw, a constable who reports to Sheriff Ned Peebles, has confessed to the Iron City Post that he placed a bomb in the church on September 15, killing County Commissioner Samuel Grey, the Reverend James Smallwood and 10 members of the church's congregation.

The bombing occurred during the 50th anniversary celebration of the first bombing of the church that killed four teenage girls. It set off weeks of violent rioting in the streets of Iron City, causing many deaths and injury and extensive property damage throughout the city.

Crenshaw, who was identified through an investigation by the Post, was turned over to the FBI and Iron City Police Department Friday night after being returned to Iron City from north Florida. The FBI took Crenshaw into custody. Where he would be held was not disclosed.

Before his arrest, Crenshaw was shot at twice by an unidentified sniper. Among those injured in the shootings was Clay Johnson, the city editor for the Post.

In an exclusive interview with the Post, Crenshaw confessed that he placed C-4 explosive in the basement of the church prior to the Wednesday night service. The FBI had earlier discovered that the explosives were purchased in Dothan. Crenshaw was trained to detonate explosives by the Army National Guard and served in the war in Afghanistan.

Crenshaw said his motive for bombing the church was to "kill that (African American) commissioner because he was getting too big for his britches." He told the Post that he wanted to "send all those (African Americans) a message about who is in charge in America."

Sheriff Peebles was out of the county and could not be reached for comment on his relationship with Crenshaw. Deputy Assistant Sheriff Linus Martin would confirm only that Crenshaw is a constable and is currently on vacation.

After an extensive investigation, Crenshaw was found by the Post in a motel near Panama City, Fl. He had been staying at the Pelican Seaside Hotel and Resort, but moved

Thursday to the Bayou Inn Motel after the FBI released a sketch of the bomber. He returned voluntarily by private airplane to Iron City with Post editor Joe Riordan III.

In two separate incidents an unidentified person shot at Crenshaw, but in neither attempt was Crenshaw hit. The first attempt was made Thursday night at the Bayou Inn in Florida. Johnson was shot in the leg during the shooting. He is being treated in a Florida hospital.

On Friday afternoon, a sniper again tried to kill Crenshaw outside the Post/Examiner building as Riordan was escorting Crenshaw into the building. Private detective Nicki Fabrini, who assisted in capturing Crenshaw, was shot in the shoulder.

Despite the two apparent attempts on his life, Crenshaw claimed that he does not know who is trying to kill him. He declined to identify any others involved in the bombing, including someone who paid him $2,000 to help him "get out of town."

Crenshaw was taken into custody by Harrison Pitts, chief of the FBI Iron City office. Assisting in the arrest was Iron City Police Chief Billy Bates. Crenshaw strenuously objected to being arrested by Pitts, who is African American.

"I really don't know what all the fuss is about," Crenshaw told the Post. "It was just a bunch of (African Americans) I killed."

Crenshaw, a native of Demiola, a town on the Alabama-Florida border, expressed pride in his ability to "blow things up." He said the bombing of the church was "not a real tough job."

The Post began to track Crenshaw as the result of a taped conversation he had with Mark Hodges, a freelance reporter and former staff writer with the Post, in the Aces Wild bar. Prior to his death in a traffic accident, Hodges gave a copy of the recorded interview with Crenshaw to the Post.

The article continued, quoting Crenshaw extensively from our videotaped interview and the audiotape Mark made.

A second article gave a chronology of events since the bombing of the church. Rachel put together a question-and-answer interview with Crenshaw that gave our readers another chance to read in his own words why he killed Grey and blew up the church. My sidebar gave an account of the effort to track Crenshaw and bring him back to Iron City. I hoped Clay and Nicki would be pleased. And finally I wrote an editorial column in tribute to Mark. Without him we would not have known about Crenshaw. There are pieces that are easy to write. This was one of them. Maybe I had been storing up my thoughts about Mark for a long time.

Mark was listed as a contributor at the bottom of the lead article. Ed questioned it because Mark's name appeared in the article. I told him it was a tribute to a good reporter.

When I returned to the newsroom, the staff had gathered with a toast of cheap champagne, hastily bought at the liquor store down the street that did not cater to the suburban crowd. A great moment.

"To the *Post*," we said in unison. "And to Clay, Mark and Nicki," I said. Clay would see the stories on our on-line edition when the pain killers wore off. I planned to take a copy of the paper to Nicki myself.

"And to our daredevil editor. May he live long enough to get us raises for this," said one of the assistant copy editors.

"Amen to the raises," I said.

The news wires had the Crenshaw arrest story out in minutes. The *Post* was credited with identifying and capturing Crenshaw. One columnist for the *New York Times* the following day called the arrest a "throw-back to the swashbuckling days of newspaper journalism." I felt Howard smiling down from what my mother used to call his "pink cloud."

I did interviews with Associated Press, Reuters, the *Times*, *Post*, CNN, MSNBC and Fox and others I can't remember. It was a long night, and it was going to get longer.

After all the festivities and champagne, after the interviews, after the story was written, laid out and printed and most importantly after the trucks were throwing on door steps across the city the most important paper we had produced in many years, I had to deal with one of the most distasteful tasks I had ever faced. I asked Pat to come into my office for a chat. Ed joined us.

I felt sick inside, fearing that a nightmare was about to be confirmed. I sat for several minutes staring at my hands stretched out on the top of the desk. Pat and Ed chatted away about the story, about Crenshaw and how we had scooped the world. I stood up and shut the door of the office, something I rarely do. It made the room even closer. Ed, letting his fatigue show now that the Crenshaw story was out, lay back on the sofa, his legs resting on the coffee table. His eyes were shut. Pat sat in the armed chair beside the door, his legs spread wide in front of him

"Pat, nice job on the story. You and Rachel wrote a great article on deadline," I said.

Ed didn't move. Pat smiled, enjoying the compliment. It made me sick. "But the story is only half done." Ed didn't move, his eyes stayed shut. Pat held out his hands, palms raised. "We need to find who paid Crenshaw. He is too stupid, too lazy and too self-centered to plan and execute a bombing like this."

Pat whistled. "You are ambitious. Going after some big boys, are you?"

I nodded and took a deep breath. "So, you agree it is probably someone big. Who would you say we are looking for?"

He sat forward and pulled his legs under him. His feet were flat on the floor. He shook his head. "I really don't know. I haven't heard a peep."

I stared at him for a long time. Pat was someone I had called a friend for almost half my life. I liked the man. He was a good reporter, good with the cops, which wasn't easy for many reporters today. It would be hard to find someone to replace him.

"Pat, I believe you know more about who we're after than you've told us."

Ed opened his eyes. As city editor and now managing editor, Ed had always protected Pat. When Pat got arrested for fighting in a bar, Ed bailed him out. If he got beat on a story by the *Examiner*, Ed found an excuse. I had not told Ed my suspicion. I did not look forward to his reaction to what I was to say. If I was right, it was important for Ed to see Pat as I now saw him.

My suspicion had started the night Sandra had come to ask for a raise. Her threats had made me uneasy, made me wonder. She was his weakness, but not his only one. He had to have money to pay for their lifestyle, to keep her happy. But there was more.

"Who paid you to tell them about our hunt for Crenshaw?" I asked, pausing to let the implications of my question sink in.

"What? Joe. What the hell? Shit, what are you talking about," he said, indignant, frightened.

"Leaking information is terrible enough, but don't lie to us on top of it. Tell us who paid you," I barked.

Ed sat up, eyes now wide open, his feet on the floor. "Whoa, Joe. You've got this all wrong. Pat wouldn't do anything to hurt us."

Pat stared at me. He nodded at Ed, his lifeline. "Joe, I really have no idea what you are talking about. All the power and fame gone to your head? You're crazy thinking that."

I sat back and pulled out my desk drawer. I pulled out a photo and looked at it. I then handed it to Pat.

"Nice car," I said.

The photo showed Sandra driving out of our parking lot in a new red Mercedes SL coupe. One of the photographers had shot what he thought was just a young, sexy woman driving an expensive car on our lot, not something you saw often. Newspaper photographers are like that. He had emailed it to me for a laugh. No one in the office was laughing now. Pat stared at it, then at me. Ed was shaking his head.

"Her father didn't buy her that car, did he? And I know you can't afford to buy such an expensive car."

Pat wanted to say yes, her father had bought it, but he couldn't. His pride contributed to his downfall. If he lied, if he bluffed, he might get away with it. But he knew I knew. He raised his head defiantly. He stared hard back at me, trying to make a decision. Seconds ticked by, maybe the longest half minute I had ever endured. Finally, he dropped his head in admission and submission. I had won, but I didn't like it. Part of me had hoped I was wrong.

"I don't know," he said almost in a whisper. "Some guy called me at home, said he was willing to pay me five grand and get me a good deal on a new Mercedes if I would tell him when and where you went after Crenshaw."

He paused and looked pleadingly at me. Stone faced, I stared back.

"I didn't want to do it, but Sandra ..." He wrung his hands. "Well, you know. She was in to see you. She told me she asked for a raise. When you said no .. Shit, Joe, you wouldn't understand. She was determined to stick it to you. When I gave her that car, it made her think she was invincible. She thought she could make you give me more money."

"Who was it?"

"I don't know."

"What number did you call him at?" I asked.

He shook his head. "No number. He called me every few hours for days. He was sure you knew where to find Crenshaw. I kept trying to tell him we weren't even close. How was I to know you were going to hire that private detective?"

"But then you told him that we were going to Florida?" I said.

Pat sighed, then nodded. His head hung low. "It was all over the newsroom that you were flying down," He coughed. His throat must be dry. "In a few minutes the guy called me. He was in a panic, hollering at me, putting the pressure on. He held on the phone while I called Ed."

He looked at Ed, his only hope was fading.

"You son of a bitch," Ed barked at him. Ed's face was bright red. "I never dreamed you were selling us out. I trusted you. You were part of the team. You slimy son of a bitch. You Judas, you sold us out for money and a damn car. Shit."

Ed came up off his chair. He was ready to take Pat on. Pat didn't move. I held up my hand to stop him from punching Pat. It wouldn't have been much of a fight. Pat was good with his fists.

"So Ed told you we were flying to Florida, right?"

Pat nodded. He no longer could look at Ed, and it was a good thing he didn't. I don't think I had ever seen Ed that mad.

"You know you got Clay shot," I said quietly. "All of us were almost killed because of you. Is that worth it to you and Sandra?"

Pat looked liked he had been kicked in the groin. He turned pale. His hands shook. His whole life was coming apart. He was probably wondering what he would do for a job. Would Sandra stay with him after he was humiliated?

"When I heard Clay had been shot, I, uh, well I felt like I would throw up. I hoped, I prayed that it wasn't that guy who did it, that maybe somebody protecting Crenshaw had shot Clay. But I guess I knew. I wanted to kill him with my own hands."

Pat closed his hands together as if around someone's neck. At that moment, I was sure he could do it.

"How'd you get the money?"

"I found it in a big envelope in my desk in the press room at the police building. I didn't see anybody. And nobody else noticed anyone hanging around looking for me."

"Did you keep the envelope?"

"No. I tossed it. But if you were thinking about checking it for fingerprints, forget it. This guy's too smart for that. He wouldn't touch it without gloves."

"How do you know?" Ed asked, recovering from his shock and anger.

"It's just the way this guy is."

I paused and let it all sink in. There had to be a way to track this guy.

"You got the title transfer on the car?"

Pat nodded, but it won't help. "It was transferred from some company. I ran the name through the Secretary of State's database. The company was out of Delaware. I got the names of the incorporators. I will give them to you."

"Probably lawyers. Never get anything out of them," Ed said.

"What'd the guy's voice sound like: old, young, black, white, educated, what?" I asked.

Pat sat back and tried to think. "Not real young. I would think white. Educated, I guess. We didn't exactly talk long."

"He always called you at your phone at the cop shop?" Ed asked.

"No. He had all my numbers. Sometimes he called me at home, sometimes on the cell, but mostly he called there."

The press room at the Iron City Police headquarters was a small space filled with desks. There was no privacy. Dropping off five thousand dollars in an envelope in Pat's desk there was risky. It had to be someone who knew the press room routine.

"Any idea how he got on to you?" I asked.

"No. He seemed to know I needed money. Yeah, well, that's no secret." He left unsaid that somehow the man knew he was willing to sellout his newspaper. And that took more than just being desperate for money.

I paused for a minute, letting the betrayal sink in. Ed was like a volcano trembling before spewing out built-up molten lava. He hated disloyalty even more than most. And if that was not enough, I asked, "And the FBI? Did you tell Pitts too?"

Pat looked at me, what was left of the color drained out of his face. He shook his head and wrung his hands. The bottom of the hole he had dug just fell out. "No. Not at first. But then they were all over me. Promising me exclusives on other stories, threatening to cut me off if I didn't help them. There was lots of pressure from Pitts."

What little was left of Pat's pride was gone. He sat silent. He had nothing left.

When he spoke again, it was softer. "I trade in favors like most reporters. You know that. I give some. I get some. When I heard that you had some inside stuff on the bombing, well, I wanted somebody big to owe me."

"You thought somebody here had heard something, not Mark Hodges?" I said.

"Yeah. I thought maybe somebody had called you or Mike Rose had stumbled onto it. Pitts said you lied to him. He was really pissed. You don't know what pressure D.C. was putting on those guys. They were getting hammered every day."

"Why didn't you tell Pitts it was Crenshaw?" I asked.

He shook his head and trembled slightly. "The guy on the phone. He told me if I mentioned his name to anyone, particularly the FBI, that it would be the last thing I ever did. I am pretty sure this guy would think nothing of killing me, Sandra, my whole family. He scared the shit out of me."

I nodded. "But you were willing to get into bed with him, take his money and the car?" He couldn't answer. Tears welled up in his eyes. "So why did you tell Pitts that we were headed for Florida?"

"He was pushing so hard. I told him you were on your way to find the bomber. He knew you were headed somewhere in a plane. I guess he had somebody tailing you. He figured you would go yourself, and you did. He said you've got a huge ego and wanted to rub the bomber in the FBI's face personally." Pat had a trace of a vicious grin on his lips. "But for some reason he kept saying you were headed for Biloxi. When I told him Florida, I think he shit in his pants."

Tension hung like rain clouds inside the room. There was no room for any oxygen. I so wanted to open the door. Betrayal is not one of the seven deadly sins, but should be at least the eighth. It doesn't show on the outside; it grinds you up inside. I thought about what the bombing story had cost all of us. And I doubted if the full bill was in yet.

"Pick up your last paycheck in the morning. Your story on Crenshaw, that is the last byline you'll see in the *Post*," Ed hissed at him. "Come early. I don't want to see you."

Pat stood up and turned to open the door. He looked back to me. Tears rolled down brown splotchy cheeks.

"You son of a bitch. I've worked for this damned newspaper for almost twenty years, put up with those asshole cops when nobody else would. You know what it's like being stuck on the cop beat for your entire career. It's the same thing day after day. And you just climbed right on up the ladder. You think your shit don't stink."

He stopped talking and glared at me.

"I've got a lot to pay for, but think about this: God Almighty, if you'd given me more money when Sandra begged you for it, well, she wouldn't have come threatening to divorce me and drive home in her new car to live with her parents. I wouldn't have been so pissed and scared and maybe none of this would've happened."

He opened the door, banged it against the wall and walked out, his head down, his body stiff. I wondered how he was going to tell Sandra. Probably not until after he stopped for a few drinks.

Ed and I sat for a while. He stared at the floor. I looked at the old Indian prints, glad for the air pouring in the open door. I thought about how Howard would have handled this. There's very little worse than being sold out by a friend. I hoped I would never have to see Pat or Sandra again, but Iron City is like a small town. I always seemed to run into people I never wanted to see again.

Clay would have to know he needed to find a new police reporter when he got back. I doubted he would be very forgiving of his former police reporter.

It was after midnight when I left the building. I stayed until the final edition ran, making changes and watching over the layout. This was the biggest story I'd ever worked on. I wanted to handle some of the details myself.

It was raining hard, and I took the side entrance where we had brought Crenshaw in hours before. I pushed open the door and stood looking at the spot where Nicki had been face down on the steps. I shivered at the image in my head.

Nicki was recuperating in the hospital from a bullet Pitts said I helped put in her back. I had called the hospital several times. Things were going well, nurses told me. But a combination of love and guilt made me want to check on her in person.

The large and growing complex of hospitals, clinics and medical office buildings that were part of the university medical center is now the heart and soul of the Iron City economy. There were lots of memories here, none pleasant. My grandfather had died here. So had my mother and Sheila. Seeing the old red brick buildings always sent waves of depression through me. My grandfather was my best friend. He took time for me and taught me how life worked, while we played silly, childhood games. He reinforced the confidence my mother instilled me as he and I ran circles in the backyard, pretending he couldn't catch me. I would run ahead of him cackling. The neighbors would stop and stare, an old white man chasing a small black kid.

Then on my way up the career ladder, chasing and writing stories, reading my byline on big stories and feeling important, Sheila was the center of my world. I loved to sit and talk with her for hours about the stories I was covering. It was exciting, comfortable and safe. When she died, I felt the world no longer worked. Everything went out of sync.

Nicki had been moved to critical care, a level down from intensive care. She needed fewer nurses and machines watching over her. Her doctor, somewhere in the gigantic hospital, came on the phone at the nurses station and told me not to worry. "She's strong. She is in great physical condition. I am very optimistic."

She lay in a bed in a small glass room, connected by wires to monitors. She smiled wanly at me. Monitors beeped and purred behind her head. She closed her eyes and flinched as pain went through her. She didn't look like she was in any mood for conversation. So I sat and held her hand.

I thought about our first night together. After Nicki had rescued, I wanted to see her again. Riding in her car, she looked stunning in the glow from the dashboard. I had no illusion that she thought of me as anything more than a job and a moral degenerate. I had grown thick callouses on my soul asking women for casual sex, but Nicki was not about to fall for my blarney.

She was the tough private detective, letting me see only glimpses of the soft, refined Philadelphia girl underneath her armor. "You planning on hitting the bars again tonight?" she asked me as we pulled up beside my car. It was well after midnight. "Since you know I'm being paid to protect you from whatever, I thought I'd make it easy on myself and just get an advanced itinerary."

I told her I was going to take the night off, that I was not as young as I used to be.

"I beg to disagree. You've been at it most nights for weeks. That takes a lot of stamina or a lot of Viagra," she said.

What she had seen was not pretty. I was embarrassed.

"How long exactly have you been following me around?"

"Long enough."

"And you're not going to tell me who paid you to follow me?"

"Nope. Wouldn't if I could. I'm not sure you deserve to know about angels as good as that."

I thought about possible angels in my life. Most were dead. Others, like Weitzman in Virginia, had their own reasons for keeping me out of trouble. A few, like my mother-in-law, could be ruled out. I couldn't see her hiring a private detective. I shook my head at the mystery.

"Well, since you have to follow me around anyway tomorrow night, how about we just stop for dinner? We can sit at the same table and that way you can keep an eye on me."

It was Friday night, and Saturday the only night I didn't work. She turned and smiled at me. Then she started laughing. "Deal. Eight o'clock. Pick an Italian restaurant. I'm in the mood for pasta and a glass of Merlot," she said.

I never went back to prowling the bars and frequenting sleazy hotels. We had dated exclusively ever since.

"I'm real sorry I got you into this," I whispered in her ear as she lay resting in the hospital room. "You are wonderful. I love you."

She opened her eyes and smiled. Her lips were dry and almost stuck together from the surgery she had been through. But the message that beamed out of her eyes was clear: "If it takes getting shot for you to tell me that, I'm glad to take a bullet."

14

"**D**addy, can we go climb that real tall guy?"
Saturday morning started early. Chris was up and eating his Honey Nut Cheerios. All I wanted to do was lie in bed, read my newspaper, surf the web for other stories about Crenshaw's arrest and watch the network news shows. The attorney general had scheduled a press conference in Washington. I had a regular tennis match on for this afternoon, my only exercise this week, other than the sprint to the van across the Florida motel parking lot. There hadn't been much time for Chris lately. So Saturday morning was his.

"Sure, buddy. We'll go climb Vulcan. We can go after I watch something on TV."

Still in his pajamas, Chris crawled into my bed and snuggled under my arm as a CNN anchor told the story again of how the *Iron City Post* had captured the church bomber. It was a lead-in to the attorney general's press conference.

"Daddy, is that man talking about you? He said your name," Chris asked.

"Yes, son, he is."

"Does he know you?"

"No. He is talking about something I did at work."

Chris stared back at the television.

"Was it something good?"

I hugged him, thinking about how one usually hears his name on television or reads it in the newspaper after being arrested or indicted. "Yes, son, it was a very good thing."

When I telephoned Nicki, she was groggy and only grunted her answers. I didn't tell her about the press conference or my plans to spend the morning with Chris.

"Who was that you were talking to, Daddy?"

"A friend who is in the hospital."

"Oh, is he sick?"

"Yes. But I think she will be better soon."

"Does she have a boo boo?"

I smiled and rubbed my fingers through his hair. "Yes. A big one."

"Can we take her a Band Aid?"

Chris was fascinated with any cut that required attention.

"Yes. We can. She would like that."

The tall, thin attorney general and friend of the President stood behind the podium at the Justice Department. He had used the same podium to announce the capture and arrest of several accused terrorists, including the guy who burned a hole in his pants trying to set off a bomb in a plane to Detroit and again after a terrorist bungled a bombing in New York City's Times Square. I felt Iron City, Crenshaw and the *Post* had made it to the big leagues.

The attorney general announced that the bomber had been apprehended and was in custody awaiting arraignment. He thanked the private citizens who assisted in the capture of the bomber. "We solemnly hope that this arrest will bring to an end weeks of unrest in Iron City." He called the bombing one of the most "heinous acts" in American history and described the church as "a sacred place in the history of the struggle by all people for freedom and justice."

Beside him on the stage was Allison Keene and the two U.S. senators from Alabama. The Republican senators rarely voted with the President on any legislation, but the administration kept trying to build relations with them, so the White House let them have their faces on the camera at this historic moment.

The attorney general was asked several questions, including whether the investigation was over. He turned to Keene, who whispered in his ear. Then he turned to the cameras and said, "The investigation continues." But he did not elaborate.

Finally he called on a thin young woman, who identified herself as being the *Iron City Examiner*'s Washington bureau reporter. She asked the attorney general if the Justice Department condones newspapers capturing criminals and bringing them across state lines. "Wouldn't you call this cowboy journalism?"

He did not respond immediately, nodded a couple of times, then said, "We never want private citizens to put themselves at risk, and we understand there was some violence committed from an unknown person during this suspect's return to Iron City. However, we in law enforcement know the value of a watchful public and appreciate all assistance. We want to offer a special thanks to the *Iron City Post* and its courageous staff."

He turned and left the podium. I don't think that he or Keene or any of the Justice Department team was happy with the way the *Post* helped in Crenshaw's arrest. His last sentence seemed to be said out of obligation. I chuckled several times at that thought on our way to climb the statue of Vulcan.

Chris had wanted to climb the statue on top of the mountain since he saw it one day as we drove on the street below it. Besides, climbing Vulcan was a tradition in the family. My father and grandfather had climbed the statue with me. My father never liked heights, and I remember him leaning flat against the wall away from the railing. He really hated the open grate flooring that let you look down to the concrete hundreds of feet below. Granddad and I walked right up to the railing and looked down at the city that spread out across the valley below us. It was great.

Except for several years when the statue had to be taken down and rebuilt, Vulcan had been a landmark for the city. It faced downtown Iron City, and to my amusement as a child and thousands of other children, the statue showed the son of Jupiter's naked rear end to the wealthy suburbs to the south of the mountain.

"He's really big, Dad," Chris said as we parked the car at the base of the statue.

"Yes, he is really big."

Chris asked if he could go first. He was wearing a new pair of bright-orange tennis shoes, his first big-boy sneakers, which he never wanted to take off. The tropical storm had turned east overnight and was marching across Florida making landfall north of Tampa. The rain from storm had stopped in central Alabama, but not before it washed the air, leaving it smelling cool and fresh.

"Sure, Chris, you lead. But don't go too fast. My legs aren't as fast as yours."

He looked up and smiled. "I'll hold your hand, Daddy. I don't care if we go slow. We'll make it."

We stood at the base and leaned back to look all the way up. To Chris, I said, "You sure you're going to make it all the way?"

"Of course. You think I'm a baby?"

We climbed the one hundred and fifty nine steps, which wound in a circular pattern within the base of the statue. Chris led until halfway up, he slowed. I offered to carry him, and he put his arms around my neck as he climbed on my back. It seemed we had been climbing for an hour. My legs were jello.

When we arrived at the top, I breathed easier. The view from the top of Vulcan was as spectacular as I remembered. "Wow wee!" Chris yelled. "Grammy said I'd really like it up here. See, Daddy. You can see far."

You could see across the expanse of the valley. Downtown buildings, the old iron and steel mills and the medical center complex were almost close enough to touch. Old Ramsey High School and Mark Hodges' house were at the base of the mountain below us. We walked slowly around the statue, taking in the view in every direction. As we came back to the side facing downtown, the doors opened for the elevator, which ran to the top for sane people who did not derive pleasure in climbing the steps. In the summer dozens of children and their parents would have bounded out, but today only Walt Simpson stepped out at the top of the statue. It was no co-incidence that the best political mind in the city had arrived at the top of Vulcan while Chris and I were there. Walt had called after the attorney general's press conference saying he would like to talk. I could have put it off, but it sounded urgent. Besides I wanted to know what he and the white establishment in town thought of our catching Crenshaw. So I told him where Chris and I were headed.

"I haven't been up here in twenty years. Ought to come more often," he said looking out at the city that spread at our feet. "Good place to take in what's happening. Too bad they never put a bar up here. Be a real good place to sit and sip."

I reminded him that there was a private club that offered a great view and some of the best drinks and food in the city. "It is called The Club," I said.

Walt smiled, and we started walking around the statue. Chris ran ahead of us, running back every few minutes to point out something he saw or ask a question.

"Are you my Daddy's friend?" he asked on one return.

"You think your Daddy's got friends?" Walt joked, leaning down to rub Chris' head.

I agreed. It was hard to be a newspaper editor and have many real friends. We looked out across the valleys to the south. The af-fluent neighborhoods lay peacefully at our feet seemingly oblivious to what was happening on the other side of the mountain.

"So you got the bomber, this Crenshaw? Dragged him back from Florida," he said. His tone sounded like he was impressed, which I knew was hard for anyone to do.

I nodded, but clarified that Crenshaw had come willingly. I was sensitive to Pitts' accusations. We stood in silence, looking out at the valley below. I sensed that he wanted to tell me something, so I waited.

"You know Crenshaw didn't do this by himself? He ain't got what it takes to pull it off."

After thirty hours with the dumb redneck, I agreed. And there was the discussion with Mark about the Jackson Group. That could not be swept under the rug.

Chris ran back with a little girl in tow. They were holding hands. "Daddy, this is my new friend." The girl was a bit older than Chris. She had dark hair and green eyes and wore a bright red scarf around her neck. It wasn't really cold, but she had dressed for cold weather. "Can she come home with us?"

"Starting a little young, isn't he?" Walt teased.

I gave Walt a dirty look and said, "No, Chris. I don't think it would be okay with her mother. But you can play with her while we are up here."

That was fine with Chris and the girl.

"So who put our boy up it?" The trip to Florida and long interview session Friday had drained me. Tomorrow would be soon enough to catch the guys who paid Crenshaw. Besides, Crenshaw would probably break when the FBI questioned him. He would fall all over himself trying to please the boys in matching black sedans. They would have the names of his co-conspirators in a few hours. Our job now was to make sure we got the names when the Justice Department indicted them.

I said that to Walt, who shook his head. "Don't think so. Crenshaw's not talking. He's scared. You probably got as much out of him as Pitts has, and our chief FBI agent is not happy."

"Walt, how do you know this? I don't know that, and I've got reporters hanging out over at the jail and the FBI office. They are talking every hour with Pitts."

Walt laughed. "You should know, or at least have guessed, that Pitts is not about to let you or your people have any information. He's put out the word that you and the *Post* are personal enemies of the bureau. You should be flattered."

Tweaking Pitts' nose was one thing, but not crippling our ability to get the rest of this story. It happened some times. We are threatened regularly with being cut off from news tips and advertising if we print something. Most of the time it didn't matter, but right now being shut out by the FBI and Justice Department, particularly with Pat Galloway fired, we would probably be running behind other news sources.

"I know one of the detectives questioning Crenshaw. Don't worry, if Crenshaw starts talking, I'll let you know."

We walked around the platform, keeping an eye on Chris and his friend. The city below us was eerily quiet. "You think we're going come through all this?" I asked.

Walt tapped a cigarette out of a pack and lit it. He took a long puff and stared ahead. "Give it six months and we'll be back to normal. The real casualty is the city's image. The state, the city and the chamber of commerce have spent a lot of money promoting the image of Iron City as a nice place to live and work, low taxes, great place for raising families. And it was working. The national media had been writing stories about a thriving Iron City with new businesses and new population growth, particularly among young professionals living downtown and on the southside. But that was before the riots. Now what? Do the companies pull out? Do any of the companies from Europe, New Jersey or California come here?"

He paused to take a longer drag on the cigarette. Neither of us knew the answer.

"Iron City's tough. Always has been. It's been through a lot. It'll survive this too," he said.

"Vulcan bounced back from getting thrown off Olympus. Maybe we can be like our friend here," I said.

Walt looked at me with his wry smile. "Yep. He got the girl, a gift from his papa. But Venus, as the story goes, cheated on him pretty often. He was short, ugly and crippled, and she was off the charts in the beauty department. He had a temper, a typical Greek male. Every time she stepped out on him, he would stir up a volcano in his forge. Does that sound like a good choice for this city's patron saint?"

"Sounds like a country and western song," I said.

Chris and his friend ran up and Chris hugged my leg. They were playing a friendly game of tag. He chased her, she chased him. Too bad male-female relations couldn't stay that simple. Pick out a girl and ask her to play tag. You're it, now I'm it. They ran off cackling with laughter.

"You going after the guys who put Crenshaw up to it?" Walt asked.

I shrugged. "What'd you think?"

He knew the answer before he asked the question.

"We think the guys behind Crenshaw may be some of the members of the Jackson Group. Crenshaw said as much on a tape. We're following it up," I said.

"On the Mark Hodges' tape?" he asked, taking the final drags off his cigarette.

I nodded. "By itself it isn't enough to run a story. We need to know who and why."

He didn't say anything as we stood silently listening to the birds in the trees below us.

Finally I asked, "What'd you think? Are they capable of it?"

Walt dropped his cigarette on the metal floor, stepped on it with the toe of his shoe, then kicked it away. It floated toward the trees below. I knew he wouldn't lie to me, but he had a job to protect. His son was grown, and Walt and his wife of almost thirty years lived quietly and inexpensively. I was sure the Jackson Group was setting him up for an easy retirement, if he continued to protect their interests. What I was asking put him in a tough position.

"There's a lot going on around town right now. Some of it does not make sense. I don't know yet what it all means. It's related to the bombing and Crenshaw's arrest." He paused and looked at me, then smiled. "I know things are hot, real hot. Too hot to handle, even for you."

He stared off in space for several more minutes. "It could be some of my guys. Nobody's come in and confessed to me, if that's what you want to know. I'd say most of them don't have what it takes to do it." My heart raced. "Understand one thing. This ain't the sixties. Things are not so clear cut as they were. Lots of issues, different agendas, smart and stupid stuff. It all creates strange bedfellows."

He put his large hand on my shoulder. "One thing, for sure. Don't underestimate whoever did it. They know how to play the system. They are ruthless. And if they are caught, they've got nothing to lose. They aren't a bunch of lowlife rednecks who just hate blacks. Crenshaw was a tool. The guys who put him up to this are cold, calculating bastards. They plot and they plan. They do multi-million, billion-dollar deals. Blowing up any church and especially that church was a big deal. It was done by people who are very cunning, and I would say, evil. If it gets them what they want, it was all in a day's work. And if they feel threatened, watch out."

"You make it sound like a business deal, blowing up the church," I said.

He nodded. "What's not clear is who it benefits. The riots are hurting most of my guys. The bad press around the country, around the world, is crippling some of them. So who did it help?"

That was the crucial question. Who benefited from Grey being dead? Has anyone gained from the riots?

A strong breeze pushed the tops of the trees around. A few squirrels darted through the underbrush and jumped from tree to tree. From a hundred feet above them it was fun to watch the tree rats gathering nuts for the winter. I wondered what rats we were about to uncover.

"Hope we're not going to wind up on opposite sides on this one," I said to Walt.

He smiled and shook his head. "That's not possible."

He grabbed my shoulder again with his bear-like paw and squeezed. "I'll cover my ass, tell them we talked. But that doesn't mean anything. That's what you do when you take their money. They can rent me, but they can't own me."

I asked if he had any tips.

"Same advice I always gave you. Follow the money, follow the ego. What people will do for money does not surprise me anymore. What they will do to satisfy their ego," he shook his head. "well, there's no limit to that."

Walt turned toward the elevators. He stopped and patted Chris on the head. He told him to take care of me. Chris turned to look at me and smiled. Walt looked back at me, stood straighter and raised his hand to his forehead in a salute, a gesture I thought was out of character.

The little girl had left with her mother. Now with only Chris and me at Vulcan's feet. I raced with him around the platform twice. Then with me out of breath, we started the long climb down. I looked forward to a nap after tennis.

15

Sunday afternoons at the *Post* were usually quiet. With less news to cover, it was a good time to catch up, clean desks, finish stories started days earlier or begin new ones. Not today.

When I walked into the newsroom, the staff had gathered around a photographer and a sports writer who looked like they had been in a brawl. One had a swollen face, a black-and-blue eye and jaw. The other had his left arm in a sling, a cast on his forearm. Both were giving blow-by-blow descriptions of their fights until they saw me. Then they tried to dismiss their battle scars as merely the result of a tough Saturday night at the bar. "You should have seen the other guys," came the banter.

When pressed, they admitted the fights had started when word spread in the bars that they worked for the *Post*. Apparently tracking Crenshaw down had not set well with everyone. They took it out on two staff members who had little to do with his arrest. They were not the only casualty. My office was in shambles. Every drawer was dumped on the floor. An intruder, a thief had taken a torch to the safe, cutting off the hinges. The door lay on the floor. The only thing missing was Mark's article and a copy of the audiotape.

I stared at the clutter on the floor around my desk and thought about who might have done it. Ed came in and looked at the safe. "Can't say much for the security around here," I joked lamely.

"Check your office. See if they got it too." I told him the only thing missing was the copy of Mark's article and one of the copies of the audiotape. "Pretty selective, wouldn't you say?"

He left without a word, but was back in five minutes to report that his office had also been hit. "Dumped everything on the floor. What'd they want? Who do you think?"

It could be our friends at the FBI. I told him I had heard we are on Pitts' shit list. But I thought it looked a little clumsy for professionals. Could it be somebody in the Jackson Group? Walt Simpson would have reported our conversation to his clients Saturday afternoon. He knew we had a tape from Mark. If it was them, they moved fast.

The head of the building security knocked on the door and stood surveying the damage. He was a short, thin man who rocked up on his toes as he walked to make himself seem taller. He rarely said more than two words. I had probably passed him in the building hundreds of times. The only conversation I remember was about how the Atlanta Braves were doing. I wasn't sure what his name was.

"This the only place hit?" he asked.

Ed said his office was in shambles too.

"Anything missing?" the security chief asked.

"No, not really. I guess they were just after money or something they could fence."

Ed looked at me with a puzzled expression. The man nodded and looked around my office. He knelt down to study the broken safe and grunted as he looked at the burn through the hinges. As he stood up, he said he would check into it. Ed followed him to survey the other offices. None were hit except Ed's and mine. After a few minutes they returned.

"We need to get a burglary crew up here for prints," the security chief announced. "Don't touch anything. Just leave it."

I wasn't in the mood to be cleaning up the office anyway.

"Trust him much?" Ed asked after he left.

I shook my head. "Don't even know his name. Who do you think he's calling right now? The police or Daniels?"

Ed caught my meaning. I stood up and motioned for him to follow me. We went into a small room we used for conferences or guest reporters. It was regularly swept for electronic devices.

"I don't think my office was bugged before. But somebody's been in there. There may have been more than one reason to pay us a late night visit," I said.

"Do you want me to get the debuggers over?" he asked.

I nodded. "Meanwhile, let's just assume that everything we say is being listened to somewhere. Have them come at lunch in a nondescript car with everything in a briefcase. Set up a lunch tomorrow in here for some group and tell the guards downstairs they are with that group, okay?"

"You think people are watching too?"

I was getting more paranoid by the minute. "Somebody is. What do you think of the security for this building?"

"On the surface, not bad, but it would be child's play for a professional to crack. Old man Daniels didn't care much, but junior is paranoid. A year of so ago, during one of your trips to D.C., he has the guards practice for terrorists, kidnappers and hostage situations. It was pretty funny. TV stations have to do that, but newspapers?" Ed said.

We both laughed, but knew we were pretty naive about what our enemies were capable of.

"How did they know I even had a safe?"

"Probably a good guess. Maybe it was someone who has been in here. You think it is an inside job, huh?"

"Could be. Or someone who has been here recently or can roam the building after we are all gone," I said.

In a few minutes I called everyone together, all twenty people who were working in the newsroom that afternoon. It was an interesting collection of humans, reporters, copy editors, photographers, a group my wife used to call the "Bad News Bears."

"Most of you have seen the shiners Ricky and Weir are sporting this afternoon. I want you to know they got those black and blue badges of honor defending this old newspaper. It is not often we write stories that get us beat up. But this Crenshaw story stirred up a lot of emotions," I said.

"It sure as hell has," said one of the oldest men on the staff. Roy Stephens worked the rim of the copy desk. He was an old man when I came to the *Post* and might feel more kinship with those who beat up Ricky and Weir than with his fellow workers. But to my surprise, he was annoyed. "Some asshole burned one of those miniature crosses in my yard last night and cut my hoses at the nozzle so I couldn't put the fire out. Damned fool. The ground's so wet from all the rain it barely scorched the grass."

I invited anyone else to speak.

Mike Rose, writing a story at one of the desks near the windows, spoke almost apologetically. "It was nothing like what they did to you guys. I didn't get in a fight, but my phone rang all night. The guy on the line didn't say anything the first time, but then called me a `nigger loving coon' the second time." The whole staff broke up laughing. "It stumped him when I agreed with him. I told him, What else was a black man supposed to be?"

The laughter broke the tension. I wondered if Mike had made up the story. If he had, there could be a bright future for him.

Rachel raised her hand. "At first, I thought it was just some guys trying to be cute. You know, whistling and hollering at me from their car. I was crossing the street out front here and a car passed."

Every man in the room probably had wanted to whistle at Rachel at one point or another.

"But then the car stopped and a couple of the guys jumped out. They grabbed me. I thought, oh, shit, they are going to rape me. Right there in the street in front of the newspaper in broad daylight. But they just shoved me up against the car and told me to tell all the Negro lovers who worked here that we are going to hell. One of them asked me if I had sex with any black men lately.

If I hadn't been so scared, I would've told him I'd rather make it with a black man than a redneck like him. But I didn't think fast enough. I just stood there, my legs shaking. I was afraid I would fall down right in the street. They drove off and one of the guys in the back window shouted Free Crenshaw. Send all the niggers back to Africa."

I had expected things to get ugly, but not this bad. I was proud of my people, not just because they would stand up and back the newspaper, but because they were not panicking. I feared things might get worse. A letter had been left for me at the guards' desk. I thought about reading it to the staff to make them understand the danger we faced, but decided it was too alarmist. The letter was printed in child-like scrawl, the words written by an intelligent, if disturbed person. That made the message even more frightening. It read:

> *The editor and all the reporters of the Iron City Post are in league with the Damn Yankees from Washington who are HELL-bent to destroy all WHITE PEOPLE. When we see the SWASTIKA flying over the Examiner/Post building, we will have won. Our hearts will soar. The SWASTIKA is the symbol for all WHITE PEOPLE to preserve our way of life. ADOLPH HITLER was right.*

It was time to let the tensions cool down. Maybe we would get lucky and nobody else would get hurt.

"Thanks to each of you, those who were hurt and harassed and frightened, for standing up for us. We did a good thing tracking down Crenshaw. We beat every major news organization in the country, and there was a lot of them down here for weeks trying to find him. The FBI, the state police and the Iron City Police Department were all looking for Crenshaw. But who found him?"

There was a loud cheer that bounced off the walls of the newsroom. "We did!" a few shouted.

The noise died down. "I don't want anyone else getting hurt. This too will pass. But we're going to take some extra precautions around here. I want you to think about your own safety. Be careful."

I called Weitzman at home and told him about the assaults and threats. We discussed options, and he agreed that we should hire a couple of our own guards, loyal to us. Ed went off to make the calls.

A few minutes later my mother-in-law phoned. She rarely called me at work. "I just wanted to tell you that young man couldn't find the package you sent him for."

"What young man?" I asked alarmed.

"Oh, he was a nice young man. He came to the door and said you sent him to get a package off your desk, something you needed." Her voice now sounded concerned.

I started to tell her I didn't send anyone, but stopped myself. "Is he still there?"

"No, he left. He searched all around on your desk. He was very polite, even asked my permission to open the drawers to see if the package was in one of them. I tried to help him, but I didn't know what you wanted."

It was a good try. My mother-in-law being so helpful may have kept him from looking thoroughly through the drawers and in the filing cabinet that stood beside it. Whoever it was, whoever sent him was probably frustrated that he couldn't find what he was looking for.

"Tell me what he looked like. There's a couple of guys here that might have come. That way I'll know which one it was," I said.

"Oh, he was a nice looking, very well spoken."

"Was he white? How tall? What color was his hair? Did you notice his car?"

"Why are you asking me? You know him. Oh, all right, he was black, tall, about five foot ten or so, I think his hair was cut short, not a what do you call it, an Afro? I don't remember much else. He had a short-sleeve, white shirt on with a black tie."

"Yes, yes. I know who it was. That's fine, thanks. Just lock the doors and don't let anyone else in. I should have told you he was coming, but I forgot. Chris all right?"

"Sure, he's playing with his cars and little men right here. The man knelt down and played with Chris, asked him his name and patted him on his head. He said he had a good Dad. Chris liked that."

I hung up the phone thoroughly frightened. Whoever it was may have also been the person who hit my office and safe. I thought about sending Chris and his grandparents away on a vacation. But they might be followed. I could hire Nicki's friend to move in. I needed to talk to her about what we should do.

Another copy of Mark's interview was in the back of the third drawer on the left side of my desk at home. I hoped it was still there. I could always ask Pitts to make me another copy of the one I gave him. But that request might have met some resistance. I thought about why someone wanted Mark's recording. Was there something we missed? Was the guy behind Crenshaw just concerned about what might be on it?

Tomorrow, assuming it was still there, I would make an extra copy and put it in a safety deposit box at the bank. I didn't want to give anyone reason to enter my home again. Chris was too precious.

Monday passed routinely. But Tuesday was election day, and the voters of north Iron City and the nearby suburbs were asked to choose a new county commissioner to fill Grey's vacant seat. Given the tension in the city, it was too much to hope for the election to go off without incident. With all the space we devoted to the arrest of Crenshaw, there had barely been room in the editions since Saturday for the analysis Mike Rose wrote on the campaign.

To my surprise, H.T. Jones led the field of seven candidates with twenty-eight percent of the vote. Ray Smith ran second with twenty-five percent of the votes. The runoff between them was scheduled for four weeks, a long time for campaigns in routine years, but I feared it could be an eternity in this campaign. The post-election comments coming from both candidates showed it would be a painful month, the rhetoric already hitting a new low.

"You've got to understand what's at stake here," Mike said after finishing writing the election results story. "For both Smith and Jones, all the chips are on the table. At stake is control of the leadership of the black community. Coming in second is like being dead. Both of them want not just to win, but to destroy the other. Grey had no rivals. No one questioned his power among African-Americans. Now these two want what he had and will do whatever to get it."

In a press conference Saturday night after the votes were counted, H.T. accused Smith of being a "lap dog for those who murdered Grey" and promised to produce evidence for a grand jury in the next few days. He said the proof was being gathered by a team of investigators he had hired.

Smith, in turn, accused H.T. of intimidating and bribing voters. His charges probably had some merit, given H.T.'s operations, but the accusation went down as just campaign chatter. In Iron City it was hard to imagine that more than a handful of votes could have been stolen. The city had been under the scrutiny by the federal election monitors for years looking for civil-rights violations.

As a follow-up story, Mike tracked down the elections commissioner, who told him that his staff had tried all night to find a missing voting machine. It disappeared from the Fairfield Civic Center before the votes had been counted and transferred to the courthouse. He said the machine had probably a thousand votes in it. In the special election, a thousand votes could make a loser into a winner.

Smith told Mike it was not just a coincidence. The missing machine came from one of Smith's strongest areas, and Jones knew that. But to steal a voting machine, H.T. would have to pay off the poll workers and probably a police officer. It seemed unlikely that a small time political activist like H.T. could pull off such a theft.

"Why not just steal all the votes? In you taking the risk, why just take one machine?" I asked Rose.

"I wondered the same thing. Maybe he guessed that losing one machine could be viewed as an accident or incompetence. Losing an entire precinct of machines would bring on a ton of heat from federal and state investigators," Rose said.

If H.T. were guilty, he might face some time in the penitentiary instead of becoming a courthouse boss. I hoped it was not true, but H.T. did not play by the same rules others did.

To the accusations of being involved with the bombing, Smith dismissed it, saying, "Aw, that little weasel is full of shit, and he knows it. Grey was my mentor. We were close. Not as close as we once were. But I was ready to carry that man's suitcase to Montgomery, Washington, wherever he wanted to go. It is absurd to think I wanted to kill him."

Jerry Franklin, the city council member, had run third with eleven percent of the vote. If all of his votes went to Smith, the more mainstream candidate, he would win the runoff.

As I hung up, Rachel walked over to the city desk, where Ed was finishing editing the last of the election coverage. "This may be nothing, but I'll pass it on because I heard you talking about vote fraud. A woman just called, claiming she tried to vote for Franklin, but when she went to vote, they told her she had already voted. She said she pitched a fit right there in the voting place and had to be hauled out of there by a cop."

"Jesus, what is this, Chicago? Boston?" Ed exploded. "It's the crazy season. They're coming out of the woodwork."

Mike called the elections commissioner again to ask about any complaints he had gotten from people who were barred from voting. He said a few had come in and would be investigated. Mike recorded the interview and played it back for us. The elections commissioner's nasally voice came out of the machine. "Well, first, we got no way of knowing if this woman or any of these people are for real. Maybe they're just stirring up things. Maybe they were just trying to see if they could vote twice. Who knows? Let me get back to ya. We can talk tomorrow."

Mike asked how it could be done with all the checks on voters' identity.

There was a long sigh from the elections commissioner. "The precinct elections staff would have to be in on it. You'd have to have somebody signing folks in and letting them vote. There's no other way."

Ed sent Rachel to interview the woman. We needed to see if she was crazy or maybe paid off by Smith or H.T. I called the guard's desk at the front door and told him to walk Rachel to her car. She wouldn't like it, but I told him to do it anyway. My phone rang as I watched Rachel from the window as she crossed the street. The security guard was trying to keep up with her. I had to give him credit, he stayed until she pulled her car out of the parking lot.

"You know what, home boy, there's nothing worse than a brother who starts thinking his shit don't stink." It was H.T. full of himself that he had led the field of candidates.

I congratulated him and said, "I assume you mean, Mr. Smith."

"Hell yeah, I mean Mr. Tight-Ass Smith. He's out there claiming I stole this election. He's a fucking sell-out. That's bullshit, and he knows it."

"The elections commissioner says he is missing a machine and would like to have it back."

H.T. laughed. "Oh, right. I can just take myself into the precinct with a cop on the door, figure out which machine has a lot of Smith or Franklin votes in it and walk out with it under my coat. How would I do that? Besides, I could just as easily have hurt myself."

"Not if you knew he was doing well in Fairfield."

H.T. snickered. "You must think I am pure genius. I like that. I can see the headlines now: H.T. Jones Masterminds Vote Theft. Shit. If that's all he's got," his voice trailed off. "That machine is probably in a back room. Has anybody gone looking for it?"

I told him the elections commission staff had been searching for it. I started scribbling notes on a pad. We might add some of H.T.'s rant to Mike Rose's story. My friendship with H.T. was evolving into a more formal relationship between a candidate for office and a newspaper editor.

"Right." I could hear his chuckle down the line. "That old white man couldn't find his ass with both hands. You know that. He got that cushy job because he delivered votes from the white folks on the east side for the sheriff's re-election. Who do you think tells him what to do?"

The elections commissioner was appointed. If he was in Sheriff Peebles' camp, that threw another wrinkle into the fabric.

"Do you know anything about people saying they couldn't vote because somebody had already voted in their place?"

"Nope. More of the same. Elections commissioner was told to make sure Smith got enough votes to be in the runoff. Somebody filed a complaint?"

I told him about the call from the woman who said she tried to vote for Franklin. I was hoping to get a comment we could use.

"You'll find that Smith's in there somewhere. You don't know him. He's greedy. He and his preacher and funeral home buddies and all those white money men, like your old buddy Walt "The Snake" Simpson, will do anything to make sure that he does."

That was the first time I had heard a nickname for Walt. He would love it.

"I understand that Smith is quite the lady killer," I said.

H.T. laughed loudly through the phone line. "All true, Mr. Snoop. Who in the world told you that? That's good shit. You gonna write about it?"

"Probably not. Just curious why you haven't used it against him."

There was a pause on the line. "Truth is, everybody pretty much knows about it anyway. He's out at the clubs with not just one woman, but two. He's got a fine young black woman, looks good in stilettos. And the white woman, she's from Georgia, and I don't mean

Atlanta. I mean like eastern European. Tall, well endowed. I don't know how his old lady stays with him."

"So why haven't you used it against him?" I asked.

"I would if it would help. But it won't, and it would hurt his kids, his wife. He's got a nice family."

"You growing a conscience, H.T.?" I teased.

"Hell, I hate to admit it, but a lot of brothers would be pissed if I messed up a good thing for him. Some guys think only with their pecker. If they saw him in the newspaper, if you were so inclined to run a photo, strutting between those two women, well, it'd probably get him more votes than it would cost him."

The strange world of politics.

"Did this Crenshaw say anything yet about working with Smith and his buddies to get Grey?" he asked.

"You really don't believe that."

"Hell, I don't. I've been hoping you would put them together because I'm pretty sure there were folks that wanted Grey out of the way and Smith to take his place. Somebody put that dumb redneck up to it."

I agreed and asked why he thought it might be Smith.

He started laughing. "You still don't know anything. Smith was behind it all right. He knew everything there was to know about Grey."

"But why?"

"You know they had a big time falling out, don't you? How come you think Smith stopped working for him? Because Smith got ambitious, that's why. He wanted Grey's power, not just to be close to it. He liked the money too. You know how much a county commissioner gets paid, a hundred and fifty thousand dollars a year, plus a car, and whatever you can get out of the real estate developers, road builders, garbage companies and banks. You ever see a county commissioner buy his own lunch or drive around in a shabby car?"

"Is that why you're running?" I asked.

"I'm no saint. I don't really care about the money, but I do like the power. I can do a lot for this county, more than Grey did, and a whole lot more than Ray Smith could ever do."

"So you want me to believe that Grey told Smith to chill out on his ambition to be commissioner, and that's what got Greg killed? That seems a little far-fetched, even for you, H.T. There are other offices to run for, state legislator, city council?" I said.

"Not one of them pays as well. Over the table or under. Nobody cares what one state legislator does. He would be just one of a handful of black dudes down in Montgomery. He wouldn't have the stroke a county commissioner has," he said.

"How'd he know Crenshaw?"

"Probably got some help. Maybe the sheriff. You've studied history. You know that times like these make for some bizarre alliances in politics."

I thought about that possibility. Could we be way off on any conspiracy here? Were more people than just members of the Jackson Group involved? Crenshaw was scared of somebody. The sheriff seemed like a likely candidate. Crenshaw would take orders and money only from someone he respected. That meant a white guy, probably a rich white guy or a politically powerful white guy. He came with us back to Iron City because he thought we worked for the *Examiner*. That meant Daniels.

The more I thought about it, the more I was certain that Daniels was involved. Could Daniels and the sheriff be behind this? Crenshaw said he had met Daniels when he was with Peebles. Nothing this big could be happening without Daniels. And Peebles could deliver Crenshaw and keep him terrified especially in his jail.

When it did not seem like things could get worse on a Sunday afternoon, Reverend Webster showed up with his army of right-wing Christians.

"You're not gonna believe this. The reverend is out there with a bull horn and a bunch of his flock picketing in support of Crenshaw," Ed said.

We watched as the city's leading right-wing preacher directed his troops. They marched around in the parking lot, while Webster talked on his horn. He turned toward the building, and we could hear what he was saying. One sign a picketer carried said it all: *Free Crenshaw, a martyr and a hero.*

"I'll send somebody out to interview him. Not Mike, of course," Ed said, laughing at the image of a black reporter trying to interview Webster in front of his white supporters.

Through the glass windows we could hear Webster's words. "The mark of Cain is on these people. They were cast out. Should we let them back in now? No, we must stand our ground." He turned away, and the rest of his words were lost. His followers raised a fist in support.

We watched as a photographer and reporter went out to the parking lot. Webster handed off the bull horn long enough to be interviewed and pose for a photo. Before the photographer could shoot his picture, Webster pulled out a comb. A girl with him held up a mirror as he made sure every hair was in place. It took a bunch of gel to keep his hair so straight in the wind.

"You know, I have wondered if he doesn't know a good deal more about who was behind the bombing than he has told anybody," Ed said. "It sure is playing into his hands. I bet his take on Sunday offering plate and his TV ratings are way up, probably through the roof, since the riots started."

The bombing and riots had boosted fundraising for both whites and blacks. The bull horn started up again with Webster breaking into a new version of an old high school football chant: "Free Lonnie, he's our man. If he ain't free, nobody is." The words didn't rhyme, but the message was clear enough. After a few minutes the crowd wandered off, and our reporter told me they were headed for the city jail to give Crenshaw some "vocal support."

At 7:30, Mike had finished his article on the election controversies for page one. Rachel had called to say Emma Courtier seemed credible and said she was "madder'n a wet hen." She gave us a few more comments from the woman to add to Mike's story. We could then wait until the elections commissioner compared her signature against the one on the elections registration form at the voting place. These were good follow-up story to the elections, but unclear if they would hold up as a full-blown scandal.

When the police scanner squawked on the city desk, Ed dialed Rachel's number and asked, "What was that woman's address? Wasn't it on 37th North?"

He listened, then said, "You better get back over there. I'll send a photographer. There's a fire at that address. Fire trucks are headed there now, and the cops are blocking off the street."

By the time Rachel called in, we were on deadline. Ed asked for the short version, when an excited Rachel was giving him too much detail. He put her on speaker for all of us to hear.

"Three guys broke in her house and tied her up in one of her kitchen chairs and then just started burning her house down around her. They splashed gasoline on the walls and furniture, then used a blow torch on one of the couches and drapes." Ed and I looked at each other. A blow torch had been used on my safe. Was it the same guys?

"How'd she get out?" Ed asked.

"She got lucky. The men ran out when the flames caught and the smoke got thick. A friend, coming over for a visit, found Mrs. Courtier. The friend is as old as Mrs. Courtier, but she started pulling her in the chair out of the front door. Her yelling for help brought a couple of guys standing in a yard down the street. When they saw the smoke, they came running. I talked to them too. It's sort of incredible, really."

Ed, the old pro, started firing questions at her as he typed in the answers. Instant story. He sent her to talk with the firemen. The house was totaled and almost took the houses on either side. Mrs. Courtier had lived in that house for a long time. Rachel asked if she could identify the men who burned her house, but they had worn masks, the ones of President's faces.

Rachel said, "She kept saying the old cowboy done burned my house down."

"Does she know if they were black or white men?" I asked.

"I didn't ask that specifically. I would guess she is not sure, but let me ask her quickly. They are putting her in an ambulance. I'll call back."

Ed continued writing the story. The phone rang again.

"She is pretty confused. She's not sure. I wouldn't want to go with much she said right now. When I asked her what color they were, she started giggling. She said she thought they were black, but they had gloves on and no one spoke. It was strange, she said, the way they tied her up and started the fires in her house without saying a word. To her, it seemed rehearsed, choreographed."

"Okay, wrap it up. That's good enough for tonight. And be careful coming in," I said.

Ed read her the lead on the story he wrote, but would carry Rachel's byline. She was thrilled.

"Oh, Joe, you know who this woman is related to? Henry Jones, the guy running for commissioner. He's her nephew. Isn't that something for the small world category?" Rachel said.

"H.T.'s her nephew, and she voted for Franklin?" I asked.

"Yeah. She said she doesn't care much for her nephew, never sees him."

It was late, I was tired and none of it made sense, although I doubted H.T. was the model nephew. I watched the local television news from the set in the conference room. There was Reverend

Webster again on the screen, leading his flock of picketers in front of the county courthouse, denouncing both Ray Smith and H.T. Jones. He called on the governor to invalidate the election results and appoint a "responsible" person until order could be restored in the city. It was difficult to imagine what hounds of evil Webster was unleashing. I thought about more precautions we should take. But newspapers should not run scared. I hope it would not be our epitaph.

16

I like churches. The architecture, the quiet, the streaks of sunlight through stain-glass windows make churches sanctuaries for weary souls, and mine was tired. And there is the music. I have always loved the old gospels. In my college days I often finished a long night of studying in the basement of Firestone Library by stopping in at the Princeton Cathedral a few steps away. I would sit in a back pew listening to someone practice on the mammoth organ. It was so comforting to an Alabama boy, raised on good gospel music and now far away from home in the cold north. There were times when I would fall asleep only to have the janitor rouse me as he locked up.

Jimmy Marshall had invited me to a Sunday night service for the parishioners of the Sixteenth Street Baptist Church. The church faithful met in the auditorium of the Iron City Civil Rights Institute across the street from the bombed-out hulk of the church. On the western edge of downtown the institute was an elegant brick building that held a museum. Its auditorium, where noted speakers drew crowds during the week for seminars on historic and current issues, served on Sundays as the church's temporary sanctuary. There were no stain-glass windows, but it was a comfortable place for the parishioners to gather and worship.

After putting Chris to bed with three stories and a glass of chocolate milk, I drove back downtown and left my car on Sixth Street next to the park, a block away from the church. I walked slowly through the exhibits of horror in the park that depicted people being fire-hosed and gnawed by trained German shepherds. The curved path through the tree-lined park led from one stone statue to another, each more frightening and saddening than the one before. I had taken this walk many times before, each time reflecting on how much I owed to those who had made such sacrifices against the entrenched power of segregation. They had opened doors for me and millions of other black people when they stood their ground.

The bombed out church, across the street, looked sad, boarded up, broken. It was now a familiar sight to television news junkies like me. Network producers used it continuously as a background image for reporters and anchors discussing developments on the bombing investigation, notably Crenshaw's arrest. The church had become a symbol of national tragedy, much like the 9/11 ground zero site had been in lower Manhattan before it was rebuilt. That site always reminded us that we needed to be forever vigilant against terror. Tonight, with only street lights shining on its facade, the empty church seemed to scream a similar message, a warning against evil in the world. I wished the message was a bit more specific.

The music from the evening service poured out over me as I stepped through the doors into the auditorium. It made me smile to think that Crenshaw was in a jail cell sweating out his future while the folks he had tried to kill sat here singing. The large room was jammed with people, more than I had ever seen at the Sunday night service before the church was bombed. They sang:

> O they tell me of a home far beyond the skies,
> O they tell me of a home far away;
> O they tell me of a home where no storm clouds rise,
> O they tell me of an unclouded day.

On stage with the choir and a piano was a man playing a clarinet. I found a place to stand in the back. When the choir and congregation finished singing, the clarinet player broke into a solo of *Swing Low Sweet Chariot*. I saw then that was the little deacon himself playing the clarinet, making a clearer sound than I had heard in a long time.

When the music concluded, the minister led the congregation in prayer. Recruited to the church by a new set of church elders after Smallwood's death, the minister spoke about forgiveness and tolerance. He told the congregation that it was time to give up the rage they felt about the bombing of their beautiful church and give thanks to those who were helping to restore it. In a big, somber voice he told them that the engineers and city building inspector had concluded that the church building was still structurally sound. That was a miracle after such a large bomb had exploded in its basement. We had carried the story on Saturday.

"That is the sign from God we have been waiting on. He wants this church rebuilt," the minister said. "We must rebuild. We have to rebuild. Its God's will. There are those who say our church has lost its purpose, that there are other, newer churches to meet the needs of its people. I say no. Those folks who say we should not rebuild are well intentioned, but wrong. There is no higher purpose than to restore this great church. Only then can we show Iron City and the world that we cannot be beaten. Let Satan send hundreds of bombers. We will rebuild, time after time because what they cannot destroy is our spirit, the enduring spirit of this glorious church and the love the Lord has for it."

That got me. I am a sucker for comeback stories. The *Post* should help. Who better to lead this campaign to rebuild the church than the newspaper that had captured the bomber? We helped underprivileged children with Christmas presents in December. We raised money for the United Way and a dozen other charities. We could raise funds to help rebuild this church as well.

I felt someone beside me and turned to see Jimmy Marshall, his clarinet in a case hanging by his side.

"You play very well," I whispered.

He smiled and whispered back, "That's how I used to make my living." He grabbed my arm and led me out through the doors in the hallway. "When I was a lot younger, I used to play in the clubs here. It was never as good as New Orleans or Memphis, but old Iron City had some fine clubs. Lots of good musicians used to come through here, songwriters and producers, too. But soon off they'd go. Can't blame 'em," he says.

"You sound like you are pretty good yourself," I said.

"Good enough, I guess. But I never wanted to leave. Always thought this was where I belonged. I went to New Orleans a few times, but always came back. Guess that's why I've got such a crop of grandchildren, not out on the road enough."

I asked his opinion about the newspaper doing a fundraising drive to rebuild the church.

He smiled. "I thought you might want to do that." There seemed to be a lot more to the small, slight man than I had appreciated. "I want you to meet the new minister. Man named Green, not as good as Smallwood, but might be someday. Down here from Indiana, he doesn't know much yet."

After the sermon finished and the choir sang the closing hymn, we stood outside the auditorium and shook hands with a stream of people. Some I had met, others were introduced. The minister got through shaking hands and came over to greet us. He was not as tall, a lot broader and much younger than Smallwood. He looked like the good church women had fed him well on chicken and dumplings and all the fixings.

"Nate Green," he said, shaking my hand. "I am so glad you came." The minister had a precise way of speaking, like a radio disc jockey does when he forgets he is not on the air. I had not noticed it as much when he was in the pulpit. In person it made him sound a bit artificial. I wondered how long it would take for him to lose that accent and develop the lazy tongue that was essential to a good southern drawl.

"Reverend Green," I started.

"Nate, please. Call me Nate."

"Nate, I enjoyed the service, great music. And I couldn't agree with you more that it is important for this city to rebuild this church. It has been through too much to let it die now. It would be like the bomber and his friends won," I said.

The minister and Marshall nodded vigorously.

"I just told Mr. Marshall, we would like to help. The *Post* could help lead a fundraising drive, write stories about it, strip it across the bottom of page one every day for a few weeks and see what we get in the mail. What'd you think?"

Green broke into a huge smile. "God has blessed us this day."

How our white readers would respond was a question mark, but we could run a short series of stories about the church, its history, the new minister, human interest stories about people who had attended the church all their lives. I explained this concept to Green and Marshall. Green liked it immediately. He started mentioning people who could be featured in the articles. Marshall looked troubled, but said nothing.

"There was another reason I was hoping to meet you," Green said. He took me by the arm and walked me out of the institute. With Marshall trailing behind, Green and I crossed the street to the small house beside the bombed-out church that served as the church office.

"I understand you are a Baptist yourself," he said as we walked.

I nodded and told him I was afraid this was the first time I had been to church in years. He patted my arm. "Once saved, always saved, my son. The Lord is looking out for you."

He unlocked the front door of the small house and turned on the lights. I stood there trying to imagine Crenshaw in this space, talking with the women who worked there and carrying his bag of explosives. I shivered at the thought of that big redneck, standing here with a bomb.

"Feel like someone done stepped on your grave?" Marshall asked. He had been standing right behind me and could see me shiver. I marveled at his perception.

The minister led us to a back room where he had an office. It was elegantly furnished both in the selection of an antique desk and chairs and in the drapes that covered the windows. Some money had been spent decorating that office.

Standing there, I remembered being in a similar church office when I had worked with Walt Simpson to help re-elect the old U.S. senator. Walt was the senator's Iron City campaign manager. I was a teenage volunteer, eaten up with idealism and politics. Walt had carried a package to a minister who had promised to help get out the vote for the senator. He took me along, maybe because of my skin color, for certain to further my real world education.

Walt drove an old Buick deep into a black neighborhood. Kids, most with nothing on but shorts, played in the streets and on the sidewalks or hung off of rotting porches behind yards with chain link fences. The minister, in his office behind the sanctuary, was dressed in a white shirt and black suit, which covered a heavy chest and belly that shook when he laughed. His office was decorated with a carved cross and a glittering portrait of the Last Supper. The minister looked long at me when we shook hands. I wondered then if he thought I was just a token black face in the campaign or someone he should get to know.

Walt and I were invited to sit in deep, well-padded chairs before Walt handed him the package, wrapped in brown paper and tied with a simple string. It looked like the packages of candy bars and homemade cookies that my mother sent me when I was away in school. The minister's eyes shined with excitement, probably the same way my face lit up as I took those packages from the mail clerk. Inside his package were not candy bars or new underwear. It was filled with hundred-dollar bills.

"You can be sure we'll put this offering to good use come election day," he said in a deep voice that vibrated through the office. Walt thanked him for his help and told him how much the senator appreciated his support. They talked about how the campaign was going, where the senator faced problems. The minister assured him there would be no problem with the turnout of black voters in Iron City. He stood and again shook our hands. He bowed slightly to Walt, who nodded his head, leaned over and whispered in the minister's ear. Then we left.

Back in the Buick, driving back through the neighborhood, I asked Walt what the money was for. He looked at me and chuckled. "We call it walking-round money. It goes under the category of get-out-the-vote funds. Helps make sure people get to the polls and know how to vote when they get there. Understand?"

"How much of it goes in his pocket?"

Walt shrugged. "Who knows? But he earns it. For the next few Sundays, he will stand up in his pulpit and tell everyone that the good senator is the right man to vote for. And he will have some of the ushers standing at the back door handing out sample ballots with a big X beside the senator's name. Then on election day church members will pick up the old folks and others who might not get to the polls. The minister stands outside of the school gym where they vote and shakes everyone's hand. They know he will remember who came to vote."

As we drove, I tried to reconcile the vote-buying with my own idealistic view of democracy. I asked why our opponent didn't just give the minister more money.

"That's always a possibility. Most candidates don't have the money that the senator can raise. Remember he heads the Senate finance committee. The bankers and the homebuilders like the way the senator votes. He's good to them, and they keep the country's economy rolling. They remember to contribute early and often."

In the last election, the senator faced a tough race with Richard Howart, who had a lot of money of his own. Walt said the senator and staff had worried that Howart would outspend them. So they got to the ministers early. Once bought, they stayed loyal even when Howart offered more money, he said.

"There is more to it than money. Being the incumbent really helps. The senator writes this minister and every minister in the state a personal letter twice a year and tells them what is going on in Washington. They get a Christmas card every December. If any of them visit Washington, they get VIP seats in the Senate gallery and lunch in the senators' dining room. How are they going to go against him then? You and I know that any senator, at least the smart ones, would do the same, but these guys don't want to risk losing out on that access."

I sat thinking about the power a sitting senator has to get re-elected. It is a wonder any of them are ever defeated. There was the old saying: the only way he could lose is to be caught in bed with a dead girl or live boy.

"What'd you say to him there at the end?" I have always been too curious.

He didn't answer, giving me a look that said there are some things I was too young to know. Then he relented, as I knew he would, and told me that the senator had helped the minister on a business deal he and two friends had put together. A House member got it fouled up in the Transportation Department authorization bill, and the senator had to straighten it out. Walt had told him that things were worked out and the deal would happen.

Standing in Reverend Green's office next to the bombed out church, I wondered if the bag men had come in and brought his predecessor money tied up neatly in brown paper. Had Smallwood been in on some of the deals? Had one of those deals gone wrong and given someone a reason to bomb the church? Was Smallwood as well as Grey the target?

Standing behind his desk, Green picked up a piece of paper. "I was going through some of Reverend Smallwood's things here. Some interesting reading. You are welcome to use any of it in your articles. Here is something I wanted you to see."

He handed me a letter addressed to Smallwood. It was typed on blank paper.

Reverend Smallwood,

Commissioner Grey is way out of control. Make him toe the line or you and he will suffer the consequences. Believe us. We're serious.

There was no signature. No date.

"Where was this?" I asked.

"Stuck down in some papers in his drawer. The women who worked here said they hadn't seen it. I don't know whether it came in the mail or was dropped in the offering plate or maybe got here some other way. What do you think I ought to do with it?"

It was clearly written by someone who understood the intricacies of English language. Most people, even ones who are educated, would have written "both you and him" and might have written "tow the line," instead of the proper "toe the line." So who grew up reading newspapers and had spent a few years as a copy editor learning about the newspaper he would inherit? But would Daniels have written such a note to Smallwood?

"We probably need to give it to the FBI. Have you met Harrison Pitts?" I asked.

"No," Green said. Marshall gave me a puzzled look. I knew what he was thinking. This time the FBI had the resources to figure out who may have sent that note. I explained that to Green and Marshall.

"I will call him tomorrow and tell him about the letter. I feel like I owe him one, so I will do that. But it is a strange note," I said.

"Anyone could have sent it. People out in the public eye make enemies. This might have nothing to do with the bombing. But just in case, I thought it would be good to show it to you," Green said.

It was amusing to think how catching Crenshaw had apparently raised people's estimation of my sleuthing abilities. Marshall followed me out. Across the street there was a van filled to the doors with his family.

"How big is your family?" I asked.

He pointed out his wife and two daughters and several of his nine grandchildren. Everyone was introduced. Sometimes you lose track of them all, but the women keep up with them, he said.

In the van the little ones were asleep, the older children were looking bored, punching one another. The women smiled at me, probably because they were glad to be heading home. I thought of Chris and wanted to be home myself. I was also glad I only had the one to keep up with.

As I drove away, I thought there was something more that Marshall wanted to say. He gave me the sense that he knew something I should know. It was not the first time I felt I was being paranoid.

Mike Rose was badly beaten while I was at church.

A group of white men had been waiting for him in cars when he left the newspaper building Sunday night. Dressed in army jackets and heavy boots, they got out of an old Chevy as Mike walked with a security guard escort to the parking lot. The security guard Ed had hired had barely slowed them down and received a serious beating for his efforts. The attackers used bats and pieces of metal pipe. One had a gun, another a knife, but only used them to scare Mike. They hadn't come to kill. They used the bats, pipe and their boots to injure Mike, the guard and to send a message.

Ed called, telling me about the assault and that Mike was in University Hospital. "Sunday night may be better than Friday or Saturday night at the emergency room, but it is not a place you want to go."

Mike had a concussion, two broken ribs and scrapes along his right side where they had dragged him across the parking lot. His eye and right cheek were swollen, his abdomen looked the same. The guard was only slightly luckier. He had a concussion, and his genitals hurt where he had been kicked. Nothing was broken. The doctor insisted that Mike stay overnight, and barely able to keep his eyes open, he didn't object.

"I was laughing about how silly it was for the guard to be walking me to my car," he mumbled. "He was all serious, but I wasn't expecting trouble. I thought it was a lot of crap having some guy walk me to my car."

He tried to shake his head as he lay there in the bed, but it hurt too much. Mike couldn't remember many details. "It may be better if you don't remember. The pain in your head and your broken ribs are enough."

I called the guard at home to check on him and thank him. He said the attackers had said we should not write stories that made Crenshaw look like a bad guy. They called Crenshaw a hero and told him to tell me I was next for a beating.

The regular security guard found them in the street, a note tied around Mike's neck that said *Free Crenshaw*. Our church bomber had been made into a martyr. Now there were martyrs on both sides.

One of the four police officers I had rescued three weeks ago called the next morning to ask me to meet him at a coffee shop off Fifth. I would not have remembered his name if we had met on the street. But I would never forget his face. The oldest of the four, Ralph White had earned that face. Lined from years of stress and sun, it had a thick scar along his right jaw. He was the one who hung onto the top of the Blazer and held the unconscious cop on the hood with his other hand. The coffee shop had cleared of its lunch crowd, and we sat at the counter.

"Glad you caught that son-of-a-bitch Crenshaw," he said after the coffee arrived. "I've lost three good friends in the last two weeks, all because he's got to go blow up a black church. Jesus, I ain't got no love for all black folks, but any fool could see that blowing up that church again was gonna stir them up real good."

"Maybe that was the point," I said, still perplexed at why someone would put Crenshaw up to it.

He shook his head in anger. "I hope they bury him."

"Have you seen him since he was arrested?" I asked.

"Just in passing. Not to talk to or anything. Some of the guys went to see him, stood around and talked with him like he's some celebrity. Dumb. My old patrol partner is assigned to him."

I asked if Crenshaw was talking to the FBI.

"Bragging a little, but not much new."

"Anything about who paid him?"

He shook his head. "The FBI interrogators keep asking. They are even talking about taking the death penalty off the table if he fingers who paid him."

"Anything about the Jackson Group?"

"That keeps coming up, but Crenshaw ain't saying one way or the other."

White finished his coffee. "They may cut him a deal. Maybe twenty-five years if he talks. That means he could be out in eight." He turned to me and said, "That ain't right. We'll have more riots in the streets."

"He knows this is a death sentence either way. He won't live long inside, even in a federal penitentiary out west. The brothers will carve him up for Christmas dinner. His only hope is the white gangs. If they make him into a fucking hero or becomes someone's bitch, maybe they can protect him."

I thanked him and told him I would appreciate anything else he hears. He smiled and left. I headed back to the newspaper. When I parked in the lot, I was met by a different security guard who walked me to the side entrance. I felt a little foolish. But then I thought about Mike and the message they had given the guard. "Thanks. Keep it up, no matter how much my people complain."

He nodded and smiled. "I like walking the women out."

Rachel, showing signs of fatigue, met me as I walked in the door. Dressed in another long, flowered skirt, she asked, "You know what the real problem is?"

I smiled because I knew a joke was coming.

"Guys don't shop. We all know that shopping is the cheapest form of therapy. If we could just teach guys to work the malls right, well...then we would have world peace."

Rachel had called several members of the Jackson Group. I knew she had been making the calls because several of business leaders had called me to complain.

"I can't say this is going very well. I've only really talked to two. They just told me they had no comment. I'm waiting to hear back from a bunch more."

The two she had interviewed admitted they were members of the Jackson Group, but denied any knowledge of the bombing or Crenshaw. Rachel explained that Crenshaw had mentioned the Jackson Group, and we believed the FBI was now looking at whether members of the group were involved in the planning and financing of the bomb at the church.

"That got a lot of sputtering on the other end of the line. When I mentioned the FBI, it sounded like panic set in," she said.

The two who had called me were major advertisers. They told me, one at the top of his voice, that they would not stand for an article linking them to the bombing. They would pull their advertising and as the yelling one said, "sue the *Post* for everything it has."

The president of the bank my father worked for also called. "Look, Joe, you've known me for most of your life. I am a member of this Jackson Group, but it's mostly a social deal. We get together over at the country club, have a few drinks, talk about business, politics, that sort of things. It's good for business. The other bankers are there. I have to be there. Your old boss used to be a member. To think this bunch had anything to do with the bombing. Well, that's ridiculous. I would never be involved in anything like that."

I told him we had information from Crenshaw himself and from other witnesses that the bombing and who did it were openly discussed in some of the group's meetings.

"Well, of course, the bombing is discussed. Joe, these damn riots are horrible. We've got customers going out of business every day. Its worst than the damn recession we just went through. Iron City's image is really taking a hit and that hurts us all. We'd be stupid to have been involved in something like this. We're the victims. Use your head, Joe. Oh, congratulations on capturing this jerk, but you're barking up the wrong tree now."

Rachel and I went over the calls I had received. She could use some of the quotations to give balance to the story.

"Well, I feel a little better. I was beginning to think they were just going to stonewall us," she said.

They could go silent. Put up a wall. That is one way to fight a newspaper. But it would be more in character for them to lash out, try to kill us off by withholding advertising dollars. There were other ways they might come after us. We had to be ready.

Mrs. James, wearing a matching pink scarf and glasses, held up the phone and waved it at me. I had wandered across the newsroom, talking to the sports guys. Bud Shaw, the sports editor, was telling Ed and me about his latest conversation with the mother of high school football star, Eugene Crabtree. The multi-million dollar question was where he would go to college.

"It's Mr. Weitzman," she said a little flustered. "He insists on holding while I found you." It wasn't like Maury to hold on the phone for me. I was afraid I knew why. "We need to talk," he said, when I picked up.

"Okay, talk," I said, trying to keep any anxiety I felt from being heard down the line.

"No, not on the phone. Here. How soon can you get here?" he asked.

"Tomorrow if I have to be. What's the deal?"

"We need to talk about this stuff you're working on about Daniels. That could be trouble."

"How so?" I said, knowing the answer.

"How about ten o'clock tomorrow?"

"I'd have to fly tonight. How about one o'clock? Then I can come tomorrow morning."

"Okay. See you here at one," Weitzman said.

Weitzman was a duck out of water when he got involved with the editorial side of a newspaper. He had come up through the ranks of the advertising side. He knew exactly how many column inches of ads we needed to make a newspaper profitable, but had a poor idea of what makes for a good news story. Unfortunately, he thought he did. It frequently led to some heated discussions with me and other editors in the chain.

I knew he would not want to do anything that might jeopardize our agreement with the *Examiner*. Under our joint operating agreement, if the advertising space sold for the *Post* fell significantly for the year, the *Examiner* had to make up the difference. It was a way to keep us operating and the *Examiner* honest. Otherwise it would be too easy for the *Examiner* to back off selling our ads and delivering our newspapers. A little sabotage could put us out of business. The agreement forced the *Examiner* to share in our risk. It had worked so far.

If all the major advertisers in the city, particularly the department stores, grocery stores and car dealers, pulled their ads for the rest of the year, we would be lucky to survive. Thanksgiving to New Year's is the heaviest advertising season. If they cut back during Christmas, it would cost the *Examiner* a bundle and might force the two newspapers to renegotiate the agreement. That could be the end of the *Post*. Daniels could decide we weren't worth the trouble. I doubted if the Justice Department would raise the anti-trust issue if the *Post* voluntarily went out of business.

The age-old dilemma. Do we do what's right? Or do we stay in business to fight another day?

Ms. James started booking my flight to Washington, while I turned back to the immediate problem of Bud Shaw's story.

"So Crabtree is thinking about going out of state, to Tennessee or Texas?" I said.

The sports editor nodded. "I have called his mother to confirm, but I hear he thinks he will have a better shot at a national championship at one of those schools."

"But Auburn just won the national championship," Ed said.

"Yeah, but it was almost a full senior team. Auburn's recruiting the last couple of years has been weak. The offensive line is small. Crabtree is getting some good advice."

"Well, that is page one for sure," Ed said.

I nodded. "That'll sell some papers. Good job. Are you dating Ms. Crabtree?"

Ed left laughing.

Shaw stood up. He was my height, although he outweighed me by a lot. "Newsroom gossip is that you are looking into this guy Braddock."

"You know him?"

He smiled. "Yeah, he was a player, likes to talk about his glory days. He's had me out to the house in Shoal Creek a couple of times for parties. That is quite the house."

"Does he really have a whole bunch of Alabama memorabilia on his den wall?"

He laughed. "You wouldn't believe it. He even plays tapes of his old games during parties. I don't think he was in many games and always points out when he is on the field. You would think he led the team to a National Championship." He paused. "So what are you looking at him for?"

I looked at him hard. Pat's betrayal flashed before my eyes. Was Shaw pumping me for Braddock?

"It is a wild possibility, probably nothing to it. He's in this Jackson Group, and it might be that he knows something about the church bombing," I said.

Shaw whistled. "Wow. I don't know him that well. He is a tough guy, all smiles and handshakes, but behind those blue eyes, you can see he is not someone to mess with. Do you want me to look into it?"

I smiled. "Sure. But know you are probably going to stir the pot pretty good. You may not be on his invitation list anymore."

He laughed. "His booze was good. I would miss the free Crown. But I can afford to buy my own. I'll let you know if I hear anything."

I turned and started to head back toward my office. Mrs. James was on the phone and I figured it was for me. But I had one more question for Bud. "Where did you hear that Crabtree is thinking about going out of state?"

Shaw laughed. "Weird thing. I was at the gym, talking with the guy lifting weights next to me. Young guy, I thought I knew him. You probably do. He's running for county commissioner, used to work for Grey. Name is Ray Smith."

As the saying goes, I didn't see that coming.

The call waiting for me was not unexpected. From the way I heard Ms. James talking, I knew who it was. And it was not someone I wanted to hear from.

"Son, son, Joe is that you?"

"Yes, Dad, how are you?"

"I'm okay. You ought to drop by, see how well I'm doing."

He sounded drunk. But that was normal these days. Dad was almost seventy and had been retired from the bank for five years. He spent most of his days sitting in a two-story townhouse on a golf course he bought after my mother died. He didn't play golf, mostly he sat drinking and reminiscing. When I did stop by on holidays or his birthday, he would talk about events that happened years ago, of people I did not remember. But that wasn't the reason I didn't want to see him.

"Son, I see you got that son of a bitch church bomber. That's good. Maybe all these idiots will calm down now. You think?" he said.

I told him I hoped so. I wasn't sure what idiots he meant – whites, blacks, probably both.

"So how come you going after our friends? They didn't have nothing to do with the bombing thing, you know that. They're all good guys, good friends. Our kind of folks," he said.

Of all the options the Jackson Group members had of getting to us, I had expected they would try to use my father. I knew how the executive level of the good-old-boy network worked. When it was needed, they called in favors, and my father thought he owed a few. Dad would want to help, want to intercede with his son, not just because he owed them, but just for a moment, they would be talking to him again, not walking to the other side of the room.

"It does seem pretty ridiculous, Dad, that these guys might decide to blow up a church and kill a bunch of people. But that's what the FBI is looking into, that possibility. You know I've got to look into it too. That's what I do."

It stumped him for a minute that the FBI was looking into it. He was of a generation that believed the FBI was infallible. "Well, just let the FBI handle it? Why do you have to investigate it too? It's just not good to be investigating our friends," he said.

"Your friends, Dad, not mine."

"That's where you're wrong. That's where you've always been wrong, Joe. You are my son and they are your friends too."

We had been through this a dozen times. He thought I had forsaken the family heritage by becoming a journalist. Making editor had helped, but I was still not a banker, a lawyer or a rising utility company executive, a position he would consider an equal to the men he idolized.

Dad was half white, his skin lighter than mine. I did not get his patrician nose or chin. I look more like the men in my mother's family, wider face, flatter nose, more black, than white. I always thought my father was disappointed that I was not born with more white features. Maybe he should have married a white woman. His father had married a black woman.

He had the looks and the brains, but he always knew he belonged only because the men in the corner offices on the twenty first floor needed someone like him. If he had been all white or all black, he might not have had his job.

One afternoon when I was a kid, Grandpa came to our house. His neck had been cut, and there was a deep gash above his right eye. Blood still flowed out of the wounds. He asked my mother to patch him up because he didn't want my grandmother to see him bleeding. I stood beside the rocker, soaking up his every word. He lit a cigar while my mother bandaged him on the front porch. "I guess some guys don't like me stirring up the boys too much. We walked out, laddie, and I took the whole lot with me. Boy, did that make the bosses up north come a'runnin. Yes, sir, they know we're determined to make a stand."

When my father came home, he found his father huddled on our front porch with other workmen from the mill. My father ordered them to leave. "I don't want anyone to see you here. They might think I..."

"What, Joseph, my boy, spit it out," my grandfather barked. "Am I not welcome in my son's house? Has my son sold out to the bosses, to the English?"

I did not understand then what the fight was about. I looked it up years later when I was studying the American labor movement in college. My grandfather had led one of the longest and bloodiest strikes of an iron and steel mill. At the time I was angry at my father for sending my grandfather away. I missed his ready laugh, his stories, the smell of his cigars. Grandpa always made me feel special. Only later did I understand the fear my father felt at having a union leader for a father. It would not cost him his job because the bank needed him. He was the face of a New South bank, a smiling, handsome black man who proved that Iron City was no longer a racist place. But I knew one of the demons that sat on his shoulders was that he would be fired from that job and have to find one where he did not wear a coat and tie.

As the strike wore on, men died. My grandfather had a cross burned in his front yard because he had a black wife, but he always thought it was the owners' strikebreakers who did it. I didn't see Grandpa for almost six months. He came at Christmas, full of whiskey and carrying small presents. Things got better after that. But he and my father rarely spoke. It was sad for my father that I took more after my grandfather.

"Don't you ever let them call you the N word." My father was getting deep into his bottle. The sun was almost down. I knew he would be asleep in his chair soon. "Don't drive no black man's car. Get you a white man's car. I know you keep your house good, like your mother taught you, not like they say we do. You still living with those white people. That's probably good."

I wanted to interrupt, but a hand seemed to hold me, stopped me from speaking.

"How's that boy of yours? My grandson? You need to bring him by, let me see him."

It wasn't that I deliberately kept Chris away from my father. It was just I wanted something better for him. Let the past be the past. Things, deeper, more painful hid in the past. Those memories would raise their head late at night, when I was alone and afraid. I never wanted my son to know those fears. I never wanted him to be locked away in a closet.

"Dad, I've got to get ready to go to Washington." Silence on the telephone. Going to D.C. impressed him. "Tell your friends that if they are innocent and most of them probably are, they won't be dragged through the ink of my newspaper. Tell them, Dad. I hope it's enough."

"Son, son," he said before I could disconnect.

"Yes, Dad. I have to go."

"I know. I know. I just, I am worried about you," he mumbled. I was not sure he really knew what he was saying. "You're young and idealistic. Be careful out there. These men, these white men you are after, well, they are not used to being questioned by anyone, especially by one of us. They won't take it."

I felt that twinge of fear once more. Too many people had told me to watch my back. But I thought it was time that some of these people got used to being challenged by our kind.

17

Landing at Reagan National Airport has always been a thrill. Airplanes fly in low over the Potomac River, so close to the Fourteenth Street Bridge that those in window seats can almost wave to the cars on the bridge. The flight path gives a panoramic view of Washington's best landmarks: the boxy, elegant Kennedy Center, the majestic Lincoln Memorial, the almost ethereal Jefferson Memorial, the glowing white Washington Monument and the Capitol overlooking all of it from its high perch. The White House is almost too small and sandwiched behind the massive buildings along Constitution Avenue to be seen from a landing airplane. When the terrorist attacked New York and Washington, it was speculated that the terrorists were aiming for the White House, but couldn't see it so they crashed the hijacked airline into the much larger Pentagon instead.

My five years in the Washington Bureau for the Babcock newspaper syndicate had been my best education. Before going to Washington, I reported on Alabama politics, covering two sessions of the state legislature in Montgomery. I expected Washington to be only a larger version of the rough and tumble of Alabama politics. In Montgomery there was little subtlety. Opponents tried to bludgeon one another to death during the day, while the real work of writing laws was done at the bar late at night in the Holiday Inn across the street from the state Capitol.

In Washington, the process of lawmaking was more profession-al. More of the work was done in the daylight. But the infighting, while mostly civil, was fierce. Memories were long. Elected officials would wait for years to extract vengeance for a real or perceived wrong. The Washington I found taught me never to accept any-thing at face value, always to ask why something was happening, why someone took an action at that moment and who stood to gain. In Montgomery the answers to those questions were usually obvi-ous. In Washington less so.

Sheila and I had lived behind the Capitol in a small apart-ment on Fourth Street, S.E. From my front window I looked out on Pennsylvania Avenue. It was a glorious time to be there, to be young and in the newspaper business. Crime was bad, but not out of control. The Redskins had winning seasons. And every day I talked with senators, congressmen, cabinet secretaries and occa-sionally the President for a living. Because I wrote for a national chain of newspapers, we were invited to foreign embassy parties on Massachusetts Avenue, or as it is often called, Embassy Row. Life in Washington was always interesting.

The Delta Airlines plane landed to the southeast, and I could see ahead of us down river the red brick building in Alexandria that housed the offices of the owners of the *Post*. From their offices the Babcock owners and staff looked at the District of Columbia across the flat, widening river. It was a perfect place for a newspaper chain to have its headquarters, close to the action of Washington, yet detached and objective.

Nicki sat beside me, dozing until the wheels touched down. The plane hit the runway hard and jolted her shoulder. She bolted up-right with a sharp pain. Maybe bringing her was a bad idea, but she had insisted. I had called her at the hospital to tell her I had to go to Washington. She didn't say much, but a few minutes later she called back and asked if I would take her home.

I expected to have to referee a fight between Nicki and the doc-tor. But she was already sitting in a wheelchair. In the hallway was her boss. He had commandeered his own wheelchair and sat facing Nicki, his back to me as I walked down the hall. He remained a mystery. Nicki never talked about him and would change the subject when I asked about her work. As I got closer, he rolled himself away in the opposite direction. Nicki turned to greet me with a wide grin. "I'm so glad you're here," she said, forestalling any questions about her boss. "I'm excited to be going home." I assumed she meant her apartment.

But no. My unpredictable Nicki had other ideas. Having helped her into the front seat of my car, she told me as we drove that she planned to go with me to Washington. "I feel up to it," she said, anticipating my objection. "I talked to Doctor Shepherd. He's cleared it." She smiled at me. "Oh, and since we will be so close, while we're there, would you drive me to Philadelphia to see my parents? You've never met them, and I would like for you to."

Her sudden desire to visit her parents seemed out of character, particularly with the pain in her shoulder. I wondered if the pain or the painkillers were affecting her thinking. But something in her voice made me know I should not say no. She had not been close to her parents since she wheeled her Harley out the driveway three years ago. She called her mother weekly for a chat, but that was the only communication between them. I thought her brush with death may have given her reason to rethink her relationship with them. The years had taught me that with women there are times to go along and times to put up a fight. The trick was knowing which to do when.

"And Philadelphia has some pretty good hospitals if I need anything," she said, smiling at me.

We caught the earliest flight to Atlanta. An old joke in Iron City goes that even when you die, whether you are headed to heaven or hell, you have to stop in Atlanta. I checked us into the Marriott in Alexandria, directly across the Potomac from Washington. Both the hotel and the office building next door, where Babcock occupied the fifth floor, were built in brick to match the old town colonial architectural motif. Alexandria seemed somewhat unreal, faux colonial buildings standing beside the real thing. When you turn a corner, you expect that George, Ben or Tom might be standing there arguing some issue about the new republic or more likely deciding where to have an ale.

Nicki lay in bed with a room service plate of steamed vegetables and a fruit juice from the mini-bar when I left to see what Weitzman wanted so urgently. I had a bad feeling about his sudden interest in the bombing investigation. I walked out along the river to try to clear my head of the fear, worry and pride that clamored for dominance. The Potomac flowed placidly along under gray skies. Upriver it rushed through a narrow gorge and over a falls named inappropriately Great Falls, but here in front me it meandered between wide banks toward the Chesapeake Bay. I wished I could step in a boat and float off with it.

Weitzman was waiting for me in the large conference room. A receptionist ushered me in like a visitor and took my request for coffee. Weitzman and three other men I barely knew were seated on one side of the long conference room table.

"We don't want a confrontation with Daniels," Weitzman said after the coffee arrived and questions about my flight were out of the way. "Our deal with the *Examiner* isn't the best in the world, but right now it is better than being out of business."

"Did Daniels call you?" I asked.

"We've talked," Weitzman said.

"Did he threaten us if we printed a story about who's behind the bombing?" I asked, nervous and excited at the same time.

"No. He wouldn't do that."

"So what did he say?"

"Joe, it is just not a good time to be burning bridges with Daniels, okay?" he said.

"Why?"

"I can't say right now."

Weitzman was a fleshy man who smoked a pack and a half a day. He often slipped into his private restroom where he thought no one knew he was violating Arlington law despite the tell-tale ash flakes on his jacket lapels. The man beside him was the polar opposite. Thin, dapper with a small mustache and neatly trimmed hair, George Casterly was the chief numbers cruncher. He distrusted editors and sat frowning at me with several file folders in front of him.

The other men in the room barely spoke. Even when I came in and shook hands with each one, they merely smiled. I was on the griddle.

"You could have told me that on the phone. Why did you bring me here?"

None of the men answered. They sat looking at me. I kept my eyes on Weitzman. He was my boss. He had made me editor. I had known him for years and expected him to tell me the truth.

"Are you selling the *Post* to the *Examiner?*" I asked, expressing the deep fear I had harbored since he had called me here.

"It's a point of discussion," Weitzman said.

"But that's only on a need-to-know basis," Casterly chimed in.

The Pentagon was upriver a few miles from where we sat. The CIA was a little further up the river in Langley. It never ceased to amaze me how national security jargon crept into everyday D.C. lingo. The phrase sounded silly coming out of Casterly's mouth. I might have laughed if the news hadn't been so depressing.

Our chain of papers was slowly becoming extinct. Out of the original twenty two Babcock newspapers from New York to San Diego, we were down to twelve. Newspapers in Texas, California and Tennessee were sold before I joined the chain. The owners had jettisoned three others in Michigan and Illinois during the last recession. And the international wire service the chain owned had been allowed to go bankrupt and sold. Now the *Post* was on the block. I felt weary, yet angry at the owners and these men they employed who seemed to have no vision, no courage.

"You've seen what the *Examiner* is all about. It isn't a newspaper any more. Most days it is a waste of trees," I said.

"That's not our concern, Joe. We're in the news business. Note the emphasis on the word business," Weitzman said as if he was talking to a radical college student.

I started to argue the merits of having a good newspaper for the people of Iron City, but none of these men gave a damn. They had sold advertising or were accountants. They knew nothing of writing a good story and watching its impact on the readers.

"The excitement over the Crenshaw story last Saturday was the boost we needed. We can keep it going, drive up the circulation numbers over the next few weeks."

We had sold more papers on Saturday than ever in the history of the *Post*. And the national publicity we were getting was helping sell more and bring more viewers to the web site. It was helping the whole chain. The *New York Times* ran a feature on our bringing Crenshaw back from Florida. The *Columbia Journalism Review* and, of all things, *People* magazine had called for interviews.

"We, not the *Examiner*, are in the driver's seat. Let's press our advantage now," I argued.

Both Weitzman and Casterly shook their heads. The other men joined in like robots. The publicity was nice, they conceded, but they did not think it would translate into more than just a blip in the circulation figures.

Casterly, his weasel face in a frown, said. "I doubt it will improve the bottom line, which now is the only thing that will impress the shareholders."

"But they can't be too upset. We're not losing money in Iron City," I said.

"Well, yes and no," Casterly said. "It depends on how you look at it. We could be making more money, actually a lot more money, investing in other properties or even in T-bills."

Considering what Treasury notes were paying, that was not a ringing endorsement of the *Post*'s financial picture. The writing seemed to be on the wall. Iron City would join the ranks of cities with only one daily newspaper and someday maybe none. I could not imagine doing something else, not being involved with the newspaper every day. It was all I had ever done. Other staff members would drift off to newspapers in different cities. Others would find work in Iron City. A few might go to the *Examiner.*

I also felt sorry for our readers. They would be ill-served by this decision. I would miss them and flattered myself that they would miss us.

"I guess you're right. I've never thought much about the *Post* as a business. I always thought it had a higher purpose," I said.

"Joe, maybe newspapers should not be a business. Maybe they should be structured as not-for-profit corporations, as a public service. But they aren't. Our investors want their money to pay dividends. Some of the properties are making a good profit. Most aren't," Weitzman said, pausing to change the tone. "I don't want you to worry. We'll find a place for you. You are one of Babcock's stars, and maybe a few of your people."

The other newspapers in the syndicate were a mixed bag. Some were dominant in their markets, others like papers in Ohio and Pennsylvania were the weak sister like the *Post* was in Iron City.

"Are you looking at closing all of the papers that are not making a big profit?" I asked, not really expecting a detailed answer.

Casterly warmed to the topic and began to explain that a new owner had asked him to examine the return on investment for each property. Both he and Weitzman seemed to think of the newspapers more like real estate, than as living, essential organs of a city.

"New owner? We have a new owner?" I asked.

Weitzman shook his head at me. "You don't know? Don't you read what we send you?"

I raised my eyebrows. Lately emails had not been my highest priority. Mrs. James often reminded me to check them, but then there were so many, I would go through them as quickly as I could. I must have skipped an important one.

"I've been a bit preoccupied lately."

"Well, yes, I understand. What we sent out three weeks ago was notice that two of the family members had sold their shares." Weitzman paused conspiratorially. "What we didn't say was that two of the daughters, it's not important which ones, needed cash. They overspent their trust allowances, I'm afraid. So they sold their stock to an outside investor, a successful investment group, which now owns about forty percent of the stock. That makes the investor the largest stockholder." Weitzman looked around at Casterly and the others, as if checking to see if he was telling me too much. "He is the one, who is holding our feet to the fire."

"Who's the new owner?" I asked.

Weitzman shook his head and said it really didn't matter. "It is an investment group that owns a lot of real estate, called Temple Investments. It has never invested in newspapers before. You probably never heard of it. It stays under the radar. I hadn't run across it until the chairman suddenly stepped in and bought the Babcock daughters' stock. Things change. We adapt."

Our newspaper chain had been created by Louis Babcock, who put together a media empire before World War II. The old man had started as a copy boy at the *New York World* and every week put away a few dollars to buy stock in his newspaper. Through the years he worked his way into management, finally becoming the newspaper's publisher. After the war, he bought up and started newspapers around the country and built the Babcock Newspaper Syndicate into an influential force in national economic and political affairs. Babcock had one of two afternoon papers in Washington, which gave him influence with Congress and at the White House. His newspapers were in many congressional districts across the country. Before television and the Internet became so pervasive, Babcock had more reach than almost any other media, other than the *Washington Post* and *New York Times*. From the White House to the Pentagon to the State Department, his reporters were called on among the elite journalists at news conferences. He was a tough old bird even into his eighties. He picked John Kennedy over Richard

Nixon in the 1960 election with many of the local editors screaming against endorsing the young senator from Massachusetts. In his
memoirs the old man wrote that it was one of his finest moments.
He died not long after Nixon was impeached. Since his death, the
syndicate in the hands of his children and the bean counters had
been deteriorating.

Babcock's heirs, four daughters and two sons, were not carved
from the same wood as the old man. The syndicate prospered financially until recently when most newspapers took on too much debt
and began to fall on hard times. To the old man, profits were second-
ary to the power the newspapers wielded. Now the bottom line was
the only barometer. The children needed to keep up their dividends
to support lavish lifestyles. Two lived in the Hamptons. One was married and lived quietly in Ohio. One son had divorced, spreading the
stock ownership. The other son had died in the first Iraq war. The
fourth daughter was the toast of Carmel. I was glad Babcock was
dead and could see his empire only from his perch in heaven, where
I imagined he played poker with the likes of H.L. Mencken. Now
with a new owner, which I took to mean a non-newspaper person,
controlling the Babcock syndicate, I doubted that we would survive.

A memory flashed through my brain. When I was a young reporter, one of the veteran editors had stopped to talk one afternoon.
He chewed tobacco and carried a Mason jar with him to catch the
spit. "You know you'll probably outlive newspapers, at least as we
know them today." I thought then he was being dramatic.

"So why are you focusing on the *Post*? Are we the worst of the
papers?"

"Actually no," Casterly said, showing off his on-going analysis of
the newspapers' finances. "Several other papers are bleeding red
ink. The agreement with the *Examiner* keeps the *Post* in the black,
though not by much."

"So why are you thinking of selling us?"

Weitzman sighed. "It was suggested by the new owner that if we
got an offer for any of the weaker papers, we should take it. And

then Daniels called. It would be our first opportunity to sell off a weaker paper, that's all. Don't see a conspiracy behind everything, Joe."

Under-performing, hell. We had just captured the church bomber, driven up circulation, been on several national television shows. I had learned from Howard, never trust coincidences.

There was a knock on the conference room door, and the secretary who had shown me in came in the room. She apologized as I watched Casterly frown at her and snatch from her hand the piece of paper she carried.

"I'm sorry. They said it was urgent." She backed out of the room.

I assumed it was from Ed. Something had probably happened. Had the FBI broken Crenshaw?

"The Deputy Attorney General's office called for you," Casterly read with a smug sneer. "They want to know if you could see Ms. Keene in her office at three." He looked up at me. "It would seem you have been summoned for a command performance."

The bean counter was jealous.

"Well, that should be interesting," Weitzman said. "I wonder how she knew you were here."

Me too. Maybe they had called the *Post* and Mrs. James had told them. Or did Pitts still have agents tracking me?

Weitzman said, "Let us know what she has to say, and don't do anything to piss off Daniels. That's an order."

What was he going to do, fire me? There is a little rebel in all of us. I was born with more than my share of it. The African and Irish stew I was spawned from made me want even more to write the story linking Daniels to the bombing.

"We don't know how he would react to a story in the *Post* about some group he is in," Casterly said.

I snickered. "You mean Daniels might not like to be named a co-conspirator in the bombing of the church?"

Weitzman and his three colleagues stared at me like I had grown an extra nose. I realized then that they had not known what

"Hell, no. Why would you write that?" Weitzman said, recovering from his shock.

"Because it may be true. That's what we are working on. That's why Daniels called you. He assumed you knew."

"I had no idea. He said you were making a big deal out of the Teddy Roosevelt group or some civic thing. I don't remember. I thought you were investigating it just to embarrass him."

I looked around the room. The other men sitting around the conference table looked like the wind had been kicked out of them.

"Why, in God's name, would you think that Daniels was involved in the bombing?" Weitzman asked.

I explained about the Jackson Group, about Mark's interview with Crenshaw, about the waiter's tentative identification of Daniels. And then I told them about the phone calls between the *Examiner* and Crenshaw and his willingness to come back to Iron City with us because he thought we worked for Daniels.

Weitzman sat staring at the table. Casterly sputtered. They were trying to figure how they could still sell the *Post* if Daniels were in prison.

"That isn't enough to run a story," Weitzman said finally.

"That's right. You don't have enough evidence." Casterly lept at it like it was a life preserver in a storm.

I nodded. "Of course. That's why we haven't run it, yet," I said with a lot of emphasis on the last word. "It is just a possibility. It might be him. It might be some of his friends. We don't know yet. But that's what got him spooked." I leaned back for effect. "Interesting, huh?"

They were still recovering from their shock. Weitzman knew that the Babcock Syndicate would be a national laughing stock if it was discovered to be negotiating to sell the *Post* to a man indicted for conspiracy to bomb the church, especially after the *Post* brought in Crenshaw. Negotiations with Daniels could land Weitzman and

Casterly on CNN and the front page of newspapers around the country. But they also knew that Daniels was probably the only person that would be interested in buying the *Post*. He could kill our investigation and keep us going or close us down, whichever made the most money.

"Just back off for now. Let some water flow under the bridge. Watch yourself. You are playing with fire. Lots of important people, and not just Daniels, really want this deal to go through," Weitzman said in a monotone, clearly distracted by the possibilities involved.

He looked up and asked, "Isn't the FBI still investigating?" I nodded. "Let them do it, not you. You stick to reporting what happens, okay?"

He sounded too much like my father. As I walked out, that knot was in my stomach again.

The Justice Department is housed in one of the most elegant of many beautiful office buildings along Pennsylvania Avenue. When I stepped out of the cab, the air was crisp and clean. Two intense-looking men in pin-strips and carrying fat briefcases jumped in and told the driver to take them to the Rayburn House Office Building. I knew I was back in Washington.

I crossed the sidewalk, dodging a gaggle of tourists, bicycle messengers and government workers coming back from late lunches. I made my way slowly through a phalanx of security and metal detectors, then up the elevator to be greeted by an assistant, who led me finally into the inner sanctum of Allison Keene. Being summoned to the Justice Department felt like being sent to the principal's office. I expected a paddling or at least detention hall. The deputy attorney general worked in an office with windows behind her desk that looked down on the broad avenue. The walls of her office were paneled in dark woods, an austere, formal room, relieved only by fresh cut flowers on her desk, two watercolors of San Francisco Bay and brightly colored upholstery on the chairs and sofa. On the wall beside the door was a framed photo of her boss shaking hands with the President.

Keene, who had come to Washington as the corporate counsel for one of the rising Silicon Valley titans, entered her office from a door hidden by the paneling. Her face was familiar from all the media coverage, but I had not expected her to be so tall. Even in low heels she stood eye to eye with me. No wonder she had all the men at the Justice Department and the FBI jumping.

"I am so glad to meet you," she said smiling broadly. Her handshake left little doubt that she was in charge. "Wayman has given me a lengthy description of you and your work to bring the bomber to justice. I am impressed."

"Thank you," I said, uncertain when the flattery would stop and the waterboarding would begin. Oh, I forgot, they don't do that any more.

She guided me across the office to a sofa where we sat together. On the table in front of us was a pot of coffee. She poured the coffee into small china cups and asked if I liked a Sumatran blend. I laughed and said I rarely drank coffee from halfway around the world.

"I know you are busy, and I appreciate you coming on short notice. Let me get right to the point. This investigation in Iron City is critically important. Thanks to your efforts, the *Post*'s efforts, we have a man in jail who has confessed to you and to us that he is the church bomber. His arrest has helped quell the riots. So we very much appreciate your role in his arrest." She paused for effect. "You believe, I'm told, that this man, Crenshaw, did not act alone."

"I believe there are others."

"What is your evidence?" she asked.

"Crenshaw just does not seem bright enough or ambitious enough or maybe even crazy enough to have thought this up by himself. As you know from the confession he made to us, he admits he was paid by someone. I don't think that was just a friend, or someone who admired his work."

She nodded. Her whole body seemed coiled. She was abrupt, almost curt in her manner. But instead of being offensive, she radiated strength and determination. "That tracks with what we are getting from the interrogation. He is frightened. He continues to be cooperative on how he placed the bomb, but not about who put him up to it. When asked that, he shuts down. Even when we have offered to take the death penalty off the table, he has said only that he would not live long, especially in prison, if he told us who was behind the bombing. We believe, and this must be totally off the record, that the person behind this offense is very powerful politically, financially and has made threats that our bomber believes."

I nodded, but said nothing.

"The transcript is vague, yours and ours. I've gone over that part of it several times. Crenshaw qualifies everything. He talks in circles, coming close to giving up some intel at one point, then shutting down. Our most experienced interrogators are working with him now. I'm hopeful they will get something soon."

I guessed they had not moved him out of the jail or I would have heard about it from my new cop friends. I said, "Good. It will be great to bring this bombing to a close. Iron City can not take much more."

She agreed. "The President, as you know, has been very concerned about more riots in Iron City. There is the real worry among law enforcement that the riots might spread. The protests in other cities have not turned to violence yet, but could. FBI intelligence reports are worrisome. All inner cities are dry kindling, ready for a spark of their own to erupt. Just let another policeman shoot another black child, and we could have violent protests all over the country," she said.

If Grey had been a national figure, as he might have been one day, riots would have broken out around the country, she said. He wasn't Dr. King, but the African-American community may be more volatile, more prone to act today than it was even in the sixties. She paused to sip her coffee. "Things are different, more dangerous today. That's why it is critical that we indict everyone involved, no matter who they are. One of the worst black eyes on record for this department was its failure to indict Robert Chambliss and his accomplices in the sixty-three bombing. That is not going to happen again."

Chambliss, known to his klan friends as Dynamite Bob, was free for more than a decade before he was sent to prison for the first bombing of the church. And it was not the Justice Department that got Chambliss. Bill Baxley, a colorful and ambitious young Alabama attorney general, pieced together the case against him and his fellow bombers. Chambliss died in prison. Crenshaw was a lot younger than Chambliss, but no one wanted him to die in prison before he told us the names of those who put him up to this.

"I've reviewed the records on the sixty-three investigation," she said, leaning forward, her long arms placing her cup on the coffee table. "I thought there might be a connection. And I wanted to see what had been done then, what mistakes were made. I'm a big believer in learning from others."

A connection to the first bombing? That hardly seemed possible. Did she believe that some group of old klansmen had come out of retirement for one last attempt to keep blacks from gaining more political and economic power? Or was it just that they had gotten away with it once, and they thought they could do it again?

"Now I read confidential documents with Bobby Kennedy's name on them, memos to his brother about how difficult Governor Wallace was making it for the Justice Department in the investigation. I understand why this department failed back then. This time we don't have any of those problems, only an aggressive, uncooperative newspaper editor," she said.

She turned to face me. She sat very straight, her knees tight against the sofa. I smiled. "I didn't plant the bomb or pay Crenshaw to do it. Like you, we are trying to find out who are Crenshaw's conspirators."

"Yes, maybe I misspoke. As you know, this investigation transcends any commercial interests or even ego you may have," she said.

I bristled. "Our investigation had nothing to do with money or ego." I was reminded of the conversation with Weitzman about the business of newspapers. Did anyone understand the role of a newspaper in our society? "We are doing our job, giving our readers information they should have. Sure, I could have given the information we had to your guys and let them go to Florida and arrest Crenshaw. Undoubtedly you would have found him faster, and maybe two of my people would not have been shot and others beaten up. I feel bad about that. But we worked hard to bring that information to our readers."

She turned and looked out the window. Down Pennsylvania Avenue, the sun bathed the Capitol's dome in full sunlight. She stood up and walked slowly behind her desk and picked up a red folder marked Iron City. She opened it and read again for a minute.

"Before I ask you one more question, I want to tell you how much of an interest the President has taken in this case. He has called personally with questions, and he has told me he wants to go to Iron City once we have this wrapped up and everyone involved is incarcerated. He wants to help people like you rebuild Iron City without the racial tension. He wants to help nurture young black leadership in the city for the future."

I smiled. "That would be great. Iron City could use his leadership." I thought about H.T. and his corps of young black men and how, if I could help arrange a meeting with the President, they would benefit from his attention.

She nodded. "Now, let me ask you one more question. You don't have to answer it, of course. I know that you are continuing to search for the same people we are, so I will understand if you don't want to answer. But I also have a condition. I must insist that you agree not to publish anything about this part of our investigation. Do you agree?"

I thought about the dangerous area I was getting into. If she asked me about the Jackson Group or some members of it, my answer could limit what we could report. But I wanted to know what the FBI and Justice Department were working on.

"There are some leads we are working on where I can not restrict our reporters. If you ask about those areas, I will not answer one way or the other. I promise not to report what you ask me about it, nor will I attribute any of the information to the Justice Department. Does that work for you?"

"Yes." She closed the file. She paused considering her words. "Is it possible that Crenshaw bombed the church on orders from Sheriff Ned Peebles?"

I had a sinking feeling. Had we ignored Peebles when it was right in our face?

"That possibility has occurred to us. As you know, Crenshaw worked for Peebles. It was Peebles who got him the constable job. We suspected that the sheriff probably knew where Crenshaw was hiding. And clearly the sheriff has the power and could easily order his guards, another prisoner or one of his loyal followers to take Crenshaw out. The sheriff was also no fan of Grey's. He has to get his funding for the jail and his department appropriated by the commissioners. He and Grey tied up for months over the number of black deputies he had and how black prisoners were treated," I said.

Keene looked down at her file. I wished I could read it. But red folders, I knew, required a high-level of clearance. And I doubted she was going to leave it on the table in front of me while she went for more coffee.

"Is that enough for Peebles to kill Grey?" she asked as much to herself as to me.

"Only if he thought it would gain himself something worth the risk. Peebles is no dummy. He would've known the heat would be white hot and outside of his control," I said.

"Would you be surprised if the sheriff was behind it?" she asked.

I thought about it for a few seconds. "No. It would give me another great headline."

She stood up, smiling. I realized she was bringing an end to the meeting. She had made her point and gotten my views on something being debated by her team in Iron City and here. She was not the type to sit and chat. "I wanted to meet you in person. I am a fan. Maybe you should come to work for us," she said as polite flattery.

"Well, I'm impressed by your information network. Very few people knew I would be in Washington today," I said.

"Yes, we're very good at tracking people down once we know who we're after," she said. The double meaning was not lost behind her smile.

We walked to the door. "There is one thing, a favor I would ask, if I'm allowed."

She stopped and looked hard into my eyes. She knew it must be important if I was asking.

"If I can," she said, clearly curious.

"I believe there are serious negotiations going on that would lead to the Iron City *Examiner*, the afternoon paper, purchasing my newspaper. If that happens, it would reduce competition significantly in the Alabama media." I did not have to say it would also kill one of the few moderate voices in a very Republican state. I stopped almost afraid to ask, but it could be our only hope of stopping Weitzman and the new owners from playing out this hand. "I would hope you might take an interest in that merger and make certain that the people of Alabama are being well served."

She laughed a deep, hearty laugh. It was very contagious. I almost laughed myself. "Wait until I tell Wayman that we now have to save the *Post* from its natural predators. After embarrassing him and, let's say, inconveniencing me, my boss and his boss, you want us to save your precious newspaper. You do have some balls."

I smiled. "Yes ma'am." I chuckled all the way to the elevator. At least she hadn't said no.

18

Interstate 95 out of Washington took us north through Baltimore and Wilmington before crossing into Pennsylvania. Before leaving the capital, we drove up the broad avenue named for Nicki's home state, lunched at the Hawk & Dove restaurant on Capitol Hill and drove by the Washington, Jefferson and Lincoln memorials. We stopped to let her dip her toe in the cold water of the Reflecting Pool and drove down Sixteenth Street to view the White House across Lafayette Park. She had come to Washington with her eighth grade class, she told me, but did not remember how beautiful it was. "It reminds me so much of Paris," she said. Pete L'Enfant, the French designer of early Washington, would be pleased that she noticed.

The drive north was easy. I had rented a large car to give us a smooth ride and her plenty of room. She settled in the front passenger seat and seemed happy watching the countryside glide by. It was cold with occasional snow flurries, something you don't see often in Iron City.

"I never finished this part of my drive on the Harley. I went west out of Philadelphia, across the northern states to the west coast. I never completed the loop. Maybe someday I'll hop on the bike and head north. This is pretty."

"Not without me," I said, trying to imagine me on the back of a motorcycle.

"I'm really glad I made that trip. It was hard on a motorcycle. I went through all kinds of weather, ran into some people I would not want to meet again. There were others who were great. For the first time, I felt really free."

"A horse that finds the gate open?" I offered.

She laughed. "Maybe a gerbil escaping her cage."

She snuggled back in the seat, resting her shoulder on a pillow I had pilfered from the hotel. She looked relaxed and comfortable wearing a green pullover and jeans that showed off her lower half to perfection.

"I am excited, maybe a little anxious for you to meet my parents. I don't know how they will react. When I left, they were upset. My father was really angry, my mother in tears. I hated seeing them like that. But I had to go, not just to a school that my father paid for, but really away on my own."

"Are you going home to stay?" I trembled inside that she might be tempted to return to Philadelphia and that life for good.

All night I had tossed and turned in the hotel bed, my mood swinging from depression over the chance of the *Post* being sold or closed to the excitement every news person feels at being in Washington. Having Nicki with me was comforting, but now I was worried about losing her. I was a bundle of mixed emotions as I drove north.

"I like what I do. I like Iron City. I haven't told you, but I'm going to be a partner in the detective firm. That is what my boss was talking to me about at the hospital. And of course, I sort of like you." She gave me a big smile. "I am not going anywhere. I just need to come here and put things back together with my parents, if I can. It'll be all right. You'll see."

That made me relax a little, but the closer we got to Philadelphia the more tense she seemed.

"Maybe I'll learn a little more about what makes you tick, about your childhood," I said.

Nicki rarely talked about her life before me, and she didn't take my comment as a cue to open up about herself now. I tried to imagine what her parents would be like. I always try to anticipate situations. It probably stems from some insecurity. If I can think about it ahead of time, then maybe I could handle the situation better. It rarely helped. Unfortunately people and things usually turned out different from what I expected.

"You really believe people are good, don't you?" she said as we passed Wilmington.

"I guess so."

"Not me. I grew up assuming people did good only when it was in their selfish interests," she said.

"That's pretty cold," I said.

"My mother, you'll see, is not like that. My mother is a very good person. I miss her." There was a long pause. I waited to hear the rest of that thought. Glancing at her as I drove I could see she was deep in thought. "I guess I've been reevaluating a lot of things lately."

We rode in silence. I thought again about my grandfather, the eternal optimist. He faced a lot of adversity, even evil in his life, but he believed that people were basically good with the exception of the bosses, who turned bad by the quest for money, status and privilege. My father was the pessimistic. He assumed everyone was out to get him, to take from him whatever they could, particularly his self respect.

"People are just people," I said.

She smiled. "Maybe that's why I like being with you. You always try to see the good in people. Pretty amazing with what you've seen being in the news business. You'd think you would be all chewed up by now. I worry about that in my business. We only deal mostly with the lowlifes."

"Like me?"

She nodded. "And then some."

We laughed and drove on. Nicki asked for more details about my meetings in Washington. She mostly wanted to hear about Allison Keene, who has become a role model for many young women.

Nicki seemed almost resigned that the *Post* might be sold. "What would you do if that happened?"

Just hearing her say the words out loud sent chills up my neck. My fears were not just about collecting a paycheck or telling my in-laws to pack up, that we were leaving everything they knew for another Babcock newspaper. It was about who I was. When I opened my eyes in the morning, I told myself I was the editor of a newspaper. If I didn't have that, I worried that I would fall into such depression I might not want to open my eyes.

"Do you think Daniels wants to buy the *Post* to stop you writing a story about him and the bombing?" she asked.

That could be a big part of it, I thought. He is rich and powerful now without owning the *Post*. Would buying my newspaper make him richer, more powerful? Probably not. It would give him something that his father never accomplished. It might make him stand taller in his father's shadow.

"Sometimes things that look like a duck, walk like a duck and quack like a duck are just that, a duck," she said.

"That's true. Maybe, just maybe, we can tie this whole mess around Daniels' neck and solve the bombing and save the *Post* all in one deal of the cards."

"And you and I will walk away into the sunset, right?" she said.

We crossed the Pennsylvania state line thinking about the future. I talked to her about Howard and old man Babcock, both fighters for what they believed in. She listened quietly as she sat staring out through the windshield at the leafless trees amidst the evergreens that lined the highway.

"You're lucky. You still have heroes," she said.

I had never thought about Howard and Babcock as heroes. But they were. Without them I couldn't be who I was. Howard had allowed me to see how I could put my values into action and not let the world erode them.

"Whatever happens, don't go down without a fight. You'd never forgive yourself."

We passed the Philadelphia airport and the Navy yard, and Nicki found her old favorite radio station. She told me with pride that several of the old rock groups had grown up around South Street in Philadelphia before hitting the big time. The Schuylkill River was deserted, its gingerbread boat houses cold and silent. On the far bank were remnants of several old mills. Once the foundation of the Philadelphia economy, the mills were now condominiums, offices and labs for the biotechnology industry. There was an interesting parallel between Philadelphia and Iron City, both industrial towns that had turned to science-based industries to replaced departing jobs. Was it also a metaphor for the news industry? Old relics of newspapers turning into something new and entirely electronic. Could I ever be happy managing news web sites and blog writers?

We turned west toward the wealthy western suburbs of Philadelphia. Nicki's parents lived in Radnor, a beautiful old town where estates with broad lawns rolled down to tree-lined streets. The Fabrini family lived in a house large enough to house the starting lineup of the '76ers pro basketball team. Nicki told me as the car rolled up the curved stone driveway that the house, built in a French manor style, had nine bedrooms and six bathrooms, on four acres of lawns and woods. I wondered if Nicki's Italian-American father, like my African-American father, had bought the house in the WASPish neighborhood to acquire social acceptance.

Nicki chatted away about things she had done as a teenager on these grounds. "I used to ride my bike through there. I had a life-size doll tree house over there. Oh, it's gone."

"It must have been pretty extraordinary to have your own private park to play in."

Before we could ring the bell, a woman answered the door. Clearly waiting for us, she yelped in delight at the sight of Nicki, stepped through the double doors and grabbed Nicki in a huge bear hug. I could see Nicki wince in pain as the large woman squeezed her, but she never uttered a sound. The woman let her go, stepped back and looked her over.

"Well, you don't look too bad for all your adventures."

"Thank you, Mattie. It is great to see you. I love you," Nicki said, recovering quickly from the pain. She managed a smile at the older woman and turned to me. "Joe, this is Mattie. She helped raise me. I don't know what I would have done without her. We used to play dolls together. Remember?"

Mattie was almost as broad as she was tall. She had a huge bosom counterbalanced by a wide set of hips. It was hard to imagine her chasing after a young Nicki.

"You know, I haven't had anyone to play dolls with since you left. Sweetie, it is so good to have you home. And you, young man, are you with Nicki?"

Nicki laughed. "Yes, Mattie, this is Joe Riordan. He's with me."

Mattie looked me over. From her expression, I was not what she had hoped for. "I guess you'll be all right. But I'm keeping my eye on you. I want to see if you're good enough for my Nicki."

Nicki had told me that her parents were in their mid-thirties when she was born. Her father had built a small empire of automobile repair shops around Philadelphia, and he owned apartment houses in south Philadelphia and two older office buildings on south Broad Street downtown. His proudest investment was as a minority stockholder in the Philadelphia Eagles football franchise, which brought with him access to the players and a stadium box on game day. It also gave him bragging rights when the Eagles were winning.

Mattie, who told me she had been with the Fabrinis since Nicki was born, brought us in to the large foyer with a limestone floor. As I looked into the formal rooms, I could see the life Nicki had left behind. The furniture and furnishings were extraordinary. A huge stone fireplace with an elaborately carved mantel dominated the living room. A mirror in the foyer was framed in gold leaf. A table in the hall looked like it belonged in one of the restored houses of Europe, while light danced off of a chandelier hanging from a barrel-vaulted ceiling. It looked like the Fabrinis lived in a museum, but to showcase what or to impress whom was unclear.

At the bottom of a staircase that spiraled upward stood a woman in her sixties waiting to greet us. Small and fragile looking, she stood rigid, holding herself with her arms wrapped tightly around her waist. Her features looked drawn. Nicki set down her purse on the antique hall table and walked quickly to her. "It's good to see you, Mother. Are you well?"

"It's good to see you too, Nicole." Her mother's voice was hardly more than a whisper. It seemed to require an enormous effort for her to speak. "We are well, your father and I."

The two women could not take their eyes off one another. The prodigal daughter returning home, after years of being away, having been shot in the shoulder in a far-away city, bringing with her a man. It was probably not what Elena Fabrini had planned for her only child.

"And father, is he home?" Nicki asked.

"Yes. He is in his study on a phone call, I think. He will join us in a few minutes. I wanted to see you first. It has been so long." She hugged Nicki again, holding her like she did not want to let her go. "I am so glad you are home."

Her mother turned her eyes on me for the first time and drilled a hole. I wished I was younger and thinner and named Rafael. I did graduate from Princeton, just a few miles north, but that thought was cold comfort under her appraising stare.

"Mother, I want you to meet Joe, Joe Riordan, my Joe. But you probably guessed that. Joe's become famous lately."

Nicki reached out and took my hand, "Joe, I want you to meet my mother, Elena Fabrini."

The older woman nodded and with minimal enthusiasm, said, "Yes, we have taken a considerable interest in you. Congratulations,

Mr. Riordan. I, we were so relieved when that man was arrested. We have been so worried about Nicki living in a city with riots, so much death and destruction."

Her voice, now louder, was almost devoid of an accent. Like Nicki, she graduated from Smith College and had devoted much of her life to St. Joseph's Hospital in one of the tougher neighborhoods of north Philadelphia. One of the few stories Nicki had told me was of her mother taking her to the hospital to play with the children patients. The mother and daughter would also bring flowers to the sick and dying. Ms. Fabrini's portrait hung in the hallway outside the administrator's office as a tribute to the years she had spent raising millions of dollars to keep the charitable hospital expanding. She looked like delicate piece of china, but this was a woman made of iron.

We shook hands, her thin hand merely resting in mine. She held my gaze with strong green eyes set in her porcelain skin that looked like it had never seen the sun. "It's so good to meet you," I said. "Nicki has told me so much about you and her family. I look forward to getting to know you, and of course, more about Nicki."

Could these situations be any more awkward?

She nodded. "I have arranged for you to stay in your old room," she said more to Nicki, than me. "We left it as it was. I thought you would like that."

"Thank you," Nicki said. At least there wasn't going to be the hassle about our staying in the same room.

"Vincent will be down in a few minutes. Meanwhile I will have Benjamin bring up your bags." A young black man, dressed in a suit, appeared from a room behind the staircase and held out his hand for my car keys. He took them from me, running his eyes across my face. He merely nodded and left.

Mrs. Fabrini followed him with her eyes as he opened the front door and went out to collect our bags from the car. "Benjamin is my husband's new chauffeur. He found him looking for work at one of my husband's businesses. He was hungry and had a no place to live.

His parents are dead, and his uncle treated him rather badly. He doesn't talk much, but he has been a tremendous help around the house and to my husband. He is devoted to Vincent."

As she spoke his name, her husband appeared at the top of the staircase as if he had been waiting out of sight listening to our conversation. With Benjamin's sudden appearance and now Nicki's father, the scene seemed staged.

"Nicole." Her father's voice bellowed out as he started down the stairs. "Oh, Nicki, my little darling, how fabulous to see you. And you're looking good considering what you've been through. How are you feeling? Does your shoulder hurt?"

Vincent Fabrini was as robust as his wife was frail. Tall and broad at the shoulders, he had a deep olive skin tone and a well-trimmed Van Dyke-style beard that made him look like a 1930s film star. His angular nose looked almost sculpted beneath a pair of piercing brown eyes. He wore a three-piece gray suit that must have been hand tailored, it fit him so perfectly. He trotted down the curved staircase with the agility of a much younger man and held out his arms to embrace his daughter.

"Father." Nicki seemed less happy to see her father than she had her mother. She leaned forward into his arms. He kissed her cheek and wrapped his arms around her. She said her shoulder did not much and that she was recovering nicely. "And you, you're looking well too," she said.

"Oh, I could lose a few pounds. Always a struggle," he said, patting his abdomen held in by his vest that covered a expensive-looking tie. "And you, young man, you must be the famous Joe Riordan I have heard so much about." He reached out and grabbed not just my hand, but my arm as well, holding my right forearm with his left hand.

I did not like my reaction to him. Vincent Fabrini was all bluster and show, like many of the politicians who had come to my grandfather's house when I was a child. They smelled of after shave that covered a much nastier scent. Vincent Fabrini wore expensive cologne, but that only made me think the price of a relationship with Fabrini was just that much higher.

"Thank you for having us to your home," I said.

"Oh, you are most welcome. Nicki, of course, this is her home. A friend of our daughter is always welcome," Fabrini said, turning again to Nicki and putting his arm around her waist. "It is so good to have you home. We have missed you very much. It is not the same without you."

Nicki tensed at his words. "It is good to be here, though I feel my home is now in Alabama." She was laying down the rules from the start. This was a visit, not a return for a permanent stay. A grimace locked Fabrini's jaw. He was disappointed, angry and frustrated in that moment. The look was gone in an instant and the broad smile across perfect teeth returned. I hoped we would escape unscathed.

"Yes, yes, yes. We understand. It is just so good to have you both here." He reached out and put his arm around my shoulders while keeping Nicki close. Flanked by the two of us, we strolled into the living area. Mrs. Fabrini followed behind. Mattie stood in the doorway.

While I soaked up the view out the windows of the manicured lawn, of the furnishings and the decor of the living room, Nicki told her parents that they should come to Iron City.

"Well, maybe we will do that, once all this unpleasantness is over. I'm sure Elena and I would like to see Iron City. We've never been anywhere in the south except for a short vacation to Miami once. We didn't like it much and came home."

The room was filled with antique French furniture I had seen when I toured a few palaces in Europe in the summer before my senior year in college. There were inlaid walls of marble and gold that looked like something lifted from the Palace of Versailles.

"Iron City is very different from Miami. It is more like Philadelphia, an industrial city built by immigrants. Many of them, including my grandfather, came from Pennsylvania, up around

Allentown," I said, hoping it would make them think I was not such an outsider.

"Allentown, well, it is a small world. I'm from south Philly myself," Fabrini said.

"I understand you went to Princeton," Mrs. Fabrini said.

I told her that my parents were big believers in education. My father had wanted me to follow in his footsteps and attend a college in Alabama, but my mother had fallen in love with Princeton. While she hovered near me in the kitchen as I did my homework, she told me often that she thought her little prince should go to a college named for one. Fortunately my grades, test scores and probably my ethnicity made me attractive enough to be admitted and receive a scholarship large enough that my father could not say no.

"Oh, that's wonderful," Fabrini said. "Of course, Temple was all I could manage, and I had to drop out after a couple of years. But I've managed pretty well without an Ivy League education."

"Temple is a great school. Philadelphia has so many great colleges and universities," I said.

Silence filled the room as the Fabrinis looked at one another.

"That's right," he said. "Now it has been a long trip for the two of you. Would a glass of wine interest you? Dinner will be served about seven after you've had a chance to rest up and change."

Mattie brought the women white wine in Riedel glasses. She gave Vincent Fabrini and me large glasses of red wine.

"I took the liberty of having Mattie pour us a Cabernet I found. I thought you might like it. A bold taste," he said.

It was clear the Fabrinis had given some thought to our visit. We sat in the living room, swapping stories about Nicki's childhood and our recent adventures. I caught myself staring at the Renaissance-style mural painted on the ceiling and wondering how much that cost and why Fabrini had spent the money to have it painted. Nicki told them I had met with Allison Keene while we were in Washington. They smiled politely, but seemed more interested in how Nicki's shoulder was recovering. Fabrini asked questions about the tracking of Crenshaw, leading up to his capture and the attempts to kill him that put a slug in Nicki.

He nodded and said he had some experience with guns as a young man. I saw Nicki and her mother exchanged glances and wondered what the story was, but dared not ask. "It would seem that there is someone out there trying to kill him," Fabrini said. "Do the FBI and the police have any real idea who it is?"

I explained that we all were working on it. Everyone hoped that either Crenshaw would break and tell us who was behind the bombing or the conspirators would make a mistake and show themselves.

"Well, let's hope for a quick resolution to this so your city can return to normal," Fabrini said, holding up his wine glass as if he was making a toast.

"Amen," Mrs. Fabrini said.

Clay was back at work. He told me when I called in that he couldn't stand being away another day. Mike Rose with his ribs wrapped had returned to city hall. Ed, when he took the phone, joked: "It's beginning to look like a convalescent home around here. I had to move Clay's crutches just to sit down. Don't you come back with any busted bones. We'd have to hire a full-time nurse."

He told me Mark Hodges' wife, Peggy, had called. "I thought it might be something important, so I took her call. She said to tell you she found the name of the man who kept calling Mark. It was on a note in one of Mark's jeans she was giving away."

"Who?"

"Ray Smith. Why would a guy who is running for Grey's seat call Hodges? Mean anything to you?"

Peggy had said Mark was talking on the phone with some guy before his death. "Maybe. I don't know. I'll think about it, and we'll talk when I get back."

I asked if there had been any developments on the break-in at our office. Ed said he had talked to the head of security, but there was nothing new. The sweep of the offices had found two bugs.

The technician asked if we wanted them removed or left in place. I chuckled at the thought of sending false information, but without knowing who had bugged the offices, that was pointless.

"Anything else happening?" I asked.

"Oh, yeah, Camille said we got a couple of checks in off the fundraising promo we started for the church." Ed was the only person at the *Post* who called Mrs. James by her first name. The rest of us wouldn't dare. "Not much money. Tens and twenties. But they came with some nice notes. You want to use any of them for stories."

"Let's wait until we get some more in. Then we'll have more to write about. It might look pathetic to run something now."

I wanted to know how Rachel was faring on the calls to the Jackson Group. Ed laughed and said she had been slamming things around on her desk all day. Daniels was dodging her, and none of the other executives were returning her calls. The bank guys were putting her off onto their public relations staff, who talked in circles. He said she could probably use a bit of pep talk from me.

We went through the routine stuff that Ed was more than capable of handling. The football recruiting scandal at Alabama continued. The alumni and fans just couldn't stop giving the players money and cars. The NCAA was threatening to ban the Alabama football program from the playoffs for a couple of years. The sports desk was trying to track down two young men who had taken the gifts. With Clay back at work, Ed could focus his attention on the football stories and keep the rest of the paper moving.

"Anything from the *Examiner*?" I asked.

"Nawh, pretty normal. They're squeezing some on the space, claiming the advertisers are still not buying ads. But circulation's okay. We've picked up a bunch of new subscribers. Not bad, huh?"

Maybe we could keep the new owner placated with the increased circulation for a while. I didn't want to tell Ed on the telephone about the possible sale to the *Examiner*.

Nicki lay in her old bed, taking a nap. I watched her while I talked on the phone. Nothing else would keep me from catching the next airplane home. "Forward Weitzman the new circulation figures. Ed, hold things together until I get back. I should be in the office by mid-afternoon."

I gave him the number at Nicki's house in case he could not get me on my cell. He noted the area code. "That's not Virginia or Washington. Where are you?"

I told him I was outside Philadelphia in a house whose furnishings alone would support the *Post* for a year. When I told him it belonged to Nicki's parents, he began to get the picture.

"I mean, with Nicki and all, is this serious between you two?"

Ed had been married to the same woman for thirty-plus years. It bothered him that I was not married. His matchmaking efforts were more subtle than those of the women reporters and editors, but he was probably the most persistent. I hated giving him any ammunition.

"Keep it to yourself. Okay?"

I heard Ed chuckling as he transferred me to Rachel. I was surprised that Rachel had not said anything to Ed about Nicki and me. Maybe she was too focused on getting members of the Jackson Group members to talk with her. Now that Ed knew too, Nicki and I would be the subject of much speculation throughout the newsroom.

"Do you want me to keep calling them, or what?" Rachel said when she came on the line. Her tone sounded like smoke was coming out her ears.

"When did you call them all last?"

She had started mid-morning, waiting outside Daniels' office for an hour with no results. It made me smile to think of Daniels being corralled in his office with Rachel sitting crossing and re-crossing those long legs in his waiting room. She had finally given up when a secretary told him Daniels was too busy. She had tried calling a dozen other likely members of the Jackson Group, but had talked to none.

"Why don't you give it a rest for today? Try again tomorrow. Go ask Clay if there's a feature you can work on today. Take a breather and start fresh tomorrow."

"I'd rather take a day on the beach somewhere if you don't mind," she teased.

"Sure, you've earned it. Just be back by one o'clock tomorrow. No problem."

I could use a beach day or two to calm my rattled nerves. The next best thing was a nap lying beside Nicki. So that's where I spent an hour, blissfully ignorant of approaching storms.

Formal dinners at home always seemed so pointless. My father loved them and tried to make my mother set the table and have us dress for dinner. He would come to dinner wearing his coat and tie, which made him look uncomfortable and even harder for me to relate to him on a casual basis.

"Wouldn't you be more comfortable in a sports shirt? It has been so hot today," my very practical mother would say.

He would dismiss her comment and say that she and I should want to dress up after tending to the house and my going to school. He thought we would want to sit there with the candles burning and enjoy a romantic dinner. The candles were fun, but it seemed to slow down dinner, and I had friends waiting. When they saw the lighted candles through the windows, they asked who died. My father persisted, but it never really took. Good intentions were way-laid by my mother's reality of getting the food on the table.

The Fabrinis dined formally. But then they had servants. We all dressed for dinner; Mattie and Benjamin served. Benjamin looked particularly uncomfortable in his white jacket. Mrs. Fabrini complemented him on it, which brought a faint smile. The dining room resembled a miniature version of the Louis XIV's Hall of Mirrors at Versailles. There were large mirrors on the doors and walls, which during the day reflected the light from the tall ornate windows.

The light from the glass chandelier and white candles bounced off one mirror to another. I hoped I would not spill my red wine on the rug that looked like it cost more than my annual salary.

Nicki's parents wanted to hear more details on the shooting. "My dear, what did it feel like?" her father asked from the far end of the table. "I have never been unfortunate enough to have been shot, and I guess I have always wondered what it would feel like."

Nicki again exchanged looks with her mother, who focused on her salad. She sighed and said she didn't really know because she was knocked unconscious immediately. "I just remember a sharp pain in my shoulder. Then nothing, until I woke up in the hospital with Joe sitting there." She smiled at me across the table. "It aches more than hurts now."

"Will there be any long-term damage?" her father asked.

"My doctors say no. The bullet tore through ligaments and ripped some muscle. It lodged in my chest, which took some tricky surgery to get out. But in time and with exercise I should be back to normal."

Fabrini said that was good news. As he pushed around some lettuce on his plate, he asked how I felt about Nicki being shot. He stared daggers at me. This appeared to be the point of the conversation. I was being set up. All I could do was play out the hand.

"Scared, really scared, as you can imagine." The memory of her bleeding from the exit wound onto the concrete steps was still fresh. "I was so frightened with Nicki lying there. I was afraid she might die. Then after she was out of danger, I felt guilty, bringing her into something that got her hurt. But it looks like it'll be all right now."

Fabrini nodded his head vigorously. I had no idea what he really thought.

Nicki and her mother chatted while we ate. The lamb and roasted potatoes were excellent. I noticed that neither Nicki nor her mother ate much. Fabrini finished off a very large slice and waited while Benjamin cut him another. He was on his third glass of wine that I had seen.

"How's the newspaper doing?" he asked after he had started on the second helping.

"Okay, I guess. I'd like to say we're thriving. But the truth is we are barely hanging on and in danger of being sold to our competition. But then newspapers everywhere are struggling. Until the Internet takes over the delivery of news completely, we've got to be more efficient. It costs so much to buy paper and ink in such large quantities and pay people to deliver it. Ad sales are off and have not yet proven themselves on web sites."

It was hard even to talk to strangers about the possible sale of the *Post*. I wondered how I would ever be able to tell my staff without breaking into tears.

"So you wouldn't recommend that I invest in newspapers?" Fabrini said.

I laughed. "Not if you are hoping for a good return. Anyone who buys a newspaper is buying in for another reason: ego, power, to win friends and influence people. Maybe they think they can run it more efficiently. And the Lord knows, newspapers have never been accused of being very efficient. But I think they will be surprised at how difficult it is to change the way things have been done for centuries," I said.

Fabrini stared at me as if he was trying to follow what I was saying. Then he broke into a large grin. Benjamin took away my plate, and Mattie poured coffee for Mrs. Fabrini and Nicki. I waited for my silence to draw him out more.

He chewed his meat thoroughly. "Would you mind quitting the newspaper business?" he asked finally.

That was the question I did not want to face. How could I do anything else? More importantly, how could I be anybody else? There is a joke about printers and newspaper people: that somewhere along the way ink has seeped into their veins like a drug they can't live without. I was clearly addicted.

"I can't think of anything I could possibly hate more. My wife died a few years ago. My mother and grandfather before that. I thought that would kill me. I have a wonderful son, but when my eyes open in the morning, my first thoughts are about the paper. I get up and grab the last city edition. Most days I have seen it already or know what's in it, but I take great pleasure in seeing it."

That shadow crossed Fabrini's features again. I wasn't the only person who saw it. Mrs. Fabrini's face turned to stone. Nicki was staring at her father as well. She too had seen it. The shadow passed as quickly as it came. "Well, that's wonderful. I admire a man who is devoted to his work. In today's world you have to be dedicated if you're going to get anywhere."

As the dinner neared its end, I found myself looking forward to getting out of this beautiful room. The vaulted ceiling gave me room to breathe, but I realized how uncomfortable I was with my host. I counted the hours until we could leave in the morning.

Ms. Fabrini turned to me as we were getting up from the table. "Joe, it is delightful to have you in our home. I do have one question." I nodded and waited. "What church do you go to?"

I smiled and told her I was a lapsed Baptist. My family had gone to a large Baptist church not far from the airport. I remembered how much I loved the music, but after mother died, my attendance had slipped.

"Well, we raised Nicki in the Catholic Church," she said.

"That's right," Fabrini blustered. "Every Sunday, hurricane or blizzard, we are at the Cathedral Basilica. That is Elena's church. Of course, I was happy at St. Paul's in the old neighborhood. I still sneak down there once in awhile, play a little backgammon with the priests. Maybe it will get me a better seat in heaven."

Somehow I doubted that was the only reason Fabrini went back to the old neighborhood.

After dinner Nicki was quiet. When we escaped to our room, she lay down on a four-poster bed beneath lace canopy. After a few minutes she told me her mother had asked her to stay a few more days. There was a fully equipped workout room in the basement, including a heavy bag and a speed bag that Fabrini worked out on. And her mother wanted the physical therapists and doctors at the hospital to check her out.

"I know," she said raising her good arm to silence me, "some of the best doctors and hospitals in the world are in Iron City. But you know that Philadelphia has some pretty world-class doctors and hospitals here too. If mother wants me to be checked out here, a second opinion and all, it'll make her happy. So I want to do it."

I just smiled, although my guts were turning inside out.

"It will give me a chance to get re-acquainted with them. They've clearly missed me a lot. And I think it would be good to spend some time here. You won't miss me anyway. You'll be busy chasing your phantom conspirators."

I understood that she needed to spend time with her family. I didn't argue. Her mind was made up. Trying to change it was probably futile.

"Please don't stay too long. I like having you around."

She smiled and we snuggled together in the bed. Much had happened since we had been in the Tutwiler Hotel. We came together slowly, gently. It seemed like it had been a long time. I feared I might hurt her if I entered her with the passion I felt. So I rubbed and kissed her back, moving down slowly nibbling on her muscular rear end and legs. I thought how different she was physically from her mother: Nicki strong, her mother frail. She was built more like her father, which probably pleased him. But she was emotionally more akin to her mother. They were strong, compassionate women. The difference was that Nicki could tackle a huge man like Crenshaw. She was complicated, having been raised by two such different parents. She carried a gun and wasn't afraid to use it. At the same time, she could talk about art or play with sick children in the hospital.

She loved for me to kiss her toes. She slid out of her nightgown, and I shed my clothes. Nicki was like no one I'd ever been with. I kissed her inner thighs, my tongue and fingers brought her quickly to an orgasm. She moaned quietly as she came. Then I entered her softly and thrust slowly, deeply. Her next orgasm came quickly. And I was not far behind. We lay quietly, feeling the tension drain from our bodies.

"You are the best," I said.

She looked up into my face and smiled. "Not bad for a woman you got shot?"

"Sorry about that."

"No worries. I would take a bullet again if you promise to make love to me like that for the rest of my life."

"I promise. But let's try not to step in front of a bullet again."

19

Nicki and I ate breakfast alone. Her mother was not downstairs yet, but her father was up early and we could hear him in the basement gym. Last night he had insisted that he drive me to the airport, a prospect I hardly looked forward to. I had planned to return the rental car at the airport and fly home. But Fabrini had a different idea. He said he would have Benjamin and another man who worked for him return the car in the afternoon, giving him time alone with me. I was not sure why or that I wanted to know.

"Did I say anything wrong to your father last night?" I whispered to Nicki.

She shook her head. A sadness seemed to engulf her. She stared across the table at the doorway to the foyer for several minutes. It made me anxious.

"Be careful, Joe," she said in a voice I had not heard since the night she pulled me out of the Downtowner motel. It was stern and, if it were not come out of her mouth, would have been frightening. It was easy to forget that my beautiful Nicki, who loved with such passion, could be so tough. "My father is a proud man. He always gets what he wants." She waved her hand at the house and its extravagant furnishings that surrounded us. "He didn't take a dime from my mother's family. That all went to debts her mother ran up after her father died. Vincent did this all himself, at times by being ruthless. I hoped when we came here that he would accept my decisions about my life and you. I still have my fingers crossed."

"Am I missing something, Nicki? Does he want something from me?"

"Maybe. I don't know. You'll know before you get on your plane. Just be careful. I love you, or have you forgotten about last night?"

I slipped my hand over hers as it lay there on the table. "No, I will never forget that, no matter what happens. I love you too."

She nodded and seemed to relax. Her mother came in the room through the kitchen and sat at the far end of the table. Mattie appeared carrying her coffee and a small plate that included a sliced bagel and half a grapefruit.

"Vincent loves Nicki very much," she said, picking up on our conversation as if she had been a part of it. "There seems to be a special bond fathers feel for daughters, much like the one mothers have with sons. She is our only child, and he and I have very high expectations for her. I miss her not being here, to talk with, to go places with, to share the things that mean so much to me. I had hoped after school that she would live in Philadelphia and help me again at the hospital. I am not as strong as I once was."

Nicki stared at her plate.

"I understand. My son is little more than a baby, but I find myself already thinking about what he might be when he is grown. It's natural."

"It is difficult to explain my husband," she said as if I had not interrupted. "Nicki was more than a daughter to him. She is a validation of all he has become, all he has accomplished. To have her turn her back on the life we made for her... ." She paused and picked up her spoon, but did not use it. "Well, I think you can see it has been difficult for him."

She picked at the grapefruit. "Sometimes I think I should have been stronger with Vincent. He can be like a wild animal. He grew up mostly on the streets, worked since he was six to support himself and what was left of his family. I've loved him since I met him at a party in town when I was in college. Maybe my father, if he had been alive, would have stopped me from marrying him. But I fell in love with a proud and at times fierce young man. We struggled. We were very poor for years. But we made it. Vincent has been very successful. Now all he wants is to have his daughter here to prove to himself and his friends from the old days how far he has come. Is that too much to ask?"

I felt sorry for Nicki. I knew the pain of disappointing a parent. My father had made it clear I had failed to meet his expectations. In some ways it would have been easier for my father if I had lived in a different city. For Vincent Fabrini it was the opposite. He needed Nicki near him, to see and be seen with a daughter who had graduated from Smith College and toured Europe. For a street kid from south Philly she was the ultimate validation.

Benjamin came to collect my suitcase and told me we were leaving at eight thirty. Nicki watched him as he walked out carrying by bag.

"What is it?" I asked as she stared after Benjamin.

Nicki smiled and shook her head laughing. "I was just thinking how much Benjamin looks like you. Not as handsome, of course, but from the back he's built a lot like you."

I didn't care for that. "So now I have to worry you falling for him?"

She reached over and hugged me. "Oh, don't be goofy. I love you, all of you, your sweetness, your smarts." She paused. "And your integrity, not just the way you look. I do like the way you look." She leaned over and whispered, "And I love the way you love me. I can't imagine another man loving me the way you do."

Standing in the front hall, we hugged tightly for several moments. Before I left I called Chris to tell him I would be home tonight and we would watch cartoons together tomorrow morning. He wasn't much yet for talking on the telephone and wanted to eat his cereal, so our conversation ended quickly and I finished the conversation with his grandfather. I was saying goodbye to Nicki and her mother when Fabrini came downstairs. He had changed into a suit after his workout and seemed very proud of himself. He put an arm around Nicki and said, "Just finished twenty minutes on the speed bag. I've still got it."

"I'll be home in a few days," Nicki said, pulling away from him and standing close to me. "Go get your conspirators and I'll be there to celebrate with you."

I didn't like the look in her father's eyes.

We kissed, and I stroked her hair. Fabrini was suddenly impatient to go, his smile gone, the shadow of anger I had seen was just below the surface. When I thanked Mrs. Fabrini for her hospitality, she hugged me and stepped back.

"That's the only coat you have?" she asked, looking at my thin raincoat.

I shock my head. "You'll freeze before you get on the plane," she said. She told Benjamin to get one of Vincent's coats from the closet. "You'll be much more comfortable."

"Yes, yes, yes. That will be great. And you will look good too," Fabrini said, laughing as he hugged and kissed his wife and daughter. He stepped back smiling broadly at Nicki as if he was seeing her for the first time.

In his Cadillac Benjamin drove, Fabrini and I sat in the back. Traffic was moderate as we headed south again along the Schuylkill River. It was even colder than it had been the day before with a thick cloud cover. I appreciated the loan of the coat. The landscape was winter bleak and depressing, but Fabrini did not seem to notice. He suddenly appeared to be in a good mood. "Before you go home I wanted to show you one of my car repair malls. You ought to see it because if you are lucky enough to marry my Nicki, well, you might be owning them, you and her, someday."

Just what I wanted to do, inherit his car repair shopping centers. That thought really depressed me. We turned east on a cross-town expressway that took us through downtown. Close up, the downtown skyscrapers looked even more spectacular. I complimented the architecture of the buildings, but Fabrini seemed indifferent.

"I'd never build one of those. Too big a risk. Too high a profile. Might bring around people you don't want to know about you. Too easy to go broke. Some of those guys did. Better to invest a little in something that can't wipe you out if it goes south."

"Like your automobile repair malls," I suggested, trying to be gracious.

He turned and looked at me to see if I was putting his business down. "Yeah, and buildings that are already built and available at the right price. Just got to keep them up, and keep the tenants one way or another." A trace of his Philadelphia twang showed through. I had not heard it last night. Maybe it came out the closer he got to the old neighborhood.

We passed the exit for the national historic district that included Independence Hall and the Liberty Bell. It had been years since I had been to Philadelphia. I told him how I would like to bring Chris here and show him the crack in the bell. He asked if I had a photo of Chris. I pulled out my phone and showed him one of the latest shots of my beautiful son. He looked at it and said without feeling, "Nice looking boy. Whiter than I figured."

The expressway brought us to the Ben Franklin Bridge, and Benjamin kept driving. I watched in silence as we crossed the Delaware River. The Camden waterfront came into view on the New Jersey side. I had not expected it would take so long to reach Fabrini's car repair mall. I thought we would stop at one of his shops in south Philly, nearer the airport. I wanted to say something about getting to the airplane on time, but decided I was in his car. He was Nicki's father. I would not complain.

"It's not far now," Fabrini said, reading my mind. Was I fidgeting in the seat? "It's just about a mile here down this highway."

The Cadillac turned onto the access road at the next exit and pulled into the parking lot of a squat row of cement-block buildings, badly in need of some paint. On the end nearest us was a dingy office with neon signs and posters on the walls advertising auto parts companies. Behind the counter was a calendar of a well-endowed blonde in red shorts and partially unbuttoned top standing in front of a pile of truck tires. Customers sat looking bored in plastic chairs, flipping through magazines or playing with their phones. In the bays were several repairmen, dressed in oil-stained overalls. They moved around the cars with little sense of urgency or enthusiasm. I would not have left my car here. I wondered why anyone did.

"Not much to look at, huh?" Fabrini said. He had expected my reaction, and I wondered if this was the reason he wanted me to see the it. Was he taking a perverse pleasure in my revulsion? All I really wanted to do was to get to the airport and back to my world. I did not care much for his.

Fabrini and Benjamin got out of the Cadillac, dashing my hopes for a quick drive through. Even inside his heavy coat I shivered as I stepped out of the car. My thin rain coat would have been no match for the cold wind, which was blowing even harder and dropping the temperature even lower than it was when we left Radnor. Fabrini walked around the car and stood beside me. His fur-lined top coat looked out of place here.

"You have to understand the way your customers think. When I opened my first malls, all but this one was really bright and clean. The men who worked in them wore orange coveralls with their names sewn on. Elena did the sewing in those days when we were just getting started. I paid a night crew to come in and clean all the bays. We played music for the customers and gave them coffee. But I didn't have as many customers at the two shops in Philly as I did here. My plan was to borrow some money and fix this one up during the second year. Then I realized what the problem was. People who need their cars fixed prefer a place like this. Give them crappy chairs to sit on and make them pay for their own coffee, and you know what?" He paused a split second for effect. "They think they are getting the best deal on their car repair. At the other shops, they knew clean costs money, paint is expensive. Who's going to pay for it? They know they are. So they drive past a clean place and stop here. Amazing, huh? So now all my places look like this."

The purr in his accent that I had listened to over dinner was gone. The pretenses he kept up in Radnor had evaporated. Here with his men surrounded by filth he wore like a badge of honor, his south Philly roots showed in his speech, his body language. They knew where he came from and admired him for it.

Fabrini guided me into one of the bays. It was old style with concrete pits, instead of metal lifts, for the men to work underneath the cars. One mechanic looked like he was doing an oil change in one pit. Another changed a tire near us. Two other men in the closest pit were removing a muffler. The concrete floor was so oily I was afraid I would slip in my street shoes. Fabrini's shoes had rubber ridges on the bottom. Why did he want me in the bay? I looked back at his car, wishing we would leave.

"Joe, I want you to meet Steve." He pointed to a wiry little man, who looked to be in his mid-thirties, as he walked into the bay and stood in front of us. "Steve has worked with me for years. How many years have we worked together, Steve?"

The small, intense-looking man held up several fingers on both hands. His ring finger on his left hand was partially missing, cut off below the knuckle, so I didn't know exactly how many years he meant. I knew I didn't like Steve. His large yellow teeth protruded between tight lips curled almost in a snarl. He never took his eyes off me. Why did Fabrini want me to meet this guy? I started to turn and head back for the car. It was warm there.

"Steve, you may have seen Joe on TV. He's pretty famous. He's the hero down in Alabama that caught some redneck that blew up a Negro church." He said it with derision in his voice. I didn't take the bait. "What do you think about that, Steve?"

The man didn't say anything. Fabrini took off his coat and handed it to Benjamin.

"You do a lot of special jobs for me, don't you, Steve?" Steve nodded. "If I asked ya, would ya kill for me?"

What kind of question was that? Steve grinned, his hideous teeth bared between his lips.

"Go ahead then, kill this guy for me. He sleeps with my daughter and thinks he is going to marry her. For sure, that is not going to happen. Kill him. It won't matter. He is a Baptist. The priests won't even think that is a sin," he said laughing. "We'll put his body in the foundation of the new building we're putting up for the hospital. A fitting memorial to this famous Alabama Negro newspaper editor."

Fabrini's words were uttered so flatly, I thought it was a joke. For a second I wanted to laugh, but stopped. Fabrini was serious. Steve stepped toward me. I was afraid he was going to bite me like Mike Tyson or one of the *James Bond* movie villains I had abhorred as a child. Instead he pulled a knife out of his pocket. Fear squeezed my chest and throat. My legs shook. My arms froze beside me.

"Hey, I need some help here," I yelled, hoping the mechanics would come to my defense or at least look over and make Steve question whether he could get away with stabbing me in front of witnesses. The men didn't look up, acting as if nothing was going on. In the shop things got very quiet. Benjamin hit the switch and the giant old garage doors between the bays and the parking lot came rattling down. I was trapped.

"Okay, Fabrini, what the hell? Call off your dog. You've had your fun. I get it." My fear showed.

Steve swung the knife at my chest. I jumped back and almost lost my footing. Fabrini caught me by the shoulders and turned me around to face him. He stepped into me and rammed his fist into my gut, knocking the wind out of me. He laughed. "I told you I like to work out on the bags." I staggered back away from him toward the car that a few minutes before had been getting a new tire, hoping to find an escape. Steve came at me again. I grabbed a tire iron that lay on the floor beside the car and used it to block his next lunge with the knife. I couldn't believe I was fighting for my life in a grimy New Jersey car repair shop. I didn't appreciate then the irony that I might die in the state where I had gone to college. Princeton is a long way from Camden.

Steve came straight at me, trying to puncture, rather than slice. That made it harder to block with the tire iron. I dodged one jab and brought the metal bar down on his wrist. He jerked back in pain and dropped the knife. I tried to kick it across the floor, but missed. Steve charged into me, his shoulder hitting me in the chest and driving me hard against the side of the car. That knocked the air out of my lungs again and the tire iron slipped out of my hand. I held my ribs hoping they weren't broken. My back stung and my legs went numb, but I managed to kick the knife across the floor. Steve reached down for it, but grabbed my outstretched leg instead of me. I fell and landed on my side. I rolled over trying to get away from him. I crawled gasping for a breath toward the pit hoping to get to the knife first. Fabrini yelled at Steve, "Get on with it." I couldn't believe the man I had dinner wanted me dead. Benjamin kicked me in the ribs, flipping me on my back and sliding me across the slick floor until my arms hung over the edge of the pit. What little air I had was gone. I lay there managing to breathe again. The mechanics scrambled up from under the car. I turned over to see where Steve was. He was searching the floor, looking for the knife. Where was it? I had to find it. Then I felt it. Damn, I was lying on it. He saw me reaching for it under my shoulder, dropped to his knees and punched me in the throat with his right hand. He felt under me with his left hand, trying to wrap his fingers around the blade. I rolled over on his hand. He yelled and fell back, holding his wrist.

Behind me I heard Benjamin. "Here it is." He picked up the knife. I pulled myself up off the floor, my legs still shook, but they worked. Steve and I were back where we started. We stepped in a circle, facing one another like two old prize fighters. He grinned at me, baring those teeth I so wanted to knock out. Benjamin handed him the knife. I knew I could not let him attack again. I doubted I could dodge the knife again. I charged, tackling him. We slid, rolled toward the pit. My only hope was that I could pin down the smaller man and keep him from using the knife.

"You niggers fight good," Steve said. His breath almost finished me off.

I outweighed him, but he was stronger. We wrestled for a few seconds until Steve pushed me off. As I fell away, I shoved him with my legs. He slid on the oily floor and fell in the pit. The two mechanics who had been working in the pit stared down at Steve lying in the grease and oil below the car. They looked as if they wanted to laugh, but dared not.

A car pulled in the parking lot just outside the door. Fabrini saw it and looked furious. I stood ready for whatever was to come next.

"That'll be enough of that," he said. He stepped to the edge of the pit as Steve scrambled to his feet. "Well, Steve, our newspaper editor was a little tougher than you thought. Too bad."

Fabrini turned to me. I could barely talk, but grunted, "Why?"

He snarled, "You piece of shit. Did you think I'm gonna let you, some African buck, sleep with my daughter, keep my prize baby girl away from me? She's my princess. I raised her, I sent her to the best schools so she could be somebody in this city. She won't have to claw her way to the top. She can have it all right now." He shook his head at me and pointed a finger at my chest. "Then you come along and she wants to live in some hick southern town. You think I will let her marry you? She's going to marry someone important here, rich, powerful and white. Her children, my grandchildren will run things here. I'll see to it."

He stopped and looked around at the men who listened to his every word. They were smiling. To them, trying to kill me was great fun, something to joke about. Fabrini's image as a tough bastard was still intact. "Just because you are some big shot from an Ivy League school, you think you can take my daughter away from me. Understand me. You're still just a nigger."

"You think killing me will stop her?" I tried to collect my senses and get my breath back. I was almost as angry as scared.

He shrugged and raised his arms in victory. "Maybe. With some people that's all you can do. Kill 'em, bury 'em, get 'em out of the way. Nothing else you can do."

He spoke of killing as a normal way to resolve disputes. He wanted me to know he had killed before and would do so again if I did not give him what he wanted. From the pit with the muffler dangling behind him from underside of the car Steve glared at me. He pushed himself up on the side and climbed out. "Hold him. I can still do him for you."

Fabrini shook his head. "No, this guy is supposed to be real smart. Let's see if he has learned his lesson. Maybe he is thinking there are some other women he can fuck."

What could you say to a man like this? Reason wouldn't work. But I would not let him think I was weak. "Nicki and I love each other. We may get married someday. Maybe we will live in Iron City. Maybe not. If you think I'm going to quit seeing Nicki just because you try to kill me? No way."

He stepped closer, his head only inches from my face. "You don't get it. I've got you by the balls. I own you. I own your Goddamn newspaper. I can sell it right out from under you. I can tear your heart out. What are you without your newspaper? You said so yourself, you're nothing. I'd probably be doing you a favor to let Steve finish you off now."

The man who might be my future father in law smirked at me. My face must have registered my confusion. Fabrini was the new owner? He was Temple Investments. Of course, why hadn't I figured that out?

Benny hit the switch again, as a second customer pulled his car into the lot. One of the giant doors rolled up to let Fabrini leave.

"You call my daughter. You tell her you've changed your mind. You've found somebody else. Whatever you want to tell her. You tell her that, and I'll let you keep your damned newspaper. You hear me?" He turned and walked away. Benjamin opened the trunk of the Cadillac and pulled my suitcase out. He hurled it by the handle, end over end towards me. It landed on the asphalt, the locks popped open scattering my clothes and toiletries.

"I guess I ain't going to Iron City, Mr. Fabrini?" Benjamin said.

Fabrini laughed and turned back to look at me. "Yeah, too bad, Benny. Maybe another time. The last good thing this asshole would have ever done was give you your first ride in an airplane."

He laughed as he got in the backseat of the Cadillac. He rolled down the window and threw my raincoat on the ground. I don't think he wanted his coat, now covered in grease. Benny shook his head as he opened the door and got in the Cadillac. I walked over and put my suitcase back together. I wanted to get out of there. I looked around and Steve had disappeared. All the garage doors were down again.

On the street, no one even looked at me as they drove by. I didn't exist. If I filed a complaint with the Camden cops against Fabrini or Steve, nothing would happen. They would have witnesses to say I had attacked Steve.

I was an unwanted stranger in a foreign land.

It was only nine thirty, only an hour since I had left Nicki, but it seemed like a lifetime had passed. I called a cab and waited down the street, while I tried to brush the grease and dirt from my coat and pants. My shoes were beyond help. I ached from my shoulders to my ankles, not to mention a bruised ego. I had no gloves against the sharp wind. When I shoved my hands in the pockets of Fabrini's coat, in the left was a yellow sticky note with a phone number scratched on it in blue ink. My mouth must have fallen open when I saw it was for a number with an Iron City area code. And I knew that number. It was one I had saved in my phone. The number was the direct line to Robert Daniels' office at the *Examiner*. Of course, that made sense. Daniels wanted the *Post* to stop the investigation of the bombing and consolidate his media empire. Fabrini wanted me dead because I was keeping his daughter from him. What an unholy alliance.

I walked onto the Delta Airlines flight as a crewman was shutting the door. I don't remember much about the flight to Atlanta, except that I took my suitcase down, leaving the greasy coat in the overhead, and changed my pants and shirt in the tight space of the airplane toilet. By the time we landed, my body was so stiff and sore I moved very slowly down the long concourse to the gate for Iron City. I still did not understand how someone like Fabrini had come into my life.

What would I tell Nicki? How could I tell her that her father had tried to kill me? How could I say that he had given me an ultimatum: the *Post* or Nicki. I had no illusion that Fabrini would not carry out his threat to use the power of his money. He and Daniels could take my newspaper away from me in a heartbeat. Fabrini could also kill me in Iron City as easy as he had tried in Camden. Fabrini was as ruthless and focused as Nicki and her mother had warned me.

I should have listened better.

The afternoon staff meeting had started when I arrived at the *Post*. I knew Ed had told everyone I had been summoned to Alexandria, and such trips usually meant trouble. I could not think of a single command performance at the Babcock headquarters that had turned out to be good news.

On the drive from the airport, I recovered my senses enough to consider whether to tell the staff about the possible sale of the paper. Would it depress everyone, something we did not need right now? Or would it motivate them to produce the best editions for the next several weeks? We were facing a critical time for the city and us. Iron City was like a blast furnace with the iron ore, coke and limestone boiling, ready to be poured into the shape it would take for decades to come. The *Post* needed to be part of that shaping. We could not leave it to men like Daniels.

"As y'all probably know, I was up in D.C. visiting with Maury Weitzman and his team," I said after we had been through the routine stories for the day. "They were real concerned that we were stirring up the *Examiner* folks a bit too much, beating them to the Crenshaw story and generally outclassing them all across the board. So I want to tell each of you I am really proud of all of you. I like being summoned to Alexandria to be told we are doing too good a job."

Several of the editors, I could see in their faces, were waiting for the other shoe to drop. Too smart and too cynical, they did not believe that Weitzman would have me fly up just to receive even a backhanded compliment.

"The *Examiner*'s response to our outclassing them is to try to buy us out. What they can't beat, they try to buy. That seems to be Daniels' business plan." I paused to let that bombshell sink in. There was a rumbling around the room. Most of the staff knew that it had always been a possibility that the *Examiner* would put us out of business. We had been vulnerable for years, but had avoided it until now. Most probably thought it wouldn't happen, at least not right now. We were riding high. Around the table their faces looked stunned.

"I don't know that the buyout will happen. It may be a ruse by Daniels to stop us from continuing the investigation of the bombing. There will be a lot of negotiations between the *Post* and the *Examiner*. And then I suspect there may be a review by the Justice Department over this sale, merger or whatever it is." I stopped and looked around the room.

"So I think we have time, probably months to let this resolve itself," I continued. "Meanwhile I hope you will join me in trying to kick the *Examiner*'s butt as many times as we can. We have to turn up the heat on Daniels. Maybe in our own little way we can make his blessed life a little miserable."

Their expressions turned from being stunned to angry to committed.

"Are you suggesting," Ed said, trying to hide a smile, "that we should do everything we can to scuttle this merger?"

All faces turned to look at me. "I never said that." I faked my shock. "Did anyone hear me say that? Ed, I'm surprised at you. That would be disloyal to our owners. I'm sure that they think it is in their best interests to sell this newspaper and put their precious money to work elsewhere. And as editor of this newspaper, I am committed to maximizing their profits, right?"

The sarcasm was not lost on the group.

"So you would not mind if we ran stories that would upset this apple cart?" asked the senior copy editor.

I just smiled. Electricity flowed around the room as they each thought about ways to bedevil the *Examiner.*

Waiting outside my office was a man Mrs. James said had been there for fifteen minutes. A short, white guy with shoulders broader than most men, he was dressed in a suit that fitted him poorly, probably saved mostly for Sundays and funerals. He wore a wide striped tie.

"Mr. Riordan, I'm Jim Jessup. I own the CMI mill. Well, the bank and I own CMI." He shook my hand firmly while I tried to place where I had heard of his company.

I smiled, thanked him for dropping in and asked him to tell me about CMI.

"CMI is a new mill. If things keep going the way we hope, we might grow some bigger."

Then I remembered. We had written a story about his company as an example of the rebirth of the steel industry in Iron City. It used techniques that streamlined the steel-making operation, a process that used fewer, but higher skilled workers and paid better salaries, as I recalled from the article.

"I read in the newspaper yesterday about the money you're trying to raise to rebuild that church that was blowed up," he said.

I nodded, uncertain where this was headed. "We're just getting started. It'll take a while to catch on."

"Well, I am not the type usually to get involved in things like that. I mostly work and go home to my family. But when I read that article about the church and what it meant to black people in this city, well I thought it might be important to some of my guys."

He stopped while Mrs. James handed him a Coke. Jessup smiled and thanked her.

"So this morning I called all my guys together and asked them what they thought. I've got about fifty working in the mill and the office. About half are black. Two of them, one a foreman, go to that church. They said they wanted to do something. So I decided to give a thousand dollars to help rebuild that church." He handed me a check.

I was stunned. When I started the campaign and we had written the first couple of stories about the need to rebuild the church, I thought we might get a few thousand dollars out of the banks and utilities. I never dreamed that a company as small as this one with little to gain from it would come through with such a large contribution.

"Thank you," I finally stammered out. "This is fantastic. It will really make a difference." We sat there smiling at each other. I wasn't sure what else to say, nor apparently was he.

"Well, good, I need to get back." He stood up to leave.

We shook hands and I thanked him again. As he turned to leave, I asked him how he wanted the gift listed. We planned to run a list of those who contributed.

He looked surprised. "You're gonna run a story that we gave this?"

"Yes. I mean we can list it as anonymous if you like. A lot of contributions are," I said.

"Oh, no. I want everyone to know we gave the money. Can you list our company and the two men who work for us who go to that church?"

"Sure. Just give me their names."

He wrote their names on a sheet of paper. We shook hands again, and I walked him to the elevator.

"You don't, by chance, belong to a local civic group, called the Jackson Group, do you?" I asked as we passed Rachel's desk and I suddenly worried that this check might be meant to buy something else.

"No, never heard of it. What is it?" he said.

"Oh, nothing. Just a bunch of the CEOs of the large companies, banks, that sort of thing," I said.

He shook his head. "No, we're too small to run with those guys. Maybe someday we'll get there, but not now."

"Thank you," I said as the elevator doors closed. As I walked back into the newsroom, I felt a little more hopeful about the future of Iron City.

20

It was almost six p.m. when Joiner knocked on my door. He usually just walked in, showing the lack of respect most *Examiner* executives had for the *Post*. Maybe catching Crenshaw and being on national television had created a new attitude. When I looked up from my computer, he announced solemnly, "Mr. Daniels would like for you to come to his office on a matter of some urgency."

A dead weight filled my stomach. Fabrini must have been on the phone with him negotiating a price. But that was a little too quick. Fabrini was waiting for my call to Nicki telling her we were through. The urgency must be closer to home. Daniels' phone had been hot for days. Members of the Jackson Group were looking to him to get Rachel and the *Post* off the story linking them with the church bombing. Daniels, as publisher of a rival newspaper, wasn't going to talk to Rachel. He would try to lean on me because he knew he had leverage. He also knew I had been summoned to Virginia and had waited until I returned. I wondered if he also knew I had survived a visit to a New Jersey auto repair shop

"Well, if Mr. Daniels would like to talk with me, I'll be here. He can come down here," I mocked poor Joiner. I was in a fighting mood, not the cowering editor I probably should have been. It was often the way I felt before disaster fell. The Greeks understood. Every time their heroes got a bit overconfident, Olympus sent a lightning bolt their way, just to keep them humble. The gods must still be on duty.

"There are several people in his office who would like to talk with you. It would be easier if you would come upstairs," Joiner almost pleaded. I could imagine who was sitting in Daniels' suite of offices. Joiner could not tell Daniels in front of a room full of his friends and senior staff that I refused to come. So I relented and said I would be there in five minutes. Was I was waltzing again into the lion's den. I had not seen the danger from Fabrini and Steve coming. I didn't know what to expect upstairs, but I doubted it would be pretty.

Walking to the elevators, I reasoned that it would be a mutual squeeze play. We had Daniels and his friends in a vice with Rachel's questions. He was squeezing me through Weitzman and Fabrini. How good it would be for Daniels if I were buried in that Philadelphia hospital foundation.

I routinely rode the freight elevator mostly because it was closest to the newsroom. Daniels and the senior *Examiner* management used a semi-private elevator at the front of the building. The freight elevator creaked and rattled as it went up and down among the floors. It had no carpet, no tapestries on the wall, no recorded voice to welcome you. The men and women who assembled and printed the newspapers rode the freight elevator. I enjoyed talking with them, hearing their take on the news and events around the building. For this trip upstairs the elevator was crowded.

"Enjoyed working on that Crenshaw story Friday night," one of the men said.

"Yeah, I saw you on TV. Way to go," said another wearing overalls over a t-shirt, carrying a homemade sack lunch.

I nodded and smiled. "You guys know me, anything to sell newspapers."

"Give'm hell, Joey boy," said an older white man standing in the back. I turned to look at him. I had never seen him before, and I knew at least by their faces most of the people who worked in the building. He looked much like my grandfather, who had always called me "Joey boy." Goosebumps ran down my arms. Stress does weird things to the mind, but my grandfather coming back as an angel was a comforting thought. I could use his confidence and his strength.

In a corner of the building overlooking Fifth Street Daniels' suite of offices had a better view and made my office look too much like a closet. He had a private bathroom, and adjacent to the wood-paneled conference room was a small private sitting room, where a tall, black man I had not seen before stood waiting to take my order for a drink. It appeared he had already served the others, maybe more than one. The furniture in that room was antique and dark woods, original paintings hung in wood frames on the walls, including a large oil painting of old man Daniels that dominated the room. What did the son really think of his father, an old bastard like most thought of him or a loving father who had given him an incredible inheritance?

"Thank you for coming," Daniels said, standing to welcome me. We shook hands, but no one else did.

He offered me a chair. I sat down in it carefully, protecting sore ribs and resting tired legs and arms. Daniels looked like he could model for the cover of *Gentleman's Quarterly*, his gray and chestnut hair well trimmed, an olive-colored suit covered well his growing paunch, his Guccis glistened. I assumed there was a Benjamin at the Daniels' home.

Four men sat in the well-upholstered chairs in the room. All but one I knew or had seen photographs of. On my left was the editor of the *Examiner*, Jim Wendom, a squirrel of a man who served primarily as a foil for Daniels, mollifying insecure and creative writers and editors. Across from me on a green-patterned sofa was a man I did not know, but suspected he was the man the waiter Jerome had talked about in the meetings at the country club. He looked like a lawyer and someone to whom Daniels would defer.

"Can Michael get you anything?" Daniels said, his warmth and charm at the max. An antique wooden bar that looked like it was older than Iron City stood open against the far wall. The man I assumed was Michael waited attentively beside it.

"A water will do. Thank you. I still have some writing left to do this evening," I said.

Daniels looked like I had farted. No editor in his world actually wrote stories. "Well, I am sure you are busy. So we'll get right to the point. We wanted to talk with you about a story we understand the *Post* is preparing."

By "we" he meant the other men in the room. Sitting on the couch with the unknown lawyer was Harden Braddock. A large man physically, probably thirty pounds heavier than the photo I had seen of him during his college football playing days, Braddock was dressed in a blue blazer and yellow shirt that did little to disguise his bulk. He had glared at me from the moment I walked in. If he was trying to intimidate me, it was working. While Daniels tried conciliation, Braddock sent psychic waves of raw hatred across the room at me. Daniels took the chair to my right.

"We understand you are working on a story that links the so-called Jackson Group to a conspiracy to bomb the church. Is that correct?" Daniels asked.

I looked around the room at the men who were assembled. "Not exactly. If you or Mr. Braddock had returned any of our phone calls over the last three days, you would know what we are writing a story about. Of course, I am not used to telling the *Examiner* in advance about stories we are working on." I paused to let that point hit home. "In this case the story says the FBI is looking into a possible conspiracy between members of the Jackson Group and Lonnie Crenshaw to place the bomb in the church."

Silence filled in the room. You could hear the antique clock on a table ticking. I was confident that the *Examiner* would not try to scoop us on that story.

"That would be very unfortunate," Daniels said.

He looked at the mystery man on the couch and at Braddock before he answered. The mystery man shook his head, Braddock fumed. Neither spoke, but they were clearly communicating with Daniels, who continued to lead the conversation.

"A story that accuses the Jackson Group of any criminal activities would not be accurate, and of course, many fine businessmen and government leaders in this city would be hurt," he said.

"Are you denying that the group or any member of the group was involved in the bombing?" I asked.

He shook his head at me. I guess I had committed another social faux pas. Damn, maybe Princeton should offer a course in social etiquette for editors.

"Off the record, I deny it," he said. "And it is off the record because I do not want to lend any credibility to such an absurd accusation."

"When did I agree to having this conversation off the record? In fact, how about we tape this?" I said.

Braddock exploded. He raised his large body out of the chair and shouted at Daniels, "Tell this son-of-a-bitch not to print any God-damned story about the Jackson Group and the bombing. You own the son-of-a-bitch, just tell him."

Daniels stared at the coffee table in front of him. Several books on the Civil War were positioned in the middle. The cover of the large book on top was a reproduction of a painting of Pickett's Charge at Gettysburg. As Yankee and Confederate armies battled hand to hand, you could feel their fear and excitement. We had no muskets or bayonets, no one was bleeding or dying, but the tension in this office was suddenly almost as thick. Daniels look surprisingly embarrassed. He always seemed under control, stoic. Braddock was the opposite, a bull in his china shop.

"No one in the Jackson Group, to my knowledge, had anything to do with the bombing," Daniels started again. "I assure you of that. You do what you must with my statement. Because of our business relationship, I would hope that you would use good judgment in how you run such a story."

He wanted me to remember Weitzman's command not to ruffle his feathers.

"I would like for you to let this story rest for a while. You and the *Post* had a marvelous coup in bringing this man Crenshaw to justice. Rest on your laurels for a week or so and let things cool down," he said.

An old adage in the newspaper business was that yesterday's papers were only good to wrap fish. What counts are the stories you print today. His father understood that. I doubted if the younger Daniels did.

"I appreciate your perspective. But I don't see how we can honor it," I said.

Daniels studied his hands in his lap. "Please forgive Mr. Braddock's comments. Of course, the *Examiner* does not own the *Post*. It is an independent newspaper and can print any story it chooses. At least for now," he said.

His comments were a signal. The joint operating agreement was a joke. The *Post* was hardly an independent newspaper. We could be crushed at anytime.

"Oh, horse shit." Braddock spoke up. "Robert, have some God-damned balls. Give him the order, damn it, Mel." He motioned to the man sitting beside him. "I've had enough of this. I want to get out of here."

Daniels' mouth fell open. The man I didn't know sat forward as if on command. He cleared his throat. "Mr. Riordan, I don't think we have ever met. I'm Melvin Goldschmidt. I am an attorney with the firm of .."

"Aw, Christ, get on with it, Mel," Braddock barked. Goldschmidt looked with disdain down his nose across half-rim glasses at him. Braddock did not care.

Melvin Goldschmidt was an attorney with the largest law firm in the city. I had heard about him for years, read stories about his cases in court. He opened his briefcase and pulled out an official looking document.

"This is an order from Judge Jacob Strong of the One Fifteenth District Court. Your attorney has probably told you about it. Judge Strong's order, signed this afternoon, enjoins the *Post* from printing any article that in any way links the Jackson Group with the bombing of the Sixteenth Street Baptist Church or this man Lonnie Crenshaw," Goldschmidt said.

He handed me the order.

I was stunned. "You can't do this. You can't stop us from printing a story. Has the to the First Amendment been repealed?"

Goldschmidt realized that I had not known about the order. "I'm sorry. Your attorney, you are represented by Mr. Anthony Roberts, I believe, should have informed you. The *Post*, of course, will have an opportunity to contest this order. And you may prevail on the issue. But until then the *Post* is enjoined from printing any article described in this order. I suggest you contact Mr. Roberts. He has a copy of this order and can explain its full implications."

I wanted to scream. We were so close to nailing the bastards responsible for the bombing. And now they were sitting here, right in the same room with me, and I couldn't write about them. I didn't hear anything else he said. Where was my lawyer, playing golf? Why do we pay him? This was not a contingency case where lawyers do as little work as possible, looking for a settlement. We were paying him his hefty hourly fee.

"Furthermore," Goldschmidt was saying. "Judge Strong has enjoined the *Post* from reporting on this injunction until a hearing can be held."

"On what grounds can he seal this order?"

"Judge Strong agreed with our arguments that in view of the volatility of the community at this moment it would be best to restrict disclosure of this order until such time as it is deemed safe to inform the public," Goldschmidt said.

It was an old argument that the press had won time and time again. In 1971, President Nixon had tried to stop the *New York Times* from publishing the Pentagon Papers during the Vietnam War. There was hardly a newspaper in the country that hadn't been hit with some gag order, trying to restrain it from publishing an article that was detrimental to the public safety.

I was tempted to yell "to hell with the consequences, we'll publish the hardest hitting story we can." I looked at Daniels. He studied his manicured nails. I stood up. My legs felt weak. Daniels looked up. I'm not sure what I read in his face.

"Sad day," he said. He looked up at the painting of his father. "I'm glad he didn't live to see this."

"You fucking weenie," exploded Braddock. He got up, stepped over the coffee table, stared down at me with what I took to be contempt and stomped out of the room. Goldschmidt followed him, stepping around the table and stopping to tell me to have Roberts call if he had questions.

I looked down at Daniels. His whole body had sagged. I was not sure if he was upset at the prospect of leading an attack on the First Amendment or something more personal. Maybe, Daniels had inherited at least a little printer's ink that had surged through his father's veins. The son wanted to buy the *Post* and probably shut it down, something his father hadn't done. But he wanted to do it himself, not have a judge do it.

There was nothing left to say. Daniels was still a pompous ass and our enemy. Maybe he had also conspired to have the church bombed. At least for one more day we could not let our readers know that.

Back in the newsroom, I kicked a trash can beside a desk. It landed against Ms. James' desk, not far from where Ed and our lawyer Tony Roberts sat waiting on me. Fortunately she had left for the day or I might have given her a heart attack. The noise startled the whole newsroom. Clay and the reporters looked up from their computers and telephones to gawk at me. I looked for something else to kick. Ed jumped up and intercepted me before I could.

"Calm down, Joe. Take it easy," Ed said.

Instead, I threw the court order at Roberts, who looked startled behind his wire-rim glasses. "You fucking lawyers, you're all the same. You don't create anything. You just stop things from happening. You gum up the works. And you sit there on your ass and collect fat fees."

"Jesus, Joe, it's not the end of the world. We'll find a way around this," Ed said.

Roberts was too stunned to speak. I sprawled in a chair at the nearest desk, but after a moment couldn't sit still. I couldn't breathe. I jumped up, grabbed a handful of old newspapers and threw them across the room. The papers flew across other desks and onto the floor. Ed broke out laughing, while Roberts looked like he wanted to run. Ed's laughter was contagious. My rage subsided. I took several deep breaths, and soon I started to laugh at myself. My hands still trembled. I could not remember ever being that mad. Long gone was the fear I felt this morning.

"What the shit?" Roberts finally blurted out as he looked around at the papers littering the floor. "I've seen temper tantrums before, but..."

"Oh, shut up, Tony," Ed said.

I still couldn't believe we were being stopped by some court order. "Where the hell have you been?" I barked at Roberts, but not as loud as before. "The *Examiner*'s attorney has been eating your lunch at our expense."

"I've been trying to get you on the phone for hours. Where have you been?" he barked back.

"On an airplane, then upstairs in Daniels' office getting my ass handed to me. You read that order?"

"Yes. I got called to Judge Strong's chambers with five minutes notice. I didn't know what it was about until I got there. I've been trying to get in touch with you ever since. When I couldn't get you,

I called Maury Weitzman in Virginia. Then I rushed over here to make sure you weren't getting ready to print a story about Daniels. Weitzman said you were hot under the collar, but I didn't expect this." He waved his hands at the mess I had made. "Weitzman said you had promised you wouldn't write anything about Daniels without clearing it. Is that right?"

"Hell, I don't know. Maybe."

Ed looked away from Roberts to hide his smirk.

"So what story are you working on that got Goldschmidt over to Strong's courtroom this afternoon? Goldschmidt told the judge that it would blow the lid off the city, make things a lot worse than they are now," he said.

Ed told Roberts about the Jackson Group and the possibility of the group's involvement in the church bombing. My head was still spinning.

How could they stop us from printing this story? It was bad enough to have to compete on a tilted playing field with the *Examiner*. But to bring in some judge to stop us when we were winning. That was changing the rules of the game at half time. I told them about the meeting in Daniels' office.

Roberts whistled, "You really have kicked a fire ant bed. No wonder they got Goldschmidt out of his office and over to see Strong so fast. You guys have been asking for it."

I stared at Roberts, then asked how a judge could stop us from printing a story on such a flimsy pretext.

"Well, you know there are a lot of scared people out there. It wasn't hard for Goldschmidt to persuade him that this story was more dynamite."

Neither Ed nor I smiled at the unintended pun.

"This is a legitimate story. Tell me how this happened?"

"Oh, you know how the system works. Goldschmidt and his firm have been the key fundraisers for Jacob Strong for probably ten years. Goldschmidt, I heard from the judge's clerk, just met him in his chambers and had the order ready for his signature. They talked for a few minutes and then called me in so we couldn't say the *Post* hadn't been represented," Roberts said.

"Well, have you got a judge that will countermand the order?" I asked.

Roberts shook his head at me. "We do know several friendly judges, but Joe, you know that's not how it works. Since the case is in Strong's court, it has to stay there, until he rules on its merits. Then we can appeal."

"That could take months!" I shouted at him.

The newsroom was quiet. Everyone had stopped work to listen.

"Oh, no. We're in court tomorrow morning. Nine o'clock. I already have two associates working up the briefs we will file tomorrow morning. I insisted on an immediate hearing, and Strong scheduled it," Roberts said. He seemed to believe that was an accomplishment that would appease me.

"That isn't good enough. That will cost us a day," I shouted at him.

He put out his hands with palms turned up. "It is just one story, Joe. What's the big deal?"

I couldn't believe our own lawyer didn't understand our business. "A day's delay will run the risk of some other newspaper, TV or some damned blogger getting the story before us. Don't you understand: timing is everything?"

All eyes remained on me.

"I know. I know," Roberts said, his hands in front of him as if warding off an attack.

Behind Ms. James' desk is a cheap wooden cabinet where I kept alcohol for special occasions. I led the two men into my office. I poured Roberts a glass of bourbon, which I knew he liked, and Ed his favorite scotch. I swigged a beer I got out of a small refrigerator. Clay told everyone to get back to work.

The legal merits of Goldschmidt's arguments, Roberts began to explain, were based on the doctrine of clear and present danger, an arch rival of the First Amendment. The bourbon seemed to help calm

Roberts' frayed nerves. It would take more than one beer for me. "It falls in the same category as prohibiting someone from yelling fire in a crowded theater when there is no fire. Strong, with Goldschmidt whispering in his ear, is interpreting this doctrine to mean you can't print a story that will unnecessarily inflame the public."

"Do you know Judge Strong?" I asked.

"Oh, sure. Been in Jacob's court many times, been to lunch with him, talked with him at bar functions," Roberts said.

I wanted to know everything about this judge. Roberts asked what I wanted to know. I told him everything. The more I knew, the more likely we were to find a point of leverage. Roberts looked doubtful, wondering what his out-of-control client had in mind and what he could do to stop it. But he sat back and dredged up what he remembered about Strong, hoping to impress us that he was close to the judge and thus worthy of his fees.

Before being elected a judge, Jacob Strong had been a personal injury attorney, who had graduated from a small South Carolina law school. About seven or eight years ago he represented the families of two teenage girls whose car had been rear-ended, the gas tank had exploded and the girls had been burned to death. Strong won millions in a judgment for the families. His forty percent fee had been enough to make him think about becoming a judge.

"He's got a real need for acceptance," Roberts said.

I got up and stood in my office doorway, where it was easier to breathe, and asked Clay to get someone digging up everything we could on Strong. In a few minutes, the assistant city editor came over carrying a photo of the judge. I walked over and handed it to Rachel. "One more for Jerome to look at," I told her.

"Now?"

"Right now." I looked at my watch. "It's getting late. He may be gone, but let's try."

"Is this more important than the story on the Jackson Group? I'm trying to pull it together and it's taking me some time to wade through all this material."

Ed said he would get someone to help her. In a few minutes Todd Smith, a rookie reporter, came over and said he had all the stories we had written on Strong in his computer.

"Todd, I need you to call the judge, he's probably at home and interview him." Roberts and Ed looked at me like I had lost my mind. "Tell him that it is for a routine feature in tomorrow's editions. Apologize for bothering him at home, but say that we have to move quickly on this story to fill out the paper."

Roberts stood up and said he did not want to be around for what I was about to do, but told me to email him any story we decided to write tonight. "Remember, we have to be in his courtroom tomorrow."

Todd, a serious young man, looked like I was sending him into battle, which, of course, I was. I told him to record the interview and let me know what he said.

"Me too," Ed shouted. "I am still managing editor 'round here, aren't I?"

A dart thrown in my direction. I knew we were playing with fire. Judges have a lot of power, and this was no parlor game.

Todd called the judge. On the recording, Todd sounded like the young reporter he was, which may have saved him from the judge's wrath. Strong did not believe that the *Post* had randomly chosen today to write a feature story on him, but Todd kept insisting that it was routine, part of a continuing series of profiles on elected officials. He apologized repeatedly for calling him at home. The judge could barely contain himself and wanted to lash out at Todd, but was torn by his desire to see his name and photo in the newspaper.

He answered the basics: Why did he want to become a judge? Is being a judge what he expected? Is it more satisfying than practicing law? What would he change about the judiciary if you could? What was the most exciting case he ever presided over?

Strong clearly wanted to question our motives, but couldn't find an opening in the questions Todd was asking. I was glad Todd

did not know about the restraining order and could play the innocent he was. There were numerous pauses and silences as Strong
thought about the dilemma. I loved it. Payback is such fun. What I
failed to understand was that this game we were playing was tennis,
not golf. The ball might be in our court tonight, but tomorrow it
would be a soft shot in the middle of the court waiting for Strong
to hit it back at us.

Todd finished the first draft of the profile on Strong just as
Rachel came back from country club. "I think I should become a
member. They seem to think I am, they've seen me in the club so
much lately," she said, dropping her purse and notepad and flop-
ping into one the chairs.

"So, was Jerome there?" She nodded at me with a wry grin. "And
what did our source say?"

"Jerome was not sure," she said in almost baby talk, mimicking
me. "He thinks he comes and just eats and drinks and doesn't say
much. That's why he didn't remember much about him. Besides, he
told me all old white men look alike."

"I take offense at that comment," Ed said laughing.

"Okay, here's what I need you to do. Call the judge and ask him.
He's at home. Todd has his number. He just finished an interview
with him for a feature we're writing in the morning. And after you
talk to the judge, write up the story on the Jackson Group, everything you've got, but we can't mention the bombing."

Rachel looked at me, then Ed, clearly not understanding what
was going on. "Did I miss something, while I was socializing with
the rich and not so famous?" she asked.

Ed told her about the court order, signed by Strong, not to
write about the Jackson Group being linked to the bombing. Her
mouth fell open. A quick study, she saw where I was going. "Great,
I'm now an arrow being shot at a brick wall. You know I deserve
combat pay."

We discussed the possible repercussions. I suggested that she
play it innocently, but expect Strong to explode and accuse the *Post*

of harassing him. One call might be a strange coincidence. Two calls and a question about being a member of the Jackson Group stretched credibility.

I sat in a chair next to the city desk, hoping to be distracted. I so wanted to listen, but did not want to make Rachel any more nervous than she was.

"You gotta hear this." She almost ran to the city desk and turned on the recorder. She introduced herself and explained that we had a couple more questions, and that she was working with Todd. Strong didn't like it, but agreed. When she asked him if he was a member of the Jackson Group, he sputtered and stammered and then denied it.

"Well, we have other people who say you are a member and regularly attend the group's meetings at the country club," she said.

"Well, they're liars. They're damn liars. I would not be a part of that group. I'm a sitting judge. How dare you?" he was shouting.

"Are you saying, judge, that there is something wrong with being a member of the Jackson Group?" she said.

"Uh.. uh, well, uh.. No. I didn't mean to imply that. It is just that it would be inappropriate for me to be a member of any business group like that, you understand. It might force me to recuse myself in cases."

"What do you mean a business group like that?" she said.

"Well, you know. An elitist group, where you have to be invited in," he said.

There was a pause. Then Rachel said, "So if I understand you, your honor, you are saying the Jackson Group is elitist and that is why you are not a member?"

The honorable Judge Jacob Strong was twisting in the wind. If we quoted him as denying he was a member of the group because it was elitist, he would have hell to pay from his friends in the group who probably financed his elections and glad-handed him at parties. He could say goodbye to some of the social acceptance he had achieved. If he admitted to being a member, he would have trouble getting the labor union and black votes he needed.

The taped conversation continued until finally Strong said, rather pleadingly, that he would prefer that Rachel not write the profile on him. Rachel stopped the tape. "You don't want to hear him beg do you?"

I did. But it would be unseemly for me to appear eager to hear it. "He asked if he could talk to you," she said. "He's waiting for you to call him back."

Strong picked it up before the second ring. "Judge Strong, this is Joe Riordan, editor of the *Post*. Can I help you?"

"You son-of-a-bitch, this is blackmail. You are having your reporters threaten to write some story about me, linking me with those Jackson Group folks, and you're doing it to try to intimidate me because I signed an order this afternoon stopping you from printing some damned lie of a story," he shouted. Having to wait a few minutes for me to call him back hadn't helped his mood. I could hear ice tinkling in a glass.

"What story is that, Judge?"

"You know damned well what story I'm talking about. Tony Roberts was in my chambers today when I issued my order, and Mel Goldschmidt told me a few minutes ago that he explained it all to you this afternoon."

"But your honor, do you know what story you stopped from being printed?" I asked.

There was a long pause. 'Well, I don't ... , I mean I don't have to know the details. I just know it was a story that would have caused more riots in the streets. That's what Goldschmidt said."

"I'm sure that is what you were told. But you really shouldn't believe what attorneys tell you. As you may know, they get paid to lie, as opposed to newspaper editors who are paid to tell the truth." There was some coughing down the phone line. "Let me tell you what the story really is. It is a legitimate piece of reporting that would inform our readers about the direction the FBI's investigation is headed. Now don't you think the citizens of Iron City have a right under the First Amendment to know what the FBI is doing?" I said.

"Don't you try to lecture me on the First Amendment. I was writing Law Review articles on the First Amendment when you were still in grammar school," he barked.

"Yes, your honor, I know you have a much better understanding of the protection for free speech. That's why I think you know that under the First Amendment a newspaper should be allowed to print this story."

There was silence on the other end of the line. "Not if it might cause more riots. If this story will cause more panic, more people could get hurt, then it's my responsibility to stop it, to stop you. People are scared, real scared of these riots," he said.

"Your honor, if we could put all the bombers behind bars, don't you think that would calm the streets and end the riots?"

"You've got that man Crenshaw. I thought he was the bomber?" Strong said.

I told him that Crenshaw had confessed to placing the bomb, but it appeared there were others involved, that someone had paid him.

"Oh, I see. Well, you will have an opportunity in my court in the morning to present your arguments for writing this damned story of yours," he said.

"Judge, we would like to move ahead with the story tonight. If you would lift your restraining order, we could resolve this now. I think you will agree that the facts are different from what you were told."

"We have due process. Tomorrow morning is the best I can do. In my courtroom. I will do nothing until then," Strong said.

There was a long pause. "What about the story on me? You going to print it?"

I paused to let him sweat. "Well, we've got a pretty full paper tonight, although we are one story short on the front page because of your gag order. We could put it there. On the other hand, maybe not. They tell me there is something happening in Russia that may fill that space."

The judge's sigh could be heard across town. "We'll just hold it for now. But if this gag order stays in place tomorrow, we may have a hole on page one where it would fit nicely. Good night, judge. See you in the morning."

I looked around at Ed and Rachel and Todd, who had heard my end of the conversation and could guess what the rest was. We all smiled, except for Todd, who looked perplexed, wondering if he was to supposed to write his story on the judge. Sometimes working for a newspaper was better than sex.

The articles Rachel and Todd wrote on the Jackson Group were scrutinized word for word. Whole sections were rewritten by committee. Tony Roberts, at home reading the story on his computer and talking to Ed, argued against running the article at all. But when that suggestion was rejected, he made only a few changes to minimize the potential of law suits.

By the time we sent the story to the layout group, Rachel was so tired she could hardly stand up, and Todd was questioning whether he wanted to be a newspaper reporter.

The lead article ran across the bottom of the front page and jumped to page six. It read:

SECRET POWER GROUP HAS MAJOR INFLUENCE IN CITY

A secret business organization in Iron City, known as the Jackson Group, wields great influence over the decisions by the city and county governments that benefit the members of the group, according to an investigation conducted by the Iron City Post.

The group, made up of about 20 senior corporate executives in Iron City, meet regularly with Mayor Jason Martin and other city and county officials to discuss elections and legislation. They also discuss who will be awarded city and county contracts, members of the group said.

The purpose of these meetings, often held in private at the Iron City Country Club, is to influence key government decisions and ensure that members of the Jackson Group receive large contracts and other benefits from local government, according to several members of the group and local officials.

"We all have influence individually, but together we are a powerhouse," said one member of the group, who requested anonymity. "Together we have a lot of leverage and know how to use it. It's the way the game is played. We just play it better than other folks."

The Jackson Group influences city and county decisions because of the size of the political contributions its members make to local election campaigns. An analysis by the Post of contributions to local election campaigns for the last two years shows that the members of the Jackson Group have contributed more than $500,000 to local candidates for city and county offices.

The members of the Jackson Group also have significant influence with local officials because of the implied threat that they could move their companies out of the city. They represent a large percentage of the local economy and tax base. During the recent riots, several members of the Jackson Group threatened to move their companies out of the city to the southern suburbs.

"These riots are killing most of us. They are killing Iron City," said the Jackson Group member.

The article named the members we were certain of, including Daniels. And we ran photos of six members listed in the piece. It also printed a list of group's contributions to the mayor, city council members, county commissioners and school board members. They totaled more than five hundred thousand dollars in local elections, but we decided to use the lower figure to allow some margin for error.

Mike Rose had pulled together a list of city contracts that went to the companies controlled by the Jackson Group. A woman he had cultivated as a source in the computer services division ran a full list of transactions the city had with corporations controlled by members of the Jackson Group. The transactions ranged from the interest-free accounts the city kept in the large banks to the purchase of a fleet of cars for the building inspectors from Harden Braddock's dealership.

Rose had also developed a list of zoning variances and decisions that the city zoning commission had made on properties owned by the corporate or individual members of the Jackson Group. Several zoning decisions clearly benefited the owners, including Braddock, the banks and public utilities. All of the deals were legitimate, but our article painted a pattern of influence and benefits that was unmistakable.

The articles did not mention that the FBI was investigating links between the Jackson Group and Crenshaw. That's where it belonged. And that's where it would have had its greatest impact. Alone it was a great story, but linked with the bombing investigation story, it would have given our readers a complete picture.

We ran a small story on the Metro page inside that the FBI was offering Crenshaw a twenty-five-year sentence if he identified any co-conspirators in the bombing. We promoted that story on the front page in bold type. We placed the promo bug in the Jackson Group article, hoping the readers would make a connection between the two stories. I smiled at the power newspapers have with juxtaposition.

That ought to put the fear in the people behind Crenshaw. If they start hearing footsteps, maybe they'll do something stupid and come out of the shadows.

I called Walt Simpson to tell him we were publishing the story on the Jackson Group and why. He would want to tell the leaders of the group what to expect when they opened their morning paper.

Walt laughed and said, "I always knew you had a mean streak. My guys won't like it, but they will survive. Maybe we'll disband the Jackson Group and form a new one that even you can't find. But for now watch your back. You're painting a big old bull's eye on it."

Probably the last person I expected to see was leaning on Mercedes. His vanity plate read: "Luv Bama". A smug looking Harden Braddock was waiting for me as I left the building. I wondered how long he had been out there. He had changed clothes somewhere. Now he was wearing a dark suit and a tie over a white shirt. Maybe he had downed a few more drinks and come back to see if he could intimidate me more.

"What the hell do you want?"

"Just a chat, Mr. Riordan, a wee bit of talk between two men, who, I think, if I'm not mistaken, have some mutual interests that need some attention."

I shook my head. "What mutual interest could we have?"

The former second-string college quarterback shook his head at me like I was the class nerd who just didn't understand anything about girls.

"Our city, the businesses that run it. That's what we both should be worried about. We can't let all these businesses be destroyed, run out of town. That wouldn't be good for you, now would it? You would go from conquering hero to terrorist," he said.

I waited for the other shoe to drop.

"Now I know we jammed your shorts today, and we'll tussle over that in the morning. You may win. But what happens if you do win? You write a story about the Jackson Group or whoever you think is behind this guy Crenshaw and the bombing, then you're just inviting these blacks, oops, I meant your people, the African Americans, to get all worked up again. And that's not good."

His arrogance filled the parking lot.

"Maybe it settles everything down once the guys behind the bombing are in jail," I said.

"Wrong. You're dead wrong about that. You're being manipulated. The Yankees, like the ones that own your newspaper, they're enjoying it. They're laughing at us down here, saying we can't keep our blacks in line. It's good for some folks here too. Some of these politicians or would-be politicians may see a silver lining. But it ain't good for Iron City."

I didn't want to listen to the paranoid ranting of this rich redneck. It had been a tough day with Fabrini trying to kill me and these jerks using an insecure judge to stop us from reporting the news. It was all boiling up in my gut so much that I wanted to punch someone, if my arms and torso didn't hurt so much. Braddock would do.

"Mr. Braddock, just answer me one thing. Did you pay for Crenshaw to bomb that church?"

"Aw, go to hell, asshole. I'm really gonna stand here and confess to you and whoever else might be listening that I had something to do with murdering a bunch of people. Yeah, I'd love to sit on death row or spend the rest of my life in a jail cell."

He turned to leave.

"Well, I just thought you might want to confess. You know what they say, confession is good for the soul."

He sighed and shook his head at me. "Where'd you learn to run your mouth like you do. Your father's got a good gift of gab, but he never had the balls you do," Braddock said, turning again to walk toward his Mercedes.

He was right. Dad never said anything that would get him in trouble, unless he was drunk. My father would not risk his position at the bank.

"Maybe, then, you'd like to tell me about your new land developments up north?" I said.

He turned around and looked at me. "You mean Stonebridge and Highland Lakes?"

"Yes. How did you get the state to build the interstate through your land?"

He laughed. "The attorney general sent a guy to ask me that question. He drove up from Montgomery just for that. I'll tell you what I told him. I gave the state the land. Simple as that. The transportation boys were having trouble buying up the right-of-way for the highway further north. So I made them a deal. Build it three miles to the south and take the land free and clear. They jumped at it."

"But it makes the highway have a sharp curve. Did you bribe the highway officials to get them to make that change?"

He laughed. "You got nothing. You're fishing. Besides I didn't have to. There are so many ways to pay government folks off. There are fundraisers almost every night in Montgomery and Washington. Bureaucrats need to send their kids to college or take a vacation. I own some nice properties in fun places. You want to take your son and white girl friend, just let me know. Besides it saved the state a ton of money. You know they are bringing that highway in on budget. That's a first. And it's all because of me."

"It didn't hurt the value of your land much, did it?"

"Hell no. Mama didn't raise no stupid kids, but it doesn't take a genius to give away near worthless land if it makes all the rest of it valuable. Real valuable."

"It must've pissed you off to have Commissioner Grey trying to stop it."

I expected him to blow up again. He shook his head at me. "Yeah, that son-of-a-bitch didn't know what he was talking about. But it was all right. He was all worried about the blacks who live up there in those shacks. Lot can happen to those shacks, I told him. Fire, earthquakes, maybe skinheads will go on a rampage. When I told the late, great commissioner what could happen..." Braddock laughed at the memory. "He really lost it, started yelling at me that I was some racist bastard."

I stood there holding the first edition of the paper, wishing it was a tape recorder.

"Hell yeah, I'm a racist if it means I don't think want a bunch of low-lifes living up there on land I own trying to stop me from turning my land into something special. Stop and think. There's not a quality shopping area in all of the northern part of the county. I've already signed a contract with one of the best mall operators in the country. You wait, North Lake Mall will be a gem in this county. Thousands of people who live up north will have a great place to shop. And I am going to build some of the best houses in the whole area. Make it a showplace. But then you probably don't really understand why what I'm doing is important. Most Negroes don't have a brain for business."

He knew how to turn the knife. Here was what my father was afraid of, being disrespected because of my skin color.

"And I'm sure you're going to donate your profits to charity, right?"

"Nope. I've got a better idea. I plan to use that money, and there will be a lot of it, to buy me a few more politicians. And maybe some high school star athletes for 'Bama."

"That sounds more like your style," I said.

Braddock stepped up really close and leaned his face within inches of mine. I tried not to flinch. "Grey swore he'd get me. But I've got too many powerful folks on my side. Slow me down, maybe, but he couldn't stop me. Did his getting blowed up help me? Sure, it did. But that is not the real problem. What's stopping me now is these damn riots. They have put everything on hold. If anybody is getting hurt by all this shit going on in the streets, it's me. It sure as hell, ain't your raggedy-ass newspaper."

He turned to leave. I handed him my copy of the morning edition. "Here, take a copy of my raggedy-ass newspaper."

He looked down the front page and saw the story on the Jackson Group. He swore. I slammed the door of my now-restored Blazer as I heard him questioning my parents' marital status at the time of my birth.

The insults about me bounced off, but I was getting tired of the insults to my newspaper. Wayman Wright had called it "two-bit." Now one of the richest men in the city called it "raggedy ass." Maybe I was being overly sensitive with the threats that hung over the *Post*. But that didn't make them hurt less.

The phone call I had dreaded all day came as I was driving out of the newspaper parking lot.

"What happened between you and my father? He came back smiling and has been in a good mood all day. It looks like he won something big, and I assume it has something to do with you."

How do I answer that question? "I learned a lot on the way to the airport."

"What?" The anxiety in her voice was strong.

"He needs you very much. He doesn't want you coming back to Iron City. And he is willing to do whatever it takes to make certain that you don't."

On the airplane, I knew it was not in the realm of possibility that I would do what Fabrini told me to. I could not live with myself if I gave her up to save my job. And she would see right through any lie I told her to break up. Besides she had left home before. I doubted she would willingly return to the gilded cage.

I knew she was on her cell phone, not the house phone where Fabrini might be listening. She said she was downstairs. Her father and mother were upstairs in their room. I could hear her close a door.

"Your father is a new owner of the Babcock Newspaper Syndicate, a majority owner. That means he owns this newspaper. He told me he would force Babcock to sell the *Post* if we stayed together and you lived here. That's the bottom line."

Nicki exploded. Sputtering rage bounced off the satellite. "That bastard, I won't have that. I won't. I'll walk out right now. Dammit, he can't tell me where to live and who to be with. No way am I going to take that."

"Nicki, please listen. There are ways to handle this, but it is going to take you and your mother to solve it. Your father's ego is riding on this, and as you know, he has quite a temper. You have to be careful. I'll fight the battle of the newspaper. But I don't want to lose you. You and Chris are the most important people in my life, more important even than this newspaper, as much as I love it."

There was a long pause. "You mean that?"

"Yes, I love you. I want to spend the rest of my life with you, if you will live with a lapsed Baptist." She didn't laugh at my poor attempt at a joke. "Your father doesn't want you living here, being with me. He is willing to go to great lengths to stop it."

There was another long pause on the line, then in anger, she almost hissed the words. "If he goes through with that threat and sells your newspaper just to try to stop us from being together, I will write him off. I will never see him again. I'll tell him that. If he ever wants to see me in Philadelphia again and strut around, showing me off to his friends, then he had better keep the newspaper just like it is."

I was worried that she would stomp into his room and tell him off or worse, pack up and call a cab to the airport without even a word of goodbye. She needed to calm down, be as cold and calculating as he was.

"Let your mother help you. She still has the most influence with him. Like you, she gives him respectability. Use that. And don't make any threats you don't plan to keep. He is a master at making threats and carrying them out."

She was quiet. I didn't know if we had been cut off. After a few more seconds, she said, "There's something you're not telling me. What? He's my father. I know him a lot better than you. What'd he do?"

The fight in the greasy shop came rushing back in my mind. I recoiled again at the memory. For most of the flight from Philadelphia to Atlanta, I thought about what had happened in that repair shop. I had first breathed a sigh of relief that I had escaped. But then I tried to figure out what Fabrini was thinking. How would he explain my disappearance? It was then I remembered the odd comment by Benny that he was not going to get to go to Iron City. I hadn't given it much thought at the time. My mind was still in shock.

Staring out the plane window, it came together. Benny, whom Nicki had said looked a lot like me, had been promised his first plane ride, a trip to Iron City. That is how my disappearance would have been explained. Using my plane ticket, license and wallet, Benny would have flown to Iron City, his first trip on a plane, Fabrini said. The last Fabrini would have seen of me, he would say, was when he dropped me at the airport. He would hint that some of Crenshaw's supporters in Iron City must have kidnapped and killed me, certainly a more believable scenario than being killed and entombed in concrete by my girlfriend's father.

After a few days Benny would have made his way home, using his own identity, leaving the police searching in Iron City for me. It may have been her worst nightmare, her father trying to kill me. Nicki was tough. So was her mother. But I was not sure they were a match for Fabrini.

"Let's just say I believe he is as focused a man as I've ever met. He made it clear what would happen to me if I continued our relationship."

Nicki's anger exploded again. She ranted for several minutes before she slowed down long enough for me to talk. After a half hour, she promised not to say anything until morning. She would talk with her mother, get her advice before confronting him. Maybe together they would talk to her father.

"But I promise you. He is not going to win this time. I will be home soon. Then you and I can talk about our future, my wayward Baptist. I love you."

The tensions of the day drained out of me. Maybe things would work out. I couldn't wait for her to come home.

21

It was clear the next morning just how angry we had made Judge Strong. The night before we had jousted on our court. Now I was in his.

Strong's courtroom on the fourth floor of the state district courts building had a high ceiling with walls of marble and dark woods. The large room exuded power. To the customary "All rise," Strong entered, while we stood, and took his seat in a high-backed chair behind a large desk on a raised podium. The seal of the State of Alabama decorated the wall behind his chair. He looked much like the head shot photo I had looked at last night with a trimmed mustache and a bit of a comb-over hairdo that glistened with hair gel in the light streaming from high windows. In person he wore half-rim glasses and projected an attitude that we were all peons and only he was important in the courtroom. But I had heard him stammer as he broke into sweat on the phone. Beneath those judicial robes and autocratic bearing he was hardly tough. Unfortunately he knew I knew it.

The courtroom was packed, mostly with reporters, which was unusual for a case that did not involve a murder or some celebrity. Rachel and Mike Rose sat in the back and waved when I turned around to look at the crowd. To my comment on the number of reporters in the courtroom, Roberts whispered: "Goldschmidt does love to see himself on television and read his name in print. Good for business and feeds that ego. The CNN reporter from Atlanta, he's sitting three rows back, told me he got a call last night from the public relations firm Goldschmidt has on retainer, telling him he should be here this morning. Besides anything you do right now makes for a good story."

Great. Now every reporter in the country would be all over the story we have been working on exclusively.

"Let's try to make sure he doesn't win, but we need to win without giving away what we are working on. Right? That would be winning the battle, while losing the war," I said.

"I'll try, but to win, I may have to be a little aggressive. Leave it to me. This is my game," Roberts said.

The judge unfolded the morning edition of the *Post* and sat on the bench reading the front page. I felt pride at seeing him hold our newspaper for all to see, but a bit anxious at what was coming. Strong turned to an inside page, probably to read the FBI story. We all sat quietly watching. Then he closed the newspaper and stared straight at me. He banged his gavel and asked, "All parties to this matter present?"

Both Goldschmidt and Roberts stood and introduced themselves. Then Strong asked me to stand.

"You play it pretty close to the line, don't you, Mr. Riordan?" Strong was speaking in a deeper voice than the one I had heard. "I think it's time we taught you a lesson about disrespecting this court's orders." Strong banged the gavel three times. "I hold you and the *Iron City Post* in contempt of court and order you to be held in the Iron City Jail until this court deems that you have learned a bit of respect for judicial mandates. Bailiffs, escort Mr. Riordan to the jail."

The courtroom erupted. The noise from reporters and other spectators bounced off the marble. Roberts had to shout to protest Strong's order. I couldn't believe it. Not only wasn't I getting the ban on the article lifted, Strong was locking me in a cell. Reporters madly typed on tablets or texted on their phones to their news desks. Television cameras captured the exchange with the judge. My arrest would be on the Internet before I could be booked.

"Your honor, there is no article in the *Iron City Post* this morning that in any way violates your order of yesterday evening," Roberts argued. "There is no reason to incarcerate the editor of the newspaper."

"Well, what is this bold type here? It says: Turn to page B-one for news of the bombing probe. That would seem to me to be linking this story on the Jackson Group with the bombing," Strong said.

Roberts looked down at me. "No, your honor, that is simply a promotional reference on the front page to additional news inside. It directs the reader to other stories inside. If you'll look at other editions of the *Post,* the same promo is placed on the front page stories. It's just where the layout people thought it should go. Those men and women work for the *Examiner* as well as the *Post* and probably didn't even know about the court order. Pure coincidence."

Coincidence? Hell, I had gone to the fourth floor where the newspaper was laid out and made sure the promo bug was placed in that story. It was my way of reminding the judge that I had power too and was willing to use it.

And Strong knew it.

The courtroom quieted down. Two bailiffs, large, going to fat white men, were standing next to me. One smiled a crooked grin at me with handcuffs dangling from his left hand. I figured he was a Crenshaw supporter, enjoying having the tables turned on me. The judge nodded to him, and the smiling bailiff turned me around and snapped the handcuffs on my wrists. I had my answer. Strong was making me pay for the game I played with his fragile ego.

Several reporters ran out behind me. "What's your reaction to being sent to jail?" one of them asked.

"Oh, I love going to jail," I joked. Then the smart ass in me came out. "As the monument says over in the park, I ain't afraid of your jail." It was one of my favorite comments from the civil rights battles that took place in Iron City. At least, I would not be beaten, bitten by dogs or killed where I was going. The reporters followed along behind other silly questions, like "How long do you think you'll have to stay in jail?"

I told them to ask the judge.

One asked what was the Jackson Group. I suggested they read the article in today's editions.

Rachel walked with me across the street. "Sorry my story got you sent to jail." She tried to look serious, but broke into a giggle. "I've heard of reporters who went to jail to protect their sources. I have never heard of a reporter who got her editor sent to jail. This may be a first."

"At least, I will get to the see the inside of the famous Iron City jail. Maybe they will book me in a cell with Crenshaw. Wouldn't that be fun?" I joked with her to put her at ease, even if it did little to quell my fears.

The jail cell was brightly lit and clean, a world of difference from the "narrow jail cell" that King recalled in his dream speech, where he and his fellow protestors had spent time and spawned one of the better civil rights songs. I was in a large holding cell by myself. No Crenshaw. I wondered where they were keeping him. All the overnight drunks and other petty offenders were already out or headed to court. I sat down on one of the bunks. If Pat Galloway was still working with us, if he hadn't sold us out, he could make things a lot easier for me in here.

It was not more than a few minutes before my pulse started to race. Sweat broke out on my forehead and neck. A trickle ran down my back. This cell was not good for my claustrophobia. I tried to think of other things, let my fantasies take me away. I thought about some favorite places I had been, the beach, London, Venice. But nothing worked. I sat locked in my fears, thinking about how I was going to get out of this cell.

Was Strong acting on his own, irritated at me for the way I handled him last night, or was he earning points with the Jackson Group? What was Roberts saying? Would we have to appeal to a higher court? That would take time. I wanted to print the story today, not next week, not next month. The story was hot, and there were too many other reporters in the courtroom trying to piece together what we had. Strong couldn't stop them from publishing, particularly the out-of-town papers. Our best alternative might be to publish the story in another city, in one of the other Babcock newspapers. Then the wire services would have it, and it would be a national and international story. I didn't like that idea. We couldn't run our own story.

The clock ticked slowly. I loosened my tie, took off my jacket. I was sweating. I wished Dr. King and Reverend Shuttlesworth and their band of warriors were here to chat with. I tried to gain strength from their spirits, but guessed they had moved on and did not haunt the new jail.

What was going on in the courtroom? How was it being handled on cable and Internet news? Was Nicki watching? I hated for her to see it on television. What if some teacher said something to Chris? That would scare him. I felt helpless. My father would hear about it. He would be mortified, his son in jail. My grandfather knew the inside of the old Iron City jail. But not my father. Had I let him down?

Sweat rolled down my cheeks. My breathing came hard. I wanted to scream. How much longer would he keep me in here. There was no one to ask.

It was almost after ten when a bailiff showed up outside my cell and told me the judge wanted to see me again. Had Roberts convinced him? Or was I in for some more intimidation? Before we left, I asked if I could towel off my face. I didn't want to be photographed looking like I was having an anxiety attack.

When we walked in the courtroom, the number of reporters had swelled in the short time I was in the cell. They broke into a round of sympathetic applause. I bowed my head in acknowledgment. I wanted to hold my fists high, but didn't want to piss off the judge even more. This was an early round, a long way to a decision.

Strong still had his game face on. "You're back here because I'm tired of listening to your lawyer argue that I have mistreated you. You probably could use a few weeks in a cell to cool off that hot head of yours." My chest tightened at the thought of spending weeks in jail. "But that will have to wait. I want to get on with the arguments in this case. Sit down, Mr. Riordan, and try to learn something."

Goldschmidt went first. In the courtroom standing beside his table, I could see him better than in Daniels' office. He was short, round and exuded confidence. He had seemed taller sitting on Daniels' couch. His balding pate and thick, black-rimmed glasses made him look smart. He launched into an argument for civil order and against anything, especially the *Post*'s proposed article, that might further disrupt the city. He painted a picture of the city racked by riot and destruction. With a broad flourish of his hands over his head, he compared Iron City to Paris during the French Revolution, when the city was trashed by revolutionaries, and more recently to Ferguson, Missouri and New York City. I thought his comparison a bit dramatic. He made the *Post* sound like a tool of the revolution and the root of the rioting.

He cited various precedents, especially the opinions rendered by Justice Oliver Wendell Holmes. I thought I preferred Sherlock to Oliver.

"A single spark may kindle a fire that, smoldering for a time, may burst into a sweeping and destructive conflagration," Goldschmidt quoted from Justice Holmes. He called our proposed article a "trigger of action" that would incite more violence in the streets. Goldschmidt, working his associates overnight, had found additional precedents and asked Strong's permission to add them to his brief.

Strong nodded his head as if agreeing with every word out of Goldschmidt's mouth. I began to regret my decision not to go ahead with the story on Strong. But then I would have no leverage. Roberts kept smiling and looking confident. I tried to be optimistic.

Goldschmidt introduced into the court record the written statements of several residents of Iron City who claimed they were afraid the city would be burned down and their homes or businesses destroyed if there was one more spark. The implication was that the *Post*'s article would provide that spark.

Finally Goldschmidt wound down. It was our turn. Roberts talked of the importance of free speech and how courts at all levels had protected that fundamental right against encroachment.

"The greatest danger to our freedom today is not that some individuals will engage in civil disobedience. The primary danger to our way of life is that too much government power will be used to erode our freedoms of speech and assembly in the name of security and safety," Roberts argued. "There is nothing in the proposed article that will incite riots. I submit to this court that no group or person has worked harder than the *Iron City Post* to end this period of unrest and disorder."

As Roberts made his arguments, I gained a sliver of hope. He talked of the Pentagon Papers and the attempt by President Nixon to stop *The New York Times* from publishing those Vietnam War-era documents. He cited numerous other cases and concluded with the argument that Iron City could withstand the risks of allowing the *Post* to publish an article. And that article might bring to justice other people who were involved in the church bombing.

The news reporters behind me hung on every word trying to understand what was at stake. I shook my head at Roberts. I wanted him to be a bit more circumspect, but he only smiled at me. He cited numerous attempts to keep the press from publishing articles thought to be detrimental to someone. In each case attempts to impose "prior restraint" on the media had been rejected.

Roberts had warned me that there would be only one witness, me. We had rehearsed on the phone for an hour last night and again in person this morning for thirty minutes. I expected a tough session, but with Strong glaring at me as I was being sworn in, I knew it would be grueling. I only hoped the reporters in the courtroom would keep the sides balanced. We went through the preliminaries. Then Roberts asked me to describe the article we proposed to write.

If looks could kill, Roberts was dead. The last thing I wanted to do was give away our story.

"Answer the question," Strong barked at me when I hesitated.

I looked up at him on the bench. He smiled, knowing the vice I was in and enjoying it.

"It is a routine article. It reports or would have reported this morning that the FBI and Iron City police are investigating the possibility of a conspiracy involving in the assassination of Commissioner Grey."

I had to grit my teeth as I watched reporters from the wire services, cable news reporters, out-of-town newspapers and the *Examiner* taking down every word.

"Are these individuals residents of this city?" Roberts asked.

"Most of them."

"Are they white?" he asked.

I paused. "I expect so."

"Would your article accuse these individuals of conspiring to commit mass murder?" he asked.

"No. It would state that the FBI is investigating that possibility."

"Do you believe this article could incite additional riots or civil disobedience in our city?" Roberts asked.

"I believe that the riots will end and the city can begin to return to normal only when the people of Iron City are convinced that all of those responsible for the church bombing are in jail. There is no reason to believe that this article would incite further disturbances."

Roberts sat down, and Goldschmidt, armed to the teeth, approached me on the witness stand. He kept me there another forty five minutes asking pretty much the same questions over and over.

"If the *Post* named the alleged conspirators, wouldn't these individuals become targets for the riots, their businesses, their families, their homes. Would they be safe in this city?" he said.

I shrugged. He waited for a verbal answer. "Anyone who instigated this heinous crime will undoubtedly be at risk, but I feel certain that the FBI and Iron City Police would provide the necessary protection until they can be brought to justice."

Goldschmidt avoided mentioning the Jackson Group, probably because members of the group had him on retainer. But any good reporter could put together the business group and the conspiracy to bomb the church.

"Do you have first-hand knowledge that there is, in fact, a conspiracy?" Goldschmidt asked.

I said no.

"So this could be false and damaging information. Correct?"

"We do not knowingly print false information or willfully damage anyone's reputation. We report facts and what people, like FBI agents, tell us," I said.

"Will you verify this story?" Goldschmidt asked.

"We were in the process of doing that until you had this court stop us."

Goldschmidt sat down, and I escaped to my seat. When neither side offered to call any other witnesses, Strong declared a recess while he considered the arguments.

Roberts remained confident, but Goldschmidt also looked pleased. I feared his firm's political contributions would outweigh Roberts' arguments.

Rachel brought me a message, asking me to call Nicki. I left the courtroom, avoiding questions from the other reporters, and phoned her.

"Mother heard on the news that you had been sent to jail," she said anxiously.

"Not for long. I'm out now. It was just a judge flexing his muscles. How are you? Things calm there?"

"I wouldn't say calm. But the tiger is in a tight cage. My mother's a fighter. She can be tough in the clinches. She told him that he would lose her and me if he tried to sell your newspaper to stop us from being together. Father got angry and stormed out of the house. But mother thinks he'll be back in a few hours in a more reasonable mood."

With my luck lately Benny and Steve were headed for Iron City to finish the job he started. But I didn't want Nicki to worry. Maybe Fabrini would cool down. I hoped he would. There was a lot at stake.

"Great, when do you think you can come home?"

"Maybe tomorrow, but it may take a few more days. I want to see things through here, and then I'll be back. The compromise I proposed was that I would come back here four times a year for a week or ten days at a time so I can help mother. But I plan to live in Iron City, or wherever you live. That okay with you?"

"You bet. That's the best news I've had today." I smiled and felt pretty good, even if I had Strong, Daniels, Braddock and Fabrini breathing down my neck.

After a quick call to Ed to update him, I headed back to the courtroom, again dodging reporters in the hall. Strong took his time getting the proceedings started again. I felt like a prisoner in the dock, waiting to hear if I would live or die. He stared at me as he began speaking. His first words sent shock waves through me.

"This court shares the plaintiff's concern about the potential for continued civil disobedience and criminal activity in the streets of this city. This is a dangerous time. Our city is a tinder box with a lot of people holding matches," he said very solemnly. "However, the right of free speech must be protected. It is the cornerstone of our democracy." He paused while the reporters typed and scribbled and the television guys played with their cameras.

"So I will not grant the injunction. But let me warn the defendants in this matter, the *Post* and specifically its cowboy editor, Mr. Riordan, that if there is damage caused unjustly to certain individuals, it is within the jurisdiction of this court to award damages. During my deliberations I took a moment to look up a passage from a decision that I consider quite similar. For the record it is Bernard v. Gold Oil Co. I'm sure you know it, counselors, but let me read it for the benefit of Mr. Riordan."

He read: "*There is no power in courts to make one person speak only well of another. The Constitution leaves him free to speak well or ill, and if he wrongs another by abusing this privilege, he is responsible in damages or punishable by the criminal law.*"

"Mr. Riordan, you may proceed with printing the article in question. But exercise care, or you may find yourself and your newspaper in a whole lot of trouble."

Winning is sweet. In this case there was no runner-up trophy. Roberts clapped me on the shoulder. "I'm not sure it was my arguments or your threats to tie the judge to the Jackson Group that did it, but we won."

It didn't matter. There was one less crack in the foundation of the First Amendment, and we could print the article we wanted to yesterday. Tomorrow's editions would carry it and a story on our court victory. We were on a winning streak.

Pride goeth before destruction, a haughty spirit before a fall was one of my mother's favorite proverbs.

I thanked Roberts, told him he did a good job and walked toward the back of the courtroom. Rachel stood there smiling. Mike sat on the wooden bench. His ribs still hurt, but he managed a wave. "Way to go, boss," he said.

Several reporters stopped me to get my reaction. I was not getting any more comfortable answering answering instead of asking the questions. "We're very pleased Judge Strong ruled in favor of freedom of the press. The story we wanted to print was stopped by people who had an interest to protect. This is a victory for the people of Iron City over special interests."

I watched them scribbling on notepads and recording my words on tape recorders. Several other reporters gathered around me and asked for details on the article. I laughed. "Read it all tomorrow morning," I said.

"Is the story about this group, the Jackson Group, being involved with the bombing?" asked a woman reporter with short blond hair in her thirties. I had never seen her before. I assumed she was with one of the out-of-town media.

"Same answer," I said, smiling at her.

"Yes, but what makes you think this group was involved in the bombing?" she pressed me. Her accent was clipped, northern. She was also better dressed than most home-grown reporters.

"I may be able to discuss it more tomorrow."

"You mean, after you print the story?" she said.

"Something like that," I said.

I walked toward the back of the courtroom. Harden Braddock sat in the back row, scowling darkly at me while he talked on a phone. I wondered if he was selling cars or bribing some bureaucrat while his side went down in defeat over the story we were about to publish. I walked past him without either of us acknowledging the other.

"When you were a boy, did you like swatting hornets' nests with a stick?" asked a voice I recognized over my shoulder. I turned to see a smiling Walt Simpson. His bear-like frame gave me comfort. Seeing him, I was suddenly thirsty. I wanted to down a couple of beers and replay the courthouse victory. But that would have to wait. I wanted to get to the newspaper.

"And twisting tigers' tails," I joked, standing in the hallway outside the courtroom.

"Well, you're doing that all right. I can name twenty of the richest and most powerful men in town who wouldn't pick you up if you were run over by a truck," he said.

"Then I will have to watch myself crossing the street. How are you faring? Are your clients taking this out on you?" I said.

He laughed. "After I called some of my guys last night, you'd have thought World War III had been declared. Needless to say, you're not playing by their rules."

The swirl of people who had been in the courtroom passed us, making jokes and clapping me on the back. Several looked at Walt and wondered who he was. Few people knew he was more influential than almost anyone in the courthouse. He did not seem to care that he was being seen with the enemy of an organization that paid him a hefty fee each month.

"Never said I would. I even gave Braddock his own copy of the paper last night. No charge."

Walt snorted in laughter. "I heard about your little conversation. Did you really ask him if he paid Crenshaw?"

I nodded and smiled. That dark look on Braddock's face in the courtroom said it all.

"Someday guys like Braddock are going to learn, we're a newspaper, not a voice of the old boy network like the *Examiner.*"

Walt shrugged and turned just as Braddock walked out of the courtroom and down the hallway away from us. "I thought I taught you better'n that," Walt said. "Just remember your laws of physics. I gotta go."

He walked away quickly down the courthouse hallway in the same direction that Braddock had gone. His comment about physics was puzzling, but that was Walt, his mind always an anomaly. I watched him walking quickly away until he stopped to talk with a small black man standing down the corridor. As they talked, they looked back at me, and I realized it was Jimmy Marshall. I waved. Why was the little deacon, jazz player and civil rights warrior in the courthouse today? It surprised me too, but probably shouldn't have, that he and Walt knew each other. At times, politics creates strange relationships.

Outside the courthouse, the sun shined down out of a blue sky, creating a perfect sixty-five degree day. It had rained before dawn, which at the time I feared was a bad omen. But it had left the air feeling soft and smelling clean. The pretty black weather girl on television this morning had promised a bigger storm would roll through this evening, but for the moment, it was a great day to be alive. This morning I had walked across downtown from the newspaper to the courthouse. Rachel now offered me a ride with Mike and her, but I was glad I could walk the few blocks back. I was so excited I knew I couldn't sit still for hours. I needed to burn off some of the adrenaline flowing into my blood stream.

I didn't make it more than two blocks.

22

As I started to cross Nineteenth Street, a black Lincoln Continental slowed to a stop. The driver, a young man, dressed in a dark suit and pale blue tie, rolled down his window. Distracted by my own thoughts, reveling in my joy at beating Daniels and the Jackson Group in court, no alarm bells went off in my head. I was sure the driver just wanted directions. This was my city, I was pleased I could help.

No good deed goes unpunished.

I stepped off the curb, leaned closer to the open car window. The back doors swung open, and two other young men jumped out on either side of the car. They too were dressed in suits, white shirts, ties. The driver and the man closest to me on the street pointed a gun at me. The other man ran around the back of the car, grabbed my arm and pulled me toward the open door of car. Startled, I planted my feet and resisted and yelled, hoping that someone would see and be alarmed at the sight of me being pulled into a car by two young men at gunpoint. I hoped someone would call the police. My captors, much stronger than I, dragged me into the backseat.

"You yell one more time, and you will be dead meat right here on the street," one said. The other man jabbed the gun in my side. A thin woman in a patterned dress carrying a sack of Sneaky Pete's hot dogs on her way to her office saw the scuffle, heard my cries and screamed herself. The two men in the backseat pinned me on either side. The car sped off, leaving the woman screaming, her hot dogs and fries in a heap on the sidewalk.

Oh, my God. What was happening? Panic. I was going to be killed. These guys were not smiling. I was being kidnapped. Images raced through my mind: hostages in the Middle East, businessmen seized in Mexico, South America. So few ever came back. Some had their heads chopped off.

"What are you doing?" My voice cracked.

After a long pause, the man on my left said, "We're going to take you to see The Man, so just you settle back and shut your hole. Nothing you can do about it."

I struggled in my seat, but to no avail. The two men had my arms pressed tight against my sides and one had a gun against my ribs. The car drove west out of downtown and turned north. It was unreal. It moved smoothly as if there were no bumps or potholes in road. A full symphony orchestra blared from the surround-sound speakers. My captors rode in silence. No rap. No jive. All buttoned down and serious. They hadn't bothered to blindfold me, so I guessed it didn't matter if I knew later what they looked like or where they were taking me. Neither Benny nor Steve had tried to hide their identity either. These men planned to kill me too. I pushed my feet against the back of the front seat and started trying to push my captors in the backseat away from me. I wiggled and shoved. Useless. I looked at the one on my right. He just smiled showing a full set of white teeth at my useless escape attempt.

The driver took the entrance to the interstate that ran north to Tennessee. Were they taking me out of the city where it would be easier to bury me? But we only stayed on the highway for a few miles, then he turned the car off at an exit just north of downtown and cruised through back streets to what looked like an old factory. Piles of dirt and coal lay in hills taller than the one lone building on the property. He stopped the car in front of it, a large, one-story metal building that looked like it might once have been a small factory or warehouse. He pressed a button on a remote opener and the large garage door went up. The car rolled inside. He pressed the button again and the overhead door rattled closed, trapping me again just like in that New Jersey car repair. The only light came from a row of narrow windows at the top of the front and back walls. In the dim light the place looked cavernous and empty.

My captors dragged, half walked me out of the car. I tried to struggle again, but that only made the four men laugh. Were these guys working with Benny and Steve? Were they waiting in the building for me?

"Come on, get him in there," the driver said.

The other three men pushed and pulled me toward the back of the building. I kept my legs stiff to make it a little harder for them. But they moved me along. As they forced walked me across a polished concrete floor toward the far corner of the building, I saw an interior wall with a door. The driver pulled out a key ring and unlocked it. When he swung the door open, I could see there was a room behind, but in the half light I could not see what or who was inside. They pushed me through the door. The room looked a lot like the jail cell I had just left. There was a bed against one wall, a sink and toilet against the other. There was no other furniture, no table or lamp, only a light hung from the metal ceiling. Had someone lived in here? At least it was not a closet.

"You have got to learn, don't mess with the man," the driver said. They patted me down and found my phone and keys. They took both. "He's clean," one said.

"Then leave him," the driver said.

I ran back through the door. But the four of them, younger and much stronger, pushed me back. One hit me across the top of my head with his fist. Another shoved me back against the door jam. My back hit the frame and my legs went numb. The muscles in my shoulders and back were still sore from the earlier brawl. This only made them worse. I slowly fell to the concrete floor. Two of my captors grabbed my arms and dragged me inside the room. One kicked me in the back and laughed. The driver barked at the man who kicked me, "Don't do that. You know what he said. If he is to be harmed, he will do it, not you." The other man straightened, held his head up and walked out of the room.

The other men stood over me smiling. Then the driver reached down and grabbed my left arm. He pulled back my sleeve and slid my watch over my hand. He looked at it, "Pretty cheap watch. How come you don't have a Rolex?"

Then they stepped around me and walked out the door. One of the guys who had sat in the back seat bowed at me as he shut the door. I heard the key turn in the lock.

"No, please. Help me. Please," I shouted at them without really knowing why. It was clear they weren't about to let me out just because I begged. But that required rational thought.

I lay there on the concrete and tried to stop shaking. My head and back hurt. I worried that the blow to my back had smashed a vertebrae, and I wouldn't be getting the feeling back in my legs. After a few minutes that worry subsided, I moved my legs a little. Slowly the numbness ebbed, and both legs got a tingling sensation in them like when they used to fall asleep in church.

When I tried to stand, my back and side had sharp pains. My head throbbed. I thought of Mike Rose, stooped over as he walked, holding on to his ribs. I hurt all over. I tried shoving the door to see if it would budge, but it did not move. The room had a closed feeling. Was there enough air? Was I supposed to suffocate? Did they know I hated little spaces?

On the wall I found a light switch. The wattage on the bulb couldn't have been more than forty, barely enough to see around my new cell. But it made me feel better. This was a lot more frightening than being locked in the brightly lit Iron City jail. I knew then that the judge wouldn't keep me there long.

"No bail bondsmen going to get me out of here," I said out loud.

Here, there were no rules. I began to sweat. I tried not to panic by forcing myself to think of other things. What were they thinking at the newspaper? Were they wondering yet why I had not shown up after the hearing? For a few hours they would not worry, thinking I had some place to go, maybe I had stopped for lunch.

Would Ed go ahead with the story on the FBI investigating the Jackson Group, the court ruling? Deadlines were still hours away. What was the *Examiner* writing in its final afternoon editions? What were the television news shows broadcasting? What if this went on for days? What would Chris think if I wasn't there in the morning? That was the hardest.

Why was I here? Why would four, well-dressed thugs, who liked big cars and classical music, grab me off the street and bring me here? It was no random kidnapping. They must have followed me from the courthouse. Why? I sat on the bed and tried to think it through. But thinking came hard.

I wiped my forehead with my sleeve. I loosened my tie, took off my jacket. Maybe it was because I had become high profile with the arrest of Crenshaw. Did someone want to show how tough they were? Maybe they would try to ransom me to Weitzman and the Babcock folks. That would be a joke. I doubted if the bean counters would pay a king's ransom for me, especially if it had to come out of Fabrini's pocket.

Fabrini. This was his style. He wanted to erase me from his daughter's life. Nicki had said he left home angry and had not come back. Was he on the phone setting this up? He could make it look like someone in Iron City killed me. That was straight out of the Italian mob playbook. My captors said I had messed with the man. Is that Fabrini? He could hire people here. Maybe this was his backup plan.

Sitting on the bed, I lost track of time. My nerves were exhausted and my head pounded. The walls closed in. This was a nightmare. Locked away in a small room, no food, no watch, nothing to do, nothing to read, nothing to listen to but my fears. What would happen when the door opened again? Would they kill me, or was I to be left here to die alone?

I tried to shake off my fears, but the anxieties were determined to stay. They came every time I was in a small space. I tried again to take my mind away from the room, to someplace nice, a hike in the Smokey Mountains, lunch at Gladstones on that rocky beach in Los Angeles, a drive with the top down through the Alps, any place where the air was clean and fresh. But the sounds in my head won out. I knew where they came from. My mother's bed. My father, drunk again, would pull me out of her bed, shove me in that closet and shut the door tight. Tears rolled down my face while I heard him tell my mother how beautiful she was. She would never say a word. Then I would hear his hand slap her face. It would always leave a welt, an ugly bruise she tried for days to cover with makeup and by combing her hair forward across her face. The bed springs would creak as he shoved her down. I could only hear, which made things worse, straining for the next sounds, yet holding my little hands over my ears. He would grunt and the bed's headboard would bang against the wall. It lasted only a few minutes, but seemed like hours. When I got a little older, I thought about pushing open the door and running to her side to save her. But my legs would not work. When I told her my hopes of saving her, she would hug me, cry and tell me to forgive him. It was only the booze that made him crazy, she said. In the darkness, when it was over, my mother would open the closet door and pull me out. She would cover her face, but I knew the damage was there. It was always there on her face and both of our souls. Being held by her, wrapped in her nightgown, I felt warm and dreamed silently of killing my father.

My father snored in the bed. I hated him, was afraid of him. She and I would go to my bed and cuddle all night. She would tell me I was a brave boy, but I didn't feel it. I had not saved her. By the time I was old enough to have fought him, my father sent me to a boarding school.

Now I had to deal with another monster. Fabrini had reached out to finish what he had started in a dirty repair shop in New Jersey. I prayed my mother would bring her band of angels and pull me out of this room, just like she did when I was a boy. But it was not likely. She was in heaven. I was here in hell.

No coherent thought came for what seemed like hours. Fear and confusion blocked real thought. Rational thought was hopeless, a rat racing around in a loop.

"Okay, think, Joe," I said out loud, mostly just to hear a sound other than those in my head.

I had to figure it all out. Only then could I get out of here. I focused on the bombing and Mark's death. His article on Crenshaw had thrust me into the middle of a whirlwind of events. Coming back from the cemetery, I had witnessed the attack on the four policemen and jumped in. We had printed the story, given it too much play. Then Walt told me that some people did not like it and to watch my back.

Was that what this was all about? Retribution from the gang that wanted to kill those cops? Saving them seemed like a long time ago, but was really only a few days. So much had happened since then, the hunt for Crenshaw, more riots in the streets, finding Crenshaw and bringing him back to Iron City, the two attempts to kill him. Or were they attempts on my life? We assumed someone was trying to kill Crenshaw. Could someone have been shooting at me?

No. Of course, it was at Crenshaw. "C'mon, Joe, think," I said again out loud, trying to force my brain to concentrate.

We fought with and made an enemy of the judge. Who were we really fighting with? Members of the Jackson Group? Or were we just fighting with Daniels and Braddock? Would they hire a black gang. Were they the man?

Fabrini. It always came back to Fabrini. He was the driving, evil force, determined to finish killing me off, while claiming ignorance. Nicki would not return to live in Philadelphia or would she? She liked it here, liked the work. She would use her skills and her connections to find out what really happened to me, but I doubted that her father could see his little girl as a tough private detective.

Oh, shit. When my captors said we were to meet the man, well, maybe Fabrini with Benny and Steve was flying in to kill me himself.

On the bed I held my head in my hands. Sweat beads dropped off my nose onto the concrete floor.

What was it that Walt said? Something about physics. What the devil did he mean? That piece of the puzzle seemed important only because he said it right before the guys in the car grabbed me. As I walked happily down the street in the sunshine and fresh air, I remember thinking I would tease Walt about his obtuse message. Then the car pulled up and they grabbed me.

What could physics have to do with being put in a small room, locked away? It had been a long time, the last year in my boarding school, when I last thought about physics. I never cared much for it then. Old Mr. Hagood tried to force some physics into my brain, but all I cared about was making good grades to please my mother and go to college, while I played tennis and dated, oh, what's her name … ? Melissa, yeah, Melissa, that's right. Thinking about Melissa, who went to St. Anne's Academy, was better than thinking about physics, then and now. What was it that Mr. Hagood was always talking about? If something's standing still, then it will continue to stand still. But if something is moving, then it will continue to move. I never did understand that exactly.

And there was another one. Newton had a bunch of laws. For every action, there is always an equal and opposite reaction, or something like that. You push an object in one direction, there is an equal force pushing against it in the opposite direction. Was that what Walt meant?

Then there were the policemen I saved. Did the gang of men grab me to show they were still in control? If they killed me, would they then have their pride restored? Did they want to kill me to keep the riots going?

And then there was Daniels. Since he owned the *Examiner* and had always influenced the *Post*, at least until I became editor, he had never seen negative publicity about him. The story we wrote this morning mentioned him as a member of the elite political group. The one we were preparing for tomorrow would be more to the point and he wouldn't like it.

Walt made the comment about physics right after Strong ruled against the Jackson Group's motion. The pendulum swung hard, pushing me into this room because we had pressed hard against the Jackson Group. Back and forth the pendulum swung. I shoved back, and now I was being pressed against a wall. Newton be damned, each push seemed to be getting stronger. Pretty soon, maybe this time, it would be too strong, and I would be brushed off the game board.

More sweat rolled out of my hairline and into my ear. The room was not even warm. I had to get out. I stood on the bed and gripped the top of the wall. It ran up to the bottom of the metal beams that held up the roof. The beams were about eight inches thick, leaving a six-inch hole between the roof and the top of the wall. I stood on the bed and pulled myself up so that my head was between the beams. No use. The room was solid. No holes big enough to try to squeeze through. I tried yelling, a wasted effort, but it made me feel a little better. The silence overwhelmed.

I was hungry. What time was it? It could have been minutes or hours since I was thrown in here. The first deadlines must be coming up. Damn. What was happening at the paper?

Suddenly in the silence, the garage door opened. I felt a whoosh of air rush into the building. A car pulled in, its tires squeaking on the concrete. Was this help? Or were my captors coming back to kill me? From the footsteps on the concrete it sounded like two or three had come. A key was inserted in the lock. The door opened a crack. "Stand back," a voice barked. I did as I was told. The man pushed it open. Two others from the limousine stood beside him. They had me outnumbered and blocked the doorway. Of course, that was purely academic. My knees were shaking so that I doubted I could outrun a cripple.

"The man figured you were hungry." He tossed me a white sack. In it was a burger and some fries. He set a drink on the floor. Big spenders. But I didn't voice any complaint. I was glad to have the food. At least they didn't mean to starve me to death. Anger slowly replaced some of the anxiety.

"I want to get out of here. There's not enough air in here. I don't like small places. I might die." I tried to sound tough, but undoubtedly failed.

They laughed. "That'd be too bad, now wouldn't it? One less Oreo in the world. What a shame." He was showing off for the other guys.

"What do you guys want? Money? What?"

They just shook their heads at me like I was a wayward child. They started to shut the door. Panic gripped me again. I begged them not to leave. The guy who had thrown me the food, opened the door again and asked if I needed anything else.

"Yes, please, let me go. I need to get out of here. This room is too small. I need to get back to work."

They sniggered at me. "Get used to it," he said. "You may be here awhile. The man's coming, but not soon. Yell all you want. Make yourself hoarse. It won't do you no good. Nobody'll hear you."

I sat down on the floor and cried. Fear consumed me. I did not want to die. I wanted to get out of here and get back to the newspaper where I was safe, where I knew who I was. Not knowing what was happening, who these guys worked for drained me of my energy. I had to know.

"Do y'all work for Fabrini?" I yelled as the door was closing again. As they walked to the car, I heard them laughing, but couldn't make out what they said. "Do you work for the Jackson Group? Daniels?" I shouted louder. They laughed harder.

I sat on the bed and ate the burger and fries. I hardly tasted it, though I have always liked fast food. Chris and I would sneak off occasionally to have a Happy Meal and a burger. It was a great time. Nicki would shake her head at me when she finds a McDonald's sack in the car. If you are going to be dead in a few hours, who checks your cholesterol count? The medical examiner would hardly care.

Chris is such a good kid. I thought about the fun we would have this year shopping for Christmas and writing Santa Claus, if I could get out of here.

I needed to get out of here. If I had a hair pin or something to pick that lock. I looked in every corner of the room and under the bed to see if there was anything that might work. The room was clean. I turned on the water in the sink, flushed the toilet, just to see if they worked. It didn't get me any closer to escaping.

Suddenly I heard pounding on the roof. The weather girl was right. It was raining again. I lay on the cot and tried to think more. There was a missing piece in the puzzle, a big one.

The garage door creaked open again, breaking the silence, metal sliding on metal as the motor in the ceiling raised the large door. I was glad it had not been oiled. I didn't want Fabrini, Benny or Steve sneaking up on me, not that it would probably have mattered. I stood up ready to face whatever was coming. What was I going to do, fight them again with my bare hands against Steve's knife or maybe he would bring a gun this time to finish me quick.

A car drove in. A car door slammed, and a pair of what sounded like street shoes echoed in the cavernous space. Not two or three pairs of sneakers like before. If it was Fabrini, he was coming alone. A key turned in the lock, and the door opened. A familiar, but unwanted face stood in the doorway.

Harden Braddock hissed at me. "Step back. I came to see if you were okay."

How did this jerk have the right to kidnap me? Seeing him, my blood boiled, more angry than frightened. It made sense. This had to be his warehouse, one of the properties he inherited from his father-in-law. Braddock was the Man?

"I have to get out of here. You can't hold me here. This is kidnapping. You know that. It's illegal."

"I told you before, you talk too much," he barked. "You don't know why you are here. Your mouth just keeps on running like you got something important to say."

It was hard, but I shut up.

"I'm thinking I'll let you go. But first you gotta promise me you won't write any story tying me with the church bombing. You understand?"

Could I agree? I would not be bound by what I said standing here locked away in this little room. But then he would know that. What was his game?

"Look, you're a pain in the ass. If it wasn't for you, there wouldn't be this problem. Everything would be fine. I had things under control. But now, it's gotten way out of hand. It's gotta stop. I thought about just killing you, but that wouldn't solve anything. Your guys at the newspaper would still print the story. The world, from the President to the talking heads on TV, would make a martyr out of you."

He paused and let out a deep sigh of frustration. Discussing my death so cavalierly sent chills through the muscles in my neck. If I took his advice and said nothing, maybe he would let me go.

An agitated Braddock paced in front of the door, rubbing his hands together. The rain was still pounding on the roof, but Braddock was dry. He must have been in his car when the rain started or used an umbrella. He was dressed like he was taking his wife out for a casual dinner, blazer over a blue shirt with no tie. As I watched him pace, I wasn't sure what really disturbed him. The threat that the *Post* wanted to write a story about him, even one that implicated him in the bombing, did not seem enough to upset him this much. He was tougher than that. He would make us prove it. He would have Goldschmidt file a multimillion-dollar libel suit. And maybe he would win.

So why did he throw me in here? Why had he come here now? Not to help me. There had to be another reason. Was there something that scared him more than bad publicity.

374

"I don't understand," I blurted out.

He looked at me and shook his head. "That never stopped any of you newspaper guys from writing stuff. Details be damned. It don't matter who you hurt. Go for the big headlines and sell those papers."

"You're right," I tried to be conciliatory hoping I could get out the door. "Sometimes we are not as good as we would like to be. We walk a fine line."

"Oh, shut the fuck up." Braddock started pacing again, more agitated than before. "I didn't start this thing. I just got dragged along into it. Now I've got the FBI sitting in my office waiting to talk to me, all because you wrote that damned story this morning about the Jackson Group. You mentioned my plans for North Lake Mall and my housing developments. The FBI and the police, they think you know something that you haven't told them. You out-smarted them once. You embarrassed the high and mighty from Washington. They are not going to let that happen again."

He continued to pace. Could I make a run for it? I might get past Braddock. He was a big guy, but he wasn't in as good a shape or as strong as the four guys who put me in here. My feet just wouldn't move. My brain was not connected to them any more. Besides, I hated to admit it, I wanted to hear the story, and it looked like Braddock was wound just tight enough to tell me.

"I mean I've had all kinds of assholes from state and federal agencies crawling all over me, trying to get something on me. Just because I made some money and give a lot of it to politicians and the university, that means I gotta be crooked. Well, I ain't a crook. It is just business." He hardly stopped to breathe. "The assholes from the attorney general's office down in Montgomery, they can't prove anything. But the FBI, they're different. They will spend millions to prove someone is guilty. You can't buy them. Buy all the congress-men you want, but it doesn't do much good. The FBI does what it damn well wants. They don't listen much to congressmen or gover-nors or even the fucking President of the United States. Now thanks to you, they're after me."

He stopped talking, a jumble of mixed emotions. He hated me and sure didn't trust me. But things had gone so far wrong for him that he seemed to want me to understand.

"You're interested in the truth, aren't you? You want to know how all this got started, the real truth?" he asked.

"Sure," I said, trying to sound nonchalant. Next to getting out of here safely what I wanted most was to hear him admit he was the guy behind the bombing and who else. What role did his friend Robert Daniels play in blowing up the church. And of course, I wanted to see it printed in banner headlines in the *Post*. I wished I had a secret recorder.

Braddock looked down at the floor. I was afraid he would change his mind. His whole body shivered. "Aw, shit, you wouldn't believe me anyway. You're convinced that I'm some bad guy, a greedy white bastard that would do anything to make more money, have more power. Ain't that right? Even mass murder, right?"

"I'm listening. You got a story to tell? I'm here to listen."

"No. No way. Daniels I can trust, but not you, no. Robert says you're too old school, spent too much time listening to that old editor of yours, Howard somebody. You're too much into the old newspaper values, right or wrong, the story comes first."

This was not the time for a debate on my values. I waited. Braddock seemed torn. He needed to tell somebody how things had gone wrong. I waited, hoped. Time seemed to stand still. I was afraid to breathe. Would he regain control of his emotions and walk out, leaving me to rot in this make-shift cell?

Braddock was one of the most powerful men in the state, the biggest supporter of the Alabama athletic program, friend to university presidents, governors, senators, mayors. He had more money than he knew what to do with. He could intimidate anyone. But right now, standing in this dim light in a cavernous mill, he looked broken, scared.

His need to talk won out.

"You wouldn't believe it. I still don't, and I was there. This guy calls me one afternoon, gets past my secretary, telling her he wants to buy a fleet of cars, will only talk with me. Why should I care what he wants to buy? I got salesmen for that. But he insists on meeting with me. So he comes by the next day, and we sit down.

"He was black, darker than you, but sounded like a white man on the phone. I never met him, never even heard of him. It pissed him off when he asked me what I knew about him. I told him nothing. He then told me how important he was. He said he knew people in Washington and Montgomery and down at the courthouse that could get me anything I wanted. Contracts, zoning changes, that sort of thing. What the shit? I do all that already myself. I should have thrown him out.

"After we talked about cars a bit, he gets up and shuts my office door, real spooky like. Then he tells me he has this dream, just like old Martin Luther the Almighty King, that he is going to be elected the next county commissioner. I thought about it, the funny way he had come round to it. I told him we already had a couple of black commissioners, and I didn't think there would be more any time soon. He would have to wait. No, he says. He wanted Grey's seat. I told him that was fine if he wanted to run. I would have loved for someone to beat that loud-mouthed, self-important son of a bitch. But I didn't think anybody could."

He paused and looked around like he was suddenly worried someone else was listening. Reassured, he started up again.

"I figured he was just going to ask for money. I'd have given him some. Anybody who wanted to take on that bastard Grey, I would have helped him. Like you said, Grey did get my goat. I don't mind a little civil rights agitating. I know they all got to do that to keep the money and votes flowing their way. But Grey really meant it. He took it too far."

He stopped and seemed lost in thought. I wanted to keep him talking. The pieces to this puzzle still didn't fit.

"So was that it? Did he run for county commissioner?" I asked.

He shook his head. "I only wish that had been all it was. This guy, he just up and said it, right out. Can't beat him, we gotta kill him. Then he sat back and smiled at me." Braddock paused to let that sink in. "I'll tell you I've heard a lot of shit in my time, spun a little of it myself. But that floored me. I couldn't believe it. I still can't believe it."

Braddock clapped his hands, as he probably had a thousand times on the sidelines watching his team play. The sound bounced off the bare walls. He laughed. He was in no hurry to get on with the story. We stood in the small room. There wasn't any place to sit except on the bed or the floor, and neither of us did that.

"Grey was a real pain and could have cost me a lot of money. At first, he was just an aggravating, but a manageable problem. That is until the Yankees decided to put a black man in the White House. That changed things. Grey stopped preaching and started meddling. He and Smallwood were asking questions about all kinds of deals. He came after my land deals up north. But the worst was his ranting about Bama having a black football coach. I know there are a few black coaches in the pros and some colleges, but not here, not at my university. I heard him start in on that rant after a commission meeting one day. I went home and told my wife. She spit her bourbon across the carpet."

The coach of a winning team at Alabama or Auburn can make a fortune, not only for himself, but for people and businesses that support him. Over the years we had written stories about the Alabama coach's business deals. Braddock was one of the guys who backed Coach Sprengler financially. He had his name on a chain of men's clothing stores and showed up to bring in customers. He had been given ownership in land deals and probably a whole lot of other things we didn't know about. He was reported to be a part owner of two rehab hospitals in Selma and Montgomery, places you go to dry out. The joke was that he bought or was given a stake in the hospitals to give him some place to send players, coaches and contributors. He was paid well by the hospitals to encourage doctors around the state to refer patients there.

Those deals, which went well beyond the usual arrangements for college football coaches, made Sprengler a very rich man. All he had to do was keep on winning Southeast Conference championships, compete for national titles and, of course, beat Auburn. Wherever Sprengler went, he drew a crowd. Grey's plan to replace Sprengler with a black coach would upset many of those deals.

"I give a lot of money to support Bama football. The coach likes to come to my house. We sit around with some of the guys and sling the shit. He drops by the car dealership a few times a year. It sells cars. I have invested in several deals with him and want to make sure those investments pay off. How is that going to happen if we replace Sprengler with some black coach Grey helped pick?"

He paused and looked through the door for several minutes. "How am I supposed to invite a black coach to my house in Shoal Creek? My wife said 'no way.'"

Then I knew. Braddock had written the note to Smallwood, telling him to get Grey under control. I asked him if he had. He gave an exaggerated shrug, then nodded. "I wanted Grey stopped. I had a lot riding on those land deals. At first, I figured he was just raising the price I would have to pay him and the other commissioners. But no, he wanted to stop any roads or sewers the county would build to those properties. That would kill them and leave me holding several bank notes on that land."

He turned to the wall and slapped his hand against it. He looked at me. He had been so lost in his rant that he seemed to have forgotten whom he was talking to.

"So I told this guy, I could see the need for getting rid of Grey. That is when he reeled me in real smooth." Braddock wrapped his arms across his chest. He seemed almost angry with himself. "I should have thrown him out of my office and called the police chief. I could have dealt with Grey somehow."

He blew out a chest full of air. "But I didn't. I asked him how he planned to do it. He told me about this old boy that would kill Grey, shoot him or something. The only problem was the guy was a real redneck, hated black people. He would need a white man, somebody Crenshaw would respect, to front the deal."

Braddock shook his head, "Sounded easy enough, the way he laid it out. I could call this Crenshaw, who was big time lazy and dumb, but we needed some dumb ass to do something like this. He and I talked about things, met him over at a bar. He really hates Negroes, well, you know. He told me he had some trouble in the Army with them, got cut by one. There was no question he would do it. He seemed to think it would be a great thing for humanity. All we had to do was point him in the right direction. I gave him some money and told him that I would give him more if he needed it. I told him I would give him some traveling money. It would be good if he were gone."

He paused and looked around again like he was expecting a ghost or someone to walk in. Sweat rolled out of his hair line. The small room seemed to have closed in on us both.

"Crenshaw called me in a couple of days. We met again. He said my friend had a great idea. He wanted to blow up the church. A bomb? Why a bomb? I asked him. That might kill other people and stir up all kind of trouble." He shook his head again. "Guess I was right about that, huh?"

He swore and asked, probably not for the first time, why Crenshaw had not just shot Grey. It would have been easier, he said, and nobody else would have gotten hurt.

"But no, this guy wanted Crenshaw to bomb the church and Crenshaw liked to blow things up. I guess he learned how in the Army." Braddock wrung his hands. "He said this would be big and would really show the niggers, I mean Negroes, who's boss."

Braddock was still trying to make sense of it. I hoped he would keep talking. The more he talked, the more I would know. And maybe he would decide to let me go. I assumed Braddock planned to leave the country or something.

"That's when I think it really started to get out of control," he started again. "Crenshaw was all fired up. I don't think I could have stopped him even if I'd tried. A few days later the bomb went off and killed all those people. I laughed when I saw it on TV. I didn't care at first. But then the whole town started coming apart with these damned riots. I knew there'd be trouble, but not this much. Shit, now we've got the Guard patrolling the streets. Nobody's bought a damn car in weeks. All the land I own ain't worth a fart as long as this is going on."

He was talking to the floor, but then looked up at me. "They almost got you one day, didn't they? That was pretty funny, you getting it by a bunch of your own." He chuckled. "Then I got a call from this guy that started it all. He says he wants to start running for commissioner. You know what he said? I had to give him five hundred thousand dollars off the books for his campaign.

"Well, I know what a commissioner campaign costs, and that's way too much. Maybe two hundred total. And this was a special election, which cost even less. But he insisted it had to be five hundred because other candidates were going to run, and he needed to scare them off. He said he had lots of expenses. As if I'm supposed to care," he said.

I was trying to guess who the blackmailer was. Ray Smith? He had fallen out with Grey. He had made it clear he wanted to take his place. I could see Braddock and Smith working together. Smith would know how to get to Braddock.

"When I started complaining about the price, he threw in a kicker." He laughed. "He knew my hot button. You want to know what he offered to get me to go through with the deal. It's crazy."

He reached inside his coat and pulled out a small flask. He unscrewed the top and put it to his lips. He drank enough for two shots, then wiped his lips on the back of his hands and smiled at me.

"Eugene Crabtree. That's what he offered."

"The high school football player?" I asked. That floored me.

"Yep. The best damn running back since Herschel Walker. I've seen him run. He is amazing."

He took another swig. "This guy said he had Crabtree and his mother in his pocket. That he could get him off the fence and sign with Alabama, not Tennessee or some other school. Sprengler would bend down and kiss my ass if I could deliver Crabtree. I could be on the sidelines for every game. I'd make tens of millions off the deals we would do with Alabama headed to the national championship for the next four years." He nodded at the thought. "I told the guy I would get him his half million by the end of the week."

He stood smirking at me. "Dumb, huh? Should've known better. Blackmailers are all the same."

I was pretty sure we were talking about Smith. Bud Shaw learned about Crabtree's decision to go out of state from Smith. Somehow, I never thought Smith was capable of all this. There was clearly a dark side to him.

Braddock said he got other members of the Jackson Group to make contributions. By then he said they were so scared of the riots, they didn't know what to do. "Typical. Sitting around with a thumb up their ass. So when I told them to, they just paid up."

He delivered the money and hoped that was the end of it. It was hard not to laugh at his naivete.

"Were many of the Jackson Group involved in this?" I asked.

"Nawh," he blurted out. "Bunch of wimps. Some of them are afraid, now that you have exposed it all, that they will lose out on their sweet deals. But most of them are just glorified bureaucrats, trying to make sure that no shit happens on their watch."

I took a deep breath. "What about Daniels, did he know?" It was a question I had wanted to ask from the start. I didn't want him to know how important his answer was, but he knew instantly.

"You've got a real thing for Robert, don't you?" He laughed. "I think he knew I was behind it, or at least I always thought he knew.

We never talked about it, but he had to know. He's not like you, always wanting to find out stuff. He doesn't think of himself as some big-time reporter. He's always been an owner, trying to fill those shoes his daddy left him. And mostly feeling a bit small. You should feel sorry for him, not threatened by him."

We stood there saying nothing for a few minutes. He was trying to figure where it had all gone wrong. I was trying to figure a way out. I had a hell of a story to get in the paper, Braddock, Smith conspiring to bomb the church. The clock was ticking. Deadlines were coming. But there was more to learn.

"I laughed when the FBI put out that photo that was supposed to look like Crenshaw," Braddock said. "It was so far off. I knew we were in the clear. Nobody would recognize him from that picture. But then I heard you had something."

"Were you the one who called him and told him to change hotels?" I asked.

"Yeah. I wanted him to lay even lower than he was. The guy had scared him pretty good. It was funny, he didn't even know he was taking orders from a black man. They only talked on the phone. But he told me he knew that if he ever talked, he would be dead. Me too. When you found him, that is when the real trouble started. Ol' Lonnie and I were the only links to him, and those had to be cut."

Braddock didn't seem to be talking to me any more, just confessing to the only priest he had.

"Who tried to shoot Crenshaw down in Florida and outside the paper?" I asked.

"Not me. Probably him. He told me not to worry. He would take care of Crenshaw, but I had to put another fifty grand into the campaign. Campaign, my ass. The money wasn't going to the campaign. It was just a game. I was pissed, but there was not much I could do about it. I needed Crenshaw dead too before the redneck started talking."

"But he missed," I said.

"Yeah, he missed. Maybe on purpose, I don't know. Kept the pressure on me. Then we couldn't get at Crenshaw. He was somewhere with you. When the story came out, we knew the FBI had him. I was just waiting for him to point the finger at me."

"We were interviewing Crenshaw in the Tutwiler Hotel. Then we brought him over to the newspaper and turned him in to the FBI," I said.

"Yeah, so I learned. But too late."

He ran his hands over his face. He seemed very tired. I had to make my escape soon. Could I get out of this room, out the garage door? I hadn't heard it come down after he pulled his car in. Maybe I could make it outside.

"Then you had some girl calling to ask about the Jackson Group and the bombing. I knew that was just a cover. You were really on to me. So I told Robert to stop you, but he kept saying he couldn't because of some agreement he has with that company that owns you."

He shrugged. "You know the rest. I had Goldschmidt pull Strong's chain to get that court order to stop you printing that story. But, you, you son-of-a-bitch, you wouldn't quit." He turned his anger on me. "You sat there looking so tough in Daniels' office. I thought we could scare you, get Daniels to threaten to shut you down. But he wimped out. All we did was piss you off. I should have known."

"So did you grab me and throw me in here? Are you working with that bastard Fabrini?" I asked.

"Fabrini? Who the hell is Fabrini?" he said.

He started pacing again. Now I was confused. Was this just Braddock?

"Sitting there in the courtroom, I knew you would go print your article fast. My name would be in big headlines. I didn't think there was much else to do. So this guy said he would take care of you. Without you, the newspaper would hold up on the story. I thought that might work, buy us some time. Then my assistant called saying there were two FBI agents waiting in my office. Hell, that did it. I drove out to one of the mines I own. I thought maybe I'd just keep on going. Find some island where I couldn't be extradited, spend my money and live quiet. But first, I was going to kill you, just for the hell of it."

He giggled at the idea. Was his mind coming unhinged?

"Then I thought that wouldn't do any good. They'd hunt me down." He shook his head. "So I decided I'd just come let you go and then go tell the FBI everything and see if I could make some deal."

I breathed easier for the first time since he had walked in. Braddock was delusional if he thought he would go free by making a deal with the FBI. But I wasn't about to tell him.

"Come on, I'll drive you back," he said.

I turned toward the door. I was excited. I wanted to get back to the newspaper. What a story we had for tomorrow's editions. I still needed him to confirm he was talking about Smith. But before Braddock changed his mind I wanted out of this little room.

23

"Like hell you will," came a voice from the other side of the wall. I knew that voice. I should have guessed. Maybe I did know. Maybe I had always known. I just couldn't bring myself to believe it. I still didn't want to believe it. I guess that is why it was hard to wrap my mind around Ray Smith as the head of the conspiracy.

Three of the men, his men, who had brought me here, stood behind my friend, H.T. Jones. At least now I had my answer. My mind was whirling, my throat dry. I knew we would probably not survive the night.

H.T. just looked at me with disdain. Then he turned to Braddock. His eyes flashed in anger. "So you were just going to roll over on me, were you?" he stood in the doorway, his chest and biceps bulging under a black, sleeveless T-shirt. He was dry, no sign of rain drops on his perfect attire. He held a black checked sports jacket that he handed to the driver. "And who's going to believe your silly white ass? I was in the church when the bomb went off. If I had know'd about it, would I have been there?"

"That's why you were there in the back of the church away from the bomb. The perfect alibi," I muttered almost to myself.

"Shut up, Mr. Know-it-all Editor-in-Chief," H.T. said to a chorus of cheers from behind him. "I'll get to you in a minute. First, I got to take care of this Mr. Rich-and-Powerful, White-Muther-Fucker."

I did not know how much of Braddock's confession H.T. had heard. He and his men must have walked in through the open garage door. They had not made a sound.

"Now, boy, you gotta understand, the FBI is all over me. I had to do something," Braddock said.

H.T. did not show any reaction to being called boy. "I'm gonna tell you what you got to do. You're going to do one of the few things you know how to do well. Pull that checkbook out of your pocket and sign one of those beautiful checks. This runoff election is getting mighty expensive, you know. Old Ray Smith is a bit tougher than I thought."

His smile showed a lot of teeth.

"How much you got in that bank of yours?" H.T. asked, not expecting an answer. "Oh, that's right, I forgot, white folks can't bounce checks. They got that overdraft protection. Man like you being a VIP at your bank, you have your own personal bank officer answer your calls on the first ring. Ain't that right, Mr. Editor-in-Chief. White folks can write checks for any amount of money they want. 'Course, not black folks. They gotta write their checks and hope the bank'll cash 'em, even when money's sitting in the account. Right?"

He was talking more for the benefit of his guys, who were giggling and punching one another behind him.

Braddock stood straighter. "I'm not writing you any more checks. You've soaked me for too much already."

H.T. shook his head and stepped closer to Braddock. In what was little more than a whisper, he said, "So then what good are you? If you're not going give me any more of your money, maybe it'd be best if you were some place you can't do any more talking.

Without you around, the ties with me and that asshole Crenshaw are broken."

He leaned back and the man, who had driven the car when they brought me in, handed him a handgun. He looked at it. It was big, cradled in his left hand. He smiled at Braddock. H.T. was serious. He meant to wipe out the threat Braddock posed. But what about me? I could still put H.T. away. So I had to die too.

"Okay, okay," Braddock said breathlessly. "How much you want? I got my checkbook right here." He pulled the checkbook out. "How about fifteen hundred? That's about all I've got in this account right now." He was panting and really spooked. "I can get more later."

"Shit. You think that's all your life's worth. Fifteen hundred dollars. You probably got more'n that in your wallet. You just date the check yesterday before all this started and sign it. Make it out to the North Iron City Good Government Fund. That'll do. That's my new campaign fund. How you like it? I started to call it just the Rich Negro Fund."

Braddock's hands shook so that it took what seemed like several minutes for him to write out the check. He paused several times. He didn't look up, but just shook his head. He left the amount blank and tore off the check and hesitating for a heartbeat before he held it out for H.T. It was a few seconds before H.T. took it, like it was not all that important to him. Then he held it up for his entourage to see. He smiled. He was a happy man, in control. He folded the check and slid it into the hip pocket.

"Why?" I asked. "Why did you bomb the church and kill Grey?"

H.T. stared at me. "Well, you probably should know that. But it does get a bit complicated." He laughed. "Well, maybe not. It was actually real simple. Grey was a big obstacle to my plans for me and my boys. He was in the way." He paused for effect, letting that sink in. He stood with hands on his hips, looking menacing. "Hell, I had people talk to him about running for the Alabama Senate or go to Washington and be in the United States House of Representatives. Now wouldn't you think he would be interested. But no, he took a pass. He wanted to stay right here in old Iron City and be the commissioner. We couldn't jump over him. He wouldn't get out of the way. The commissioner can step up to a bigger office, but not some street guy like me. I need to be the commissioner for a few years, build me a reputation for good government, create a huge war chest of beautiful money. Grey wouldn't help." He looked at Braddock and then back at me. "So he had to go."

That tracked with what Mike Rose had said and the man I had seen when Grey sat in my office. He was ambitious, but thrived on being a local politician. It was all he wanted, a new black version of an old-fashioned city boss. Grey felt it was the right place for him to do good for his people, the whole county. If he went to Montgomery or Washington, he'd be too far from his neighborhood. He would be out of his comfort zone. He never dreamed it would get him killed.

H.T. smiled even bigger. He looked more unbalanced than I ever imagined. "I got this white motherfucker to front for me. It wasn't hard. He hated the commissioner too. Talked him into getting me that crazy redneck Crenshaw to do the bombing. Can you believe it?"

"I want out," Braddock said, regaining some of his bluster.

"You'll be out soon enough. I've got a few loose ends to clean up. Then everything'll be all right, now won't it?" H.T. said. His gang broke up laughing again. "When I'm commissioner, you and your bitch wife won't have to worry that you'll have to serve some nigger football coach a drink in your big house or watch replays of the Iron Bowl game with him on your giant screen TV. That's not going to be your problem. Your problem will be persuading that white cracker coach you like so much to cut me in on some, let's say, all the deals you two are doing. Then I will be rich as you."

He smiled. "Don't you worry about the county building you roads and sewers to your mall and all those beautiful houses. Just get ready to pay double what they would cost. And you can just build me one of those houses. I'm tired of living in a shack."

Braddock looked like he had been kicked in the balls.

H.T. turned to me, the gun shifting from hand to hand. "The big problem, as I see it, is you, Mr. Editor-in-Chief. You're getting a bit too close to the truth. I can't let you print anything that might put a needle in my arm. You always were kind of smart and even more bullheaded when it comes to a story. Should've figured you would be tough to manage."

I started to beg. "H.T., I thought we were friends. How could you do this?"

He shook his head and waved the gun around. "Friends, hell. We ain't never been friends. I played you like a song. A lot of other people too. That Mark Hodges guy, friend of yours, he was easy once I figured out what made him tick."

"What do you mean?" I asked.

"All he cared about was a story that would get him on the front page of some newspaper, any newspaper, even your newspaper." He was trying to get a rise out of me.

"D'you kill Mark?"

He laughed and turned to his guys to share the laugh. He turned back to look at me. "Hell, yeah, we killed him. See what I mean? Nobody, not the cops, but you, you would figure out that he was even killed. That's how good my boys and I are."

"That's right, that's right, we did him," the black men behind H.T. chanted.

H.T. smiled at them, then looked back at me. "You wanna know what happened, right? Just like your friend, always got to know about things. Didn't you ever hear that curiosity killed the cat? In this case a black cat."

I didn't answer.

H.T. laid it out with pride. He have given Mark the list of possible bombers I found on his desk. Crenshaw's name was on it. That was the beginning of the end for Crenshaw.

"Why? Why did you turn him on to Crenshaw?"

H.T. laughed, twirled around to face his gang. Then he turned back to me. "That neck was just too dumb not to get caught. I knew he would get drunk in some bar and start bragging. It was just a matter of time. I needed to control it." He waved the gun at Braddock. "And I used your friend to keep the pressure on this fool. I could squeeze more money out of him if you newspaper boys were breathing down his neck."

"Why didn't you tell the FBI?" I asked.

He laughed. "Can't manage those guys. I could always keep you in my sights, know what you were doing, how your investigation was going. Can't do that with the FBI."

Dawn broke on my thick head. He had bugged our offices. He laughed, when I asked him, and said that he had also bugged my home office. I wondered how he had done that, but then remembered the unknown delivery man. I should have hired some security for my house.

"But why would Crenshaw take orders from you?" I asked.

H.T. chuckled. "That's the beauty of this plan. Old Lonnie thinks I am another white redneck. We only spoke on the phone. When I try, I can talk like any white man." He imitated the rounded tones of a television newscaster.

Proud of how he engineered the bombing, H.T. waved at Braddock. "Crenshaw only saw this jerk, when they first met and he paid him his money." He started laughing. "You know what I told the old redneck asshole to get him really riled up. I told him Daniels was a standup guy for the cause, but he had this Negro working for him as a senior editor, who could be a real problem. That got old Lonnie's blood pressure up good."

Mark had met H.T. with me years ago at city hall. He would think him a good source. He would never have believed a black man, particularly H.T., could be the mind behind the bombing. When Mark finished talking with Crenshaw in the Aces Up, H.T. said he came to him and played the recording. Whoever said there was no good irony left in the world?

"D'you know I tried to get him to take the story to the *New York Times*? But no, he wanted to take it to you. He said you deserved it. I told him not to be a sap. He would get more money and fame if the story ran in a big time newspaper, not in your old rag. But no, he said it was a story you should have first," H.T. said.

I wanted to kill H.T. My brain reeled with anger, frustration. No one likes being made a fool, and H.T. had played us all.

"What were you doing, following him?" I asked.

"Most of the time, one of my guys was." He turned to look at his men. "We don't leave much to chance. He stopped in a bar over on the Southside. He had started asking questions about the Jackson Group and looking for a conspiracy. Those were the wrong questions. I went to meet him, made sure he downed a few beers. He was so excited about the story."

"He served your purpose, right?" His cool commentary about killing Mark scared me, but made me just as angry. Mark deserved better. "So how'd you kill him, run him off the road?"

"There you go, you too, asking too many questions for your own good. What'd you care how I did it? You ain't ever going to write about it."

He smiled at his guys. They smiled back. This was fun, showing off their power, more control than they ever dreamed they would have. H.T. could never resist showing off. It was part of his style even from the early days. "We followed him to a Sack 'n Save on Green Mountain Highway. It was about eleven, he was well on his way to being drunk. No problem to pop him on the head, drive his car up to one of the cliffs, put him in it and over it went. So long Hodges, you nosy bastard."

There were cheers from the chorus.

I tried to smile, despite the pain in my soul. If I didn't look frightened, maybe he wouldn't kill me too. "So it was you shooting at Crenshaw in Florida?"

"You got it," he said.

"Why? I don't understand why you didn't kill Crenshaw when you had the chance. Why did you wait until we found him to try to kill him? You went to so much trouble keeping an eye on us."

"You figured that out, did you, Mr. Editor-in-Chief. With all that Ivy League education, you done figured that I had a mole in the organization, spoon feeding you smart assholes just what I wanted you to know. And making sure I knew what you were up to. I admit I'm proud of you, you spotted my snitch. Your friendship with that cop reporter didn't blind you. I thought it would. Maybe there's hope for you after all. Make you an official street nigger," he said.

I thought about Pat and, to my surprise, felt sorry for him. With his need for money, he was easy prey for someone like H.T.

"You had enough information to write a story that Crenshaw was the bomber. I wanted him talking some, but not too much. With Hodges' tape and once you found old Lonnie, you could write a story. Then when he was dead, the trail would stop right there. You wouldn't be satisfied, not knowing the rest, but the TV guys and other newspaper reporters would be, and they would move on to the next story. Then it would be over. I'd get myself elected commissioner. And this son-of-a-bitch would go on making me rich and powerful for years."

I remembered that H.T. had asked me if we would write a story even if Crenshaw was dead. I thought his question was a odd at the time. Now I knew why he wanted to know.

"Crenshaw had to go. If the FBI got him or if he had told you about Braddock, then it wasn't much of a leap to me."

"But you missed," Braddock said angrily. He clenched and unclenched his fists. He was not accustomed to having no control. "Now the FBI guys are sitting in my office."

That annoyed H.T. "Don't you dis me," he said, brandishing the gun. "That was a tough shot in the wind."

I have never seen a relationship change so quickly. The wealthy car dealer, real estate developer, white power broker, university benefactor had walked into his own warehouse a half hour ago thinking he might still get out of this mess. Now he knew better.

For me, there was still more to learn.

"I assume you really did steal the votes from that Fairfield precinct, right?" I asked.

H.T. just smiled. "Politics is a beautiful thing, ain't it? You've just got to know what you're doing. Then it's fun and profitable. A little money spread around to folks who need it bad, then you can get them to do what you want."

"Was that also your guys who burn down the Courtier woman's house?"

He nodded and smiled an evil grin.

"But isn't she your aunt?" I asked.

"Yeah, a great aunt. She never liked me much. She was rich, always looking down on my mother and me. I had to scare a few folks. D'you hear any of them talking now? Besides who would ever think I would burn down my own kin's house. The honkey sheriff or that useless elections commissioner can investigate all they want. They'll never get anybody, except her, to say anything. And now she knows how close to the pearly gates she came. I already sent a press release down to the newspapers and the TV stations that when I'm commissioner, I'll raise money and do one of those home makeovers on TV. She'll get a new house. That'll play good in the neighborhood."

"So you burn the house down, and then have other people pay to build them back, right?" I said.

The men behind H.T. started laughing. He laughed and nodded at me. I wanted to keep H.T. talking. When he ran out of stuff to say, he might start shooting.

"So what are we going to do now with Riordan?" Braddock asked.

"I don't think that's really your concern, now is it?" H.T. said with a sneer. His contempt for Braddock was escalating dangerously.

"He knows it all. We had to grab him to see what he knew, what Crenshaw might have told him. But now if we let him go, we'll be on the front page tomorrow morning," Braddock said.

H.T. shrugged as if to say not to worry. He turned and motioned to the men behind him. One of them pulled out a phone. In a minute the fourth member of H.T.'s team walked up behind the others.

He reached behind his back and pulled a child in front of him.

Chris! No! No, damn it, no! They had Chris! I heard myself yelling, and I stepped toward Chris. But H.T. came between us and pushed me back.

"That's right. That's right. I got myself a little insurance policy against any more of your exposes about the church bombing. What d'you think, Mr. Editor-in-Chief, you think I'm stupid. I've got your number."

My whole body shook with fear and rage. I, my need to chase a big story, had put Chris' life in danger.

"You think we can make a deal? Your kid's life against a story about who talked Crenshaw into bombing the church?"

"No, you can't!" I heard myself scream. "Not Chris. Don't hurt him, don't scare him, please. He's .. he's only a child. Give him a chance, please, H.T." I was pleading. "Do anything to me, but not Chris."

Why hadn't I hired some security?

"That makes your decision real easy, now," H.T. said, half smiling, half laughing at me. "You see you are not an Oreo, gooey and white on the inside, black on the outside. No, you are a brown egg, like the ones that church lady with the turned up nose would bring my mother, all white on the inside, brown on the outside and yellow to the core." He laughed again and turned to see if his men appreciated his metaphor. For a guy, who dropped out of school, H.T. was one smart man, dangerously smart.

"There'll be lots of other stories to write. And I will be telling you what to write."

H.T.'s cruelty showed through his smile. What had seemed to be an aggressive, tough mentality with lots of potential for positive leadership was unbalanced, cruel and amoral. If I had a gun, I could pull the trigger.

Chris had been squirming in the man's grasp. He dropped to the concrete and broke free. He ran to me, wrapped his arms around my legs and buried his face between them. He sobbed soundlessly. He was terrified. My whole body trembled with rage.

"You son-of-a-bitch!" I said, losing control when I felt Chris's terror.

"Yeah, and then some," H.T. smiled.

I lunged at H.T., but it was a useless gesture, even if Chris wasn't holding my legs. What could I do? I had to distract H.T., knock him off his stride. He was too much in control. If I didn't agree to his deal, he would kill us.

"What would your mother think of her precious little Henry now, threatening little boys so you can get rich and powerful?"

H.T. turned the gun over in his hands and looked down at it lovingly. Then in a small, but menacing voice he said, "Don't try to play no mind games with me. You ain't even in my league. I made my peace about my momma a long time ago. All that stuff I told you I made up. The truth was worse. But you bought it. You go all soft, mushy inside. I thought about grabbing your old man, but then I figured you don't care all that much for the old drunk. Hell of a father to have, ain't it?"

The truth hurts.

"The better option was this pretty little boy. I knew he was the only thing more important to you than that damned newspaper. I see I was right, as usual." His men launched into a chant, "You right. Man's right. You right."

He paused to wait for my nod. That was all I could manage in response.

We only lived two blocks from Chris' school, and his grandparents picked him up every afternoon. On nice days like today they walked home together. Chris knew not to get into anyone else's car. I should have hired a bodyguard, picked him up in a car at school.

My in-laws were old. They were no match for H.T.'s men. If they could grab me, they could easily grab Chris. My mother in law must be hysterical. I hoped the police were searching with an Amber Alert for Chris. The folks at the newspaper would know something was happening.

"This is outrageous," blurted out Braddock. "I'm not going to be part of this, kidnapping this boy."

He started toward the door. H.T. hit him in the stomach. His punch doubled Braddock over, buckled his knees. Gasping for breath, Braddock knelt on the floor, his head down.

"What? You care?" H.T. yelled at him. "Is it 'cause this boy's skin is more white? What is he? I figure he is more than half white, right? His nose ain't as wide as mine or his daddy's? Would you care if he looked like me?"

Braddock looked up at H.T. trying to follow his rant. "I don't know, maybe," he whispered.

"Maybe if he could play football." H.T. shook his head. He put the gun barrel against Braddock's temple and pulled the trigger. "Goodbye, asshole."

The blast of the revolver was deafening in the small room. The bullet took off the far side of Braddock's head. His body writhed and fell limp. Blood splattered the wall opposite me. More blood poured out of his head and pooled on the concrete. Chris screamed. My mind reeled. The smell of gun powder overpowered. But H.T.'s face showed no emotion. I stepped into him, hoping to grab the gun, but he was quicker. He moved back and pointed the gun at me.

"Easy, my old friend, we still got plans for you," he said. "Death would be too easy."

I stepped back. My legs were so weak, I fell on the floor beside the bed. Chris knelt beside me, and I pushed him under the small bed.

H.T. looked down at Braddock. He stepped over his body and kicked him. "That'll teach you, you son-of-a-bitch. Fry in hell, white man. We'll be here spending your money."

The four guys behind him cheered. They laughed and pointed at his body. One reenacted the shooting, pointed his finger at him, said "pow" to simulate the gun's sound and then blew on his shooting finger as if it was smoking. They were all happy.

The guys who had driven the car that brought me to this nightmare took the gun from H.T.'s hand and gave him another one. He wiped the first gun thoroughly, taking off any fingerprints. Then he knelt down and placed it in Braddock's lifeless hand. He pulled out a thick metal box with a hole in the side and wrapped first Braddock's fingers, then his around the gun. He placed the muzzle in the hole and pulled the trigger. Another explosion, not as loud as the first one, bounced off the walls of the small room. Chris whimpered. I wanted to scream. After a couple of minutes, the man opened the box and pulled out the smashed bullet and held it up for H.T. and the others to see. He smiled a toothy grin. Then he loaded the gun with a bullet, leaving only one chamber empty.

H.T. turned to look at me cowering on the floor. "Now it's your turn." he said. "If you want to live, if you want this boy to live, you will write what I tell you. As smart as I am, it may even win you a prize. What are those things called, Nobels? No, Pulitzer prizes, right?"

I kept my head down, my nose inches from the concrete. I was too scared to think.

"Now here's what I want," H.T. said leaning down to put his head close to mine. "You'll write stories that say I am a great guy, maybe stories about how I am solving serious problems, working to bring whites and blacks together in old Iron City. I want a story and what do you call it, an endorsement, for how I've helped these young men, how I am a good role model for them. You will write those stories and editorials and get white folks and black folks thinking they are glad Grey's dead and I'm the commissioner. I will be bigger than Grey, more powerful. You'll help me do that."

He paused to let that sink in. "But first, you are going to clean up this mess. I want to see a story about how Braddock was the brains and the money behind the church bombing. He gave Crenshaw the cash. Now the son of a bitch has gone and killed himself because the FBI was closing in. You are going to write that, just the way I say."

I didn't say anything.

"It's going to be like owning my own newspaper." He turned and smiled at the men who stood close behind him, watching my every move. "And you know what they say about newspapers. Don't mess with guys who buy ink by the barrel. Ain't that right?"

I still didn't answer him. There was no answer. It was either give in or he would shoot Chris and me.

"You hear me?" he shouted.

My hands were shaking and my brain felt like oatmeal. "Yeah, yeah, I hear you."

"Now, Mr. Editor-in-Chief, know this. I can grab this boy any-time I want, whether I'm sitting in my new office on the fourth floor at the courthouse or in jail or in hell. If you try to move him out of town, I'll find you and him. There's no place safe. I promise you that."

I looked at Braddock's body, lying still on the floor. The pool of blood was growing larger. His face didn't look like him anymore. It wasn't hard to imagine Chris or me lying dead, looking much the same. I knew H.T. meant what he said. He was too disciplined, too smart, too evil not to carry out his threat. And with his gang of loyal followers, he would be able to get to us even if I could get him sent to prison.

H.T. saw me looking at Braddock's body. "Don't worry about that honky. He served my purpose. His death, the conspiracy of rich white folks to kill the great black hero Grey will sell you even more papers, get you on national TV again. See, everybody wins. Stick with me. H.T.'ll take care of you," and after a pause he bent down and added, "and this sweet little boy."

That prospect was terrifying. Being controlled by H.T. was not a life worth living. Every time he called, I would relive this horror.

I would have to go to the FBI and ask for protection. Wouldn't that make Pitts laugh? We would have to leave town, change our names. Sending him and his guys to prison would not be enough. I couldn't live like that.

I had to get us to safety. The only hope was to agree to his plan and hope for the best. I reached back and squeezed Chris' leg. He didn't deserve this. Poor Chris. First his mother, now him and me. A whole family wiped out.

"Okay, okay, you win," I said, holding up my hands in surrender. My head was still bowed. Babcock was going to sell the newspaper anyway. My life as a newspaper editor was coming to an end. I knew that. I just didn't want to face it yet.

"Just don't hurt my son."

I looked up to see him smiling in victory, pointing the gun at us. "I am smarter'n you. No use fighting me. I was always going to win. Just a matter of time. Maybe you got too much white in you," he said.

His turned to look back again at his guys. They were loving the victory. They had beaten me. They had killed a rich, powerful white man and were going to walk away free. They had me cringing for my life. They controlled a newspaper. They felt important.

Lightning crackled outside, followed quickly by thunder above the building. Through the storm, I heard another noise. H.T. and his guys heard it too. He motioned with a flick of his head to go investigate. A loud pop; then glass broke on the concrete floor outside the room. Another pop. It didn't sound like the storm noises. This was something else, something man-made. The guys crouched outside the room. H.T. stood still inside the room. Then the smell. My eyes stung. My throat was on fire. White gas flowed through the building and into the room. Tear gas. Someone had fired tear gas canisters. Two more followed.

H.T. yelled to his guys to pull their coats over their faces. He barked orders through a handkerchief he held to his face. Like a military unit, they took up positions nearer the open garage door. Their precision was surprising. No panic. They followed his orders.

More glass broke. Something, was it a bullet?, bounced off the metal walls. H.T. and his guys held their ground, waiting. Somebody was outside. But who? I hoped they were marksmen and knew Chris and I were in here. Two of H.T.'s guys fell backwards, bullets in their chests. H.T. swore and yelled for his men still standing to shoot back. They started firing. The pistols near us boomed inside the warehouse. Chris screamed, his face against my leg. My fear was that H.T. would shoot us if he was out of options.

Through the water rolling out of my eyes, I saw a third of H.T.'s men fall. He didn't make a sound. I couldn't see the last man through the smoke. But then I heard him scream. He called for H.T. to help him.

The gas filled the room. Chris whimpered that his eyes hurt. Mine did too. I could barely see. H.T. turned and lowered his handkerchief. "You ain't worth this shit, Joe. If you are dead, I've got a chance. Damn, I had other plans, but this is the way it has to be."

He picked up the gun that had been placed in Braddock's dead hand. Chris, behind me, crying, clung to me. He was protected under the bed for the moment, but I thought we would never again see anything outside of this room. The tears streaming down my face were not just from the gas.

"Get up. I got to make this look like that asshole shot you."

It hit me. In the last few seconds as his men were being shot around him, H.T. had devised a backup plan. With us dead, no one could link H.T. to Braddock and Crenshaw. He could claim he and his men were trying to rescue us from Braddock and we all got caught in the crossfire. He could claim he didn't know the police were outside. Strangely, even as he was about to end our lives, I remember thinking that I admired his quick thinking.

My legs trembled as I pulled Chris up and kept him on the back side of my body away from H.T. He stood over Braddock, his back to the door. All I could see was the gun barrel rising to aim directly at my head.

I heard a shot. Did he miss? His face looked stunned. The handkerchief fluttered toward the floor. He smiled as he fell forward on the concrete.

Lying there, his face turned towards me, blood gushed from his mouth as he spat out his final words, "Remember, I'm the good guy. Write it like I told you, or I'll get you."

He coughed, then died with his eyes open.

Frozen in place, hanging onto Chris, I heard heavy feet running. Men in blue uniforms and Army fatigues burst through the door, rifles and guns in hand. They wore gas masks.

"Here," I croaked out the one word. The soldiers and police officers surrounded us, then led us out of the room and toward the open garage door. The fresh air and rain felt wonderful on my skin. The burning in my eyes still blinded me. We cried and coughed, my lungs still felt like they were imploding. I could barely breathe. The soldiers pulled off their masks and gave Chris and me oxygen. Two of our rescuers were the cops I had helped save weeks before. They smiled big at us. Other policemen and National Guardsmen surrounded us, their helmets, clothing soaked from the rain. Someone was talking on the walkie talkie, saying five were dead and one wounded inside. He was instructed to bring the wounded man out of the tear gas.

The dozen cops and soldiers outside looked ready for a major assault if necessary. Standing in the heavy downpour, God washing us all clean, two officers knelt to check on Chris, who was again squeezed between my legs. Suddenly he vomited on my pants and shoes and the asphalt. I didn't know if his stomach was upset from the tear gas or from the gun shots or the gaggle of strangers around us. What did I care? We were alive. I hoped there wouldn't be too much damage to his psyche. I knelt down and held him. Someone held an umbrella over us.

Commander Howell walked up and asked how we were. I nodded vigorously and thanked him.

"Now we're even," I told the two policemen I had rescued.

"No, sir. Are you kidding? We were doing our job, getting rid of bad guys," one said.

I wanted to ask questions, especially how they found us. But first I tried to get my hands and legs to stop shaking. My eyes, nose and throat still burned from the tear gas. A crowd had gathered. There was even the public relations woman for the police department. She too leaned under our umbrella to ask how we were.

In the back of the crowd I saw two men coming towards us. Walt held a large golf umbrella over Jimmy Marshall. Both looked pleased. I was struck again at how odd they seemed together. So different, one white and bear-like, the other black and small.

"What are you two doing here?"

The old saxophone player, who had survived his own brush with death at the church, knelt down and whispered quietly in Chris's ear. The boy's trembling slowed. To my questions, Walt started to answer, but Marshall interrupted him. "All that can wait. We need to get this boy home."

We rode away in Walt's Cadillac. I called Ed from Walt's phone to tell him we were safe. He was in a panic with no idea where I was. The police had kept radio silence, communicating only by telephones during the rescue attempt, fearing the radio was being monitored. My father-in-law had called the newspaper when Chris was not waiting at school. There had been no alert about Chris on the police scanners. Ed was at a lost to know what had happened to me or Chris. He was just hoping I had picked him up.

After breathing a deep sigh, he told me about the stories they were working on. He managed to joke that now, thanks to our rescue, he would have to redesign the front page. I promised to call him back after I was sure Chris was safe at the house. He told me he would send Rachel to get the details.

Chris knelt on the backseat of Walt's car beside me and watched out the back window the police cars following us home. Marshall sat in the front seat, turning frequently to talk in a soft voice to Chris. As we drove, I sat in silence, hugging Chris close and staring at sites I had seen a thousand times, the facades of the old Britling's Cafeteria, the Highland Avenue Methodist Church, popular Southside bars and restaurants, Vulcan standing watch on the mountaintop. Each was familiar, but in an extraordinary way, it was like I was seeing them for the first time. An hour ago I feared I would never see anything outside that warehouse prison. Now time was a commodity I had again. There was time to watch Chris grow up, to be with Nicki, probably time to figure out what life would be like after newspapers. Those thoughts helped repair my frayed nerves.

Rachel met us at the house shortly after we arrived. Mike was talking with the police, getting details of the rescue. I spent a few moments comforting Chris, getting him in his pajamas and finding his favorite bear to sleep with. I also hugged both my in-laws, something I didn't do enough of, in hopes I could reassure them that everything was okay. They had gone to the school, and not finding Chris, had rallied the whole neighborhood to look for him. The crisis now over, the neighbors were back in their homes, taking pieces of homemade cornbread my mother-in-law had baked after she knew we were safe.

While his grandmother read a book to Chris, Rachel sat in my living room and interviewed me. It would probably have been easier to write the story myself, if I could have focused.

Walt and Jimmy sat on the sofa across from us while I told Rachel the story, the kidnapping, the murder of Braddock, the rescue and of course, the plot H.T. had hatched to be county commissioner. Rachel had the recorder on. Ed listened on the phone. He said he planned to use photographs of H.T. and Braddock for page one to go with the story Rachel and Mike were writing about their conspiracy and about our kidnappings and rescue.

With our stories and the layout in motion, I turned to Walt and Jimmy and said, "Okay, you two, I want to know how the police knew where we were and what were you guys doing there."

"Just helping the police," Marshall said.

I looked at him and then Walt, not comprehending. "This part doesn't need to be in the newspaper. Just write that the police got an anonymous tip. It wouldn't do Jimmy or me any good to be in your newspaper right now," Walt said.

I nodded and looked at Rachel. "Go write what you've got. We'll talk about the rest later." I told Ed the same and hung up the phone. Rachel went into my study and turned on the computer.

Then I sat back and waited for their story. Walt led off. "Jimmy had a spy in Jones' gang. One of his grandsons. The boy joined the gang about a year ago and really believed in Jones at first, but it wore thin in the last few weeks."

"He's a good boy," Marshall joined in telling the story. "Like a lot of boys in neighborhood, he got really caught up with Jones. He thought the guy was special, liked the routine, the discipline. It made him feel strong. I was happy for him at first, but I began to have doubts."

In hindsight, the signs were there. Usually a cynical newspaper reporter, I had been blinded by my hopes that H.T. was something different, a special new leader.

Marshall continued. "When the campaign for Grey's seat came along, Jones began leaning on folks to back him. He strutted around like the black savior, while he was clearly getting money from someplace. I didn't think it was coming from the northside, from black folks. But his preaching violence really scared me and made me mad. Dr. King was right about violence. It is a no-win situation."

He leaned back in his chair and quoted his hero: "In the process of gaining our rightful place, we must not be guilty of wrongful deeds. Let us not seek to satisfy our thirst for freedom by drinking from the cup of bitterness and hatred. We must forever conduct our struggle on the high plane of dignity and discipline. We must not allow our creative protest to degenerate into physical violence. Again and again, we must rise to the majestic heights of meeting physical force with soul force."

There was no rush now, no reason to interrupt or hurry him. We had all the time in the world to listen. The tension started to drain out of me.

"I was a big admirer of Commissioner Grey," the little deacon continued again. "I believed in him. He was a good man. Nobody should have killed him. They shouldn't have killed Martin and the Kennedy boys. Too many good men gone. I thought it had to be white men who had done it, same as those who bombed the church before or that evil man in Memphis. I began to wonder that night we went to church together. I began to think about who would benefit most from Grey being dead. I could think of several possibilities, but Jones seemed to be at the top of the list. He wanted to step up into Grey's shoes so bad. Smith too, but he seemed less ruthless. I talked with my grandson about Jones. He and the other guys thought Jones was great. They liked being in his gang."

He smiled at Walt, who had heard the story before. "I tried talking with Jones. He didn't hide how much he resented Commissioner Grey, how jealous he was of his position of power. He showed the dead no respect. I started helping Ray Smith to stop Jones."

An angry H.T. took it out on his grandson. He demoted the teenager in the ranks of the gang and embarrassed him in front of his friends. The grandson wanted to quit, but Marshall asked him to stay to keep an eye on Jones. "Once my boy, who is a lot like I was, stopped admiring him, love turned to hate fast."

Walt found the bourbon bottle I kept in the house and poured himself a full measure over a couple of ice cubes. Marshall passed on his offer of a drink. My father-in-law brought me a beer, when he got himself one. He gave my shoulder a tug as he left to go watch television.

"Jimmy called me two days ago," Walt joined in. "I'd been helping Smith some. I thought Jones was bad news, so I did what I could." He held his glass up in a toast. "Still troubled by this pesky conscience my mother left me with."

"Braddock ask you to back Jones?"

Walt smiled. "Yeah, he told me we needed to help the little shit. I should have guessed H.T. had found a way to get Braddock by the balls."

"Things began to get tense in Jones' camp," Marshall said. "He and his guys were having a lot of whispered conversations. My grandson was not part of it, but one of the guys bragged to him that they planned to grab you and they had a way to make the *Post* print stories that would give Jones the election. My grandson listened."

He did not know where they were going to take me, but guessed it must be in north Iron City at some place that Jones' white friends owned, Marshall said.

Walt interrupted. "After you left the courthouse, I talked to Braddock. He was in a foul mood. I knew something was up. I'm sorry that it took me a while to realize he might take his anger out on you directly. I called your cell, but you didn't answer. So I called the *Post* to warn you, but your Mrs. James said you hadn't come back. I didn't think anything about it, until Jimmy called me to tell me what his grandson heard."

Ed had told me that Mrs. James got the call from my father-in-law saying Chris was missing. They hoped I had picked up Chris. But then Ed realized my car was still at the newspaper. That is when they began to panic. Mrs. James called the police. Fortunately they took her seriously.

"Jimmy and I decided we would do a little detecting on our own. It was a wild guess, but I asked a friend at a title company to run me a list of all the properties that Braddock owned in the county. He came up with about a dozen, mostly apartments, his house, some raw land and a couple of old warehouses and mills. I knew it wouldn't be his house, and the apartments would have too many people around. He could have stashed you on the vacant land, tied you to a tree or something. But it was raining, so I figured it had to be one of his industrial properties, probably an empty warehouse or mill. I called Commander Howell and told him what we suspected. He didn't believe at first that Braddock was involved. So Jimmy and I went for a drive. At the second property we checked, the empty warehouse, we saw Braddock's car through the open garage door. We drove back and forth watching and then Jones and his guys showed up. Bingo, we knew we had found it. We called Howell again and stayed out of sight while the cavalry arrived."

The police and National Guard were preparing to start negotiating with Braddock and H.T. when they heard a gun shot. That left no time for talking.

"Glad it was Braddock who was shot, not you," Walt said. "Braddock could have made a difference around here. But he turned out to be a weak man, despite all the money. He ain't much of a loss. You, on the other hand, well ..." He and Jimmy sat there smiling at me.

Marshall stood up and asked if he could walk out on the balcony. The rain had stopped. I opened the door for him. The air that flowed in smelled fresh and clean. "It looks mighty pretty out there," he said.

We stepped out to the railing on the balcony and looked at the city lights that spread below us across the valley. "This is a good spot to thank God for riding with us tonight," he said.

I left him alone to say his prayers and went in to check on Rachel, who was talking with Mike as they both worked on the story. In the living room Walt leaned back on the sofa and stroked his goatee. He took another long sip of his drink. As I watched him, it hit me. I had the answer to a question that had been rattling around in my head for months.

"So it was you who hired the private investigators to follow me some months back?"

Walt always had an infectious laugh. He sat there chuckling at me. I joined in. It was good to laugh.

"You remember I gave you a hint that night at the Monteagle. You may not have put it together then, but I told you our favorite sins are the ones that do us in. Your skirt-chasing after your wife died almost did you in. It would have that night if the man on sticks had not had his team, including your future girlfriend, following you."

"Did you know the cops were coming there that night?" Walt had strong ties to the police, but even for him that would be impressive.

He shook his head. "Not that particular night. As you may recall, you were not particularly picky in those days on your choice of bedrooms."

I spread out my hands with my palms up. "All I can say is thanks. Again."

"It wasn't cheap, but worth every dollar," he said.

"Why? Why me?"

He laughed. "You don't get it, even now. You don't understand why it was so important to save you tonight, to save your black ass back then."

I didn't understand.

He sighed and poured the rest of his drink down his throat. "I know people think I do what I do for the money it makes me. Of course, that's part of it. But there is a lot more to it. I love this city. I move around in the background making things work and stopping other things people try to do because I believe this city has a strong future. Some days I ask myself why I bother. Despite all our efforts, cities seem like they are going to hell. But then you walked in, a breath of fresh air, someone with new attitudes. Yeah, you were well educated, but more important it was born in you. That is rare today."

He threw back his head, his chuckles turning into to a belly laugh.

"And the best is your skin color. You are a whole new breed of southern leader, a black man who ain't afraid or angry, who is willing to take risks, not for himself, but for the benefit of others. You're going to change this old city. Hell, you already have. You got rid of Crenshaw, Braddock and Jones. The city's a better place."

My father would not have understood anything Walt just said. But my mother and my grandfather would.

"There is one thing I didn't count on. I didn't expect the private detective I hired to fall for you." He laughed even louder and that made me laugh again. Marshall came back in to see what we were laughing at.

Walt stood up to look for a refill. "Just count what I paid her and her company as my wedding present."

After everyone left, I called Nicki. I didn't want to worry her, but I needed to hear her voice. She could help pull me back together. And she had a right to know. Her father picked up the phone. "I hoped you were dead," he spat out the words. "It was on the news here that you were missing. Nicki's upstairs trying to get a plane tonight."

"May I speak to her?"

The phone went dead. In a few minutes Nicki was on the line. "Thank God, you're all right. Father said you had called. Are you hurt? Is Chris all right?"

I told her we were fine, just recovering from being terrified. I told her what had happened, but that we were safe now. Both Braddock and H.T. were dead. "Your father said you were trying to come home, is that right?"

"Duh. With what you've been through, but damn it, I've missed the last flight tonight. I could charter a plane, but if you and Chris are all right, I can wait until tomorrow."

I told her not to charter a plane, that we were fine now and would be asleep shortly. "How are things there? What happened?" I asked.

"Father stomped around town for hours, then came home drunk. He's not happy. But it looks like he will keep the agreement we made."

"Good. I've had enough threats against my life. And I am sure ready for you to come home. I love you, and I need you."

"Maybe that charter flight does sound good," she said. "I'd hate for you to lose the mood."

I sat on the balcony where I could breathe fully for the first time since I had been dragged into that car. The little deacon was right. I looked up at the stars and said my thank yous.

The city was relatively quiet, spent from the ravages of recent weeks. Or maybe it was just me. I looked along the ridge of the mountain. The brightly lit Vulcan was on duty. His spear looked like it was protecting us, not threatening.

"Can I sleep with you tonight, Dad?" Chris asked, running onto the balcony. His grandmother followed, unable to take her eyes off him.

"Of course. Just tonight, okay? Big boys like you need to sleep in their own beds. But I'm still a little scared. So tonight we'll sleep together, okay?"

Chris nodded happily and started pulling on my arm. As I stood up, the door bell rang. Panic churned my gut. Could H.T. be reaching out from the morgue? So soon?

When I opened the front door, Ralph White and the three other policemen I had saved and who had saved us took up the whole doorway.

"We just came by to see if you were all right," White said. All of them smiled broadly. Two police cars sat in front of the house. The neighbors' tongues would be wagging tomorrow.

I thanked them and invited them in. They stepped through the door and took up most of the front hall. One of the younger officers knelt to be at eye level with my son. "Chris, I want you to look at each one of us and remember what we look like. Can you do that?" The boy, awed by the four uniformed policemen, nodded and took his time looking at each man. "Now when you see us around the school or anywhere you go, will you remember us?"

Chris again nodded, still concentrating on their faces.

"We're going to be like your big brothers," the younger police-men said, giving Chris a hug. "You don't have any big brothers, and well .. we kinda of need you to be our little brother. Is that okay?"

Chris broke into a big smile and hugged my legs. "Can I, Daddy? Can I?"

"Sure. I can't think of any better big brothers."

Chris beamed.

White said, "Joe, if you don't mind, we talked it over and de-cided we should watch over Chris for a bit until things settle down. It will be harder to watch over you, but maybe we can help keep Chris safe."

I hoped it wasn't necessary. But when it comes to Chris, what-ever it takes.

"Thanks guys. Chris and I would like that."

They filed out with White bringing up the rear. He turned and said, "Crenshaw got the word that Braddock and Thomas are dead. So he is now talking up a storm. Not that it will do him any good. Not much left for him to trade."

He chuckled and waved as he walked through my doorway.

EPILOGUE

"Too often when a city faces a crisis such as we have, we tend to focus only on the negatives, the threats to our economy, our community, our way of life. But such times also present us significant opportunities to forge change, to improve our way of life. We in Iron City have such a chance now."

I felt more than a little strange standing in the cemetery reading a newspaper editorial out loud. But I owed it to Mark. I wanted him to hear it. I didn't know if heaven had a subscription to the *Post*. Maybe he could read it on the Internet as it bounced off the satellites.

Clay and I had the front pages of the *Post* laminated with the stories about Crenshaw's arrest and the stories that ran yesterday about H.T. and Braddock. We felt they were fitting memorials for Mark, and despite feeling foolish, I taped them to his grave stone.

I read them as if Mark was there listening.

The Bold Headlines Shouted:

Church Bombing Conspiracy Uncovered
Braddock, Jones Killed; Post Editor and
Son Rescued From Kidnapping

The bombing of the Sixteenth Street Baptist Church by confessed bomber Lonnie Crenshaw was planned by county commission candidate H.T. Jones and financed by wealthy businessman and philanthropist Harden Braddock. Both men confessed the conspiracy to Post editor Joe Riordan III.

Braddock and Jones were killed last night. Jones shot Braddock after the businessman threatened to expose the plot to the FBI. Iron City Police and National Guard troops killed Jones and three other men in his gang while rescuing

Riordan and his son, Chris, who had been kidnapped ear-
lier in the day by Jones and his men.

Jones said he engineered the assassination of Grey be-
cause he wanted his seat on the county commission.

Braddock, a former quarterback and philanthropist
of the University of Alabama, wanted Grey dead because
he was demanding that the university hire a black football
coach.

The story went on to fill in the details of the conspiracy behind
the bombing, the unlikely connection between Jones, Braddock
and Crenshaw and the role the *Post* had played in exposing it. The
confessions of both Braddock and Jones were quoted in the article.
Head shot photos of Jones, Braddock and Crenshaw ran on the
front page. A photo of the police and National Guard vehicles outside the warehouse ran inside.

A second story, buried inside next to the jump, reported what
I had expected to be the lead story for the day, recounting how
the *Post* had won in court the right to publish a story linking the
Jackson Group with the bombers. That story never ran. Instead
our story said it was not the Jackson Group, but rather Braddock,
a prominent member of the group, who was behind the bombing.

As I was reading the editorial and article at Mark's grave, my cell
phone rang. It was exactly 10:07 central standard time. The display
said an unknown caller was the on the line. Panic. I could barely
breathe as I stared at the phone. It could be anybody, the media
wanting another quotation, the FBI, Fabrini. I almost didn't answer.

"Mr. Riordan? Is this Joe Riordan, editor of the Iron City *Post*?
Can you hold for the President?"

The most powerful man in the world and I talked for eight minutes. After I came down off cloud nine, I checked the timer on my
phone. We talked about the church bombing and how glad he was
that it was over, that all the conspirators were now exposed and
dead. He said he understood their deaths were having an impact

on Crenshaw, who was outraged sitting in jail, having been told that he had been duped by a black man. It was doubtful that Crenshaw would still be regarded as a hero by the white supremacists. The President chuckled at the irony.

He told me he had been in Iron City only once to make a speech at the Civil Rights Institute. He said how much the visit to the church and the park, seeing the statues of German Shepherds snarling at black teenagers, had affected him. "You know that was not my fight," he said. "I was too young to be a Civil Rights warrior with Doctor King. I wish I had. I envy you being part of that tradition and helping Iron City put its past behind it."

The President thanked me for the efforts of the newspaper in bringing the bomber and his conspirators to justice. He congratulated me and wished me a bright future. I wish I could have recorded it.

Still standing beside Mark's grave, I thought about how much my friend would have enjoyed talking with the President. He deserved the honor even more. The best I could do was finish reading him the editorial I had written.

> *Iron City has been under a microscope for weeks. The national and international media have explored every angle on our city. It is time for that attention to go away. We need time to heal the wounds. It is time for us to take constructive steps to forge new iron and steel and build new foundations for a strong city.*
>
> *If we fail to do it now, our children and grandchildren will face the same fate we have, one spawned of hatred, mistrust and miscommunication. Unless we act now, Vulcan's legacy to this city will not be Heaven on Earth, but generations of more anger, frustration and violence. We owe it to the man on the mountain to do better.*
>
> *We at this newspaper pledge to lead our city where we can to help nurture new life from the ashes.*

Clay, leaning on crutches, and Nicki waited about twenty yards away. He didn't want to intrude on my time with Mark. I helped Clay into the back seat where he could stretch out his leg. I reached in the trunk for a bottle of champagne I had put on ice in a cooler. I popped the cork and poured stiff portions in three red plastic cups.

I walked back to Mark's grave and poured the rest of the bottle near the headstone. That was probably the sentimental Irish in me. The more practical black side would never pour good champagne on the ground.

After a few minutes, I walked back to the car.

"Well, what do we do for an encore?" Nicki and Clay groaned in unison. I started the Blazer. "Let's go tweak Daniels' nose, for as long as we have a newspaper to do it."

THE END

44412407R00243

Made in the USA
Charleston, SC
23 July 2015